CHARM CITY'S BLUE JUSTICE

Dick Ellwood

iUniverse, Inc.
Bloomington

Charm City's Blue Justice

iUniverse books may be ordered through booksellers or by contacting:

iUniverse
1663 Liberty Drive
Bloomington, IN 47403
www.iuniverse.com
1-800-Authors (1-800-288-4677)

Because of the dynamic nature of the Internet, any web addresses or links contained in this book may have changed since publication and may no longer be valid. The views expressed in this work are solely those of the author and do not necessarily reflect the views of the publisher, and the publisher hereby disclaims any responsibility for them.

Any people depicted in stock imagery provided by Thinkstock are models, and such images are being used for illustrative purposes only.

Certain stock imagery © Thinkstock.

ISBN: 978-1-4759-6665-7 (sc)
ISBN: 978-1-4759-6667-1 (hc)
ISBN: 978-1-4759-6666-4 (e)

Library of Congress Control Number: 2012923335

Printed in the United States of America

iUniverse rev. date: 12/13/12

ACKNOWLEDGEMENT

I would like to acknowledge and thank my editor. She did a superb job. She was extremely patient in keeping me straight with my punctuation and grammar. If it were not for her attention to detail, the book would have never been completed. I want to also thank her for being tolerant with me during the process. Editing a manuscript can be a very demanding task. She devoted many hours and never complained.

I also want to thank her for being my wife.

Thanks Sharon, whatever success this book has, I share it with you.

In Memory of Many
In Honor of All

CHAPTER 1

The neighborhood was rough back when I was growing up, but compared to what is happening today, it was like the old TV show, Mr. Roger's Neighborhood. Back in the '60s, in the summertime you could sleep in the park across from my house. You would actually wake up in the morning to go to work or school. Today, you can still sleep in the park, but your chances of waking up are slim to none. We had our share of bad guys back then, but today it seems like everybody is a bad guy. In our teenage years, we did some crazy shit. We were stealing cars, shoplifting, drinking, and other things that are now considered minor offenses. Hell, today you can walk in certain neighborhoods in Baltimore and you are almost guaranteed to get shot or stabbed—you don't have to do anything. The mere fact that you are in that neighborhood is enough for some punk to want to impress his buddies and take you out.

I never got busted for any crimes while growing up—I guess I was lucky. When I turned seventeen, I knew that the only way out of that neighborhood alive was to go in the service. I talked to my closest buddy, Frank Favasi, about going down to the U.S. Custom House and taking the test for the Marines. We were both seventeen, so our parents had to sign for us. I knew that would not be a problem. We had both quit school and there was no doubt they would sign. I am sure they thought that the only way we would get straightened out would be to go in the service or jail. Service would be my first choice.

The year was 1960 and there was no actual war going on, except the Cold War with Russia. Frank and I both figured we would go in the Marines for a few years and see the world. There had been a few other guys from the neighborhood who enlisted in the Marines. We saw them when they were home on leave. They talked about how tough it was. What the hell—we were tough! So how bad could it be?

Back in those days guys were proud to wear their service uniforms while home on leave. I always noticed that when they were in the neighborhood bars, they did not pay for their drinks. Some of them were not old enough to drink, but the elders in the bars figured that if you could fight for your country, you could sure as shit have a few drinks. I could picture myself coming home on leave and walking the streets wearing that Marine uniform. I could get all the chicks I wanted. The drinks in the bar sounded damn good also.

The neighborhood was a very proud neighborhood and had many war veterans. We had one guy that we called Sarge. It was a known fact that he was a decorated Korean War hero. I never knew him to actually have a home. I think people just felt sorry for him. They took him in their homes once in a while and if not, the street was fine with Sarge. He was a quiet man. When he drank, which was most of the time, he was morally offensive. He was downright scary when he was drunk and very unpredictable. I think he was in the Army. When he was sober, he loved to tell anyone that would listen, about his exploits during the war. He carried a few medals around in his coat. He pinned them on when he was begging or looking for a drink. He could be found sleeping in the park on very cold days. I am not sure how he survived the weather—maybe the cold reminded him of Korea. I know that when he was sober, which was not that often, he insisted on being called sergeant, not Sarge. We had a lot of war heroes in the neighborhood, mostly from World War II and that included my dad.

I remember one very cold winter morning; I heard that Sarge had died. I am not sure why, but it upset me. I heard that his body was taken away and no one claimed it at the morgue. I assumed many years later that the poor guy was buried in Potter's Field where they buried all the unclaimed bodies. Just imagine, fighting for your country, decorated with medals, living on the streets, no one to care for you, and then dumped in Potter's Field—that sucks.

I looked up to the servicemen in our neighborhood. Hell, if it were not for them, we might all be speaking Japanese or Korean today. I am not real proud of the way we treated Sarge when he was alive. He deserved better—all heroes do.

I wanted to make the neighborhood proud. Frank and I joined the Marines.

Chapter 2

We went to Marine Corps boot camp together at Parris Island, South Carolina. Frank was a well-built tough guy and in great physical shape. He looked a little older than seventeen. I was just a scrawny teenager and probably didn't weigh more than a hundred and forty pounds soaking wet. I knew that I would probably have a harder time in boot camp than Frank and was I ever right about that.

We went by train from Baltimore to Yemassee, South Carolina. Yemassee was a tiny town close to the Georgia border. From there we were put on what the Marine Corps called a cattle car. We were taken to Beaufort, South Carolina, where we were to meet our Marine drill instructor. I know why they called them cattle cars—there were no seats. We were literally herded on like a bunch of cattle. If you were lucky, you could hold on to a strap that hung from the ceiling. I was not lucky. During the thirty minute ride, I was thrown all over the cattle car. Frank did get a strap and he laughed at me being tossed around. Looking back on the experience, it might have been one of the few laughs we had during the early boot camp days.

When we arrived at Beaufort, we were transferred to another cattle car. We were taken the rest of the way to Parris Island, South Carolina, in the nasty smelling cattle car. I am not sure why they transferred us to a different vehicle, but this time I made sure I got a strap. I think I pushed some skinny kid—skinnier than me, out of the way to get the strap.

We arrived at Parris Island and when we pulled to a stop—all hell broke loose. A Marine drill instructor got on the cattle car. He was the nastiest looking son of a bitch I had ever seen. He just stood at the front and stared at the recruits that were closer to him. He was about five feet, eight inches tall, and probably weighed about one hundred and seventy-five pounds. He looked like the Incredible Hulk in his Marine uniform.

He finally spoke up in a real deep and scratchy voice. "You maggots are now at the Marine Corps Recruit Depot at Parris Island, South Carolina. You will not speak unless you are spoken to and for the next twelve weeks, your asses belong to me. You are on an island that consists of eight thousand acres of hell on earth." He moved a little closer to the middle of the cattle car where I was standing. "Out of the eight thousand acres of land, only about three thousand are habitable and the rest is salt marsh. If you don't think you can make it through boot camp and decide to make a run for it, the salt marshes have the biggest alligators in the world." He sure as hell got my attention with that statement.

He moved to the back of the cattle car. "What a sorry looking bunch of maggots you are." I knew that after hearing the word maggots twice in a few minutes, this was going to be our group name for quite a while. He walked back to the center of the cattle car. "The only thing you have to remember now is that my name is Gunnery Sergeant Victor Stafford and you are assigned to platoon 299. I will be with you twenty-four hours a day for the next twelve weeks." He walked to the front and his face got real red and he shouted, "Get your sorry civilian asses off this bus and form three lines in the marked areas on the sidewalk!"

We ran off the bus, making sure we did not have any contact with the drill instructor. I got in a line next to Frank. He whispered, "Are you okay?" I told Frank I was fine. It was a good feeling that he was next to me; just like he was back in the neighborhood.

Boot camp was really rough. I did things that I would have never thought I could have done without the prodding and pushing of Gunny Stafford. I don't know if I ever saw him smile. It appeared to me that he always had a chip on his shoulder. I always thought of the Gunny as a guy that lived and died with Marine Corps tradition. Without the Marines, he would be nobody in civilian life. We did find out over the twelve weeks that he was a single man. When he was not living with a boot camp class, he resided on the base in the enlisted men's barracks. We also found out that he had fought in the Korean War and was highly decorated. He was well respected by the other drill instructors.

Boot camp in the '60s was still probably the toughest training for any military unit in the world. Back then, drill instructors were allowed to beat you to get their point across. I don't mean push or shove—I mean they could smack the shit out of you to get your attention. I saw some things while in boot camp, that would make you cringe. I always knew that the training would be vigorous. I found out very early that the Marine brainwashing was the way they wanted every new recruit to think about combat. The teaching throughout boot camp was that you were a part of the greatest fighting force in the world. They constantly told you that no matter what the odds were in combat, you were superior and thus would come out a winner. I bought into this Marine thinking. I now know many years later that it served me well in all that I have done or at least most of what I have done.

Frank and I did what was expected of us in boot camp. Frank was always the guy that topped everyone in the unit when it came to physical activities. He was far more superior physically to most recruits in the platoon. He always looked good at whatever he did. This was noticed by Gunny Stafford who always said to the other recruits, "Do it like Favasi does it." I really owe getting through Marine boot camp to Frank. He didn't do the training for me, but he was always giving me the nod that things would be okay and that pushed me to get it done.

Toward the end of boot camp, I think that Gunny Stafford picked up on the relationship that Frank and I had. When I was struggling to do something like swimming, Stafford would say, "Come on Miss Giango, you can do it or do you want your girlfriend, Favasi, to do it for you?" The Gunny had a sick perverse way about him, but that was what drill instructors were about. He talked to some of the recruits in terms that would absolutely piss you off. That was his motive. We didn't realize it then, but that is what drill instructors were supposed to do. They pushed you to heights that you never thought you could achieve. The sole purpose of a drill instructor is to mold a fighting unit that when called upon would perform at the highest level in combat. Gunny Sergeant Stafford was the guy who could do it. If you would ask Frank or anyone from Platoon 299, they would tell you, they hated him— but he did a great job.

CHAPTER 3

Frank and I graduated from boot camp on time. I still consider that the greatest accomplishment of my life. Frank was given the Dress Blues Award when he graduated. With that came a promotion to Private First Class and his first stripe. We proudly paraded across the field on graduation day. It was an honor to march on the same field as so many honorable Marines before us. After the ceremony, we were allowed some time with our families to celebrate. We knew each other's families from back in Baltimore. It was nice to get together with them. My family could not believe the person they were seeing after twelve weeks of boot camp. I was now a lean, mean, fighting machine. I must say that we looked damn good in our uniforms.

My mom asked about the stripe that Frank had on his uniform. Before I could answer, Frank said, "It's no big deal—I guess I shot a little straighter or ran a little faster than the others. I'm sure Nick will get his stripe at his next duty station." I looked at Frank and he nodded to me like he had throughout boot camp. I knew that our relationship was as tight as ever—a bond that would never be broken.

We went our different ways after Marine boot camp. It would have been great if we could have served our time at the same duty station. After boot camp, you really don't have any say on where you go. I was sent to Camp Lejeune, North Carolina. Frank was sent to Okinawa.

Frank and I served out our four year enlistment. We both received an honorable discharge. Frank got his discharge papers from Camp Pendleton on the West Coast. I got mine from my second duty station at Quantico, Virginia. We had stayed in touch with each other over the four years, but our paths never crossed. I think we both thought we would stay together after boot training. The Marines had other thoughts on that.

The four years in the Marines went slow for me. When the discharge day came, it was like hitting the lotto. I could not wait to get back home and check out my buddies. I wanted to see how many survived not going to jail or for that matter, how many were still alive. I knew that Frank would have the same discharge date as me. I could not wait to see him and bust down some beers. We were both twenty-one. We could now legally go into any bar. No more phony cards needed to get served. No more asking Sarge to get it for us. It seemed like we went in the Marines as kids and came out as men.

CHAPTER 4

The first thing I did when I got back to Baltimore was to go in Jimmy Jordan's bar. I sat at the bar—I'm twenty-one. The bartender, who I did not know, came over and asked me what I wanted. I was thinking that maybe I should have kept my uniform on for one more day. I could get the veterans to buy me beer all day and night. The bartender introduced himself to me. "I'm Mace, what can I get you? Jimmy is out of town for a few days. I'm running the bar for him." I was glad to hear that Jimmy still owned the bar. He was an interesting guy. He had been in prison a few times, mostly for gambling charges. He purchased the bar with gambling money. He had a unique location. His bar was directly across the street from the Maryland State Penitentiary. More interesting than the location, was the name. The bar was called, The Little House Across From the Big House. The characters that hung in this bar varied from steel workers, fire fighters, and cops—to riffraff that mostly gambled for a living. The fact that I was sitting there and not having to worry about being back to a barracks was a feeling that I hadn't had for four years. I talked to a few people at the bar. I just sat there and enjoyed this tremendous feeling of freedom. A few of the old guys from the neighborhood recognized me and sent beers down my way.

It was getting a little dark outside. I decided to call Frank's house and see if he was home yet. I dialed Frank's parents' number by memory. I was surprised that after four years of Marine brainwashing, I whipped that number right out. It rang several times and went to the answering machine. I cleared my throat and said, "Hey Marine, get your maggot ass down to the Little House; we got some serious drinking to do." After I hung up the phone, I was getting excited to think that after four years, I would hook up with my best friend and continue where we left off.

I was starting to get shit-faced. I was thinking about leaving Jimmy's bar and hitting a few bars where I knew there would be some girls. I started to pay my tab and the bartender said, "You don't owe me anything; it's been taken care of." I asked who took care of the tab. He pointed to an old guy at the end of the bar. I walked down to thank him. When I got off the stool, I accidentally bumped into a hard hat steel worker. I started to say excuse me. Before I could say anything, he pushed me against the cigarette machine. I was furious. I was thinking why would this asshole push me? Didn't he know I was a Marine? It hit me quick that I was not in uniform. He didn't know that I was a lean, mean, fighting machine. I was about to take four years of frustration out on his sorry ass. He walked toward me. I grabbed the pool stick off the table and cracked him across his head. I mean I hit this bastard real good. I opened a gash on his head. The blood was pouring out. I soon found out that the other guys at the end of the bar with hard hats were his co-workers. The pool stick was not much good to me any longer; it had broken into several pieces. I figured I would do the best I could, for as long as I could. The look on these guys' faces showed no fear of this just discharged killing machine. I was not doing real well, and it appeared that I was about to get a homecoming ass whipping.

What happened next sounded like something out of a Hollywood script. Walking in from the side door of the bar was Frank. He still had his uniform on. I could see a smile on Frank's face and all he said was, "What the hell did you get yourself into Marine?" He looked like the poster guy for the Marine Corps in that uniform. Over Frank's four years in the Marines, he put on some weight and it was all muscle. As only Frank would do, he calmly took off his Marine blazer, he neatly folded it, and placed it on a bar stool. He then jumped into the melee and now we got ourselves a pretty good homecoming battle going on. As Marines are big braggers when it comes to combat, I can tell you that Frank and I thought that we could take on these steel workers. It was four of them. One of them, who seemed a little older, kept dancing around and it appeared he did not want to see any action. It actually got to the point that we were all exhausted and the fight sort of petered out. We didn't know it, but the bartender had called the cops. When two cops came in the bar, we had stopped fighting. You could tell from some broken tables and blood on the floor that there had been a fight in the bar. I actually knew one of the cops—it was Billy Meyers. He had been a grade ahead of me in school, which made him twenty-two years old. Billy recognized me. He also knew the bartender. Billy probably did not drink or hang in bars. He was a straight arrow guy. When I was in school, we all thought Billy would be a priest and now seeing him as a cop was a big surprise. Billy was cool; he asked what happened. Frank, who also had grown up with Billy, told him that we were just having some fun. Frank was putting his coat on and told Billy, "It's a good thing you showed up when you did. We were kicking the shit out of these pansies." That pissed off one of the steel workers and he came after Frank. Billy and his partner interceded and stopped him.

"Listen guys, I'm going to chalk this up as a disagreement amongst friends. If I leave and have to come back, everybody's getting locked up."

Frank walked over to the steel workers and shook hands with them. "Let's get some beers. You guys can help two discharged Marines celebrate." We thanked Billy and for the next few hours, we drank with the steel workers. All was good in the Little House Across From the Big House.

I don't know how we did it, but Frank and I stayed at the bar until it closed at midnight. As the bartender was shutting off the lights and motioning that we had to leave, he gave us a dozen beers in a bag. He said, "The beer is on me. I'm proud of your service to our country and good luck to both of you." We thanked him and walked down the street to a small park where we both had played as children. We sat on the grass and reminisced about our childhood. We talked for a long while.

Frank got serious and looked directly at me and said, "Now that we are out of the Marines, what the hell are we going to do?" We were finishing up the beer and daylight was slowly creeping in over the park trees.

I am not sure where it came from, but I put my arm around Frank and said, "I got a great idea buddy." Frank was still feeling the effects of the beer and looked like he was in a coma. I shook him and said, "Listen dude, let's join the police department. They are so damn short of cops; they will hire us in a flash." I kind of hit a cord with Frank and he came around a little.

"What the hell are you talking about? They won't take us on the police force."

"Frank, think about it, they are in need of cops. We just got out of the Marines. We are perfect for the police department."

Frank started to walk away. He turned and suggested to Nick that they get some breakfast at the Brew & Chew in Fells Point. Nick agreed and they walked the short distance to the Brew & Chew which was open all night. Along the way, Frank told Nick that he would consider applying for the police department.

CHAPTER 5

We stood in line at City Hall to get sworn in as police officers. I could not believe that Frank and I were actually going to be cops. It was my idea to take the civil service test. What the hell were we thinking? We had moped around for about a month. When the Marine discharge money was running out we needed to make a decision on what we would do in the real world. We were desperate. The both of us were still taking up space at our parents' homes—that sucked. Running up bar tabs at a few joints was catching up to us. The days of getting drinks just because we served our country were getting old. I was not sure we were doing the right thing. The police recruiter jumped at the chance to sign up two lean and mean Marines. I think he told us that the police department was about two hundred short at the time, so we looked damn good to him.

I was nervous about joining the police department. I looked around at the other twelve guys at City Hall to be sworn in. Frank and I looked like we were in much better shape than they were. The job paid a lot more than we were making in the Marines. It had some benefits, like medical and a pension. With Frank's temper, he might not make it to the pension part—he would sure as hell need the medical coverage.

We were all mingling around. Some guys introduced themselves to us; they seemed a lot more nervous than we were. We knew that after four years in the Marines, a swearing in ceremony would not be a big deal? We were however getting a little impatient. Then some guy hollers, "Attention" and in walks this big guy dressed like a gangster. Well, the guy was far from a gangster. He was introduced as the police commissioner. He got up on a small platform and you could tell he was the boss. All the people with him jumped out of his way; the ones in uniform saluted him.

He had a very deep voice. He cleared his throat and said, "Gentlemen, welcome to the finest police department in the country. My name is Tom Kelly. I'm the police commissioner for Baltimore City."

I looked around and we were standing tall. You could tell that most of the others had not been in the service. They didn't know how to properly stand at attention. The commissioner continued talking. "You will be sworn in today and start your journey through the police academy to become part of a great police family."

I was watching Frank and I could not help but think that one day he could possibly be up on that platform telling young guys that he is the police commissioner. I knew that Frank would take this police career as serious as he did the Marines. He was the kind of guy that when he put his mind to something, he could overcome any obstacles. I wanted to be the best also. Most of that rubbed off on me from being around Frank. I never really told him that, but I think he knew it—he liked it. The commissioner went on to the swearing-in part. When he was done, all his flunkies clapped and that was our signal to clap also. The commissioner walked down off the platform and started to shake hands with each new police officer. When he got to Frank, he told him that he sure had a firm handshake. Frank wasted no time in telling him that he just got out of the Marines.

I think Frank pushed it a little too far when he told the commissioner, "Sir, I'm dedicating my life to making the streets of Baltimore safe."

The commissioner smiled and said, "That's great son. With a good attitude like that, I'm sure you will do just fine." Frank did what all the others did and told the commissioner a little about his background. I was surprised that the commissioner took that much time with us.

He came to me and I gave him the firmest handshake I could muster—he didn't say anything. I told him that I was Nick Giango and commenced to tell him a little about myself. He stopped me and said, "Are you related to Carmen Giango?" I told him that Carmen was my uncle. He said, "Son, it's a pleasure to meet you and a real honor to have you join the police department." I knew that Uncle Carmen had been a cop, but I was not really familiar with how his career went. The commissioner went on to say, "Carmen was one of the finest police officers that ever wore the uniform of the Baltimore Police Department." He was now talking loud and had the attention of the new recruits. "The city of Baltimore owes much to Carmen for making the ultimate sacrifice."

I was thinking that I should respond, but I was not sure what Uncle Carmen did. My family was not real connected to him. I figured out that the ultimate sacrifice meant that he must have been killed on the job. I didn't want the commissioner to think that I didn't know about Uncle Carmen, so I said, "We loved Uncle Carmen and there is not a day that goes by that the family doesn't mourn his loss."

I think the commissioner bought it. He grabbed my hand and said, "Son, in honor of Carmen Giango, if there is ever anything you need, make sure you come to me."

Someone hollered, "Dismissed" and the commissioner left with his entourage. I was thinking that I will probably never see that dude again. But if I ever did need his help, I would sure as shit use old Uncle Carmen. I am sure that's what he would have wanted.

CHAPTER 6

The police academy was a piece of cake. Frank and I were Marines. What the hell could they throw our way that we couldn't handle? It was actually getting boring when we approached the twelfth and final week of the academy. I knew that we were at the top of the class in the academics. The physical part of the training, especially the shooting was where we also excelled. We had some great instructors in the academy. Sergeant Tony Lambrosi was our class leader. He also taught several of the courses. Sergeant Tony was a great guy. He always had funny stories that fit right in with any subject he was teaching. I actually think he made up some of the stories—nevertheless they were funny. He would use every opportunity to relate some incident that happened to him when he worked the street.

He was talking one time about the importance of carrying your flashlight and making sure the batteries were good. He had a way about him that kept you awake in class and sitting on every word he said. "Men, I can remember the time I was walking in the rear of a store late at night. I heard something and pulled out my flashlight. When I flipped it on, nothing happened. The batteries were dead. I moved closer to the sound and can you believe it—I stepped in a bucket of shit. I can tell you that ever since that night, I always checked the batteries and nothing like that ever happened to me again. So gentlemen, the moral of that story is to make sure all your equipment is working before you head out on the street."

Looking back on that story now, it does not really make any sense. How do you step in a bucket of shit? Sergeant Tony tried to make his point on that subject and many others. I think he really enjoyed watching all the starry-eyed police recruits hanging on his every word. We always looked forward to seeing his name on the agenda. We knew we were in for some great stories, even if Sergeant Tony stretched the truth a little.

The time in the academy really flew by. We were approaching graduation. We were actually in our last week. Frank and I wanted to get a few drinks to celebrate. We went to Sweeney's nightclub which had a band. It was a great hangout for the ladies. The night we decided to go celebrate was the same day that we officially were issued our weapons. We were issued Smith & Wesson .38 caliber revolvers. We were told to only carry the guns to and from the police academy.

Frank picked me up at my apartment in his car. He had bought a 1958 Ford. It was a used car, but it was in great shape. When he picked me up, he pulled his coat back and showed me that he had his new revolver hooked to his belt. I was shocked that he would do that.

"You stupid shit, we were told not to carry that gun unless we were at the academy or on our way there."

"Nick, you worry too much. We are just days away from being real cops." I looked at him and was envious that I had not carried my gun.

We got to the nightclub and the place was packed—mostly with women. Frank and I found a spot at the bar and ordered drinks. It did not take Frank long to spot a very attractive blonde. She was sitting with a very large-boned woman. Large-boned woman is being nice—she was fat. Frank said, "Let's do it buddy" and started walking toward the blonde. He was smooth. I envied his talent for scoring with the women. I can't tell you how many times over the years that I scored only because Frank made the first move to talk to some women. Well, Frank and I were talking to these two ladies for about ten minutes. The blonde seemed real interested in Frank. The big- boned girl just kept talking. I'm not sure what the hell she was talking about. I was trying to tell Frank that we should move along and check out the rest of the club. Well, just when I had convinced him we were wasting our time, this big dude comes over and says hello to the blonde. It was apparent that she knew this guy. She started to direct her attention to him. I could tell by the look on Frank's face that something bad was about to happen.

"Excuse me my man—can't you see we were having a conversation before you so rudely interrupted us?" Frank faced the guy and even though this guy was tall, I could tell Frank would probably handle him without much trouble. The guy did not say anything. When he turned to walk away, he swung around and sucker punched Frank. The girls started to scream and Frank and this guy were on the ground punching the shit out of each other. I tried to get in the middle and break it up. They were much bigger than me and moving too fast. Frank rolled over on the guy and when he did, his gun fell out of his holster.

Well, you can imagine what happened next, the whole place was screaming, "He's got a gun!" I saw the gun go under a chair. I retrieved it and put it in my pocket. A couple of bouncers came over and broke up the fight. As we were trying to leave, the cops came into the nightclub and were directed over to where we were standing. The bouncer told the cop that we had a gun. I knew before they searched me that I needed to tell them that we did have a gun and we were also cops. I started to talk and one of the officers grabbed me and literally slammed me against the wall.

He put his gun to my head and said, "If you move, I'll bust a cap in your ass!" Not only did I not move, I don't even think I was breathing. Frank was being held by the other cop and then through the door came about six more cops with their guns out. The officer that had me against the wall, reached in my coat pocket and felt the gun—he put the cuffs on me. They took us to a small office in the rear of the club.

Before the cop could say anything, Frank said, "Guys, we are cops." There were so many police officers in the room you could hardly move. A sergeant arrived and took over. He was a big dude and nasty looking. When he heard Frank say we were cops, he asked for some identification. Well, luckily Frank also had his badge. I had nothing, but we both did have our police identification cards and clearly marked on the card in red was the large lettering—POLICE TRAINEE.

The sergeant said, "You two assholes are in deep trouble." He went on to tell most of the cops to go back on patrol. The original two who got the call, stayed in the room. The sergeant sat down and lit a cigarette. "How long do you two have to go before you were supposed to graduate?" When I heard the suppose, I was scared. All I could think about was that after all the weeks in the academy, we would be booted out. Frank hadn't said much while in the room and that was not like him. I looked at Frank with the look that I usually gave him when we were in trouble.

Frank finally sat up in the chair. "Sarge, can I explain what happened?"

"I think that would be a great idea and it's sergeant to you son, not sarge." Frank apologized to the sergeant and commenced to tell him that it was a mistake for him having his gun. He told the sergeant that we had no intentions of coming to the nightclub. He said that we were on our way to see his dad and show him the gun and badge. Frank said that while in the car, he got a call from an old girlfriend who asked him to stop by the nightclub and have a drink with her. He told the sergeant that he is responsible and that Nick didn't even know he had the gun. He said that if anyone is in trouble, it should be him. I was going to jump in and say we both screwed up, but the story seemed to be working.

The sergeant then told the two original officers to wait outside the nightclub for him. What happened next was amazing. The sergeant seemed to mellow a little. He moved his chair a little closer to where we were sitting. He leaned in a little and said, "I don't want to see you boys lose your job. We need all the cops we can put on the street." He sure as hell got our attention and now there was hope that we might one day soon be police officers. "I'm going to handle this as if it didn't happen. You boys okay with that?"

I think that Frank and I sounded like a boy's choir as we responded simultaneously, "Yes sergeant, we are really OK with it." The sergeant handed Frank his gun—unloaded of course.

"Now take that pee-shooter home and tuck it away in a safe place until you go back to school." We got up to leave and were walking to the door with the sergeant.

I can't believe he said it, but Frank said, "Sarge, what about that asshole that sucker punched me?"

The sergeant immediately reverted back to his original nasty looking demeanor and told us, "You two better get the hell out of my sight and it's sergeant to you boy, not sarge."

CHAPTER 7

Monday morning we were called into Major Kincaid's office. He was the commanding officer of the police academy. He held our future in his hands. He started off by asking, "How did you young fellows enjoy your weekend?"

We were standing at attention and looking like two boy scouts who got caught smoking. I could tell something was up, because there was no reason for the major to call us in his office. I looked at Frank and I figured I would take the question. Frank had already done enough to get us out of trouble. The major never offered us a chair and was ignoring us as he stared out the window. I knew I had to say something. I wanted to own up and tell the truth. As I started to say something, the major turned and faced us. He was smiling.

"Listen men, you are about to graduate from the police academy; you both have pretty good grades." He moved around from his desk and finally offered us a seat. "Sergeant Cannon called me this morning and told me about the incident in the nightclub. Sergeant Cannon is a longtime friend of mine; he worked in my squad when I was a sergeant." At this point, Nick and I were thinking how we had come so far in the academy and now it was ending.

"When Cannon was on the job for about a week, he got in a fight in a nightclub and pulled his gun." The major went on to say how he liked Cannon so much that he went to bat for him and saved his job. Frank and

I were looking a little perplexed and wondering where this story about Sergeant Cannon was going. Well, we got our answer as the major sat on his desk between the chairs we were sitting on—he smiled at us.

"Sergeant Cannon has asked me to forget what you guys did in the nightclub and give you a break." The major went on to say that when Cannon first asked him to forget the incident, he said no. The major said, "After I hung up with Sergeant Cannon, I started to think that everyone needs a break, so I'm letting you two continue through the academy."

Frank and I stood up and reached out to shake the major's hand. He didn't extend the same gesture. He just stood there and stared at us. We didn't know whether to sit back down, leave the room, salute him, or break out in a chorus of "Jesus loves me…yes he does." The major actually changed facial expressions and pointed to the door. As we walked gingerly towards the door, he said, "There will be no more breaks. When you leave this academy, you better prove to me that I did the right thing." We both turned and looked like bumbling idiots as we saluted him. We bumped into each other as we reached for the doorknob. I actually think I saluted the major with my left hand— damn, I hope he didn't notice.

When we got outside and were heading back to class, Frank said, "Listen Nick, we need to settle down and get through this academy." I started to argue with him and tell him it was his fault, but what would that prove. We were cleared and heading back to class. Life for two police trainees was good again.

CHAPTER 8

Graduation from the police academy finally came and we were excited. After many weeks of hard work and perseverance, we were about to be cops. The ceremony was held at the War Memorial Building next to the police headquarters. We marched across the stage and received our diplomas. We shook hands with all the police command staff, including Major Kincaid. He didn't even smile as we shook his hand.

After the graduation we all received our assignments. It was a tradition that the new officers would receive an envelope with a letter inside telling each person where they would be assigned. You would then go to the rear of the hall and meet with your new commanding officer. This was a very exciting time. We all knew where the busiest patrol districts were. We all wanted to see action. As Frank and I walked to the rear of the hall, we stopped to tear open the envelope. Frank got his paperwork out first. He just smiled at me. I got mine out and we were playing a game of who was going to say something first. I started to head for the rear of the hall and Frank grabbed my arm. "Come on dude, break it to me. Where the hell are you going?"

"You tell me first." We were now acting like little kids with a secret. I decided to end the mystery. I told Frank that my assignment was the Western District.

Frank looked at me and said, "Damn dude, that's where I want to go—you lucky bastard."

I was waiting for him to tell me where his assignment would be. I started to walk towards the rear of the hall. I grabbed his arm and said, "You ain't playing fair asshole. Where in the hell are you assigned?" He kept walking and that pissed me off. What the hell was new—he pissed me off routinely.

As he was almost entering the rear hall, he turned and shouted, "I'm going to the Western District with you. You don't think they would split up the deadly duo." We high-fived each other and looked for the commanding officer of the Western District. The long struggle through the police academy was over. Frank and I were heading to the Western District to fight crime and the forces of evil.

CHAPTER 9

The Western District was a hellhole of a place to work. It was situated in the middle of the most crime ridden neighborhood of Baltimore City. Just to drive through the streets to get to the station house could be dangerous. The parking lot for the personal vehicles of the cops assigned to the district was enclosed with barbed wire fencing. The doors had locks that could only be opened with a numbered keypad. The windows were covered on the outside with steel bars. The district was often compared to the famous Fort Apache which was the 41st precinct of the NYPD in the South Bronx of New York City. The precinct in New York got its name by comparing it to an army outpost. The Western District, like the 41st precinct in New York, was the worst and most dilapidated district in the city.

The Western had a reputation of having police officers that had disciplinary problems and were unwanted in other districts. The district was also known for having the most shootings and the most complaints about police brutality of any district in the city. The makeup of the officers in the district consisted of approximately ten percent black police officers. This was in a neighborhood that was one hundred percent black. It was also known for the district that had the most action. If you wanted to make a name for yourself, this was the place to be. We were told that when we got to the district, to work hard and keep our noses clean. If not, we could spend our entire careers there.

On our reporting day, Frank said that he would pick me up. We would go in together on our first day. Frank had purchased an old 1956 Chevy—he got rid of the Ford. I didn't have a car yet, but I was looking. I really didn't need one because Frank and I had moved into an apartment together in Northeast Baltimore. It was a small place. It had two bedrooms, a living room, a bathroom, and a small kitchen. Neither one of us really wanted to live with the other, but we were starting our careers on entrance level salaries. I loved Frank like a brother. I also knew that whenever the opportunity came, I would want to get my own place.

Driving through the district just to get to work the first day was an eye-opener. I kept pointing out things to Frank as we drove along: kids throwing bottles at cars, guys drinking alcohol openly on the corners, obvious drug deals going down on street corners, and just organized chaos everywhere. I mentioned to Frank that while driving to the district I did not see one police car anywhere. He just kept driving and never really responded to what I was pointing out. I finally kept my mouth shut. I got the impression that Frank was sensing a little apprehension on my part.

As we approached the district station house and it was more overwhelming than we expected. The streets around the station were filthy. There was paper, bottles, trash bags, and even a discarded mattress lying just outside the entrance to the police parking lot. As we parked on the lot, we were approached by an officer who appeared to be about fifty. He looked like he had a lot of years on the job. He motioned to roll down the window on Frank's side. As we took a closer look at this guy, we could see a filthy shirt and just a real overall nasty appearance. He had a cigar in his mouth. He blew the smoke into our car. Frank asked what he wanted.

"Are you two new? I have not seen you around these parts before." Frank told him that we were recent academy graduates and will be working in the district. He got a little arrogant as he leaned in the window. Without taking the cigar out of his mouth he said, "Boys, the first lesson in this district is that new recruits park way down at the end of the parking lot by the fence." Frank choked a little on the smoke and asked the dirtball why we could not park in any open space. He seemed to be more agitated. Then, with an obvious smoked-filled throat said, "Son, I told you the first rule and now the second rule is you pay attention to us old farts in this district."

I pulled on Frank's shirt and nodded to just go park near the fence. We did not need to start our career having the old farts pissed off.

The district turned out to be everything everyone had said and more. The inside of the district station was filthy. It was not a place you would want to sit somewhere and eat your lunch. We could not believe that police officers would want to work in such a dirty environment.

Frank and I were assigned to 722 patrol car in what we were told was the worst area of the district. Getting assigned to a car was not a normal practice for new police officers. Most new officers walked a foot post until there was an opening in a car. Our sergeant told us they were so short of officers in the district and they were putting everyone in patrol cars to cover larger areas. After roll call the first day, we went to find 722 car and relieve the officers on the day shift. On the way out to the parking lot, several officers made comments on our appearance. It was obvious they had not seen clean uniforms in quite a while. It did not appear to be a friendly bunch. There were remarks that would lead you to believe that we were the bad guys, instead of reinforcements coming to Fort Apache.

CHAPTER 10

Frank and I did not last long as roommates. It's not that I did not get along with him; it was the surprises when I got home at night. I dated some girls that actually had a little class. Frank dated some that were just toys or like Frank called them, the bitch of the week. I rarely brought a girl to the apartment because Frank was very open with his bitches. I walked in on many occasions when Frank and his bitch of the week were in some compromising positions. They made no effort to even acknowledge me. Hell, I could walk in and he'd be humping some broad and I would say, "Hi Frank how was your day?" Without breaking stride, he would actually have a conversation with me—it was weird.

I moved out after almost a year of living with Frank. I was dating a real nice girl and we had a great relationship. I wanted it to work for us. I did everything possible and that was not easy. Frank and others in the district always wanted to stop after work and knock down some beers. I did not mind the stopping, but after a few beers I was ready to go home. They were just getting started.

I guess you could consider me somewhat of a loner with the guys on our shift. I think that regardless of being a loner, I was well liked by the other officers. They knew that I would be there for them if they were in trouble. It didn't take long to realize that there was a very strong bond among the cops on our shift. In that district, you had to rely on your fellow cops or you might not be going home when the shift ended. As far as Frank and me, we were eventually split up. Although we remained on the same shift, we had new partners. I missed working with Frank. I knew I could always count on him to be on the scene when he heard the dispatcher assign a serious call to me. My new partner was a nice guy, but he was no Frank, but then again, nobody was like Frank. My new partner would prefer to just park the police car and wait until a call came over the police radio. Frank and I on the other hand wanted to keep patrolling and looking for some action—that's the way we liked it.

We had a great reputation when we worked a patrol car together. We made several arrests on some serious crimes. The supervisors in the district would always comment at roll call about the arrest we made. I got the impression that some cops were jealous. I think the supervisors made comments about me and Frank to plant the seed with some cops to get with the program. I missed working with Frank. After a little more than a year, we knew each other's moves when handling calls for service. I never got hurt while working with him. We had some scary moments, lots of fights, and lots of complaints. Frank was a nasty guy and the clientele in that bad neighborhood knew it.

The police department had a unit called the Internal Investigation Division or IID. The IID had the job of investigating complaints made against police officers, usually brutality allegations. It was a given in the police department, that if you had a lot of complaints being investigated by IID, you were probably a good cop. The reason behind that thinking was that if you were out there doing your job, you were going to get complained about. Frank led the district with complaints. Most of the complaints were that he used excessive force when dealing with the bad guys in the district. I had a few complaints myself, but they all occurred when I was working with Frank. He was the kind of guy that if you didn't move when he said to move, he would commence to smack the shit out of you and thus the IID complaints. Frank got nastier as his time in the district went along. He had a short fuse.

Working in the Western District made you hard and your outlook on society certainly changed. Police work in general made you not trust anyone and everybody you looked at seemed suspicious. I was trying my best to think that all of the people in that district were not bad people. It was hard because the bad were all we dealt with.

Frank was turning into a different person, even when he was off duty. He talked nasty to people. I talked to him about it on several occasions, but he was becoming like most of the hardened cops in that district. I had some cop friends in other districts and when we talked, I didn't feel the meanness that I felt when I talked to cops in the western. Frank did not like anyone preaching to him. He would tell me that I was turning into a real pussy. I loved Frank like a brother, but when he talked like that, it pissed me off. I could see that our friendship was slipping away the more we worked in that hellhole of a district. When I was moved to another patrol car, I was kind of relieved that getting away from Frank would be a much needed change for me.

Frank and I grew even further apart as time went on. I did see him at roll calls. The stopping after work for drinks only happened on a few occasions. I found out early in my time in that district, that drinking after work was a release for these guys. Most of the guys that stopped for drinks were married. I never knew any of them to call their wives and say they were stopping for a drink. I think they just thought that they deserved it. Hearing some shit from their wives was not something they wanted to deal with after eight hours of chaos. I also found out that there is no such thing as stopping for one drink. That would be the talk after the shift; somebody would say—hey, let's stop and have a beer. Now in the normal world of accountants, bankers, and school teachers, that might be the case, but with cops there was no end to the drinking.

There were a lot of divorced guys in the district and they usually were the ones that promoted the drinking. I found out early in my career that the divorce rate in law enforcement was very high, one of the highest in any profession. I knew that if and when I got married, I did not want to fall into that category. I was dating a very nice girl. The last thing I would want is to marry her, have children, get divorced, and pay child support for about eighteen years.

CHAPTER 11

After about three years working in the Western District, Frank and I were eligible to take the promotion test for sergeant. I really had not thought much about being a sergeant. Frank talked about it all the time. He wanted to lead men and made no bones about it. When we were together, he always said he was tired of being screwed over by supervisors. I knew that Frank's motivation to study for the test would be based on getting out of the Western District and getting into the detective unit. Frank was very smart and there was no doubt he would do good on the test for promotion. He was also a good cop. He was well respected by his peers and supervisors. If he passed the test, I was sure that he would leave the Western. He would go somewhere that would enhance his career and start his move up the chain of command. Frank always talked about promotions and how he wanted to go as far as he could in the police department. I knew that he could do it; the only thing that would hold him back would be his aggressiveness. His lack of respect for certain people would also hinder his rise in the department.

Leading up to the promotion test, Frank and I would meet at my apartment and study for the test. We knew what books would be used to come up with the test questions. We went over them until we could ask each other questions without even looking in the book. It was funny—I would ask Frank a question and he would recite the answer almost the way it was written in the book. I studied a lot when Frank was not around, but

I knew that there was no doubt about Frank passing that test. Myself, on the other hand, I would take it just for the experience of taking it. I had no real hopes of passing the test. I could not help but to be excited for Frank. He actually gave up the drinking after work to study or at least most of the time he did. When you saw him at work, he was always carrying the study material. It was so obvious to others in the district, that they started to call him sarge. Frank laughed at them when they called him sarge. I know Frank—he loved every minute of it.

We had heard about the old days in the police department, when corruption was rampant and promotions were bought. In our neighborhood, the rumors would be talked about openly that cops had to pay to get promoted. It was a known fact that if you were a beat cop and wanted to make rank, you needed to come up with some money. The department did have a test for promotion back then, but it didn't account for the only means of getting promoted. Cops didn't make much money back then. To get promoted, the money usually came from some of the affluent and well-heeled people in the area where you worked. It could be a store owner, a saloon keeper, or in some cases, it would come from those running the illegal activity in the city...like gambling. Naturally, you would be indebted to those for your entire career.

I had often heard Uncle Carmen talk to my dad and others in our neighborhood about trying to come up with the money to get promoted. Uncle Carmen didn't have any money and even if he solicited the entire family, they could not do it. I guess he could have borrowed the money, but he would probably have to take bribes to pay it back.

The process was actually a joke until the city started the Civil Service Commission. Under civil service they would give the test and then publish a list with about one hundred names on it. The names would be in order of the passing grade of the applicant for promotion. It didn't mean that the process was now perfect...it only meant that you knew your score. The bosses high in the command staff could still screw with the list. They could go anywhere on the list to promote and that's where the system reverted back to favoritism and possibly payoffs for promotions.

Frank and I had often wondered about some of the sergeants we saw early in our careers. There were some that appeared so dumb that they couldn't even correct the reports that you wrote. I knew a sergeant that would ask you to read the report out loud to him before he would sign it. It was funny, when you were done reading it, he would say, "That's a great report you wrote, son." I would thank him and walk away thinking that what he meant to say was, "That's a great report you read to me, son." I often wondered how someone like that could make it through an entire career.

It would not be like that with Frank. He was not only book smart, he was street smart. It would take a lot to put something over on him. Not only would Frank read your report, he would look for grammar and punctuation. I could just see Frank telling some of the old cops that had been around for ages to do their reports over. I'm sure he would be very diplomatic when he would tell them to make the changes. I take that back—there is no diplomacy in the way Frank handles things.

CHAPTER 12

Promotions were held in the auditorium of the police headquarters building. The mayor was there with all his puppet-like city councilmen. The governor was there; not sure why he was there except for the fact that he used to be the mayor. The command staff of the department was there—the place was packed. When promotions were held, it was a big deal. It was a time for the mayor, department heads, and all the other so-called dignitaries to pose with the newly promoted officers and their families. I don't think the politicians really gave a damn about the promotions; they were just looking for a photo shoot.

Frank did it—he aced the test. He was number five out of one hundred police officers put on the promotion list. On this day, the department was promoting ten sergeants and five lieutenants. Frank's parents attended the ceremony and a few other close friends that he invited. I didn't pass the test for sergeant. I don't know what my score was because they only tell you that you did not pass. I felt like I had helped Frank get promoted. I was the guy who studied with him and asked all the questions.

When Frank was notified that he passed the test, his first call was to me. He talked about what would happen if he got promoted. "Do you remember when I got promoted to PFC out of boot camp?"

"Yeah, that was great Frank."

"Do you remember how great I was feeling when that happened?"

"Yeah Frank, I sure remember how great you felt."

"Are you sitting down right now?"

"Frank, what the hell is going on? Quit messing with me!"

There was a moment of silence on the phone and than in the loudest voice he could muster, he yelled, "I did it Nick! I passed the test and they're promoting ten sergeants." Frank was screaming in the phone. I had to move it away from my ear. I'm not sure what the hell he was yelling. I got his attention and told him how proud I was of him and that he would make a great sergeant. Frank said, "Nick, I owe you a lot. Without you studying with me and keeping me focused, it would not have happened." I appreciated what Frank said, but I knew that he did it on his own—well, maybe I helped a little. Frank now turned to the consoling side. "Nick, there is no doubt in my mind that you will pass the next promotion test; we will study together and make it happen."

I sat in the auditorium on that promotion day with Frank's family. As I looked around the crowded room, I got that feeling that I wanted to be part of this one day soon. The new sergeants and lieutenants paraded across the stage. They received their promotion certificates from the mayor and the police chief. As each one held up their certificate, the crowd would applaud. When Frank got his certificate, I kind of forgot where I was. I jumped up and shouted, "Go Frankie, you did it man!" I was standing and clapping my hands when it hit me that I should sit down real quick. Frank had the biggest smile on his face as he crossed the stage. He gave me a big fist pump. I was really happy for him. He was a good cop and would now be a great sergeant.

Everyone congregated in the rear of the hall and a lot of handshaking was going on. Frank was politicking on his first day as a sergeant. He was shaking every hand he could get to, especially the mayor, the governor, and all the flunky city councilmen. Frank looked damn good with those stripes on his uniform. As I looked at him talking and shaking hands, I could not help but think this would be the first of many promotions for him.

Frank finally made his way over to me and grabbed me in a big bear hug. He looked me in the eye. "You are my main man; I could not have done it without you." He grabbed me again and I thought he was going to kiss me. I was right; he kissed me on the cheek. Frank came close to me and put his arms around me. "I'm going to hang with this boring crowd for a while, but me and you are going to celebrate later." I told him that I was scheduled to work later that day. Frank said, "Dude, this is big—call in sick."

I thought about it but decided to call in and ask for the day off. Frank was right—we needed to celebrate.

CHAPTER 13

I was back in my apartment waiting for Frank to call. I clicked on the answering machine and there was a message from my girlfriend. I punched the message button.

"Hi sweetie, this is Janet. I won't be able to see you this weekend. I'm going out with the girls—talk to you later." My first thought was wow—she is going out for the whole weekend with the girls! I thought that was unusual because we had made plans to be together for the upcoming weekend. I called her back and got her answering machine. I left a short message telling her that I got her message. I did not say that I was upset about the change in plans for the weekend.

While I was waiting for Frank, I was thinking about Janet. Although we were together a lot, I did not have a clear vision on where our relationship was going. We had been dating for over a year. Lately it seemed as if something was wrong. I was not fooling around on Janet. I sure hoped she wasn't fooling around on me. I popped open a beer and listened to some music. I thought more about Janet. I assured myself that everything was fine and maybe it was good that she was going out with the girls.

Frank called and it sounded like he had already started the celebration. I could hear loud music and shouting in the background. I asked him where he was and what the plans were. Frank said, "I figure we would celebrate back where it all started." I could not imagine what he was talking about—back where what started? "Nick, I'm at Jimmy Jordan's

Bar. Come on down, the place is packed—some good-looking broads also." I was going to tell Frank that I really did not want to drink in the city. I thought we should hang out in the county. I gave in and decided that this was Frank's night. I should go where he wants to go. I told him that I would be there in about an hour.

I got to the bar about nine o'clock and Frank was right—it was packed. He was right about the women also. Apparently Frank had made some phone calls and told everyone to join him at the bar for his promotion party. I did not see him when I walked in, but it didn't take long to hear him. I followed his voice to the rear of the bar. I was right; Frank was well on his way to getting shit-face drunk. I ordered a beer. I knew that if Frank continued the way he was drinking, I would have to take him home. I told myself that I would take it easy. I was also concerned that if he drank until closing time, he would probably find a way to get in a fight—he usually did.

Frank saw me and literally knocked some woman off his lap and onto the floor. He ran towards me and didn't care who he was bumping along the way. He threw his arms around me and said, "Everyone give me your attention." He then stood on a chair with a drink in each hand. "Folks, this is my best friend, Nick. If it wasn't for this good-looking dude, I would have never gotten promoted." Frank got down from the chair or I should say, he fell down off the chair. Everyone was coming over to me and shaking my hand. They were thanking me for getting Frank promoted. I was explaining to each person that I had very little to do with Frank getting promoted; he deserved all the credit.

The party got wilder as the night moved along. The owner of the bar, Jimmy Jordan, was just putting beer up on the bar. I did not see many people paying for the drinks. Jimmy was a great guy. He knew our families from when we lived in the neighborhood. He loved us for being in the Marines. He loved me and Frank for being cops. I asked Jimmy if he wanted me to start to get some money from Frank's friends in the bar. Jimmy seemed offended. "Listen, I'm so proud of you two boys; you are not paying for anything in my bar." Jimmy loved most cops and there was a reason he loved them. Jimmy owned the bar, but he also ran an illegal numbers racket out of the bar during the day. It was well known in the neighborhood that Jimmy was paying off the cops that worked that area. I knew it too, but I did not work that area. I guess I should care that cops were being paid off, but I knew it had been going on for years and I really liked Jimmy.

On several occasions I tried to talk to Frank, but he was having such a good time I let it go. I was getting concerned about his drinking; it seemed that he had a beer in his hand for the entire night. If it wasn't a beer in his hand, it was some broad's boobs. I was thinking about trying to get him out of the bar and getting something to eat. I approached him while he had a good-looking blonde up against the wall near the pool table. I think Frank was teaching her the proper way to frisk a scantily clad female. Frank saw me looking. "Hey dude, you want some of this later?" The blonde smiled; she was very attractive. I was wondering what the hell she thought her night would be with a total drunk like Frank. The blonde kind of broke loose from Frank and headed for the ladies' room. From the looks of her, she required some readjustment of her clothing. She also needed to put that thong back where it started.

Frank came over or should I say staggered over. "Are you having a good time Nick?" It didn't quite come out that way, but from knowing Frank for so many years, I could make out what he was saying. I told him that he should slow down with the drinking. I also told him that he just got promoted and if he continued to drink, something nasty usually happens. Frank grabbed me or fell on me and tried to kiss me on the cheek. I pulled away in time to avoid the leftover lipstick from the blonde. I knew that it was useless to keep trying to talk some sense into him. The blonde came back and they picked up right where they left off. I walked down to the not so crowded end of the bar and thought about calling Janet.

About one o'clock, Jimmy started to tell people that he had to close the bar. Most of the people left, but there were the ones that had too much to drink that ignored him. I was thinking—why would Jimmy want everyone to leave? He had the beat cops in his back pocket. He could stay open as late as he wanted. I was really glad that he was telling everyone that he had to close the bar. I walked to the back looking for Frank and the blonde.

I found Frank, but no blonde. She had been replaced by a short girl with black hair. Frank was all over this girl. The difference between the blonde and this girl was that she came with some dude who was sitting at the bar. I tried to tell Frank that Jimmy was closing the bar. When I put my hand on Frank's shoulder, he came around and caught me on the chin with a fist. Normally I would have been pissed, but he only grazed me.

I started to walk away when I saw a guy walking fast toward Frank and the girl. I moved to the side to let him pass and that was a mistake. Without breaking stride, he collided with Frank and landed a solid punch to Frank's jaw. Frank fell over on the pool table and was actually laughing. The guy grabbed this girl by her pretty black hair and pushed her against the wall. She took the push extremely well. She was arranging her clothing when she said, "I might have come here with you, but I'm leaving with Frank." She went over to help Frank off the pool table and that was a mistake. Before I could grab the guy, he punched her in the back of the head. She went tumbling past Frank and landed on the floor. I was moving toward the guy when Frank made a miraculous sobering accomplishment and nailed this dude with a right hand to the jaw. The guy was a little bigger than Frank, but Frank was solid as a rock. Mike Tyson could not have decked this guy any better. We all stood around and some people were apparently waiting for a classic barroom fight—but the fight was over. The guy could not even get to his feet.

Jimmy came over and said, "Frank, I have never in all my bar days seen a guy knocked out like that—it was great!" I could not believe what Jimmy was saying. Jimmy than stood on a chair. "OK folks, the fight is over and the bar is also over. You all have to leave." Jimmy asked two guys to help the poor bastard off the floor and get him some fresh air. Frank was back in the grasp of the girl. I told Frank that we needed to get the hell out of the bar.

CHAPTER 14

After the incident in the bar on Frank's promotion night, I hadn't seen or heard from him for three days. Taking Frank home that night was quite an experience. I had to convince the girl that spending the night with Frank was not a good idea. While I had been talking to Frank, he vomited every beer he had all night—this absolutely convinced her to go home alone.

I continued working in the Western District. Frank started his new assignment in the Homicide Unit. I was not sure why Frank had not called me since the party. I would have thought that getting the assignment in the Homicide Unit would have been very exciting for him. Was he still mad at me?

I was a little shocked when it was announced that he got in the Homicide Unit. Getting in that unit usually meant that someone was pulling for you or you had some big-time drag in the department. I knew Frank was well liked, but he did not talk about pulling any strings to get in that unit. It was a prestigious unit. It was a place where anybody that wanted to be somebody in the department went through the Homicide Unit. They were the elite of the department. When you saw the detectives in that unit, you would think you were watching a men's fashion show. Even though they handled bloody scenes, you could see them out there in their three-piece suits, trench coats, and some with Stetson hats. I knew that Frank would have to do some big time shopping to fit the image in that unit.

I finally got in touch with him and he apologized for not calling me. He said that he was just as surprised as anyone that he got assigned to the Homicide Unit. I told him that he must have had someone pulling for him to get there. He said the only person he could think about getting it done was Colonel McAvey. This was the first time he mentioned having a relationship with Colonel McAvey.

McAvey was a veteran cop who probably had forty years on the job. He was a grumpy old guy, but had the respect of the men and women in the department. He had risen through the ranks over the years and was politically connected in the mayor's office and probably in the governor's office. It was always rumored in the department that if you wanted a certain assignment, you would go to McAvey. I had worked with Frank since we came on the job and he never mentioned talking to or meeting with McAvey. I guess Frank was told to keep things quiet which really surprised me. He and I had shared everything over the past years. I guess something as important as going to the Homicide Unit was not something he wanted to share.

Frank told me that he was assigned to a squad in the Homicide Unit that had some very experienced detectives. He said that the captain of the unit told him that he had great expectations of him. Frank said that the captain acted a little strange at first, as if Frank was not his choice to come to the unit. He assured the captain that he would work extremely hard and that he would learn as much about homicide investigations as he could. I had my concerns on how Frank would do in that unit. He had spent all of his time in patrol and had no real investigative experience. I was excited for Frank, but to be honest, I was also a little jealous. I was getting a little tired of patrol, especially in that godforsaken Western District. I knew that I now had a contact in the Homicide Unit—maybe I would get there one day. My only concern was…would Frank stay out of trouble long enough to get me in the unit?

CHAPTER 15

I continued to work hard in the Western District, but it was getting to me. It seemed as if I was just working all the time and getting nowhere fast in the department. I had thoughts of quitting the job and trying something else. I had made many new friends in the district, but it was not the same without Frank. Once in a while, I would see Frank's name in the newspaper about working on a murder. I was proud of his accomplishments. I wanted something more rewarding than coming to work every day and putting up with the same old bullshit. I wanted to come to work in a suit and look like a banker. I was hoping that Frank would be working towards getting me down to the Homicide Unit—I knew it would not be easy.

My new partner in the district was Fred Binder. He was a salty cop with eighteen years on the job. He had spent his entire time in the department in the Western District. He did his job, but that was it. He did no more or no less—just what he had to do to get by. I found it hard to get along with Fred. Most of our conversations were about how fucked up the department was. I had somehow maintained my pride in the job. I was also well aware that I had many years to go before I could retire. I wanted to keep a positive attitude. I knew that if I got discouraged on the job and talked like most of the men in the district, I would have very little chance of getting assigned to detectives or getting promoted.

I tried to convince Fred that we were making a difference in the district, but it was a daily struggle. He had been injured a few times on the job and once seriously when he was attacked by a group of black guys. According to Fred, he let his guard down and they kicked his ass. He said after that, he didn't trust any of those black bastards. Every time we got a call for a disturbance, he would tell me to never let them get the upper hand. It got a little crazy working with Fred. If someone would do as little as make a move toward him… he would bust them with his nightstick. He would then lock them up and make up some bullshit story in court. I didn't like this, but there wasn't much I could do. I put up with it and the more I told Fred it was wrong, the funnier he thought it was. I knew that I had to get away from him or it was just a matter of time before his stupidity would take us both down.

As nasty as Fred appeared to be while he was working, he was actually a good family man. He confided in me one night that he was active in his church. He had three children—two boys and a girl. In his moments when he was not criticizing the police department and most of the world, we held some decent conversations. He worshiped his kids and always talked about them. He worked a lot of overtime to send them to Catholic schools. He absolutely despised the public school system in the city. As far as Fred was concerned, all the problems in Baltimore were the result of the poor public school system. You didn't really know what the topic of the day would be with Fred. It could start out that the Orioles sucked and he would never go to another game. He would then knock his neighbors and say that he hasn't talked to most of them in over fifteen years. He was not as dumb as he led the other officers in the district to believe. I got it out of him one day that he attended Loyola High School, which is one of the finest Catholic schools in the Baltimore area. He went on to the University of Baltimore where he majored in business with the intentions of getting into law school. He left college after the second year to join the police department.

I missed working with Frank in the district, but Fred was an interesting character. He would on occasion ask about the relationship I had with Frank. I went through it all with him. I talked about growing up with Frank, getting in trouble with him, joining the Marines, and then coming on the police department with him. I confided in him that Frank's goal in the police department was to rise to the highest rank he could. Fred on the other hand had no aspirations of obtaining any rank; he would be perfectly happy staying in patrol for his entire career.

Fred could be talking to you one minute about politics or sports. As soon as a call for service came over the radio, he changed like you would never believe. The conversation would stop and he would put on his game face and off to the call we would go. Depending on what kind of call it was, he would talk about how we would handle it when we arrived. He knew the district as well as anyone. We could be responding to a call and he would tell you when he was at that location last. He actually knew the people on some of the calls. I felt safe around Fred. I don't think it was because he was so cautious. It was probably because he had been injured in the past. I think it was the respect I saw from the clientele we dealt with in the district.

He had his little specialty moves that he would teach me when we were in homes handling domestic disturbances. A particular move that he taught me, worked to perfection one night. If we were in the house and the disturbance was on the second floor, he would always make sure the aggressive person stood close to the stairway. Fred had a way of maneuvering so that the aggressive person was facing him on the top step. He would talk to the person and if it looked like a fight was ensuing, he would simply put his hand on the person's chest and down the steps they went. Usually when they landed at the bottom of the steps, they had no fight left in them. When I first saw this, I was thinking that it went so smooth that Fred had obviously perfected this over many years. He didn't use it all the time—but when he did, it worked. Fred also did not like to get dirty on the job. In the Western District, it was not easy to go home at night with a clean uniform.

We were called to a home one night for a possible DOA which means dead-on-arrival. We arrived on the scene and an elderly black lady was standing on the steps screaming for help. I ran into the home and saw an old black man lying on the floor. There were several others standing around and screaming also. Someone said that he was dead and had just fallen to the floor minutes ago. Fred was coming in the home and apparently he heard the statement that the old man had just died. He walked toward the man and hollered to me, "Give him mouth-to-mouth."

I dropped down over the man. I guess it's a spontaneous move. I stopped short of putting my mouth over this dead old man's mouth. I got to my feet and now the small crowd in the living room is shouting for me to give him mouth-to-mouth. Fred was just standing there. I told Fred that it appears the man is dead. He said, "You never know— give it a try."

I was getting a little perturbed that Fred was giving the orders and making me look like a fool. I reached down and tried to get a pulse in the old man's neck. It was obvious this guy was dead. He was probably that way since he hit the floor. Fred was getting a kick out of all this mouth-to-mouth stuff. I told the old lady that he was dead and that I would call an ambulance to respond anyway. She started to scream. "You could have saved him. He told you to give him mouth-to-mouth. You could have saved him!"

Now the whole room is screaming and crying. I was trying to tell them that it would not have been any use attempting mouth-to-mouth. Fred calmly walked to the middle of the room. "Folks, why didn't one of you give him mouth-to-mouth? You didn't need to wait for us to get here. He's obviously a relative of somebody in this room. He ain't related to me or this officer. What the hell did you tell the police dispatcher when you called?"

The elderly woman was now slumped in the chair. She looked at Fred and said, "We told them that Henry fell and he be looking dead."

Fred got a little more serious and put his arm on the old lady. "I'm sorry Henry is dead. I know there was nothing we could have done for him. When the ambulance gets here, they will officially pronounce him dead. They will take him to the morgue and the funeral director can pick up the body in the morning. In the future if something like this happens again, just drop down and blow in their mouth. You never know what will happen."

The ambulance came and took Henry's body to the morgue. I got the information to write the report and we left. As we were driving away, I let Fred know that his little routine that he tried on me was not very funny. "Fred, I like you, but you need to remember that the people in this district are human. That was his family in that room. You didn't have to pull that bullshit about dropping down and giving him mouth-to-mouth. Those people are not that dumb that they don't know you were screwing with them at a terrible time in their life. How would you like it if the cops came to your house and fooled around while your father was lying dead on the floor? Shit Fred, you talk sometimes about your faith and sending your kids to Catholic schools. What kind of faith would do what you did in there?"

"Okay, that's enough preaching to me. I told you before that when I'm working in this hellhole of a district, I'm a cop. When I'm off duty and at home, I'm a father, a family man, and a churchgoing man. I may have pushed it a little too far in there. I was only having some fun. That old bastard was dead long before we even got in that house."

"It doesn't matter Fred. You have to start to give these people the benefit of the doubt. You may have been hurt a few times, but they were bad guys that did that to you. I believe that most of the people in this district are law-abiding citizens. Don't go through your entire career hating black people. It's against all the principles that you live by in your private life."

Nick was driving to the spot in Leakin Park where they usually parked to write reports. Fred was not talking. After a few minutes parked, Fred told Nick that he now feels bad about what happened in that house. He told Nick that he really needs to put some bad memories in the district behind him. He told Nick that he was the first cop in the district to ever talk to him that way. He said that most of the cops in the district just mess with people to make the time go by faster. Nick told him that he did not believe that most of the cops were that way.

The rest of the night went without any serious incidents. They handled a stolen car report, a dog bite, theft of some candy from the 7-Eleven, kids playing football in the street, and a traffic light out at Mosher and Laurens. Not bad for a night in the dreaded, old, and nasty Western District.

CHAPTER 16

While I was struggling to hang on in the Western District, Frank was making a name for himself in the Homicide Unit. He had attended a few schools to learn about death investigations. He was also getting a reputation in the unit as a no-nonsense supervisor. He was attracting the attention of the command staff. Frank was seemingly on the path to move up in the department. I also knew he could not wait to take the test for lieutenant.

Frank got a call from Nick while working the night shift. Nick told him that he had to get the hell out of the district or he would probably consider quitting the police department. Nick told him that he wanted to meet with him the next night to discuss it over a few beers. Both guys were excited that they would be getting together—it had been too long that they were apart.

Frank was dominating most of the conversation with a few murder investigation stories that his squad was working on. He sure had Nick's attention. The stories were much more exciting to hear than the mundane work in the district. Frank took a break from the stories and asked Nick how he was doing. Nick was appreciative that Frank realized that he was talking too much and now wanted to hear how he was doing. Nick sipped a bit of his beer. "Frank, I'm going crazy in that district."

Frank touched Nick on the shoulder. "Tell me what's wrong; you know that I am always here for you." Nick went off on how going to work every day was getting to be a struggle. He talked about all the assholes that he worked with in the district. He told Frank it was just an absolute madhouse with no real supervision from anyone. Nick continued with a few stories of the chaos that occurs on a daily basis with no one giving a shit.

Just as Frank was about to speak, Nick stopped him. "I think Janet is screwing around with someone."

"Wow, you sure know how to change the subject in midstream." Frank ordered more beer. "I think that little statement calls for a shot of some good whiskey." Frank told the bartender to pour two shots of Crown Royal. The shot was no sooner on the bar before Nick downed it and ordered another. "Slow down big guy, we got all night. I want to hear about Janet."

"Let's move to a table...I don't want anyone to hear this." Frank looked at Nick and saw a very serious side that he had not seen since the early days in the Marines—he was concerned. Over at the table, Nick did not waste any time. "Frank, I'm positive that she is seeing some guy."

"Slow down and start from the beginning. Tell me what you know and not what you think."

Nick said that he hasn't seen Janet for about three weeks and that when he calls, she always seems to have a reason not to get together.

"I thought at first it was my job; she told me she can't stand me being a cop. I don't think it's the job. I watched her apartment one night and saw her get out of a car with some dude."

"You got to be shitting me. That bitch loves you or at least she used to love you. Do you know who the guy is?"

"No, I was not close enough to see him, but they were holding hands and seemed real friendly."

Frank stood up and shouted, "That no-good son of a bitch." Nick told Frank to sit down and be quiet. Frank sat down, but it was obvious to Nick that he was really pissed at Janet. Nick was now wondering if he did the right thing by telling Frank.

"Frank, I'm only telling you this because I really don't have anyone in the district to talk to about personal things like this." Frank put his arm around Nick and did not say anything. He did not have to speak. Nick appreciated the gesture. Frank sat down and asked Nick if he confronted Janet about this guy. Nick said that he considered his options, but wanted to run it by someone and then make the decision to either approach her or just move on with his life.

Frank was comforting Nick and the Crown Royal helped a little. He asked Nick if he knew what kind of car the guy was driving the night that he saw him with Janet. Nick said he looked at the car after Janet and the guy went into her apartment. "He must have some bucks— he's driving a brand new Mercedes."

"If you were that close to the car, I hope you got the tag number."

"Of course I got the tag number, you asshole."

"Well, hello—what the fuck is the guy's name and where does he live?"

Nick told Frank that he did not run the tag number in the system because he did not want to leave a trace of his name.

"Good move Sherlock—for once you used your head. Give me the tag number; we have ways in homicide to get things done without leaving any footprints."

Nick gave Frank the tag number and asked what he was going to do. "Listen, we have been like brothers for a long time—just trust me and let's get the hell out of this place."

CHAPTER 17

It was about 3 A.M. on the midnight shift in the Western District. It was just downright hot, with no relief from the heat going into the early hours of the morning. A dispatch came over the police radio, "Burglary in progress at the Sphinx Club, 2112 Myrtle Avenue."

Nick reached for the police radio and answered the call, "724 will handle that call—we're in the area." Fred put on the running lights and the siren. He tore out of the parking lot. We had just finished a sandwich and soda. We were also planning on trying to get a little sleep. Fred was one of the scariest drivers you ever wanted to ride with. He had no regard for life or limb when he got an emergency call like this one. He rarely slowed down for stop signs or traffic lights. If anyone was in the street he appeared to actually be aiming for them. I was sadly getting used to this madness. I never really liked it and tried to drive when we worked together. I would tell Fred that we were not at the Indy 500. I don't think he gave a shit about the people; after all, it's just the scumbags of the Western District.

Fred made it to the Sphinx Club in record time and did not run anyone over or at least I don't think he did. I did experience a few bumps along the way. We had handled calls like this before and most of the time nobody was in the place. Fred shut off the lights and siren about a block from the club. He parked the car on an angle next to the club. We had worked together long enough that we knew hand signals. Fred motioned to me to take the back. He would check the front and side doors. He whistled

52

at me and signaled that the side door was partially open. I started to walk towards him and he motioned for me to continue to the rear of the club. I thought about calling for assistance. I knew that the cars would come with the sirens blasting.

Even though it was still really hot outside, there wasn't anyone on the street. I was approaching the rear of the club. I was thinking that maybe I should have gone in that door with Fred. I no sooner finished that thought when I heard a gunshot from inside the bar. My first reaction was to jump behind a large dumpster and hang out with the rats. It seemed like minutes before I heard anything after that shot, but it was probably seconds. I moved out from behind the dumpster. I had this bad feeling about what was happening.

The night was suddenly eerily silent. I moved closer to the open side door and that's when I heard Fred holler. "Nick, the son of a bitch is coming out back. I think he's got a gun." I ran to the back alley and at first saw nothing. I was moving toward the dumpster again when I heard some movement on the second floor rear porch. I directed my flashlight up towards the noise. I did not see anything, but I heard Fred holler, "Stop you bastard or I'll blow your ass away." Just then I saw a black guy jump from the porch to the alley. I don't know if he knew I was there because he landed about five feet from me. It was dark in the alley, but he appeared to have something in his hand. I told him to stop. He started to run. I fired two shots. At first I thought I missed him, but as I went further down the alley, I found him lying face down.

Fred came running down the alley and at first he didn't see the black guy. He was panting and sweating. I thought he was going to have a heart attack. He saw the guy on the ground and said, "Great job Nick, you finished the bastard." Fred moved toward the guy and was going through his pockets. I was standing there in shock. Nothing like this had happened to me before. Fred put his arm on my shoulder and said, "I could have sworn this dude had a gun. Did you see a gun?" I told Fred that it did appear that he had something in his hand, but I was not sure what it was.

We looked around the alley and we could not find any weapons. There was a broken bottle near his body. I told Fred that we need to call our sergeant and an ambulance. Fred put his arm on my shoulder and said, "Easy man, this sorry bastard won't need an ambulance—he's dead. Don't touch anything. I will call those that need to be called." I was still standing there with my gun in my hand. I stopped shaking, but I was still in shock. I was thinking that here we are in the alley with a dead burglar, gunshots had been fired, and no one has come out of their houses. The neighborhood was bad, so I guess they are used to gunshots. You would think somebody would come out.

Fred came back from the car and told me that he called our sergeant, the Homicide Unit, and the medical examiner. He told me to sit in the car for a while and pull myself together before the sergeant got there.

I was leaning against the car when the sergeant pulled up. Sergeant Jackman was an old-timer. I don't think anything bothered this guy. He was walking toward me when Fred came out of the alley. "Nick, you lucky son of a bitch; he did have a gun." Fred came over and showed us a gun that he said was under the dead guy's body. The gun was a Charter Arms .44 caliber revolver with five rounds in the gun. I really didn't know what to say. Fred was making a big deal about how lucky I was. The sergeant asked me if I saw the gun before I fired at the guy. I was about to answer when Fred spoke up. "Damn right, he saw the gun. I hollered to him that the dude had a gun." I stood there debating my answer. Did Fred really holler that the guy had a gun?

The sergeant said, "Well young man, before the assholes from homicide get here let's come up with a story." I was stumbling over my words and told the sergeant that if Fred said he hollered that the guy had a gun, then that must be what happened.

The homicide detectives arrived about the same time as the medical examiner's wagon. The guys from the ME's office were civilians that had the job of riding around Baltimore and picking up the dead bodies. You had to watch these guys, because they would just pull up and snatch the body. They did not care about preservation of a crime scene. They had no training in crime scene procedures. They just wanted to grab the body and go. It's Baltimore and they are busy.

The homicide detectives told the ME goons to just standby and not to be in such a hurry. The detectives were cool. Like most of the guys in homicide, nothing seemed to bother them.

The detectives apparently knew my sergeant. They introduced themselves to me and Fred. "Hi officer, I'm Detective O'Brien and this is my partner, Detective Solinsky. We will be working this shooting."

Fred was much more relaxed than I was. He looked at Solinsky and said, "How you doing Pollock, do you remember me? You and I went through the academy together." Those two slapped hands and hugged each other as if we were having some kind of reunion. Fred did the talking. "This should not be a problem for you guys. My man here did the right thing and wasted that piece of shit." Fred put his arm on my shoulder. I really felt uncomfortable.

O'Brien seemed to be a little more serious than Solinsky. "We will conduct our investigation and we will need to take statements from the both of you down at the homicide office."

The homicide detectives gave instructions to the crime lab guys. I was impressed how they handled themselves. I could not help but to think that this is what policing is all about. Fred wanted to tell them what happened and O'Brien stopped him. "I will talk to your sergeant first and then you can give me a brief account of what happened. I'm sure everything went according to procedures. I want to advise you both that you don't have to give a full statement to us if you don't want to."

Solinsky jumped in, "Yeah my partner is right; you're protected under the police officer's bill of rights."

Sergeant Jackman stepped in between the two detectives. "Listen fellows, my men know about the police officer's bill of rights and they will give you anything you want." I was thinking that I should say something, but when I heard police officer's bill of rights, I was concerned. I noticed that Fred was smiling when the detectives were talking. I assumed that he had been through this before. We watched as the detectives and the crime lab proceeded to do their thing. Sergeant Jackman told us that he would ride us down to the homicide office. He was not in any hurry; it appeared that he wanted to watch what the detectives were doing.

After about thirty minutes, O'Brien came over to us. "I seem to get the gist of what happened here, but can you give me the Reader's Digest version."

I started to talk when Fred moved in front of me, "Gentlemen, let me run this by you so you can understand what a great job my partner did." Well, I think O'Brien was getting a little peeved with Fred's attitude. He motioned for Fred to step back.

He stepped directly in front of me. "Officer, since you are the shooter in this case, maybe you would like to tell me what happened."

Sergeant Jackman chimed in, "Make it brief son, you can decide later at the office if you want to give a full-blown statement." I stood there listening to all the talk. I had never been involved in a shooting incident. I was hoping I was doing the right thing and getting the best advice.

I told O'Brien that we got the call for a burglary in progress. I told him that when we got on the scene, I took the back of the bar and Fred went in the side door that was partially opened. I was choosing my words carefully. I did not want to add something that would be questionable procedure. I told O'Brien that while I was in the rear of the bar, I heard a gunshot. I told him that Fred hollered that the guy might have a gun and then I saw a guy jump from the rear roof. I must have been talking too fast, as O'Brien told me to slow down a little and take some breaths. I slowed down and told him that I saw something in the guy's hand as he was running from me. I ordered the guy to stop and when he did not, I fired two shots. I started to continue when O'Brien said, "That's all I need to know for now; we can discuss it further at the homicide office."

Sergeant Jackman drove us down to the homicide office and had someone else take care of our patrol car. I had never been in the homicide office. When we walked in, we were directed to an interview room. A detective opened the door and we both started to walk in the room. He put out his arm, "You will each be in a separate room for now." I went in the room and when he shut the door, I was getting concerned about what was happening. The room was like something you see in the movies. The small room had no windows, nothing on the walls, no phone, a small table, and two chairs. The door opened and it was Sergeant Jackman. "Don't worry about anything; you can start to write your official report." He didn't say anything else and was gone in a minute. It seemed like I was in that room for a long time. The room had no clock and I did not have my watch. I was not sure how long it really was.

I was about ready to go out and ask what was going on. I moved toward the door and it swung open. I was shocked by who came in. "Nick, what the hell happened out there tonight?" I moved back to my chair and was really glad to see Frank. Yes, Sergeant Frank Favasi himself, a sergeant in the Homicide Unit and my best friend. I was a little confused and asked Frank if he was working on the shooting. "No Nick, I got a call from one of the guys that know how tight we are." Frank flopped down in the other uncomfortable chair. "Nick, this room is not bugged, so tell me real quick what happened out there tonight." He reached across the table and touched my arm. "Tell me the exact truth and no bullshit. I can make this right if it's wrong." I told Frank the story and he stood up and said, "Nick, don't fuckin lie to me; did you see the guy with a gun or not?"

"Frank, you said you were going to help me, why would I lie?"

"Nick, I didn't say you lied, but I know that piece of shit you were with. He probably put that gun on that guy."

I was not really surprised at what Frank said, because after I shot the guy, I had the thought that maybe I really didn't see a gun. "Nick, I can't stay in this room much longer. O'Brien is one of the sharpest detectives we have. Nick, if you saw a gun that's fine; if you didn't see a gun we can make it fine also, but you need to tell me."

"If Fred said he had a gun, then he had a gun."

Frank walked around to Nick's side of the table and hugged him. He whispered in Nick's ear, "You know I love you like a brother and everything is going to be OK." Frank turned away and started toward the door. He had the doorknob in his hand. He looked back at Nick with a reassuring smile. "Nick, the son of a bitch had a gun."

CHAPTER 18

The apartment lights were out. There was a Mercedes parked near Janet's car in the parking lot. Frank decided that he needed to go over and make sure it was the same tag number that Nick given him. He got out of his unmarked police cruiser and walked toward the car. He was working the midnight shift in the Homicide Unit. He told his guys he was going out to ride around for a while and if anything happened to give him a call. He was thinking that he sure picked a piss-poor night to check out Janet and her new beau. The rain was coming down as if it was being poured from buckets. Frank knew that Janet's apartment was in the front of the complex where she or anyone else would have a clear view of the parking lot. He got close enough to the Mercedes that he could direct his flashlight on the license plate—BLX-912, that's the tag that Nick gave me to check out.

Frank went back to his car. He wiped the rain from his face. He moved his car back further in the parking lot where he had a direct vantage point to observe the apartment and the Mercedes. He pulled out his notepad and brushed through the pages. Here it is—Paul Philbin and he lives at 5527 Talbot Road in Carroll County. Let's see, he is six feet tall, weighs one hundred and ninety pounds. He is twenty-eight years old and has no criminal or traffic record.

Frank sat in the unmarked police car for about two hours. Periodically he called the homicide office to make sure nothing was happening. It was about 3 A.M. when the door to the apartment complex opened and a guy fitting the description of Philbin came out. Frank sat up in the car. He watched as the guy walked briskly to his car, ducking from the pounding rain. Frank could hardly keep the guy in view as the rain was coming down as if the skies had opened up. He slouched down in his car as the Mercedes drove out of the parking lot. He waited a minutes and then he followed the car. There was not much traffic on the road. He stayed as far back as possible. Frank knew the guy was heading in the direction of Carroll County—a suburb outside the city. He was probably going home. The Mercedes pulled down a street with some expensive single houses on both sides. Frank looked around at the homes and was thinking that this guy is probably married. He was just screwing around with Janet.

The Mercedes pulled into a long driveway. The guy just sat in the car with the lights out. Frank assumed the guy was probably thinking of a story to tell his wife. Frank pulled over and turned out the lights on his car. He could not determine what the guy was doing. He had this crazy idea that he would approach the car and tell the guy he's a cop. He would say that the Mercedes was driving in a very suspicious manner and he was just checking it out.

Frank got out of his car and walked up the driveway with his flashlight pointing at the car. With the rain coming down hard and the flashlight being dulled somewhat, he could not see in the vehicle. He approached the driver side door. The door swung violently open and caught Frank in the midsection. He went down on the ground and the flashlight went flying on the grass. He was stunned and all of a sudden, along with the rain, he was feeling the weight of this guy pinning him to the driveway.

"You bastard, I know you've been following me. I'll teach you a lesson." Frank was still stunned from the door slamming him to the ground. He was taking a few solid punches to the head and chest from the guy. Frank was more embarrassed than hurt. He was thinking that this dude weighs more than his driving record indicated. The guy got off of Frank and tried to stand. Frank rolled over to get away and reached for his flashlight.

The guy screamed for help and came toward Frank. "I got something for you buddy." He swung at Frank and that was a mistake. Frank rolled away from the car. He pulled his gun from his holster. On pure impulse, he fired two shots at the guy. The guy went down like a sack of potatoes—face first on the wet driveway. Frank got to his feet and reached down to check the guy. He was reaching down when the lights came on in the house. He ducked behind the Mercedes and waited to see if the door opened. His first thought was that he could say he figured the guy was trying to break into the house and when he approached him, he was attacked. Frank decided that story did not make any sense. Why was he in Carroll County and not in the city? He was way out of his jurisdiction. He saw another light come on in the house on the first floor. Frank decided that he had to get the hell out of the area and leave the guy—he was sure that he was dead.

Frank got in his car and drove as fast as he could back toward the city. When he got completely out of the neighborhood, he pulled into a vacant lot. He was shaking both from the night chill and from what had just happened. He needed to assess the situation—that's what cops do. He called into the homicide office and asked if everything was quiet. He was told that there was a homicide on the west side, but it was being handled. He told his detective that he would be in soon. He said he had got tied up on some personal business.

Frank was cleaning himself off and checking his gun. He realized that he had shot the guy with his service revolver. He also knew that unless they recovered his service revolver, they would never be able to match up the bullets recovered from the dead guy.

He left the vacant lot and drove to his favorite all night restaurant in Fells Point, the Brew & Chew. Frank went in and was greeted by Pesto, the manager. "Frank, you look like you saw a ghost—are you all right?" Frank went to the rear of the restaurant and sat in a booth. He ordered coffee and assured Pesto he was fine. He said that he had been working too many hours and needed a break. Pesto brought him a coffee and told Frank that he needed to take better care of himself. He told Frank what he frequently told him. "The job sucks and nobody gives a rat's ass about you." Frank nodded his appreciation for Pesto's concern and assured him that he was fine. Frank knew that he had to eat something—his stomach was rumbling.

He told Pesto that he would have the usual. The usual for Frank was three eggs, fries, toast, two slices of bologna on top of the eggs, lots of hot sauce, and a Dr Pepper. Frank went to the men's room and looked in the mirror. He used some paper towels to wipe some areas that he had missed. He looked in the mirror again. "Holy shit, what did I get myself into?" He went back to the table and even though he was totally nauseous, he finished off the breakfast. Pesto came over and again asked if everything was all right. Frank was annoyed with the questioning. "Goddamn Pesto quit asking me if I'm okay. I told you I was fine."

Pesto walked away. Frank tried to grab him by the arm and apologize. Pesto pointed his finger at Frank. "Frank, I have known you a long time. I knew you before you took this shit job that you have."

"Pesto, I didn't mean to jump at you. I have some things on my mind and need to take care of them—I'm sorry."

Pesto gave Frank a great big hug. "Go ahead, get your ass out of here and fight some crime." Frank offered to pay for his meal, but Pesto would not take his money—he never did.

Frank stood outside the restaurant and his head was spinning. He was talking to himself out loud. "What the hell do I do and where do I start?" He sat in his car and looked in the mirror and said to absolutely no one but himself, "I can handle this. I know what to do. I just need to think things out." His first move was to call the office and tell his guys that he was taking the rest of the night off because he was not feeling well. He figured that his next move was to go home and clean his service revolver. He pulled away from the restaurant and screamed into the mirror, "You're a fuckin homicide sergeant— you can take care of this mess. It will just appear that the poor bastard was attacked outside his home by some thugs." Frank smiled into the mirror and drove to his apartment.

CHAPTER 19

Nick was back to work in the Western District after a short suspension for the shooting. It was routine procedure in the department to suspend an officer involved in a shooting. The Internal Investigation Unit conducted their probe of the shooting to see if any departmental procedures were violated. Nick was cleared.

Nick's first day back was like a homecoming from a war. Everyone was high-fiving him and telling him what a great job he did to rid the city of a no-good piece of shit. Nick took it all in stride. He didn't like that kind of attention, especially since someone had died.

In the Western District you had to come to work each day with your game face on. You could be the mildest, nicest, clean-cut guy in the world, but when you entered the Western District you were now a hardnosed, take no shit, kick-ass cop. Nick was finding this harder to do as the time went by. He could actually feel the change coming on him when he knew it was time to go to work. He did not like what he was becoming.

Along with the woes of the department, he was still dealing with the fact that Janet had dumped him. The guys in the district knew that he was not dating Janet. They would try to fix him up with their wives' friends. Nick was considered a nice clean-cut guy. Most guys were sincere in trying to fix him up.

He was probably also at the point in his career that he knew he needed a change. He knew he could not take the Western District much longer.

Nick loved police work. What kept him going was the hope that he would soon get a transfer to detectives and maybe even the Homicide Unit. Nick was also a realist and knew that getting out of the Western District was probably like busting out of Alcatraz.

His first day back found him working a patrol car with Salvatore Muntez or like most of the guys in the district called him—the crazy spic. Sal was not as bad as the guys would make him out to be; he just loved the women. The guys in the district would say that Sal would screw a snake if someone would hold it still. Nick had only worked with Sal once before. He actually found him to be a nice guy. He never saw the screw a snake guy at all. Sal did love to talk and it seemed like he would talk for the entire eight hour shift. In between talking about women, he would even throw in some talk about when he played semi-pro baseball. Nobody ever really questioned it, but Sal said he played double-A baseball for the New York Mets. He had some great stories about who he played with. He said that some of those guys were now in the majors. Sal said that he hurt his shoulder and that was it for his baseball career. He came to Baltimore and became a cop. NYPD had a waiting list of about six hundred and he knew he could get right on the force in Baltimore.

The shift started off quiet, so they pulled the patrol car under the Franklin Street Bridge. Sal was a big guy and he always wanted to stretch out. He opened the door, pushed back the seat, and grabbed the newspaper. Nick felt a little tired also and stretched out his legs.

Sal finished the front page and threw it over to Nick. Nick just brushed the paper aside. "I don't read that propaganda; it's the same shit all the time."

"Yeah you're right—it's the same old shit Nick. There are people getting killed, people getting robbed, and politicians getting caught taking money. The same old shit, like the poor son of a bitch that they found dead in his driveway up in Carroll County this morning."

"Damn, a murder in Carroll County that's rare—what happened?"

"All the paper said was that the guy was shot and found in his driveway by his wife."

Nick was curious and picked up the paper. He started reading the story and let out a very loud, holy shit. Sal looked over and asked Nick what was up with the holy shit. Nick got out of the car and walked away still reading the paper. He recognized the name of the guy found shot dead in his driveway. It was the dude that was driving the Mercedes and seeing Janet. Nick wanted to be sure and pulled out his case book and thumbed through it until he found the license tag from the Mercedes. He found the name—Paul Philbin, 5527 Talbot Road, Carroll County. Nick walked further away from the car. He was getting sick to his stomach. He was thinking about Janet. Did she know about this? Was she somehow involved in his death? It also became very clear now to Nick that this guy was married. Was he just screwing around with Janet?

Nick's thoughts were racing. Was Janet that dumb that she would dump him for a married man? Damn, should I call her and tell her that her lover was murdered? He was also thinking that there are not that many murders in Carroll County. Was this guy screwing around with someone's wife? Did the jilted husband find out and kill him? His thoughts were also a little selfish as he was thinking that now that her lover was out of the way, maybe he still had a chance with Janet.

Sal hollered over to Nick that they had a call for a disturbance in the 500 block of Pritchard Street and they had to take the call. Nick folded the paper. He stuck it in his back pocket. On the way to the call, Sal asked if everything was all right. He asked Nick, how come all of sudden you like the paper? Nick said he just felt sorry for the guy that was shot dead in Carroll County. He stared out the window and said, "The guy probably has kids and was a good family man."

"That's bullshit Nick, he was probably out fuckin around and his wife wasted his cheating ass."

The shift went by rather quickly. Nick could not stop thinking about the murder. He wanted to call Janet but he wanted to give her time to digest what happened. He was sure that Janet knew. She was a big reader of the paper in the morning.

Nick was leaving the district parking lot and got in his car. He just sat there for a while. He was dying to find out more about the murder. He slapped the steering wheel. "I can call Frank. He can call Carroll County and find out what happened."

Nick tried Frank's cell phone but got a voice mail saying that he was not available. He left a message asking Frank to call him as soon as possible. Nick wanted to call Janet, but he knew he had to follow some type of plan. He decided that talking to Frank was first. He was also thinking about calling the Carroll County Police Department—he nixed that thought. "What the hell would I ask them? Would they have a lot of questions for me?" Nick drove down to Jimmy Jordan's Bar. He decided to wait there for a call from Frank.

Jimmy was glad to see Nick. He asked about Frank. "That dude got promoted and now he's a big shot. He don't stop by to see us peons anymore." Nick assured Jimmy that Frank was busy working in the Homicide Unit. He had very little private time anymore. Nick and Jimmy were catching up on some gossip about the neighborhood when Nick's cell phone rang. He jumped off the stool and moved to the rear of the empty bar. He flipped the phone open—it was Frank.

"Hey dude, it's me. What's up?"

"Oh, I was just wondering how you were doing. I was thinking that we could drink a few beers."

"Nick, I'm pretty busy. We are getting slammed with murders."

"Frank, if at all possible I really need to talk to you."

"Shit man, you're right. We do need to talk—it's been too long."

"I'm at Jimmy Jordan's. How long will it take you?"

"I need to talk to a couple detectives. I will be there in about thirty minutes."

Nick had a few more beers with Jimmy. He was not a big drinker and Jimmy asked if everything was okay. Nick laughed, "I guess I'm still sad about my girlfriend dumping me." Jimmy listened to Nick while he went into the details of how Janet broke up the relationship slowly over the past few months. Jimmy was telling Nick that there are plenty of fish in the ocean.

"Nick, I would have thought you would have been married by now. You are a nice guy and any female out there would consider you a great catch. Between you and Frank, there is no doubt that you are the marrying type. Frank likes women but he's not the kind of guy that would be faithful and want to raise a family."

"I appreciate that Jimmy, but this job is crazy and there is very little time to dedicate to a lasting relationship."

"Shit, here we are talking like two sorry bastards. A few years ago, you and that crazy Frank would screw any bitch that would glance your way." Nick and Jimmy laughed. The bar was starting to get crowded. Jimmy told Nick that he needed to wait on some customers. He put his arms around Nick and kissed him on the cheek. He put another beer in front of him. He walked down to take care of some of his regulars.

Nick lifted the beer to his mouth; they were going down smooth. "Where the hell is Frank when you need him?"

CHAPTER 20

Nick woke up on his couch. When he realized where he was, he was pissed. "Why the hell did I stay at the bar so long? I feel like shit." Nick pulled himself up from the couch and stumbled towards the kitchen. He yanked open the refrigerator. "There ain't a damn thing in here to drink. My mouth feels like several squirrels died in there." He flopped back down on the couch and tried to think about what happened last night. Not being a big drinker, he quickly realized that he stayed too long at the bar and got drunk. He remembered enough to know that Frank did not show up. He made his way to the bathroom and aggressively brushed the squirrels from his mouth. The cold water gave some relief. He wanted to take a shower but decided that he needed to talk to Frank. He knew that it was not like Frank to not show up, especially since Nick had told him it was real important.

Nick dialed Frank's cell number and got the voice message that he was not available. He did not want to call the Homicide Unit and bug Frank. He wanted to find out what happened. It's uncharacteristic of Frank to not show up when he promised he would. Nick finally called the Homicide Unit. He asked for Sergeant Favasi. He did not want to ask for Frank. He wanted to keep it formal. He did not identify himself. The detective that answered told Nick to hold on and he would find the sergeant. Frank got on the phone. "Sergeant Favasi, can I help you?"

Nick wanted to be calm, but he could not hold back. "What the hell is going on Frank? Why didn't you show up last night?"

Frank decided to kid around with Nick. "Who is this? Please refrain from using that kind of language on a police phone, sir." Nick started to come back at Frank with some nasty shit, but before he could think of what to say, Frank said, "Calm down asshole."

Nick took a deep breath. "Frank, why didn't you meet me last night?" Frank started to laugh and that pissed Nick off.

"Look Nick, I'm sorry about last night, we got real busy. I could not get away."

"I really needed to talk to you. I waited so long I got drunk."

"Good, that's probably what you needed anyway."

Frank told Nick that he would finish up a few things in the office and be right over to talk with him.

He got to the apartment and looked around. "Nick, what the hell is going on? This place looks like a damn pigsty." Frank walked around the small apartment and was just shaking his head. Nick flopped down on the couch.

"You're right Frank…it does look bad. I got to get my shit together." Frank figured he had hurt Nick's feelings enough. He put his arm around him and asked what was happening. Nick told him that he really needed to talk to him last night. He said that too much was building up in him. Frank sat in the only chair that did not have junk on it. "Okay big guy, I'm here—let it all out." Nick moved over to a kitchen chair and asked Frank if he wanted anything to drink. Frank told Nick that he did not have much time. He told him to just start talking.

"Frank, I feel like everything is crashing down around me. I'm starting to hate the job. I don't like the guys I work with. I have no social life. Frank, did you read the paper yesterday?"

Frank checked his watch. "Nick, I don't have much time to talk. What the hell was in the paper that's so important?"

"Frank, you ain't going to believe this. The guy that Janet was messing around with got wasted the other night."

Frank gave Nick a big phony surprised look. "No shit, tell me what happened." Nick moved over to the couch and was shocked that Frank had not heard about the guy getting shot.

Nick said, "Dude, the guy that Janet was hanging with was murdered in front of his house. They apparently have no suspects in the case." Frank got up and walked around in small circles with his hands in his pockets. He walked over to Nick and put his hand on Nick's shoulder.

"Well, that's a good thing. He was probably messing around with some guy's old lady. He got what he deserved."

Nick jumped up from the couch and shouted at Frank, "You ain't too bright for a big time homicide sergeant! He was seeing Janet, not someone's wife. We need to find out what the cops in Carroll County know about that murder."

Frank started to walk to the door and turned toward Nick. "We don't need to find out a damn thing. Just be happy that you might have a chance of getting Janet back." Frank told Nick that he had to get back to the office. Nick was now visibly upset. He stood blocking the door. Frank reached around him for the doorknob. "Come on Nick, stop acting like a little kid. The cops in that county will catch whoever wasted the poor bastard—just calm down." Frank pulled on the door and was halfway out when he turned and smiled at Nick. "Hey dude, give Janet a call. She ain't seeing anybody now."

CHAPTER 21

Frank got to work early on the day shift. Roll call started at 7:30 A.M., but Frank got there a little after 6:30 A.M. He was going through some reports when he noticed that the captain's door was open and the light was on. He walked over and pushed the door open the rest of the way. The captain appeared to be deep in thought. He didn't even notice that Frank was standing in his doorway. Frank tapped the side of the door and the captain was a little startled.

"What the hell are you doing here Frank? Did you get drunk last night and decide to just come here right from the bar?" Frank laughed and asked the captain if he wanted some coffee.

"Yeah Frank, get us some coffee. I need to talk to you about some of these murders."

Frank walked to the coffee machine on the same floor and got two black coffees. He was heading back to the captain's office. He was thinking about the murders in his squad that were not solved. Frank liked the captain—he had a serious side to him. When the arrest rate in the unit was low, the captain could be hard to deal with. Frank walked back in the office and handed the captain his coffee. He had no sooner sat in a chair when the captain said, "Frank, I'm getting a lot of pressure from the chief about all these unsolved murders." Frank asked the captain if he was talking about the murders being investigated by his squad or was he referring to the entire unit. The captain leaned forward, "Frank, you are one of my best supervisors. I'm talking about the entire unit."

The captain told Frank that he had met with the police commissioner. The commissioner told him to do whatever it takes to turn the arrest rate around. The captain told Frank that he asked the commissioner if he could get an additional five detectives assigned to the unit. The captain sat back in his chair—he sipped the coffee. He didn't say anything. Frank just sat there not knowing if he was supposed to respond or not. Frank finally said, "That's great captain— I think we could use ten detectives. Five more detectives would be a great start."

The captain told Frank that he was very surprised that the chief would give him any additional detectives. He told Frank that he didn't want to hold him up any longer. Frank got up and was leaving the office when the captain stopped him. "Frank, I need to get the best five men from the patrol division that the department has." Frank was nodding in agreement and instead of leaving, he asked the captain if he could recommend a very good police officer. The captain told him it had to be someone from patrol.

Frank moved to the front of the captain's desk. "I have a close friend in the Western District that would fit in great in the Homicide Unit."

The captain surprised Frank and told him to contact that person. "See if he would be interested in coming to the unit."

Frank told the captain that he would make the contact. He told him that the officer would be extremely excited to come to homicide.

The captain thanked Frank. "Who is this officer that you are so high on being a good homicide detective?"

"He's my best friend and a helluva good cop. His name is Nick Giango."

Frank walked briskly back to his office. He could not wait to make the call. "Nick, this is Frank. I know you are probably sleeping. I need you to call me as soon as possible. I have some great news." Frank was excited that he would finally get his best buddy down to the Homicide Unit.

After roll call the secretary told Frank that he had a phone call on hold in his office. Frank ran to the phone. He was hoping that it was Nick. "Sergeant Favasi, can I help you?"

"Frank, what the hell do you want so early in the morning"?

Frank decided to take the call on a phone in a quieter office. He told Nick to hold on. He closed and locked the door in the outer office. He asked Nick if he was sitting down.

"Come on Frank, what the hell is it?"

Frank told Nick the information that he got from the captain about the chief giving the okay for five additional detectives in homicide. Nick was a little groggy from being awakened so early. "What the hell does that have to do with me?"

"Nick, slap yourself in the face. Try to follow this conversation. I told the captain that I wanted to get you in the Homicide Unit."

"Frank, are you serious or are you playing with me?" Frank assured Nick that this was not a joke. He told Nick that if he wanted to come to the unit, he would go back and tell the captain.

Nick could hardly hold back his emotions. "I want to come down to homicide more than anything in the world. It could not have come at a better time." Nick hung up with Frank and plopped back down in the bed. Many thoughts were running through his mind, but the most important was that he was now getting out of the dreadful Western District.

CHAPTER 22

Nick was preparing for his first day in the Homicide Unit. He had shopped for a few suits, nice dress shirts, ties, and expensive shoes. He felt like he was preparing for a men's magazine photo shoot. He knew how the guys in the Homicide Unit dressed and he wanted to fit right in. He had said all his good-byes in the Western District. He was happy to be leaving, but part of him was sad. He had worked and fought with these guys for quite a while—he would miss them. When he drove away from the district on his last day, he actually hollered out the window of his car, "I'm free—I'm free—no more Alcatraz."

Nick was so excited about getting the assignment in the Homicide Unit that he actually gave his apartment a much needed overhaul. He figured that if he was going to live a life where he dressed nice each day, he needed to have his apartment looking good. He could not wait for his first day in homicide. He did not talk to Frank about getting in his squad. He hoped that Frank would at least do that for him. He was thinking how great that would be for him and Frank to be back together.

Nick decided to call home and let his dad know about the promotion to the Homicide Unit. He was walking to the phone in his apartment when it started to ring. He looked at the caller ID and did not recognize the incoming number. He picked up the phone. "Nick, this is Janet. Please don't hang up on me."

Nick was shocked. "Janet, how have you been? Is everything all right?" Janet told Nick that she needed to meet with him. She said she had something that was bothering her and wanted to get it out. Nick told her that he could meet with her later in the evening.

She seemed to be crying and said, "Thanks Nick, I have really missed you." Nick was a little taken back by that statement and thought best not to respond. He asked her where she wanted to meet and she told him her apartment would be fine.

Nick was excited and anxious as he was driving to Janet's apartment. He convinced himself that he needed to be very cautious. Every fiber of his body wanted to forgive Janet. He was hoping to start back where they left off with the relationship. He also needed some answers on why she dumped him so abruptly and without any explanation. He was running it through his mind on how he would handle it. He still had feelings for Janet regardless of what she did to him.

Nick knocked on the door and within seconds Janet opened the door and hugged Nick. He told her that it was nice seeing her. He asked her what was up with the urgent need to see him. She asked him if he wanted a drink. As she moved to the couch, Nick felt excitement coming over him. He told her that maybe he would want a drink later, but really wanted to talk. He could not keep from staring at her. She was just as beautiful now, as she was the last time he was with her. He noticed that her hair was shorter. He tried not to stare at her, but she looked so good that he could not help it. It was very obvious that she was dressed a little enticing. She was wearing tight jeans and a very low-cut blouse. Nick also picked up on the perfume she wore; it was something that Nick remembered well. He had told her that her perfume could melt him like a cheese sandwich on a hot grill. When they were dating, Nick often kidded Janet that her perfume gave him the feeling of being anesthetized.

Janet was nervous and tried some small talk with Nick. He picked up on her being nervous. He told her to just tell him what was on her mind. He was feeling sorry for her nervousness and wanted to reach over and kiss her. He knew trying that move could be disastrous, especially since he didn't know what she wanted to say.

Janet told Nick that she had made a big mistake by breaking up with him. She said that she wanted to see if they could work it out. Although this is what Nick wanted to hear, he remained stoic and tried to show no emotion at all. Janet told Nick that she had something to tell him and she hoped that he would not get upset. Nick told her to just get it out. Janet moved closer to Nick and the perfume started to work. "Nick, I dated a married man after we broke up."

"Janet, we didn't break up; you broke up with me." She started to cry and threw herself on Nick. The perfume was in the anesthesia stage. She was trying to talk, but Nick could not make out what she was saying through the tears. He put his arms around her.

"Janet, I still have feelings for you, but I don't understand why you dumped me for another man."

Janet sat up and pulled a tissue from the box on the table. She wiped her eyes. "Nick, the man I was seeing was murdered in front of his home recently. I don't know what to do."

CHAPTER 23

The Homicide Unit, being the elite unit that it was, did not usually hold a formal roll call like they did in the patrol districts. The detectives that were working the day shift showed up around 8 A.M. each morning. Some detectives made it a point to come in early to relieve the night shift, knowing that the favor would be returned. On the morning that newly appointed Detective Nick Giango was to report for his first day in the unit, the word was out and all hands were on deck. It was not only the first day for Nick; it was also the first day for the other four officers coming from patrol. Everybody was anxious to check out the reinforcements.

Nick was the first to come in the office. His stomach was churning from not knowing what to expect. He was surprised that everyone was very polite and friendly. He shook hands with most of the detectives. There were some that never raised their heads away from their computers. Nick was never told in advance what squad he would be in; he was only told what day to show up. It was awkward at first, but as the other new detectives started to arrive, he felt a little more at ease. It was funny to watch, as the new guys seemed to all gather in one corner of the office. Most of them knew each other. They shook hands and offered congratulations.

Just as it appeared that the five new guys were going to spend the day standing in one corner of the homicide office, a well-dressed middle-aged man came over. "Gentlemen, I'm Lieutenant Anthony Valentino. I'm the dayshift supervisor in the Homicide Unit. Welcome to the best Homicide

Unit in the country. You can meet all the detectives later after we have a sit-down with your captain." The gang of five was led off to the rear of the office. "Gentlemen, wait right here. The captain is on the phone with the police commissioner talking about murders that occurred last night."

It was a small area they waited in—they felt uncomfortable. Everyone passing by gave them the once-over. The door to the captain's office opened and a very deep voice said, "Lieutenant, bring in the new gumshoes." The five guys paraded in and dared not to sit until told to do so. Nick did not know much about Captain Bobby Jenkins. He did not have much time to discuss the make-up of the unit with Frank.

"Gentlemen, please find a seat, I'm Captain Bobby Jenkins. I am the commanding officer of the Homicide Unit. I'm sure you have already met Lieutenant Valentino." Everyone nodded in the affirmative and the captain stood up after all the new detectives had sat down. Captain Jenkins was an imposing figure. He was probably six feet five inches tall and weighed at least two hundred and fifty pounds with very little fat. He was dressed meticulously. The new guys could not help but notice all the plaques and awards on the walls.

"Gentlemen, you have been selected to come to the Homicide Unit because you have stood out in patrol above your peers. There is no greater honor in the police department than to be a member of the Homicide Unit. Each and everyday you will be working on the death of another human being and it doesn't get any more honorable than that. You will be scrutinized every step of your investigation by your sergeant, your lieutenant, and me. After your investigation, you will go before a judge or jury and defense attorneys who will attempt to tear your investigation apart. If at any time while you are a member of this unit and you act inappropriate or bring any disgrace to this unit, you will find yourself back in patrol."

The captain took a deep breath and sat in his chair. He looked out over the new detectives who at this point were mesmerized by what they had just heard. The captain continued, "Gentlemen, let me end by saying that I'm thrilled to death to have you in this unit. Each one of you will bring something unique to the unit. I expect great things from all of you.

Lieutenant Valentino will now take you to his office where he will have his say on what is expected from each one of you. Lieutenant Valentino has been with me for many years. Let there be no mistake…he and I are on the same page when it comes to how this unit operates. If there are no further questions for me, then off you go with the lieutenant. I wish you much success while working in the best damn Homicide Unit in the country."

Nick could feel beads of sweat running down the back of his neck. He and the others paraded down the hallway to the lieutenant's office. There was not much conversation amongst the group. Now they had to listen to the lieutenant and when he was finished they would get a spiel from their new sergeant.

The talk from Lieutenant Valentino was not that long and really mimicked what the captain had already said. Before leaving the lieutenant's office each new detective was given an envelope that had the name of their new sergeant in it. Lieutenant Valentino told the group that this was the best way to assign new detectives to a sergeant. He explained that two of the new detectives would be in the same unit. He informed the group that there were four sergeants in the Homicide Unit. He said that this way, none of the sergeants could get someone they either campaigned for or knew from patrol.

Nick and the others walked out of the lieutenant's office. Most of the detectives could not wait to open the envelopes as they made their way back to the main office. Nick was standing off to the side when he started to open his envelope. He heard one of the detectives holler, "Yes, I got Sergeant Favasi. He's the best sergeant in the unit!"

Nick was thinking— oh shit, I won't be working with Frank and that's a bummer. He did not hear the others shout out any names. Feeling a little disgusted, he tore open the envelope.

Nick forgot where he was and shouted, "Thank you Jesus, I'll be working with Sergeant Favasi also." Nick caught himself and was a little embarrassed that he shouted so loud. He was making it appear obvious that he wanted to work for his best friend.

He and the others were told to find their sergeant's office and introduce themselves. Nick bolted into the main office and was looking for the names on the offices assigned to the sergeants. He found Frank's office and the door was closed. He could hear some talking in the office. He stood around outside the door. He wanted to knock, but thought it best to wait. The door opened and a detective walked out. Nick moved to the center of the door. Frank, with a big grin on his face said, "Get your ass in here—you great big, beautiful, brand-new, homicide investigator." Frank moved behind Nick and locked the door. "Sit down Nick… how did it go with the captain and the lieutenant?"

"I guess I survived my first encounter with the big bosses. I assume that it's now your turn."

Frank put his feet up on the desk and stared at Nick. He took a drink from his Dr Pepper soda, his favorite drink—other than beer. Frank asked Nick if there was anything he could get him to drink. Nick said he did not need anything right now. He suggested that they get a drink together later.

Frank started to talk when there was a knock on the door. He opened the door. It was McCarthy—his other new detective. "Sergeant Favasi, I'm Mike McCarthy; I was told to report to your office. I'm assigned to your squad."

Frank stepped in front of McCarthy and prevented him from coming in the office. "I have Detective Giango in the office right now. Can you come back in about thirty minutes?" McCarthy followed his first instructions from his new sergeant and walked away. Frank turned back towards Nick. He told him that he needed to talk fast because in the Homicide Unit you did not have much time to relax. It seemed like someone was always banging on the door for advice or to let you know they had a fresh caper.

Frank pulled his chair closer to Nick. He wanted to make sure he had his attention. He also did not want to talk too loud. "Nick, I'm really glad to have you in the unit. I have thought about this for a long time and it has finally happened. We are best friends and we go back a long way together. We have been through a lot of shit together. Let me start by saying that we need to treat your assignment to my squad in a very professional way. I'm sure others will pick up on our relationship and that could be a problem. Listen to me carefully. This is the way we will treat it. When we are in the office or around any other police officers, you need to call me Sergeant Favasi—not Frank. Unless you want to discuss one of your investigations, I suggest that we do not just sit around my office and bullshit. I will have to talk to you and treat you like I would any of the other detectives in my squad. I will expect nothing but hard work and dedication from you. I know that is what I will get. If you need to talk to me about any personal matters, we can meet somewhere and have those discussions. I don't want anyone in this unit to think that you got assigned here because of me. I know that you can do this job. You have been waiting to get here for a long time. I'm thrilled that you are finally where you want to be. I will do anything for you that will enhance your investigative abilities; all you have to do is ask."

Nick was sitting there just nodding his head in agreement. He knew that Frank had to give him this spiel. Frank moved closer to Nick. He leaned in close to his face and said, "Hey buddy, did all that shit I just said scare you?" Nick laughed as Frank moved back behind his desk with a big smile on his face. He told Frank that for a while he was more scared of him than he was of the captain or the lieutenant.

Frank told Nick that he needed to talk to Detective McCarthy for a while. He told him that he should go see the admin clerk to find out where his desk would be. He said there was a lot of other admin stuff that needed to be taken care of. Nick and Frank shook hands. Frank grabbed Nick and said, "What's with the handshake dude? Give me one of them big Marine Corps bear hugs." Frank told Nick to remember what he had told him about being professional around the office in front of others. Nick nodded his head and walked out to find the admin clerk.

As Nick was walking to find the admin clerk, he heard Frank holler, "Where the hell is that McCarthy guy? Can someone find him and tell him to get his ass in my office?"

CHAPTER 24

Nick's life, both personal and professional, seemed to be heading in the right direction. In the Homicide Unit, Frank had assigned him to be partners with Rod Perconti. Most of the guys in the unit respected Rod. He had been in the unit for over ten years. He would be a real asset to Nick as he learned the ropes in homicide investigations.

On the personal side he was dating Janet again and things were going well. Nick convinced her that she had made a mistake by dating a married man. He also told her that the murder should not be a distraction in their relationship. He said that it was most likely a random robbery and when the guy resisted—he was killed.

Nick was thinking better of himself, now that he was a detective. He liked going out of the apartment in a suit and watching all the nosy neighbors check him out. He also liked the fact that he was making more money as a detective. The abundance of overtime was great. Murder meant overtime and overtime meant money. He knew that just about any night shift would probably mean murder in Charm City. How ironic it is that Baltimore, the murder capital of the country, would get the nickname of Charm City.

It was a good feeling for him to be regularly shopping for new clothes. Dressing in the Homicide Unit was like a contest. Before going to work, you would think about the last time you wore a certain tie or a sport coat.

It was sort of weird how guys looked each other over. Nick's cleaning bill was growing each week.

The apartment was looking good with the new stereo, large screen TV, and decent sheets. The sheets were very important now that he was back with Janet. Janet was a neat freak. He knew that he had to keep the apartment looking good. The former man-cave was now a love shack. Janet was well aware of the hours of the shifts that Nick worked. It did not seem to bother her anymore. She was different since they had gotten back together. She knew she had made a big mistake. She also knew that Nick was the guy she wanted to be with. On occasion, Janet would ask Nick about the murder of the guy she had fooled around with. Nick would dance around it and tell her that it was something they should not be talking about. He told her not to worry.

One night when they were snuggling on the couch watching a movie, she brought it up again. "Nick, I hate to keep asking you… is there any way possible you can find out what happened to Phil?"

"Who the hell is Phil?"

"Nick, Phil was the guy I was seeing. He got killed in front of his house; it keeps bothering me. I need to know what happened. I feel really bad for the guy and his family."

Nick threw the remote across the room and it slid all the way into the kitchen. "Why in the hell do you keep bringing up this guy when I told you not to worry about him? Was there more to your relationship than you have told me?"

Janet moved closer to Nick and put her arms around him. "Nick, I told you that I made a mistake seeing him. Believe me when I tell you that nothing happened between me and him. I just can't stop thinking about the murder."

"Janet, I'm no fool. Don't try to make me out as some dumb-ass that can't find another girl. How can we move on with the relationship if you keep talking about that guy?"

Janet moved away from Nick and started to cry. Nick felt bad that he had been so strong with his language toward her. It was not like him to talk to her like that. "Janet, I'm sorry I said those things. It bothers me that you keep bringing up this guy all the time. I know he got murdered. You must feel bad for his family, but we need to stop talking about it."

"Nick, all I am asking you to do is to call the detective working on his murder and ask what happened."

"Oh yeah, I'm going to call them and say— hey dude, what's up with the murder of Phil Philbin? I guess they would say— what's your concern buddy? I would say—well my girlfriend was screwing around on me and dated him. She found out he was murdered and wants to know who did it."

Nick walked into the kitchen and picked up the remote. He got a beer. Janet was silent. Nick stayed in the kitchen for a while. Janet walked in and was still crying. Nick grabbed her and held her tight. He was upset that he had talked to her that way. "Janet, listen to me. If I call and inquire about that murder, they will ask a lot of questions. The last thing you want them to know is that the guy was murdered after he left your apartment. I know that you had nothing to do with the murder, but these guys want to find out who killed him. You will be raked over the coals because of your involvement with him."

Janet kissed Nick on the lips and pulled him back towards the couch. "Janet, let me think about it. If there is any way I can find out something without involving you, I will do it."

Janet thanked Nick and pulled him closer to her. She kissed him. Nick could feel the perfume working. Janet clicked the remote and put the movie back on—they didn't see the ending.

CHAPTER 25

Time goes by quickly in the Homicide Unit, especially when you are working murders in one of the most dangerous cities in the nation. It seems like you could come to work on a Thursday and might go home late on Sunday, if you are lucky. The only good part of working homicide in a crime ridden city is the serious overtime money. The bad part is that you really don't have the time to spend it wisely—unless you can call drinking after your shift with your buddies being wise.

Although the time was flying by, Nick still had many years to put in the department before he could even dream about retirement. He loved the Homicide Unit. He also knew that with all the years he had left, he needed to think seriously about getting promoted and build on his eventual retirement income. He knew that the thought of retirement had probably never crossed Frank's mind. Frank figured he would be a cop forever.

Nick's relationship with Frank or now Sergeant Favasi, as he wanted to be called, was just okay. Nick did on occasion meet with Frank. They had some drinks and talked about the good old days. It seemed like the relationship of detective to sergeant was keeping them from getting close like they used to be.

Frank never wanted to talk about settling down. He would never discuss if he was dating anyone. On the other hand, Nick talked about Janet all the time. He told Frank that they were seriously talking about getting married. It seemed like when Nick mentioned marriage, Frank would laugh. He would tell Nick that marriage sucked.

Nick was actually worrying about Frank. He did not know what he was involved in on his off-duty time from the Homicide Unit. Frank was considered aloof by the members of the unit. He was very secretive about where he went after work. He insisted on being called sergeant by anyone below him in the department. He would try to joke around with the guys. He could dish it out, but he could not take the return remarks. It did not appear that either way was working for him. He was hated in his professional life and his personal life remained a mystery.

Nick, on the other hand, was very well liked in the unit by everyone. It was Nick's personality to be friendly. He always asked others if they needed any help on their investigations. As time went by, Nick was not enjoying working with and for Frank. He was hoping that the relationship would get better. He knew that Frank was looking to make the next rank which was lieutenant. He was burning the midnight oil studying for the next test. Some nights on the midnight shift when things were quiet, which was rare, Frank would lock himself in his office and study.

Nick hoped for the best for Frank. He actually did not want to see him get promoted. A promotion would mean that Frank would leave the unit. Although Frank was tough to work for, Nick liked the fact that his boss was also his friend. Nick never talked about it with Frank, but he was also doing a little reading of the promotion material for the upcoming sergeant's test. He was not obsessed with it like Frank. He knew he owed it to himself and now to Janet to get promoted and make more money.

The quiet in the office did not last long. The phone rang and Michaels hollered to Nick. "Nick can you get the phone? I think you are up next." Nick reached for the phone which was a direct line to the police dispatcher.

"Detective Giango, Homicide Unit, can I help you?"

"Detective, this is Officer Forrest, Western District dispatcher. Seven twenty-four unit is on the scene of a possible fatal shooting and they need homicide to respond." Nick wrote down the address of the shooting and hung up the phone. All eyes in the office suddenly turned and stared at Nick.

Who would Nick ask to go out with him on the shooting? He would normally take his partner, but Perconti was on leave. He first waited for a response and then just asked, "Would anyone like to accompany me to the beautiful Western District to investigate some upstanding citizen's possible demise?" After a short laugh from the other detectives, some of who were now pretending to be real busy, Ronny Michaels raised his hand. Ronny didn't say anything, he just raised his hand. Nick started packing his murder investigation equipment which consisted of his gun, badge, notepad, flashlight, car keys, gloves, chalk, gum, and a cigar. The cigar was not really needed. When Nick first started, an old salty homicide investigator told him to always carry a cigar in case it was a stinker.

Ronny still had his hand up. Nick acknowledged him and said, "Unless you are asking permission to go to the bathroom, I do welcome your assistance on this case." Ronny then packed his murder equipment and they headed out the door.

Nick and Ronny pulled up on the murder scene. Nick had a hard time finding a spot close to the scene to put their vehicle. He double parked. He asked a patrol officer to keep an eye on it. Some homicide vehicles had been damaged in the past by the troublemakers who just didn't like cops, even cops not in uniform.

Nick was the lead investigator on this murder. He found the shift sergeant and asked what happened. When the sergeant started talking, Nick was a little surprised. The sergeant said, "My officer was checking doors in the rear of this store when he was confronted by some dude and he had to shoot him."

Nick looked at Ronny and they knew that they were now going to be in for a long night. They also knew they would be making some good old overtime. Nick moved a few steps back from the sergeant and said, "Sarge, when you called this in to the dispatcher did you tell him this was a police involved shooting."

"What the hell else would I have told him? My man is a police officer. He shot some asshole and that makes it a police involved shooting." Nick and Ronny had to laugh and the sergeant was laughing also.

Nick told the sergeant that when he took the call from the dispatcher, he was only advised that it was a shooting. He was not informed that it was a police involved shooting. The sergeant seemed like he wanted to argue the point. Nick told him that it did not matter, apparently it was a mix-up. He explained to the sergeant that he now needed to call the homicide shift lieutenant and the night duty officer to inform them of a police involved shooting. He told the sergeant that he would make those calls and then they would start over. Nick notified the duty officer and called the homicide office. He was advised that the lieutenant had gone home, but Sergeant Favasi was there and he would respond to the scene.

Nick went back and talked to the patrol sergeant. Ronny did the other necessary work of measuring distances, chalking off the body, directing the crime laboratory, gathering witnesses, and taking good notes. After Nick got some details of the shooting, he went around to the back of the store. He examined the body of the deceased black male. With his flashlight, he could determine that there were at least two bullet holes in his upper chest. The officer who did the shooting was sitting in the sergeant's car. He was visibly quite upset. Nick went over to the car and introduced himself to the officer. While Nick was walking over to the officer, he had flashbacks of the night he had to shoot a burglary suspect who jumped off a porch.

"I'm Detective Giango—I have a few questions for you officer." The officer got out of the car and they shook hands. Nick could see that the officer was still very nervous.

"Officer, you can calm down. This is all part of being a police officer in a very dangerous city. I only have a few questions; your sergeant filled me in on most of the story."

"Detective, I'm still a little worked up. I only know that I walked around to the back of the store and I heard something. I walked closer to the door and this guy jumped out. I shot him. It was a natural instinct. If I had my flashlight, things might have been different. I didn't see a gun, but other officers that responded said that they found a gun next to his body. It all happened so fast."

Nick was trying to write down what the officer said. He wanted to ask more questions, but it was obvious that the officer needed to take some time to pull himself together. He told the officer to sit in his car and he would talk to him later. Nick was walking away when the officer said, "Detective, am I in any trouble? Did I act too fast?" Nick knew the feelings that the officer had because he had gone through the same thing. Nick walked back to the car and told the officer to relax. He really did not want the officer to say anything, but he did.

"Detective, I really did not see a gun on that man. Before anyone else got on the scene, I checked him out pretty good. I was told that when the backup units arrived, they found a gun next to the body. I guess I missed it."

Nick and Ronny were still on the scene well after the body was removed to the medical examiner's office. They were wrapping up some loose ends when Sergeant Favasi pulled up on the scene. He shook hands with some of the uniform patrol guys. He actually looked like he was politicking for some office, instead of being a homicide supervisor.

"What do you fellows have here tonight? Has some poor bastard lost their life in Charm City? Let me guess—he decided to fuck with a cop and got the short end of the deal."

Nick took the lead and walked over to Sergeant Favasi. "Well sarge, we seem to have a situation where an officer was checking the rear of this location. When he was conducting his check of the rear door, a man moved toward him. The man surprised him and the officer shot him."

Ronny walked over and said, "We are not sure if the shooting is good yet. We still have to talk to some of the officers that responded as backups."

Sergeant Favasi moved toward Ronny and touched his arm. "Detective Michaels, I was talking to Detective Giango. He is the lead investigator on this case and that is usually who I talk to first. Is that okay with you?"

Michaels shrugged his shoulders and walked away. Sergeant Favasi was not done. "Detective Michaels, are you offended by what I said? We have procedures and I want the story from the lead investigator. At some point you can offer whatever you want. Is that okay?" Ronny knew better than to get into an exchange with the sergeant. He would not come out on top.

"Yes Sir, Sergeant Favasi, I know the procedure very well."

Favasi and Nick talked on the scene for a few minutes. While they were talking, the uniformed sergeant came over and asked Nick what he wanted his officers to do. Favasi told the sergeant that the officer that did the shooting would have to go down to the Homicide Unit and write his report. The patrol sergeant appeared to be pissed and said, "Can't he just write the damn report in the district? Why does he have to go down to homicide?"

Nick started to answer, but Favasi beat him to it. He literally got up in the sergeant's face. "We all have to play by the rules. I'm on the scene and supervising this investigation. The officer goes down to the Homicide Unit and writes the report—that's all there is to it."

"You homicide prima donnas think you know everything. Okay, I'll send him down to your damn office."

The patrol sergeant walked towards his vehicle. Frank didn't let it go. "If I need any more cooperation sarge, I will let you know."

Frank touched Nick's arm and directed him away from Ronny. "How do you feel about this shooting, Nick?"

"I'm not sure at this point. The officer is fairly new on the street. He is pretty shaken up. He said he did not have a flashlight and was surprised when the man appeared out of nowhere in the rear of the store. He said he is not sure if the dead guy had a weapon. He only knows that when the backup units arrived, someone said they found a gun next to the body. I personally think it appears that someone dropped a gun to make it look like the guy had a gun."

Frank scratched his head and smiled at Nick. "So you think that some officer threw a gun down next to the guy? Well, Detective Giango, are you like the judge and jury on this young officer? Did you forget your days in the Western District? There were times when you told me how bad it was and you hated being there. Do you remember that? So now you are a big shot homicide investigator. Do you want to report that this young officer did something wrong? He could possibly be fired or indicted for shooting a no-good piece of shit. Is that what you want?"

"Frank, I'm only telling you what I have found out."

"First of all Detective, my name while out here on the scene is Sergeant Favasi. Let's get that straight. We can move forward from there. Finish up what you have to do here and meet me in the office when you are done."

Nick found Ronny and said, "Let's get the hell out of here."

"What the hell was that all about Nick? I never really heard the sergeant talk to you like that before. I thought you guys were buddies."

"We were buddies in the past. I think when I came to homicide all that buddy shit went out the window. Let's get the hell out of here. We need to start interviewing people and writing reports."

CHAPTER 26

Nick and Ronny finished up the crime scene. On the way back to the Homicide Unit, they picked up coffee and egg sandwiches from the Brew & Chew. Nick was hoping that Frank had gone home or was in a better mood than he was on the crime scene. The office was filled with witnesses, crime lab techs, and the officers from the shooting scene. Nick put the coffee and sandwiches in the admin office. He knew they would probably never get to eat.

After about a half-hour, Nick felt confident about how the interviewing and reporting were moving along. The patrol sergeant was in the office and was sitting with his officer helping with the report. Nick walked over to where they were writing. "Hi guys, how is the report coming along?" At first there was no response and then the sergeant stood up and asked Nick if he could talk to him in the hallway.

"Listen Detective, I have instructed my man to write the report just the way it happened. He will not be giving you a detailed statement at this time. He is choosing to take advantage of the police officer's bill of rights. He will waive any formal statement at this time. When he is done with the report… I will sign it. We will be returning to our district. Furthermore, I really didn't like the way your sergeant talked to me on the scene. I will handle that at another time. I know you guys have a job to do, but sometimes we feel that you all have forgotten what it is like to patrol the crime infested streets of Baltimore. I have no more to say to you or your sergeant. Is that perfectly clear, detective?"

Nick thought for a while and felt it better to let the sergeant get it off his chest. "Sergeant, I do remember what it was like being out there in the district. I have respect for all the officers that do this shit job day in and day out. I'm sorry we had a little confrontation on the scene. I don't speak for Sergeant Favasi. I know he is under a lot of stress in this unit. I also know he only wants to do the right thing and solve murders. He's a good homicide supervisor. I do understand that your officer wants to protect himself under the police officer's bill of rights and that is fine with me."

The earlier chaos was settling down in the homicide office. The witnesses were all taken home, the police officers wrote the official report, and things were quiet—at least for now. Nick went hunting for that egg sandwich and all he found was the wrapper. The thief didn't even have the decency to throw the wrapper in the trash. He looked in the trash and was thinking maybe he could find some remnants of the sandwich. All he found was some nasty looking shit, but no parts of a sandwich.

Ronny was working on the report that needed to be on the captain's desk by morning. A police involved shooting got lots of attention in the morning when all the bosses showed up. Nick was gearing down and preparing to go home when he noticed that Frank's office light was on. He wanted to tell Frank he was going home and Ronny was finishing up the report. He knocked on the door. "Hey sarge, are you in there?" With no answer, Nick tried the door and it was open. "Hey, we didn't really know if you were still here. Ronny is finishing the report. I was going to leave if that's okay with you."

"Yeah, that's fine with me; I will walk out with you. Are you parked in the building or out on the street?"

Nick and Frank walked out of the building. They walked past the security officer on the side entrance to the building. "Hey Nick, look at that old bastard—he's sound asleep. Somebody could walk through here with a small army and that son of a bitch would not know it. I should wake that dude up and report him. I'm too tired and need to get the hell away from this building." Nick's car was closer to the building than Frank's. As Nick walked toward his car, Frank said, "Listen buddy, I hope you ain't pissed at me for what I said out there on the shooting scene. Sometimes I say shit that I don't mean. Are we still okay with each other?"

"Yeah Frank, we're fine. I was only reporting to you what I had so far in the investigation."

"Listen Nick, I have been meaning to have a talk with you. I know you are tired and so am I, but this might be a good time to have the talk. I think you are doing a great job in the unit and that has not gone unnoticed by me or the lieutenant. However, I think that sometimes you take shit too serious. We work in a very dangerous city and we deal with some of the nastiest bastards that ever walked the crime ridden streets of Baltimore. Our job is to catch these pricks and make sure they go away for life. Sometimes we have to stretch the facts to make them favor us and not the bad guys. Before you got back to the office last night from the crime scene, I talked to the patrol sergeant and the officer that did the shooting. I told them to write the report any way they wanted as long as it made some sense. I talked to the officer and he is now certain that the bad guy had a gun in his hand and that's why he shot him."

"Frank, you mean there is no doubt in your mind that the guy had a gun."

"Nick, the point in this whole thing is who gives a fuck if he had a gun or not. He's a piece of shit that ravages our city. He got what he deserved. That officer should not be put through the ringer by a bunch of assholes from our Internal Investigation Division. The reports are written and after a short write-up in the paper this morning, no one will ever give a shit about the dead guy."

"Frank, I don't feel that way and I hope I never do. We are supposed to investigate all murders the same—no matter if it's a civilian or a police officer. We need to be fair and truthful all the time."

"Well, listen to the almighty Mr. Clean, Detective Giango. Nick, you really don't believe that we give those bastards a fair shot when a police officer shoots somebody—do you? The Homicide Unit has been protecting our officers long before we came in the unit and I hope long after we leave. Nick, I have been on police shootings where there have been two or three guns found near the dead guy. The officers in the field don't give a shit—they just throw guns down. Thank God that someone on the scene realizes that we only need one gun on the dead asshole. I have been on scenes where we had to kick a couple of guns down the sewer before the crime lab started taking photos. Nick, I think it's time I tell you something that I have kept from you too long."

"Frank, can it wait? I'm really tired and maybe we can continue this another time."

"No, I want to get it out in the open and this seems like the right time. Nick, do you remember that night when you shot the guy who jumped off the porch in back of that closed bar? You told the homicide guys that night that because your partner said the guy had a gun—he must have had one. Do you remember that Nick?"

"Yeah, I remember it, but what the hell does that incident have to do with this conversation? I'm not following you, Frank."

"Well, brace yourself Mr. Goody two-shoes—that piece of shit that you shot did not have a fuckin gun. Your partner told our investigator later on that he put that gun on the guy. So Nick, you are no better than the rest of the officers on the street. I have no doubt that a gun was put on that guy last night. I'm fine with that, are you?"

"Jesus, Frank, this is too much for me to take in all at once. I can't believe what you are saying. Why did you keep this from me all this time?"

"Nick, the guys that have been in this unit for a long time communicate to other detectives on a need-to-know basis. I'm only telling you so that you can get on board with the program and quit being an asshole. The people of this city should be grateful to the guys in our unit. We are ridding the streets of Baltimore of some of the nastiest scum of the earth. Nick, I want you to be okay with what we do every day in this unit to make the city safe."

"Sergeant Favasi I have heard enough, I need to get the hell out of here."

"Detective Giango, I hope what we have discussed does not go any further or there could be consequences that you might not like. See you later, Nick. Have a nice night."

CHAPTER 27

The sun was shining in the window of Nick's apartment. He tried to cover his eyes with the blanket. He knew that he had to get up and get his ass in gear for the day. He did not get much sleep during the night. He could not get it out of his head what Frank had told him. He was thinking about how naïve he must be, to not really know how his lifelong close friend perceives his police career.

Nick was making coffee the easy way—a teaspoon of instant coffee and a cup of microwaved hot water. He never was a big coffee drinker when he was in patrol, but working in the Homicide Unit changed that. The coffee tasted like shit, but it was hot and got him moving. He was in the shower when the phone rang. He always took the portable phone with him in the bathroom so that he would not miss the opportunity for overtime. With the shampoo in his hair and dripping wet, he reached for the phone. Even with the lens of the phone foggy from the hot shower, he could see that it was Janet's number. "Hi Hon, can I call you back in about ten minutes? I'm just getting out of the shower."

"Nick, I need to talk to you as soon as possible. I will wait for your call."

Nick hung up the phone and felt bad that he did not even ask Janet if she was okay. He dried off and put on shorts. He dialed Janet's number. "Hi Janet, I'm sorry…"

"Nick, I still can't get it out of my head about the guy I was seeing. Phil getting murdered in his driveway is bothering the hell out of me. As much as I try, it stays with me. I need to have some answers. Please don't feel that I'm thinking about him in any other way than concern for his family. I really need to know what happened."

"Well, I thought this was all over and we were not going to discuss it anymore. I'm absolutely sure it was a random act of robbery or he was screwing around with someone else other than you. Maybe he was followed home by a jilted husband and got what he probably deserved; you need to let it go."

"Nick, I told you that I can't let it go. If you won't help me find out what happened, I will find out myself."

"Janet, you need to stop this and think about us. We are getting along great now and this situation only brings back bad memories for me. I have no idea how I could help you with this and not have them bring you in for questioning."

"Nick, you can help by calling that Homicide Unit and asking what happened. I'm sure that from one homicide investigator to another, they will tell you something. I cannot let this go. It bothers me to the point it could interfere with our relationship. Nick, I love you and don't want this to be hanging over our heads forever; please try and help me."

Nick ended the conversation with telling Janet that he also loved her and he would think of a way to find out what happened. He sat in his apartment and as much as he wanted to make the call to the Carroll County Homicide Unit, he could not do it. He thought of asking someone else to make the call. He knew that no matter who called, the detectives would definitely want to talk to them in person. He knew that if it was a case he was working on and got a call from someone inquiring about a murder investigation, it would certainly be someone he would want to talk to. On the other hand, he did feel compassion for Janet. He actually didn't know whether he felt her real pain or was going to do it so they could stay together. He was pacing the apartment and talking out loud. "Do I want to make the call to see what the relationship was with Janet and this dude? Do I want to make the call so that we can move on with the relationship?

Do I want to just say I made the call and say that there are no suspects and they don't know what the hell happened?"

When Nick got to work, he was trying to catch up on some reports that were due. In the Homicide Unit, you are never done with reports. You have updates of your investigations, updates that go to the supervisors, and if you have made an arrest, you have prosecution reports that go to the State's Attorney's Office. Your reports can be lengthy and it seems like you never catch up. Nick was deep into the reports when he heard Frank's voice. Frank was kidding around with some of the detectives and seemed like he was in a good mood. With Frank lately, you didn't know what you were going to get; was it the nasty old Frank or the guy who seemed like everyone's friend?

Frank walked by Nick and did not acknowledge him or even look in his direction. Nick looked up as Frank passed by and thought that it was strange. He did not say anything. Even times in the past when they were at odds, they always found a way to break the ice and talk. Nick could remember over many years that included early childhood and their Marine days, they always talked things out.

"Hey dude, what the hell you doing—writing a book?"

Nick looked up from the keyboard and was facing Frank, who was sitting at a desk just staring and smiling. He thought he would just keep typing and ignore Frank. He knew that the others in the office would pick up on it. No matter what the problems were with him and Frank, he would show him respect. Frank was a supervisor.

"When you get done with your book Nick, can you step into my office for a minute?" Nick nodded in the affirmative and kept typing for about five minutes. He did not want Frank to think that he was jumping every time he talked to him.

"Sit down Nick. This will only take a few minutes. I was thinking about our little conversation the other night. I just want to let you know that at any time you feel like you are not happy in the Homicide Unit—I can make arrangements to get you in another unit. I hope that you stay here, but you have to start to think like the rest of the guys. Nick, this is a bad city and in bad cities, bad things happen to good people. The first line of defense in this city is naturally the uniformed patrol officers. I don't have to tell you that they take shit from the bad guys all the time. When they have to shoot some asshole, it is our job as homicide investigators to make sure they get all the protection they need. Nick, there are statistics that show that when police officers have to shoot someone, the officer in almost all of the cases is justified in what he did. My point the other night was that if one of our officers has to shoot a bad guy, there is no doubt in my mind the bad guy deserved it. I know I share this feeling with the majority of the detectives and supervisors in this unit. You can call it the thin blue line or whatever you want to call it, but it does exist. Nick, I have to know how you feel about this because if you are not on board, we may have problems down the road."

Nick waited to make sure Frank was finished. He took the clue when Frank motioned with his hand to Nick; as if to say go ahead buddy…it is now your turn. "Frank, I understand what you are saying to a point. I guess I'm still a little naïve about some things. I love working in the Homicide Unit and want to stay as long as possible. As you know, I also want to get promoted and further my career. I hope you feel that I work my butt off around here. It has been a learning process. I feel that when I go out on a murder investigation, I am mentally equipped to do a good job. I also know that some things go on at crime scenes that I'm not privy to, especially when police officers shoot the bad guys. I guess what I'm trying to say, is that whatever goes on at a police involved shooting before I get to the scene, is fine with me. I believe police officers when they say they did not know the guy had a gun. I believe that because I have been in that situation and know the feeling. So if this talk is about whether I am okay with what happens on murder scenes, my answer is yes. I would, however, add that when I get on the scene, I would rather not be told later that someone put a gun in the bad guy's hand. If they do it and that becomes the justification for the officer shooting and killing someone, it does not have to be told to me later."

"Does that mean that you are on board with doing the right thing when it comes to protecting our guys?"

"Frank, I mean sergeant, I don't know if on board is quite what I want to say. I want to do my job and stay in this unit. Whatever happens on the scene of a police involved shooting before I get there is fine with me. The cops on the street have plenty of time before we get there to do whatever they want to do. I would think that in the real world, we would not have to put guns or knives on bad guys."

"Nick, quit beating around the bush. You are either on board with what I have told you or you are not. Don't be a pansy all your life. Do the right thing!"

"I want to say I'm on board for no other reason than my selfish motives for staying in this unit. I'm not really sure what being on board means. I have no problem when cops shoot people. I just have a problem with an all-out cover-up of a murder."

"Nick, nobody is talking about a cover-up; it's just the right thing to do in a fucked up city like this. Let's end this discussion for now. Are you still my compadre?"

"Yeah, we are still wop cops."

"Nick, all the guys in the office are going to be wondering what the hell we have been talking about. Just for show, I'm going to scream a little before you leave my office. When you walk out, have a look on your face like I just busted your ass. Okay, here we go—Giango, you better straighten out your shit or you won't be in this unit long. Now get your ass out of my office and do your job!"

CHAPTER 28

The Carroll County Homicide Unit was a small unit consisting of only five detectives. On the other hand, the Baltimore unit had thirty detectives and a yearly homicide count that was well into the two hundred range. Carroll County investigated about five murders a year.

Nick decided that against his better judgment, he would make the call. "Hello, this is Detective Nick Giango. I'm with the Baltimore City Police Department Homicide Unit. I understand you had a recent murder in which the victim was killed while parked in his driveway. Do you happen to recall that murder?"

"Detective, this is Carroll County; we've only had three murders this year. I could recite each one to you. Yes, we did have a murder of a man in his driveway. Do you have some information on it? I was not on the scene that night, but if you have anything important, I can call the detective at home that handled that murder."

"No, I was actually calling because we got an anonymous call from someone inquiring about a murder in a driveway. I had read in the paper that you guys had a similar murder and that is why I'm calling.

"Well, the only thing I can tell you about that murder is that the victim was shot at close range and died on the scene. We have no suspects. The victim's wife stated that she feels he was seeing some other woman. We have recovered the bullets from the victim. The neighbors did not see anything. It was raining pretty heavy when the shooting occurred. The wife heard the shots and found her husband dead in the driveway— she called the police. The family has put together a substantial reward for anyone with information about the murder. I hope this information helps you. Do you want me to notify the detective who handled the case? I can have him contact you."

"No, that's not necessary; you have been very helpful. I don't know if that person will call us back or not. I do appreciate your help and if there is anything we can do to help you with your investigation, please let us know."

Nick felt better now that he talked to the detectives working the Philbin murder. It sounded like they were at a dead-end with the investigation. He didn't leave the detectives with any reason to call him back. He could not help but think—is this what Frank was talking about when he lectured him about being on board? Why couldn't I have been more honest with the detectives and simply told them the truth about Janet's relationship with the victim? What would be the most awful thing that could happen? The investigators would come to her house and she would simply tell the truth. How is that so bad? I'm knocking Frank for covering up police shootings. Here I am possibly covering up for Janet. Is this the same thing?

Nick wanted to call Janet, but he didn't feel comfortable calling from the office. He also knew that Janet would still have some questions—she always had lots of questions. He decided to wait until they got together. Although Nick felt good about what he did, he was hoping that Janet did not take it upon herself to get some answers. The last thing he needed was for Janet to talk to the detectives and mention that she had told me the story about being involved with the dead guy.

Nick was feeling good about himself; work was now getting to be routine. He was at the point where he felt comfortable on a murder scene. He had some time in the unit and thrived on obtaining as much knowledge about death investigations as possible. His personal life was good. He had no doubt in his mind that Janet was who he wanted to spend the rest of his life with. They had talked about marriage. The talks were spontaneous, not something that warranted ordering the tuxedo and getting the ring.

Nick knew that most of the guys in the unit were married. He envied them when they talked about their wives and children. He also knew that quite a few of the detectives in the unit were either separated or just screwing around on their wives. There were nights when he was working the night shift and he would get calls from wives asking if their husband was still working. It was standard procedure amongst the detectives working the late shifts, to tell wives and girlfriends that called, that their man was on the street working. Nick did not like it, but he did not want to go against the cover-up code of the men in the Homicide Unit. When Nick would tell the wife or girlfriend that their husband was on the street, he felt bad. He always had the thought—at what point did the marriage go bad? Were there children in the family? How long can a guy lie to his wife before she figures out that he is a cheating piece of shit? If I married Janet, would I be the exception or would I one day fall into the same dilemma?

Nick had the reputation in the unit of being straight. There were numerous occasions when guys in the unit tried to fix him up. Sometimes it was strange because the guys would try to fix him up with friends of the girls that they were screwing around with. It was rare that someone would ask him to come to their home or double date with a friend of a wife. All of this was okay with him. The more he saw what was going on…the more he wanted to be with Janet.

CHAPTER 29

Frank arrived at the homicide office early for the 4 P.M. to midnight shift. He liked coming in early to relieve the dayshift, especially on the weekends. He liked the weekend action; he also knew that his early arrivals would be reciprocated down the road. The weekends in Baltimore could bring as many as five or six murders. The unit also handled all the serious shootings and stabbings.

Frank was usually friendly when he arrived in the office. On occasion, he would even bring in some doughnuts. His early arrival, not only allowed him to relax before his actual shift started, but he could read the reports on what occurred on the previous shift. There were also some quiet times when he could shut the door and study a little for the lieutenant's test.

Frank was catching up on some reports when he came across a name that he remembered. The report was about a shooting in the Eastern District of the city that occurred late Friday night. He got to the suspect's name and could not believe this guy was out of prison. The suspect in the fatal shooting was a guy that Frank had arrested about five years ago, Kenny Jackson. Frank had charged him with stabbing a guy, drug possession, and assault. The assault charge was for fighting with Frank and another cop when they went to his house to arrest him. Kenny Jackson was a bad as they come; he had absolutely no respect for the law. He was a ruthless, viscous, nasty, son of a bitch. Frank was perplexed about why Kenny would be out of prison so quick. He cranked up his laptop. He went into the Maryland Corrections website. He knew enough about Kenny to check a common name such as Jackson. He knew his age, description, and home address. Frank found the data about Kenny on the corrections website. He could not believe what he was reading. Kenny Jackson was released after serving a little over three years of his sentence. As Frank continued to read, the kicker was that he was released on good behavior.

Frank printed a copy off the website and was furious. When he went to the main copier to retrieve the printout, he kicked the trash can completely across the office. The can almost struck Detective Lenny Wilkins as he sat at his desk. "Hey dude, what the hell you doing?" Lenny then realized that it was Sergeant Favasi that kicked the can.

"Sorry dude, I just found out that a guy we want for a shooting in the eastern last night was a guy I had locked up a few years ago."

"I knew it had to be something bad for you to smash that can clear across the office."

"Detective, this bastard is a real bad guy and there is no doubt he will do some damage in Charm City real soon."

Frank retreated back to his office and shut the door. He was ordering photos of Jackson when his office door opened. "Excuse me Sergeant Favasi, can you check out this report before I put it on the lieutenant's desk?"

"Why didn't your sergeant sign it before he left?"

"I guess he was excited to get relieved early by you and just bolted."

"I don't like signing reports on something that I had nothing to do with. Just leave it on my desk and I'll look it over. Don't leave until I sign it."

The other detectives that worked for Frank were now arriving in the office for their shift. As they walked by Frank's office, they would say hello to Frank and continue to their desk. Nick came in for work and pushed open Frank's door. He asked if he could talk to him about something.

"I'm a little busy right now Nick; see me a little later in the shift."

Frank started to read the report that Wilkins had left on his desk. As he read the four page typed report, he found lots of mistakes, both spelling and procedural errors. He didn't feel comfortable signing the report. He hollered for Wilkins to come in his office. "Sit down detective. Do you really expect me to sign this piece of shit report? Where the hell did you go to school or did you even go to school at all? Detective, this report goes to the captain and others in the chain of command. I'm not putting my name on this crap."

Frank pulled out a red magic marker from his desk. He marked a large "X" through each page of the report. He threw it at the detective... Wilkins grabbed the report and said, "Did you have to do that? You could have told me where the corrections needed to be made. I have to type the whole damn report over now."

Frank smiled at Wilkins. The same smile that was so dreaded by most of the detectives in the unit. The smile that meant, I'm a sergeant and you are just a detective, do what I say. Instead of leaving the office, Wilkins leaned against the closed door. Wilkins had a few years in the unit and was known to be a hothead on occasion. "Sergeant, can I ask you something before I go and type this report over?"

"Sure detective, what can I do for you?"

"I hope you don't mind me saying this, but me and some others in the unit think you are prejudiced."

"So you think I'm prejudiced? Well detective, I am prejudiced. I don't like the Yankees, I don't like Chinese food, and I don't like cops that can't do their job. I really don't like detectives that can't write a decent report. Now, what else can I help you with before you go out there and rewrite that report?"

"With all due respect sergeant, I think you know what I mean. I mean it's the opinion of some black detectives in this unit that you go out of your way to screw with us—that's what I mean, sir."

"Detective, I will take note of what you said. Now get the hell out of my office before I write you up for insubordination. Do I make myself clear to you, detective?"

"Oh, yes sir, I am perfectly clear on what you are saying. I'm sure some others would be very interested in what you said also."

"Is that some sort of threat? I really don't give a shit what others think. I have a job to do and I think I'm doing it pretty damn good. Now, don't let that door hit you in the ass on your way out."

Frank's voice was getting higher all the time that Wilkins was in his office. He could be heard in the outer office and probably on the entire floor. Detective Wilkins walked back to his desk. Nick asked Wilkins what the hell had happened.

"Well Nick, I think your friend has pushed the race thing to the point where I have no choice but to talk to the captain."

"Lenny, you sure you want to do that? Why not give it some time. I'm sure it will all work out."

"Nick, I know you and Favasi are tight. I like you Nick, but you must see what kind of person he is. I think he is obsessed with getting promoted and he don't give a shit who he hurts along the way. I have been around here for a long time. I have seen some of the shit he has pulled on murder investigations. He makes it a point to try and go out on all police shootings. Don't it seem a little strange that on every shooting scene he is on where a police officer has shot someone— they always find a weapon on the bad guy? Also, isn't it funny that most of the bad guys that get shot are black? Oh yeah, and most of the police officers that do the shooting are white dudes. Nick, I don't won't to do it, but we can't allow him to continue like this or he will eventually take down this entire unit. I don't have that many years left before I retire. If I don't tell the captain now, no one will ever say anything. I will not let this guy destroy my career in the department. I also will not allow him to take away my chances of getting my retirement."

"Lenny, I have a lot of respect for you, but make sure you are convinced that you are doing the right thing before you act. Frank is well-liked in the department. He has a lot of friends. Proving what you think is going to be an uphill battle. You may wind up with some results that you don't like. I'm not trying to stop you, but make sure you take some time to think it over. Do you want me to talk to him about the situation?"

"Thanks Nick, I do intend to think it over. I don't think I will be alone if I do go to the captain. There are quite a few guys in this unit who feel the same way I do. I even think that some of the white detectives don't like the way he acts. Nick, you know that I like working with you. You are a good cop and a decent person. Sometimes you got to do what you got to do. Nick, I have read a lot of books and the other night I read a quote from Winston Churchill in which he said, 'Sometimes doing your best is not enough; you must do what is required.' "

CHAPTER 30

Frank's shift ended on time, which was a blessing in disguise. He had been putting in so many hours that he was getting a little run-down. Any opportunity you got where you ended your shift on time in the Homicide Unit, gave you the chance to recharge your batteries. Usually recharging your batteries meant going home and getting some much needed sleep. Frank was different—he liked to hit a few bars late at night. The bars he went to knew he was a sergeant in the police department and treated him good. It was one of the perks of the job—getting free drinks in some bars.

This night was special; there had only been one shooting in the city. The victim in the shooting did not die. Frank spent the entire shift in the office catching up on reports, working on the leave schedule, and of course doing a little studying for the lieutenant's test.

As he was leaving the office around midnight, he asked if anyone wanted to stop for a drink. Most of the detectives on his shift had already been relieved and were gone. Nick told him that he was really tired and was going home to crash for the night. There was no response from the others and Frank did not wait around or try to convince anyone to stop with him for a drink.

Frank left the building and walked to his car. He sat in his car and was thinking about where he would stop. He decided that the Pirate's Den was the closest bar. He liked the atmosphere. Frank walked into the bar and was greeted by Pam, the bartender. "Hi Frank, what brings you in so early. You usually don't get here until nearly closing time. Did they finally get wind of you and fire you?"

"Hi beautiful, I could smell your sweet fragrance as I was driving by. You know I can't resist that perfume you wear. I think I will have that special drink that I always have."

"You mean that special concoction that I do for special people like you? Well, here it is Frank—enjoy your Coors Light."

"Thanks hon. I hope it's wet and refreshing; just like the last time you were at my place. I love my beer like I love my women."

"Other than the normal bullshit, how the hell you been?"

"I could not be better. Any time you get out of that office on time, it's like hitting the lotto. I actually feel pretty good, so pour me a shot of Crown Royal."

"Wow, stepping up in the world and drinking like a real man."

"Just for the record Pam, in case your boyfriend doesn't show up tonight to take you home, I'm announcing that I'm free. It would be an honor for me to escort you home and spend some quality time with you in that very comfortable bed of yours. I love those sleep-number beds. I think your number was five; what number does that dude you are dating use?"

"Dream on buddy; I'm very happy with my boyfriend. I don't know what number he uses. Actually my number is seven. I like it hard, just like my men. If it will make you feel better, you will be my first choice if he does not show up."

Frank belted down the shot of whiskey and chased it with the beer. He did not make it a regular routine to drink whiskey. He felt good for some reason. The bar was crowded. Frank walked around just taking in the action and checking out the few women in the bar. He noticed a couple of off-duty cops that worked in the Fugitive Unit. They did not acknowledge him and that was okay with Frank. He spent about an hour in the bar and finished off three beers and two shots of Crown Royal. He was starting to feel good. He did not think he would score, at least not with anyone in the bar. His best bet was Pam, but she made it clear that her boyfriend was picking her up after work. He threw some money on the bar and hollered to Pam that he was leaving. Pam walked over towards the door and said, "Frank, if it makes you feel better, I actually wish my boyfriend was not picking me up tonight."

"Thanks Pam, I appreciate you saying that, but it don't make me feel any better. Call that dude up and tell him you are going home with a real man. Tell him that if he doesn't like it, he can call Frank Favasi to discuss it further. Tell him my sleep number is ten and that makes me harder than him."

"Good night Frank. I love a man that is as confident as you. You need to come around more than two or three times a month. I would not mind going out on a real date with you. Don't be a stranger. You have my number, give me a call. I mean my phone number, not my sleep-number."

Frank went to his car and sat there for a while. He knew the routine; chew some gum and get that smell out of your mouth. Even though you were a cop, you did not want to take a chance. Some real go- getter cop might want to make an example out of you and lock you up for DWI.

The Pirate's Den was in a fairly safe neighborhood. Frank had to drive through some bad areas to get to the beltway. It was a warm night and Frank was feeling good. He rolled down the windows and put in his favorite CD. Frank cranked up the sound. Willie Nelson blared out the window. He was driving west on Linard street to get to the beltway. When he approached the intersection of Linard and Jefferson he stopped for the red light. Frank reached over to turn the sound down a little. When he straightened up, there was a black guy standing at the driver's side of the car. Frank was startled and before he could say anything, the guy said, "You got a light?" The guy had a cigarette dangling from his mouth. Frank then noticed another black guy standing near the rear passenger side of the car. Frank had his service revolver in a holster on his waist. He had a small .22 caliber in his ankle holster. He knew that pulling the gun from his waist might be a problem. Sometimes it rested deep in his waist. Being crouched in the seat, he might not get it out as quick as needed.

In what seemed like minutes, but was probably seconds, Frank yanked the gun from his ankle holster. He put the gun up close to the cigarette and said, "Catch a light off this motherfucker." Frank pushed the door open as hard as he could and knocked the guy to the ground. He put the gun to the guy's head. The guy on the ground was stunned and not moving at all.

The guy that was at the rear of the car came running around towards Frank. He started to say, "What the…" Frank used the guy on the ground as a shield and fired two shots into the second guy.

Frank put the gun back on the grounded guy's head and said, "You want some of this?" Frank stood up and was looking around and was surprised that no one was on the street and no cars were driving by.

Just as Frank was checking out the guy he shot, he heard the sirens coming. He lifted up the guy on the ground. He pushed him against the car. The sirens were still some distance away. He grabbed the guy by the neck and said, "I'm going to give you the biggest break you ever had." The guy was speechless, as Frank had a handful of his throat. "Get your black ass out of here and forget this ever happened." He pushed the guy to get him started. The guy took off down the street and never looked back. Frank went to the trunk of his car and hurriedly went through a brown bag. He pulled out a knife with a four inch blade. He closed the trunk and with a quick slash, he cut his left hand. The sirens were getting closer. Frank put the knife on the ground next to the black guy's hand. He felt for a pulse and there was none. The sirens were almost on the scene. Frank leaned against his car. He was remarkably calm for just shooting someone. As the police cars were now pulling up, Frank had the weirdest thought—is this what Clint Eastwood would have done?

A uniformed officer bolted out of the police car. He ordered Frank to drop his weapon. The second cop in the car ran around and hollered to his partner, "it's okay—that's Sergeant Favasi from the Homicide Unit." Frank was glad that someone knew him. He knew that there had been instances where police officers had been shot by other police officers, who did not know they were cops. Frank started to tell them what had happened.

"No need to tell us sarge, it's obvious he was trying to rob you. Let's get you to the hospital and fix that hand."

"I'm okay. I was stopped at the light and he came up to my car and tried to rob me."

"I'm Officer Martin and that's my partner, Officer Bradshaw. Are you sure you don't want to go and get that cut checked out?"

"No, I'm fine, just a little shaken up. Nothing like this has ever happened to me before."

"Don't worry about nothing. I have an ambulance coming for this dude, although it looks like he won't need it. I will call the Homicide Unit and notify the duty officer."

The ambulance came and pronounced the guy dead. They took his body to the nearest hospital where the medical examiner's office could pick him up. When the body was removed, Officer Martin came around to Frank and said, "Damn sarge, you were lucky. We found this nasty knife under the dead guy when they moved his body. I'm sure you saw the knife when he was coming at you, didn't you?"

"Yeah, I damn sure did see that knife. He got close enough to cut me on the left hand. I reacted on instinct and I fired two shots."

"Well, this is one less mugger that will be on the street."

"You're right, Officer Martin. He won't be robbing anybody in the future."

Frank went back to the homicide office to give a statement about the shooting. It seemed strange for him to be on the side that was giving the statement and not taking it. His hand had been bandaged by the ambulance crew. He did not require stitches. Frank was in the office until about 4 A.M. and he was exhausted.

When all the reports were done, Frank went to his car. He sat there for a while. He was still feeling the adrenaline from the shooting. He decided to stop at the Brew & Chew. He knew he would not be able to sleep. He walked into the restaurant and took his usual spot in the rear. Pesto came walking over to him. He really did not want to go into anything about the shooting. "Hey Pesto, how the hell you doing?"

"Frank, it's great to see you. What happened to your hand?"

"It's nothing. I cut it opening a can of tuna last night—no big deal."

"Did you get stitches? It looks like some blood is oozing out of the bandage."

"It's fine. Can I get my usual breakfast? I'm one hungry dude."

"Sure Frank, I'll get it together—you just take it easy."

Frank finished his breakfast and walked out into the street. It was starting to show some daylight. Frank squinted from the morning sun as he walked to his car. He felt better now that he had eaten. He was driving home and flipped on the radio.

"Good morning Baltimore, this is your morning news. A police sergeant shot a man who attempted to rob him last night. Sergeant Frank Favasi reported that he was stopped at a red light when he was approached by a black man with a knife. Sergeant Favasi fired two shots and the suspect was pronounced dead on the scene. The shooting will be reviewed by the police department. Sergeant Favasi will be on administrative leave pending the outcome of the review."

Frank went to his apartment, changed the bandage, drank a Dr Pepper, and hit the rack. He had no problem sleeping.

Chapter 31

Nick was in his apartment relaxing. He turned to the local section of the morning paper. "Holy-shit, Frank wasted some poor bastard last night." He continued to read about the incident. Nick decided to call Frank at home. He knew he would be there. When you are put on administrative leave after a shooting, you need to stay at home. He dialed Frank's number and it rang about ten times. Nick hung up. He could not believe he wasn't home. Nick was on his regular day off and decided to go over to Frank's apartment.

Nick pulled into the parking lot and saw Frank's car. He looked in the car and did not see anything unusual. He was expecting to see a lot of blood. He went to the main door and rang Frank's bell. He did not get a response over the speaker system. He thought about climbing on the rail to get to the second floor. He decided not to do that. Frank was goofy enough to shoot anyone trying to climb on his balcony. He started to walk away, when he heard Frank calling him. "Hey asshole, are you looking for me?"

"Open the goddamn door Frank. What the hell happened last night?"

"Calm down dude, let me put some pants on. Push the door, it should be open now."

Nick pushed on the door and it opened. When Nick walked into Frank's apartment he did not see Frank. "Where the hell are you Frank?"

"I'm taking a shower. Sit your ass down or better yet, make some coffee. Check in the cabinet—I think I have some. If you don't see any, just run the hot water through the same grinds that are in the coffee pot. You remember our Marine Corps days—we drank that shit after the water was run through several times. Hell, it looked like licorice instead of coffee. Do the best you can dude, I will be right out."

"Frank, there ain't anything in your fridge. How in the hell do you stay alive?"

"I'm living off love my friend, or should I say lust. You need to give it a try."

Nick could not believe he was doing it. He took half of the leftover grounds and ran the water into the coffee pot. While he was doing it, he remembered that there was a 7-Eleven about a half a block from the apartment. He decided against the 7-Eleven. He would just stay in the apartment. He had no intentions of drinking that nasty coffee anyway.

While he was waiting for Frank to get out of the shower, he looked around. In certain areas of the apartment, Nick was actually thinking he might want to put on rubber gloves. The place was a mess. He walked into the bedroom and saw that the bed was not even on a frame—it was sitting on cinder blocks. The rest of the room looked like several sumo wrestlers had a match in the room. Nick also noticed that the smell in the room was really bad. He could not identify the smell. He assumed that it was a combination of body fluids, alcohol, and roach spray. He opened the only window in the room. "Frank, why in the hell are you living like this?"

"Quit snooping around; sit down and relax."

"I'm afraid to sit down. I haven't had a tetanus shot for several years."

"Quit making wisecracks and get the coffee ready. I'll be out in a minute."

"Frank, let's just go out and get some breakfast."

"I'm on administrative leave. I'm not supposed to leave the cave."

"I'm pretty sure they would allow you to go out and eat. You're not a prisoner; you're just on administrative leave."

"Sounds like a plan to me—let's go to McDonalds. I think there is one down the road."

"If you think they will be checking on you, call the office and let them know you're going out."

"Nick, why in the hell would I start to play by the rules? We are going to breakfast and screw them."

"I think I'm going to wait in the car for you; it stinks like shit in here."

"Quit being a pussy; I'll be dressed in about five minutes."

Frank finally came out and got in Nick's car. He was wearing wrinkled shorts, a tee shirt with the Marine Corps emblem on the front, shower shoes, and a shabby Oriole baseball hat. Frank gave Nick a fist pump. Nick checked out the outfit and told Frank that he smelled better, but he looked like a fag.

Nick pulled into the McDonalds parking lot. "Frank, what the hell happened last night? I read about it in the paper, but what really happened?"

"I haven't read the paper, so I'm assuming they screwed it up as usual. Let's go in and eat. This will actually be my second breakfast. I'm hungry as hell; we can talk about it later."

"I heard you got cut on the hand, are you all right?"

"Nick, I'm fine—the cut was no big deal. I took the bandage off this morning and it looks great."

Nick and Frank ordered. They went to the back of McDonalds. Although Frank had eaten earlier in the morning at the Brew & Chew, he devoured the sausage and egg sandwich. Nick was nibbling at his sandwich and was really appreciating the coffee. He waited for Frank to come up for a breath from his sandwich. "Frank, what the hell were you doing in that neighborhood so late at night?"

"Nick, don't question me. You read the paper and I'm sure they came close to getting it right. I was leaving a bar and heading home. I was at the red light and this black dude came up to the car. There was no doubt he was going to rob me. He had a knife. When I opened the door, he cut me on the hand. I pulled my gun and shot him. That's all there is to the story. I'm still living and Baltimore is less one low-life son of a bitch. I really don't want any more questions. You know how I feel about the criminal element in our city. The dude was just a piece of shit maggot that prays on us decent citizens. He made a big mistake and picked the wrong guy to fuck with."

"Frank, you have a perverse way of showing how sad you are that you had to take someone's life. I'm glad that you're okay, but maybe a little remorse about shooting someone would make you look at least a little human. I'm sure you slept like a baby when you got home last night."

"As a matter of fact my good man, I did sleep very well. I also had a nice breakfast before I came home. Nick, I'm not going to sit here and go over how I feel about shooting that asshole. We have had that talk before. I did what I had to do to survive. That's what we are Nick—we are survivors in a nasty fuckin city. I hope you can find your way one day and join the rest of us who want to take back the city from dudes like the one I eliminated last night."

"I'm sorry Frank for questioning you. I'm sure you did what you had to do. I was not there, so I have no right to second-guess how you handled it. I'm not sure what I would have done under the same circumstances. I'm sure you will be back to work in no time. The review of the shooting will go well."

Nick drove Frank back to his apartment. The conversation on the way back dealt with some sports talk and general conversation about what each had been up to lately. They were laughing and it seemed like for a short time, they were back to the guys who grew up together. They were for the moment, the same guys that went in the Marines together, joined the department together, and genuinely cared for each other. Frank asked Nick if he wanted to come in for a drink. Nick turned him down and told Frank that he was cutting back on his drinking. "Frank, I'm getting real serious with Janet. We are getting along great and we have talked about getting married. I wish you had someone in your life like Janet. I think it would give you a greater outlook on life and calm you down. You are too serious at work and I don't think you have many friends."

"Nick, I'm happy for you and Janet. I do wish you well. I take the job very serious. I promised myself when I came on the department that I would work harder than anyone. I intend to keep that promise. I want to get as many promotions as possible. Having friends at work is not a big priority with me at this time. You will find out when you get promoted that you have less friends. Let's end this conversation on a good note."

"You're right Frank; let's end on a very good note. I hope you get whatever you want from the job. I would really like to see you date someone so that you can have other activities in your life, other than the Homicide Unit."

Nick drove from the complex. He felt good about his meeting with Frank. He also knew that when Frank returned from administrative leave, it would not be Frank—it would be Sergeant Favasi.

CHAPTER 32

It took five days for the Internal Investigation Unit to finish with the fatal shooting investigation. They concluded after talking to officers and others that the shooting was justifiable. Frank was notified to report back to work.

Frank walked into the Homicide Unit. He was immediately informed that the captain wanted to see him. He stood at the entrance to the captain's office. "Hey Frank, welcome back. We missed your smiling face around here."

"Yeah captain, I don't think this face was missed at all—but thanks anyway."

"All kidding aside Frank, we are all glad to see you back at work. I'm glad you didn't get hurt. You did a good job. I'm sure that bastard got what he deserved. Sit down Frank. We need to discuss a few things that have surfaced while you were away."

"What the hell did I do now?"

"It's nothing serious; I just want to go over a few things before you jump back into working murders. Shut the door Frank. I want to discuss some things and we can keep it between the two of us."

"Captain, you can be assured that whatever we discuss stays in this office."

"Frank, while you were away I was approached by a couple of our black detectives. They seem to think that you are extra hard on them. They told me that you go out of your way to harass them. I think I have appeased them for now, but you need to be aware of their complaint. I don't want them to go any further than this office with their concerns. I told them that I would talk to you. Also, before you say anything, I have been told that you have been drinking pretty heavy lately."

"Captain, let me respond to you on these issues."

"Hold on a minute Frank... let me finish. I will be more than glad to hear what you have to say. Frank, I'm really pleased with your performance since you've been in the unit. You are dedicated to solving homicides and that is my main concern with anyone in the unit. Frank, you are a good supervisor. My only concern is that you need to treat all your detectives the same. The other concern is the rumor about your heavy drinking. Frank, if you feel too much pressure on you—you need to let me know. The last thing I want to see is your drinking affecting your performance. The last thing I want to say is that this conversation is over. I hope you understand where I am coming from."

Frank moved forward in his chair. He could feel the little sweat beads forming on the back of his neck. It was hot in the captain's office, but the sweat was his anxiety over what the captain had talked about. Even though Frank new that the captain was right about the way he handled the black detectives—he needed to say something. The drinking part was not a problem as far as Frank was concerned. He knew that coming from the captain it could be taken with a grain of salt. The captain was known throughout the department to be a guy who enjoyed knocking down a few drinks. He also liked the ladies and being on his third marriage was no secret. Frank was smart enough and knowledgeable about police supervision that he knew the speech he had just received was right out of the police supervision handbook. The captain had no alternative than to have a talk with Frank. If the black detectives went higher in the department with their complaint, the captain wanted to have it on record that he took some action.

"Captain, let me respond to what you have said. I don't think I treat the black detectives any different than I do the white detectives. As you know, I demand perfection in murder investigations. I have worked hard while I have been in this unit. I believe in doing it right the first time. There can't be any mistakes in a murder investigation. Everyone that works for me knows that I am fair. All I ask of them is that they do their job in a very professional manner. As far as the drinking, I'm a single guy; I do like to have a drink when I get off work. I don't think it's a problem. Captain, you know that when you are a tough supervisor, some detectives will complain. I'm sure you would agree also that sometimes the complainers are the ones that are not up to par with their investigations. I do appreciate you having this talk and keeping this between the two of us."

"Frank, let me reiterate what I said earlier—you're a good supervisor. I want to keep you in this unit as long as I'm the captain. You might be right about why people complain sometimes about their supervisor. The black guys' complaints concern me because they have their own union. The last thing I need is the police commissioner calling me in about a complaint from the black police union. Frank, keep doing a great job. If there is anything you need, let me know."

"Thanks captain, I appreciate it. I do intend to continue to work hard. I will take care of the issues we discussed."

Frank left the captain's office and walked by some of the black detectives on the way to his office. He could not help but smile at them. Lenny Wilkins was in the middle and avoided any eye contact. Frank pulled open his door and looked back at them. "Hi fellows, Sergeant Favasi is back. Did you get some pleasure seeing me in the captain's office? We were discussing how to get some detectives off their asses and on the street. I would suggest that you take a hint. I can't remember the last time anyone solved a homicide sitting in this office."

Frank closed the door to his office. He was excited to be back to work—this is what he loved. He thought about his comments to the detectives in the office. The thought didn't last long; he was back to what he did the best—fucking with the troops.

Lenny Wilkins grabbed his coat and along with some others that were in the office, started to walk down the hallway. "You know guys—that son of a bitch will never change. We know that the captain had just given him a talk about being shitty towards us. He wasn't out of the captain's office two minutes before he could not resist saying something. Let's see how things work out in the next few weeks. If his attitude doesn't improve—we need to have our union people talk to the police commissioner. We don't need to put up with his bullshit any longer. This job is hard enough without having to listen to insults, criticism, and racist's remarks every day."

CHAPTER 33

Nick frequently talked to Janet about finding a nice girl for Frank. He knew it would be a hard sell to get Frank to agree to go out with anyone he tried to fix him up with. Frank just enjoyed the spur of the moment meetings with the women he met in the bars and nightclubs. He had no intentions of getting involved in a long-term relationship. He felt that being tied down to one woman would limit his preferred activities. He had often talked about never wanting to answer to anyone. Most of the guys in the unit knew this about Frank. When the guys would be talking about family outings, kid's birthdays, and anniversaries, he would laugh at them. He would always make ridiculous comments. He would say things like: you're henpecked, you're pussy-whipped, you're on a short leash, and other absurd remarks. The guys knew all too well how he felt about marriage or even anything close to a serious relationship. Most of the guys would go out of their way to avoid those conversations when Frank was in the room. He hardly ever got invited to the homes of the married guys for parties or cookouts.

Nick, however, did not want to give up on Frank. Down deep in that hard shell, he knew there was a decent guy. He really felt that if Frank would meet the right girl, he might mellow a little. He might realize what he was missing. Nick was getting tired of playing cupid for Frank. He knew that the only love in his life at this point was the police department.

The label on Frank by most in the department was that he was a one-man wrecking ball. He hated the bad guys. He had an obsession with trying to stop the criminal element from taking over the streets of Baltimore. It was no secret in the Homicide Unit that Frank would do whatever it took to get the so-called bad guys off the streets, one way or the other.

Frank was getting the reputation in the department that he would lie on suspects or do whatever it took to get convictions in court. Even though he was a supervisor in the unit—most tried to avoid him when possible. It was all business when Frank was working. The other sergeants in the unit were approachable and for the most part, very friendly. It was a known fact that if you approached Frank, you would never know what his response would be.

One day in the office when Nick felt that Frank was in somewhat of a good mood, he approached him. "Frank, I want to ask a favor of you."

"Sure Nick, step in my office and let me know what I can do."

"Frank, I'm in a predicament."

"Oh shit, what the hell did you do now?"

"No, it's nothing like that. I want to ask you to go out with a friend of Janet's this weekend. She has a friend spending some time with her and we thought it would be fun to have you go to dinner with the three of us."

"Nick, why in the hell are you wasting my time with this bullshit? You know how I feel about dating someone I don't even know."

"Frank, this would mean a lot to me and Janet. This girl is a very nice person. I think you would have a great time. It's just a date, not a commitment."

Nick was surprised that Frank did not come back at him with some off the wall reason for not going. Frank walked toward the window and was quiet—this was a strange response for Frank. Nick did not say anything. Just as Nick was giving up and about to leave the office, Frank turned and told Nick to have a seat. Nick sat down and Frank sat on the edge of his desk. He put his elbow on his knee and just stared at Nick. He did not say anything. Nick was feeling a little uncomfortable. Was Frank going to go off on him like he usually did when the topic of dating came up? Nick was thinking that Frank looked perplexed and at a loss for words. He moved off the desk and slid around to his chair. "Nick, although we have had this conversation in the past—I think I might take you up on it this time. Maybe if I go out with you now, you will give up trying in the future."

"Frank, that's great; I can't wait to call Janet and set it up. She will be excited. Her friend has heard so much about you from the both of us."

"Nick, just set it up. Let me know when and where. Don't go into a long spiel about what a wonderful person I am—everybody already knows that. Now Detective Giango, I have things to do so get the hell out of here!"

"Yes Sir, Sergeant Favasi—I'm leaving now. Thanks for the precious time you have allowed me to be in your company."

Nick actually saw a smile on Frank's face as he exited the office. Was Frank going to follow through and go on the date? Nick was hoping in his heart of hearts that Frank was being sincere. He went to his desk and was excited as he dialed Janet's phone number. "Janet, this is Nick. You won't believe it; Frank has agreed to go out with us. You need to call your friend and set it up. By the way, what the hell is her name?"

"Nick, you know her name. I have told you several times—it's Monique. Are you sure he wants to go or is he playing you like he has in the past?"

"Janet, I really think he is sincere this time. He was in a good mood and we had a nice talk. I do have one question about Monique. Is she white?"

"Nick, of course she is white. Why would you ask such a question?"

"I'm sorry for asking; it's just something that I definitely needed to get out of the way. It's on... so call her and get back to me with the particulars."

The following weekend found Frank, Monique, Janet, and Nick in the Carousel Restaurant. Frank had gone to Nick's place to meet Monique. They had a couple of drinks and left for the restaurant in Nick's car. Things were going exceptionally well. Nick and Janet were amazed at how Frank was acting. He was very polite. He was asking Monique questions and actually listening to her responses. He was not dominating the conversation.

The restaurant was quite fancy. Nick noticed that there weren't any prices on the menu. He knew what that meant. If you had to ask the prices, you did not belong in that restaurant. It was fine with Nick. He and Janet had talked about picking up the tab for the dinner. It was important to Nick that this attempt to get Frank involved with someone went well.

During dinner, they laughed at some of Frank's jokes. Nick thought that a few were inappropriate. Everyone was laughing, so he did not say anything. It seemed like the more Frank drank, the nastier the jokes got. Nick tried to intervene on occasion. He tried to change the joke telling to conversation about what each one was up to in their lives.

Monique was a very attractive woman. She was well-built. She was wearing a very revealing dress and her breasts were almost out of the very tight dress. Frank was moving closer and closer to her. When Monique wasn't looking, he would give Nick the thumbs up. With each thumbs up, he was approving more of Monique. Frank had the biggest smile on his face. Nick was happy that things were going well—he only hoped that it would continue.

After dinner, the four of them went to Sweeney's. Frank wasted no time before he told the story about when he and Nick got in trouble in Sweeney's. Frank embellished on the story a little. Janet was hearing the story for the first time and gave Nick a strange look. He sensed her displeasure about the story. Nick reached over and touched Frank's arm. "Frank, let's change the subject; that was a long time ago. I'm sure the girls would rather talk about something else."

"Well, Mr. Nice Guy, what do you think the girls want to talk about? Loosen up Nick; we are having a good time, don't ruin it."

For the first time during the night, Nick felt that Frank might be reverting back to his nasty old self. Frank had several drinks and ordered another every time the waitress came anywhere near the table. He was slurring his speech and moving uncomfortably closer to Monique. She, however, seemed okay with his advancing moves. She was also hitting the drinks pretty heavy. Nick was the only one concerned that things could change quickly. Janet laughed and seemed to be having a good time. She had not been out drinking with anyone for several months.

Nick knew from past experiences that Frank could be a time bomb. He could be very congenial one minute and go off on a tantrum on the spur of the moment. Nick was about to say that it was getting late. He thought that because it was Frank's first date with Monique, it would be nice if it ended with him asking her out again. He was getting the feeling that Frank was going to screw it up with a very nice girl. Nick knew that if Monique went back to Frank's place, she would end up being just another one of Frank's trophies. She would be included in Frank's bitch of the month club. Nick whispered to Janet that it might be time to call it a night. To his surprise, Janet said she was having a good time and wanted to stay out longer. Nick had no choice but to hang in there and hope for the best.

It was late and approaching closing time at Sweeney's. By now it was very obvious to Nick that everyone except himself was feeling pretty good or more specific, they were drunk. Nick had a few drinks, but knew that he was the designated driver. He also knew that he did not want anything to go down that would embarrass either Janet or Monique. Frank could be a nice guy, but too much booze turned him into a nasty and crude individual.

The night air was frigid as they walked out of the club. Frank was holding onto Monique. Janet appeared to be a little tipsy as she grabbed Nick around his waist for support. Nick was thinking—so far, so good. His good thoughts abruptly ended. Frank tripped on the curb and Monique caught him before he fell. Nick saw two guys standing in the area where Frank almost fell. They were laughing. He knew that if Frank saw it, he would go off on them. Well, he apparently saw the laughing and broke loose from Monique. Before Nick could stop him, he had one of the guys over the hood of a car. He was choking the guy. Nick pulled him off and told the two guys that it would be in their best interest to hit the road. Frank had other thoughts and tried to get back in action. "Nick, what the hell is wrong with you? Are you just going to stand there and watch me get my ass kicked? I'm sure sweet little Miss Janet won't mind if you reach down between your legs and grab hold of your manhood for a few minutes."

"Frank, let's get out of here. You and I don't need to get in a fight with anyone. The girls are upset. Let's go back to my place and get some coffee. It's been a nice evening so far—please doesn't ruin it. You all stay here and I will bring the car around."

"OK Nick, you're right. Get the car and let's get some coffee. I want to continue talking to Monique. It has been a great night. She is the prettiest thing I have seen since they handed me my sergeant's badge."

Nick came around with the car. He literally had to lift Frank up and put him in the back seat with Monique. With all the drinking and foolishness that Frank had been doing, she did not seem to be upset. In the back seat of the car, Nick could see that Frank was making his move. Monique was game for what Frank was doing. She was a willing participant. Nick told Janet that they would have some coffee and then he would take Frank home. Janet surprised Nick again with her response. "Nick, leave them alone; they are having a good time. Monique is a big girl and she can take care of herself. Maybe you should take a lesson or two from Frank."

"What does that mean? You want me to act like an asshole?

Frank came up for air from an apparent groping maneuver. "Who are you calling an asshole? You big sissy—I heard what Janet said. You should take her advice."

Frank pulled himself up and slapped Nick in the back of the head. He hit Nick hard and the blow caused Nick to swerve the vehicle. Nick gained control and stopped the car in the middle of the road. "Frank, you might be my sergeant, but if you keep up the bullshit, I will drag you out of this car and kick your ass."

Janet asked Nick to stop talking like that and to please go to the apartment. She scooted over towards him and kissed him on the cheek. She told him she loved him and that she didn't want him to act like that. Frank went back to what he was doing.

Later in Nick's apartment and after some coffee, it appeared that things were getting back to normal. The normal lasted until Frank seemed to be getting bored. Although the coffee was working, it appeared that Frank was now a wide-awake drunk. He talked about how great it was that he and Nick were together in the Homicide Unit. He praised Nick. He told the girls that he hopes that Nick gets promoted soon. He told Janet that she landed a great guy. He said that he was excited to hear that they were planning their marriage. Monique seemed a little surprised at this announcement. Janet interrupted Frank and thanked him for his nice comments. "Nick and I are getting married; we have not really told a lot of people. It's still in the planning stage, but we hope to announce a date soon."

Frank clapped and stood up. "Let's get the calendar out and pick a date now. I'm sure that the first people that you guys want to tell are in this room right now. Why put it off any longer? Pick a date—you never know what the future might hold. Hell Janet, you might wind up dumping this guy."

Janet was taken aback by Frank's statement. "What do you mean Frank? I'm in love with Nick. I can't imagine not being with him the rest of my life. I'm committed and so is he. I know there is no one out there for me other than Nick. I hope he feels the same way about me."

Nick was just standing there taking it all in. He knew that he needed to respond to Janet. He also didn't feel comfortable with Frank's comments. "Janet, I want to marry you more than anything I have ever done in my life. I love you. Frank has a good point—maybe we should move forward with picking the date. We should let the whole world know we are getting married. There is no one out there that could ever take your place."

"Nick, let's stick to our plans. We will be working on the date soon. Marriage is for life. We need to move slowly along in the process. We are not going to pick a date off the calendar tonight to satisfy Frank. He will find out when everybody else finds out."

Frank was restless and asked Monique if she wanted to go to his apartment. "We can go to my place and have a nightcap. I will bring you back over here in the morning. I'm sure these newly engaged lovebirds want to jump in the sack and practice for the marriage of the century."

Monique told Frank that she would go with him. She was getting her coat and a few other things. Janet was not happy with her leaving with Frank. She put her arm around Monique, "I think you should stay here with me tonight. You guys just met; maybe you should just set up another date and see what happens."

Frank walked over toward Janet, "Maybe you should let Monique make up her own mind. You might have Nick on a string, but let her make up her mind without your two cents."

"Nick is not on a string. What the hell are you talking about? He can do whatever he wants. He knows that we trust each other. He is capable of making decisions on his own. We have been together for a long time. When two people are together for a long time, like we have, they have the utmost trust in each other."

"Does that mean if you were interested in someone other than Nick, you would give it a whirl?"

"Frank, you are crossing the line with that kind of talk. Nick and I are a team. We are totally in love; nothing can change that."

"Not even if you met someone interesting and wanted to fool around behind Nick's back."

"That would never happen because we are very open with our relationship; we talk about everything."

Frank started to walk toward the door with Monique. Nick knew that Frank wanted to get the last word. "What about the guy you were seeing when you told Nick you wanted to spend the weekend with your girlfriends? Does he count as fooling around? Was he just a friend? Was he just a confidant schooling you on how to have a successful marriage?

Janet was shocked that Frank knew about her fling. She ran over to Nick. "Did you tell Frank about that guy? I can't believe you did that. I confided in you at a vulnerable time in my life. That was supposed to be between the two of us. Who else did you tell? I guess all the guys at work know about it."

Nick walked over and grabbed Frank by the arm. "You sorry son of a bitch, do you feel better? Just when I thought you were changing, you turn out to be the same no-good bastard that I always knew you were. Get the hell out my apartment—I think we're through! I have tried for years to keep our relationship going, but not anymore."

Frank tried to tell Janet he was sorry for saying what he said. She ignored him and got her coat. She was crying as she walked toward the door. She asked Monique what she was doing. Monique called Frank a piece of shit and told Janet she was going home with her. The girls walked out the door. Nick tried to stop Janet. He offered her a ride. She refused and said they would get a cab. They left so abruptly that Frank was still standing in the doorway. Nick pointed for Frank to get out of the apartment. Frank closed the door and told Nick he wanted to tell him something. Nick was not in the mood for anything from Frank. "Get out now—you have done enough damage. What else could you tell me that would just put another nail in my coffin with Janet?

"Nick, I want to tell you something. Sit down. Do you want a drink? Do you mind if I pour myself a drink?

"I don't give a damn what you do. Just do it. Tell me what you want and then get your ass out of here."

"Nick, you need to assure me that what I'm about to tell you will never go anywhere other than this apartment. This is serious shit; you and I could go to jail for a long time if this would get out."

"What the shit are you talking about? Why the hell would I go to jail for something you did? Just get it over with and get out."

"Nick, sit down and listen to me. First, I want to apologize for running off at the mouth to Janet. It actually slipped out. I'm sorry for that. Do you remember when you told me about the guy Janet was seeing? You had his tag number. Well, I got a listing on the tag. I went over and watched her apartment one night. The guy came out. It was raining like hell. I followed him to his home in Carroll County. I pulled my car up a little too close to his driveway and he saw me. I don't know why, but I went up to his side of the car. He pushed the door open hard. I went down on the grass. I was stunned a little. He came out of the car with a baseball bat. I pulled my gun and shot him."

"What the hell are you saying Frank? You killed that guy in his driveway? You followed him home and killed him? I can't believe what you are telling me. You stupid bastard, why did you get involved? You fuck up everything you touch. Tell me this is a bad joke and you did not kill that guy. Frank, you're a cop; you can't go around killing people. Jesus Christ, Frank, how in the hell are we going to get out of this? I mean how in the hell are you going to get out of this?"

"Nick, you need to pull yourself together. I did what I had to do. The guy was about to beat my brains in with a bat. I could not have stayed there and made up any story that would have made sense. Nick, I was doing it for you. It got out of hand. I didn't want to shoot that guy—I had no choice. I can't believe it happened."

"You had a choice Frank. You didn't have to go there and spy on Janet. I never asked you to get involved. I found out about the murder when I read the paper and saw his name. I would have never thought that you would have done something as crazy as that. Frank, you need to stop living your life like you are the savior of everyone on earth. If they find out that you shot this guy, you will go away for the rest of your life. You're a cop Frank—not some crazed killer."

Nick flopped down on the sofa. Frank sat at the dining room table. He poured whiskey into a plastic cup. "Here Nick drink this—it will help you relax."

"Frank, you tell me you killed a guy that Janet dated and you want me to relax. I'm about to have a heart attack and you tell me to relax."

Frank belted down the whiskey. He sat next to Nick on the sofa. He put his arm around him. He told him that everything would be all right. Nick pulled away from him. There was dead silence in the room for a few minutes. Frank began to pace the floor. "Nick, I don't think that the Carroll County detectives will ever solve the murder. I would imagine that the wife thinks that some distraught husband of one of the females that he was fooling around with killed him. I know that it was dark and raining that night. I'm sure that no one saw anything. So they probably feel that the motive for the shooting was revenge. They have no witnesses."

"Frank, I called the Carroll County Homicide Unit last week. I talked to them about the murder."

"You dumb shit, why would you call them? What did you tell them?"

"I didn't tell them anything. I didn't know anything when I called. I was calling them because Janet was bugging me to make the call. She was upset over the murder. She asked me to find out what happened. I called from the office. I made up a story that someone had called our unit inquiring about their murder. They basically told me that they had no suspects and no real motive for the shooting. I don't think they will even call me back. I did not have anything to contribute to their investigation. It was a friendly professional call."

"Well, it was stupid for you to call. I hope you're right about them having nothing to go on. Nick, you need to promise me right now that you will never mention this to anyone, especially Janet. I have done some crazy shit in my lifetime. I can't believe I shot that guy. It has to be something you and I will take to our grave. I know you didn't do anything wrong, but you would probably lose your job over this. I know that you would definitely lose Janet. Please Nick…promise me right now that you will never talk about this to anyone."

"Frank, I guess I don't have much choice in the matter. You have just confessed to me about a murder. I guess if I were an honest cop, I would lock your ass up. However, locking you up is out of the question because I am a party to the crime. Here we are Frank—two homicide detectives talking about how we will cover up a murder. I never in a million years would have thought that you would be the cause of me not only losing my job, but possibly going to jail for the rest of my life. We have been through a lot of shit Frank, but this tops it all."

Frank was speechless. He sat slumped over on the sofa. Nick stood and stared at Frank. The silence in the apartment was broken by the ringing of the phone. "Hello, this is Nick."

"Nick, this is Janet. I just want to let you know that we are back at my place. I hope things have calmed down over there. I also want to see if we can meet tomorrow and talk about our situation. I know you are a decent guy. Frank seems to bring out any bad that is in you. I know you have to work with him. I would also hope that we don't have to associate with him after what he did tonight. I still love you. I don't want to throw away what we have together."

"Janet, thanks for calling. I know we can work this out. I will call you tomorrow."

133

Frank got up very slowly from the sofa and walked toward the door. He turned to Nick and tried to muster up a smile. He told Nick that he was sorry for being such an asshole. He tried to embrace him. Nick did not return the gesture. He told Nick that he would see him at work. Nick nodded to Frank and walked over to let him out.

"Frank, I will never believe that what you did was justified. I also will never talk to anyone about what we have discussed tonight. I have no choice in this matter because I feel just as guilty. I feel as if I pulled the trigger on that guy.

"Nick, it is what it is. I can't go back and change anything. I made a big mistake. I will have to live with it. I can only justify it in my mind that the guy would have probably beaten me to death with the baseball bat. I also know that he would not have needed the baseball bat if I did not approach his car."

"Frank, we can talk about it all night and nothing will change. I have given you my word and that's all there is to say. Nothing will change at work—you will be Sergeant Favasi and I will be Detective Giango. I just hope that somehow you can change your life—you are on a path of total destruction."

Frank patted Nick on the arm. He left the apartment and sat in his car for a short period of time. He pulled away and headed for the Brew & Chew.

CHAPTER 34

Life in the Homicide Unit continued to be a daily grind. Murders in Baltimore were spiking at a record breaking pace. It seemed like they were getting much tougher to solve. The drug problem in Baltimore was out of control—it had never really been under control. A large number of the murders were attributed to the drug turf wars. The order of succession was like this—one drug dealer would get murdered on a corner and before his body was cold, he was replaced. It was a vicious cycle. The problem was drawing national attention. It was also causing some pressure on the police commissioner from the mayor to get the violent crime stats down.

The detectives in the unit were being pressured to solve the murders. It got to the point where if you had an open investigation, you were scrutinized by anyone holding a rank above detective. The oversight began with the sergeant. He was ultimately responsible for the clearance rate in his squad. For a sergeant to be sent back to patrol because he did not perform up to expectations in the Homicide Unit was a black mark on his record. The pressure that sergeants in the Homicide Unit were under took its toll. The old saying that shit rolls down hill was never more prevalent than in the Homicide Unit. When the sergeant got his ass busted for something that was not done in the investigation, he in turn busted the detective assigned to the case. It was a period of time that did not lend to a fun atmosphere in the unit. It was getting to be a cut-throat attitude. Sergeants were competing against each other. The lieutenant would use the competition aspect as a motivator amongst the sergeants. There would be occasions when the lieutenant or the captain would walk through the office and openly talk about how certain detectives were working their ass off to clear murders. The motive behind this was to have the detectives think that they fell into the category of not working their ass off. The message insinuated that if it continued they might wind up in the Western District on the midnight shift. Although motivation is fine, this type had the total threat aspect behind it.

The Homicide Unit that was once the cream of the crop in the department was now becoming very mediocre in the eyes of the public and the police command staff. Captain Jenkins found himself in the commissioner's office a little more than he would like. It was rumored that he would be replaced if the arrest rate did not improve. The captain was well liked and connected in the department. It was getting to the point that heads needed to be chopped. It was also no secret that the captain was out drinking after work more than in the past. There were also strong rumors that he kept a bottle in his desk. He was chewing a lot of gum lately—the first sign of a booze cover-up. The captain had enough years in the department to retire. He had talked about putting about three more years on the job—just long enough for his son to finish college.

When the old guys in the police department had enough time to retire, they often came up with reasons to stay. I'm staying long enough for my house to be paid off—I'm staying long enough for my car to be paid off—I'm staying long enough that my first wife doesn't get any of my pension—I'm staying long enough that I don't have to work after I retire. One of the most often heard excuses was… I'm staying on the job because I can't stand to be at home with my wife. I think that for most of them, the real reason they stayed on the job was security.

A lot of the big bosses were from the old school. It was becoming very apparent that the modern day command staff was more educated than the older guys. The old guys were appointed to their positions under the good old boy routine. If you knew or worked with the commissioner or the deputy commissioners, you had a good chance of getting one of the top jobs in the department. Some of the top cops in the command staff stayed on the job for forty or more years. One thing that the old guys in command positions had was the gift of bullshit. No matter what went wrong under their command, they would always talk their way out of it. If it was serious, they would designate a fall guy. The fall guy would take the rap for the dastardly deed. He would be moved to another unit. He would be taken care of the rest of his time in the department.

Sergeant Frank Favasi was holding his own as far as his unit's clearance rate. He had not mellowed at all. The detectives that worked for him knew what was expected. They had also figured out how to tolerate his tantrums and his everyday nasty attitude. They knew that when they went out on a fresh murder, there were no shortcuts. Even with all the pressure coming from the lieutenant and the captain, Frank never changed like some of the other sergeants in the unit. The guys knew that Frank wouldn't change much under pressure—he was already a prick.

Frank's meetings with his squad always started the same way. He would walk in after everyone had been seated. He somehow made sure everyone was in the room before his grand entrance. He walked in with his Dr Pepper soda. He would sit at the front of the room. When he announced a meeting, he always fixed the chairs in the roll call room in the classroom style. He would sit in the front— just like a school teacher. The difference from a school teacher and Frank would be his opening remarks. "Good morning gentlemen. I use that word loosely with some of you. I'm glad we can all get together for a few minutes. I have some things to cover. Some of you won't like what I have to say. While I'm talking and you have figured out that I'm addressing you— I suggest you take some notes. I'm pleased with most of your investigations. I am totally pissed at some others. We seem to have a few people in this squad that are dragging the rest of you down. It is my job to identify the weak links. I will work my ass off to get you out of this unit. I do hope that I have your undivided attention. Are there any questions on what this meeting is about before we go any further?"

Frank enjoyed every minute of these meetings. The gratification that emanated from his every word was as if he was Colonel Jessup talking down to Lieutenant Kaffee in the movie, A Few Good Men. It was as if you were waiting for him to stand up and shout—"You can't handle the truth." This would not be out of the ordinary for Frank—after all, he was a Marine just like Colonel Jessup.

Frank always came to the meetings with a stack of papers. He never referred to the papers. Everyone figured it was something that supervisors did to lead you to believe they had the evidence against you.

Frank finished his Dr Pepper and tossed the can toward the wastebasket and missed. Detective McCarthy started to pick up the can. Frank stared him down. "McCarthy, what the hell are you doing?"

"I was going to put the can in the basket, Sarge."

"Just leave it there. Let's see how long it takes our crack cleanup crew to notice it."

"It's not a problem Sarge; I can put it in the basket."

"Do you have a problem with your hearing or are you just trying to delay this meeting so that I don't talk about people like you?"

"I was only going to pick up the can—is that such a bad thing?"

"Just stay in your seat. Leave the can where it is. With your permission McCarthy, can I start this meeting? Thank you."

Frank had a way of pissing off the squad even before his meetings would start. He would always have their undivided attention. He noticeably got a lot of pleasure from his remarks. He probably picked up some of the antics from his days in the Marines. Frank always talked about some of the comments that Gunny Sergeant Stafford made—back when he and Nick were in boot camp. Gunny Stafford would have been very proud of Frank—one prick always gets pleasure seeing fellow pricks talking nasty to people.

The meeting started and McCarthy slumped down in his chair. He wanted no more back and forth with Sergeant Favasi.

Frank went on with reading some notes that he had taken when the supervisors met with the captain. He emphasized that the clearance rate in the unit needed to increase and it needed to increase real soon. He read out the list of open investigations that his unit had. Frank had a way about him of looking directly at the detective when he mentioned an open investigation. He held the stare long enough to make the detective squirm in his chair. He started with McCarthy. "Well McCarthy, you seem to be chipper this morning. I see here in my meticulous notes that you currently have three open murders. I would ask you to talk about them in front of the group, but my intentions are not to embarrass anyone. I know all about these murders. I think that two of them need some street time. I'm going to ask Detective Perconti to assist you with these murders. I know that Perconti only has one open murder. McCarthy, I would expect you to get with him after this meeting and fill him in on what you've done. Discuss with him what needs to be done. Will that work for you McCarthy?"

"Actually Sergeant Favasi, I'm about to get a warrant for one of those murders."

"That's great McCarthy, but my question was—will Perconti helping you be okay with you?"

"Yes sir, that will be fine with me."

Nick was sitting in the back. He knew that as Frank went around the room, there would be no doubt that he would get to him. Nick had two open murders—one of them had just occurred five days prior to the meeting. Nick was always prepared when Frank called the meetings. He was known in the unit to be one of the best report writers. Most of his reports were very lengthy. Frank had actually criticized Nick at a prior meeting for writing his reports with too much fluff. He had told Nick that he needed to get to the point and leave out the superfluous bullshit. Nick knew that he was a good report writer—he also knew that Frank sometimes struggled with reports. When they were in the academy, Frank would often ask Nick to help with some writing task. Even when they were in patrol and working together, Nick would help Frank with the reports.

The unit meeting lasted longer than usual. Frank looked at the clock and told the guys he would be ending it in a few minutes. He said that he assumes that someone must need to go to the bathroom. "I got to take a leak. I think the two Dr Peppers are on their way out."

Frank stood up and walked in the middle of the classroom setup. It seemed as if he was searching for the words of wisdom to end the meeting. "Gentlemen, I know that I have been tough on you lately. I also know that some of you need me to be that way. I'm not knocking anyone in particular, but we all know that some people need that sort of guidance. I also know that I do not have all the answers. I rely on all of you to work hard. I appreciate what you do each and everyday you are working murders. This is a thankless job. There are no rewards. You work your ass off and as soon as you solve a murder, you get another one. It's a revolving door. I want to end this meeting with a couple things for you to remember. An old homicide cop told me this when I first came to the unit. He said that in homicide, there are only two rules. The first rule is that there are no coincidences and the second rule is that there are no rules. I'm pretty sure what he meant is that in this field of work, you do whatever it takes to clear these murders. You all know how I feel about the bad guys on the streets of Baltimore. If I had my way and we could identify them, I would round them up. I would personally put them in the biggest tree shredder I could find. I know that some of you think that I am radical in my thinking. My only mission in this police department is to make the streets of Charm City safe for me, you, and our families. Some people have said that I do some unethical things on murder investigations. I would only ask you and those people to look at the conviction rate of my cases when they go to court. The cases are tried mostly by juries selected from citizens of Baltimore. I don't think I have lost any cases or ever formally been accused of any wrongdoings on any case tried in the Baltimore Criminal Courts.

I will end the meeting with saying that I know some of you also think that I am prejudiced against the black community. I'm not prejudiced against any particular group of people. The only people that I hate are the bad guys on the streets of Baltimore. Now let's leave this meeting with a good attitude and work hard to clear all our assigned murders. I like working here and want to stay until I get promoted. I hope you like it here as much as I do—I'm sure you do."

The meeting ended. Frank stood by the door and shook each detective's hand as they left the room. Most of the detectives smiled as Frank shook their hand. The older guys in the unit had been through this routine before. The new ones feared Frank. He would have it no other way. Nick was the last to leave the room. Frank grabbed his hand and extended the shake longer than he did the others. Nick never wanted anyone in the unit to get the impression that Frank favored him. He avoided talking to Frank unless it pertained to a murder.

Frank asked Nick if everything was okay with Janet. Nick told him that they were still talking and they hoped they could work things out. Frank slapped Nick on the back and said, "Hang in there buddy... I'm looking forward to that wedding."

"Frank, I'm not sure what's going on with the wedding. We have talked about it. We are not in any hurry; it will happen in due time."

"Nick, you know that I am always there for you. The shit I talk about in these meetings is not directed at you. I wish I had ten guys like you in my squad—you are damn good at investigating murders."

CHAPTER 35

In the Homicide Unit when things were slow the guys tried to watch the old beat-up television set in the middle office. The captain had threatened to take the television out of the office several times. He said that it was a distraction to detectives trying to type investigative reports. He also told the lieutenant to make sure it was not turned on until late at night or early in the morning. He did not want detectives watching TV while others were working on murder investigations. The captain said he did not want any of the command staff walking into the homicide office and finding a bunch of detectives watching TV.

The detectives on the midnight shift started to arrive in the office. There was no official roll call for that shift, so they drifted in sporadically. Nick usually tried to arrive at about 11 P.M. to relieve the guys so they could either go home early or stop and get a drink. At about midnight everyone on the shift was usually in the office working on past due reports or trying to watch TV.

It was quiet for a Friday night. The quiet changed instantly as Wilkins answered the phone. "Detective Wilkins, can I help you?"

"Yes, this is Lieutenant Chelsey from communications; we have a police involved shooting in the Central District. The officer that was shot is at University Hospital—I understand it's bad."

Wilkins took down the location of the shooting and told the lieutenant that homicide would be responding. He pushed the off button on the TV.

"We have a police officer shot in the central. I'm not sure if they have anyone in custody yet. The officer is at University Hospital and it doesn't look good. Does anyone know where Sergeant Favasi is?"

"Yeah Lenny, he went down to the fifth floor to get a soda."

"I can go to the scene with Nick. Can two of you go to the hospital? We can coordinate our efforts later. I'm sure Sergeant Favasi will want to go to the scene."

Lenny and Nick headed out the door. As they waited for the elevator, Sergeant Favasi came around the corner running. "I heard about the shooting. Can you wait until I get my jacket? I'm going with you."

The three of them ran to the car. Lenny was driving. He put on the emergency lights and the siren. They were in an unmarked car, but Lenny wasted no time running every red light in downtown Baltimore. Sergeant Favasi was on the radio with the dispatcher. He asked for the location of the shooting. It was a very familiar corner to most of the Homicide Unit. There had been several shootings on and near this corner. It was a heavy drug area. Frank gave the location to Lenny. "Greenmount and Preston—I'm sure you know how to get there."

"Sarge, did they say how the officer was doing?"

"No, I forgot to ask, but I am sure we will find out soon."

Lenny tried to make it through the mass of police vehicles as he was approaching the shooting scene. He got about two blocks from the scene and Sergeant Favasi told him to just park it anywhere. They decided they would go on foot the rest of the way. Lenny put the car half up on the sidewalk and locked it. In that neighborhood it would not be out of the ordinary for someone to try to take what was in the car or just take the car. The area around the corner of Greenmount and Preston was very dangerous. The houses were old and dilapidated. The crime problem in that area was one of the worst in the city. Drug dealing was like an open market on the corners. Officers working that area were assaulted routinely.

Sergeant Favasi, Lenny, and Nick ran a short distance to the scene. It was tough at first to find anyone that was in charge. As usual for a police shooting, the area was saturated with cops. The crime lab was doing their thing. They were marking off where the officer fell, marking bullet casings, taking photos, and sketching the scene. Frank found a lieutenant and asked who was in charge. The lieutenant told Frank that he didn't know who was in charge. He told the lieutenant that he was the homicide supervisor. As they were talking, another lieutenant walked up that Frank knew. "Hi Ed, what the hell is going on?"

"Hi Frank, glad to see you guys here. It has been total bedlam out here. I'm sure you've been through this before. We're trying to get it all together— we are not getting any cooperation in the neighborhood."

"Ed, let's start at the beginning; what the hell happened?"

"All I know at this point is that the officer was chasing some guy on Preston Street. The guy had dumped his drugs when the officer came up on him. When the officer got just past Greenmount and Preston, he was shot. He radioed in that he was shot and needed assistance. That was the last time the dispatcher heard from him. When backup units got on the scene, the officer was on the sidewalk with a gunshot wound to the chest. The first officers that arrived put him in a patrol car. They took him to University Hospital. I have officers going door-to- door to try to find witnesses. I'm sure you know that in this neighborhood, that will be a wasted effort. I will get my sergeant to talk to you and fill you in on anything I have left out."

"Thanks Ed—this is Detective Wilkins and Detective Giango; they will be working the shooting. Have you heard how the officer was doing?"

"He's in bad shape. They took him right to the operating room."

"Do we have his name yet?"

"I don't know him personally. I wrote it down to make sure I didn't forget. Here it is in my notes—his name is Meyers."

"Do you happen to know his first name?"

"Yeah, it's William."

Frank stepped away from the lieutenant and grabbed Nick by the arm. "Jesus Christ Nick, its Billy Meyers."

Nick did not know what to say. They had not seen Billy for a few years. They had grown up in the same neighborhood. He went on the police department before Frank and Nick. "Damn Frank, we probably haven't seen him since the night he came in Jimmy Jordan's Bar to break up the fight."

Lenny was just listening to the back and forth from Frank and Nick. "Do you two want to let me in on what you are talking about? Do you know the officer that got shot? What's going on?"

Frank pulled Lenny to the side. "Lenny, we know this officer. He's from our neighborhood and is one hell of a nice guy. I'm pretty sure he is married with several kids."

The chaos at the scene was settling down. Frank found the sergeant in charge. He wanted to talk to the officers who arrived on the scene first. Frank let everyone know that he and his homicide guys were now in charge of the investigation. He told the patrol sergeant that anything that had already been done on the scene had to be communicated to his detectives. He told the sergeant that any officer that had any involvement in the response would have to go down to the Homicide Unit. He told him to check with his men and see if they had received any information on the shooting. He also told him that if necessary, they should retrace their initial inquiries and knock down some doors if needed. The sergeant was taking in all of what Frank had to say. Before Frank could continue talking about what he wanted, the sergeant stopped him. "Sergeant Favasi, you need to calm down a little. We have been trying to gather all the information we can. We are well aware what needs to be done. Now if you will excuse me, I have to check in with my officers."

"What do you mean to calm down? We have a police officer probably clinging to his life and you tell me to calm down. I have no intentions of calming down until we catch or kill this dude that shot Officer Meyers. Now, if you don't think you and your officers can go door-to-door and put some big time pressure on these people—I will get my guys to do it. Officer Meyers is a personal friend of mine. I'm going to see that he gets the proper investigation that he deserves. He would do the same for you or any officer in this department."

"You're right Frank, I will gather the troops. If we can't get any cooperation, we will bring their ass down to your office."

Nick and Lenny went about the business of working a police shooting. Both knew that the scrutiny of this investigation would be way above the run-of-the-mill street murder. In any jurisdiction when a cop gets shot, the entire department comes together in solidarity and respect for their fallen comrade. When the suspect is not apprehended or killed after shooting a cop, the city is virtually in a lockdown mode. It is times like this that supervisors fear. They know that the officers will use all means to catch the shooter. It has always been a handed-down tradition in Baltimore and probably many other cities that if you injure a cop, you get your ass kicked. If you murder a cop and you don't make it to your lawyer or your church, you get killed. After all, if you shoot a cop, why in the hell would any law enforcement officer want to bring you in alive? You shoot a cop and it is open season on your sorry ass. In parts of Baltimore if someone shoots one of the homeboys, there is usually a reprisal and someone gets murdered. So why in the hell would shooting a cop be any different? The men in blue in any city can be considered a gang. If you mess with a gang member, you get killed.

Frank was concerned about Bill Meyer's condition. He didn't want to make the call, but he could not hold out any longer. He called Perconti on his cell phone. "We're still on the scene. How is Meyers doing?"

"He's still in surgery. I did talk to the emergency room doctor and he said that his condition is very critical. He has a chest wound. He was not breathing when he got to the emergency room. They revived him and had him stable enough to take him to surgery. Has anyone been arrested for the shooting?"

"Not yet, we are on the scene and going door-to-door. We are hoping that someone will give us something. The area was crowded when the shooting went down. You know what we are dealing with in this part of town. Keep me posted and we will be over the hospital when we get cleared from the scene."

Nick had been helping with the door-to-door search for witnesses. At the Starlight Bar on the corner of Greenmount and Biddle Streets, Nick caught the eye of a guy motioning for him to approach him. Nick walked over to the end of the bar. A man probably in his late sixties asked Nick if they found out who shot the police officer. Nick told him that they did not have any good information. The man walked by Nick and brushed his coat. He put a piece of paper in Nick's jacket. Nick started to stop the guy but decided to look at the note first. He could hardly make out what it said. He went to the storage area in the rear of the bar. When he directed his flashlight on the paper he could make out a phone number and the name "Mooky". Nick decided to walk out of the bar to dial the number. When he got on the street he did not see the man who passed him the note. He waited a few minutes and dialed the number. It rang several times. Nick was about to hang up when a voice said, "Hello, this is Mooky."

"Mooky, this is the detective that was in the bar. I appreciate you giving me your number; I hope you can help us out."

"I want to help you, but you needs to promise me that my name will not be used. I has lived in this crazy neighborhood all my life. I knows what happens to people that work with the po-leese."

"I promise you that your name will not be used. I also have to tell you that if you are in any way involved in the shooting, the deal is off."

"I ain't involved in anything—I do knows who shot the officer."

"Do you want to talk on the phone or do you want me to pick you up and take a ride?"

"No sir, I don't want to take no ride. I was standing on the corner minding my own business. I saw this dude running down Preston Street. Right after that I saw the officer get out of his car and chase the guy across Greenmount. When the guy got across Greenmount, he turned and shot the officer. That officer did not have a chance. He didn't even have his gun out. The dude then flagged down his buddy and they drove away, almost hitting a kid in the street. The one that did the shooting lives on Chase Street. I knows his mother; he's been nothing but trouble for that nice lady. Sir, his name is Buster and his last name is Mosley. Everyone in this area knows Buster. You ain't going to get much help—there were a lot of people on the street when he shot the officer."

"Mooky, I owe you big time and the police department owes you also. I promise you that our conversation will remain confidential. I am going to keep your number in case I have to talk to you again."

Nick hung up with Mooky and could not wait to find Frank. Frank was working with Wilkins and finishing up with directing the crime lab technicians. Nick walked over to Frank and before he could say anything, Frank said, "You got that look on your face—you either hit the lotto or you know who shot Myers."

"Frank, I think I have hit more than the lotto. I will make the story short. I was in the Starlight. I was approached by an elderly man who slipped me his phone number. I called the number and talked to a guy named Mooky. He saw the shooting. He gave me the name of the shooter. I promised him that we would keep his information confidential. He is scared because of the neighborhood. The shooter is Buster Mosley and he lives on Chase Street"

"Nick, I could kiss you right here on the street. I would do it but Lenny would spread it all over the department that we're gay. Great work Nick—let's wrap up things here and head to the hospital. I'll call the office and have someone run the data on this guy. I want to have all the information available on him before we put it out to the department. I want photos also—this bastard is going to pay big time. For now, let's keep this information to ourselves."

All three headed towards University Hospital. There was not much talking on the way to the hospital. Finally, Lenny said, "Sarge, shouldn't we broadcast what we have on Buster over the radio? I'm sure there are officers in the area that know Buster. Hell, he still has a gun and might figure that he has nothing to lose by shooting another officer."

"Lenny, let's just get to the hospital. I have called the office and they will get back to me with the information on Buster. I don't want to put anything out until I'm sure of Buster's information. I would figure that by now he is hiding his sorry ass somewhere. He thinks the whole police department is hunting him down."

They arrived at the hospital. The parking area in front of the emergency department was jammed with police vehicles. Frank told Lenny that he and Nick would go in the hospital. He asked Lenny to try to park the car. Frank walked into the ER—it seemed like every boss in the department was there. He noticed the mayor and her security detachment. Frank walked by the mayor. "Good evening Mayor, I'm Sergeant Favasi from the Homicide Unit. I just left the scene. Is there any word on the condition of Officer Meyers?" The mayor looked a little perplexed and told Frank that he should talk to Captain Jenkins. Frank had not even noticed that Captain Jenkins was in the room. He made his way across the ER to where the captain was talking with a patrol colonel. "Good evening captain, I hate to interrupt—is there any word on how Officer Meyers is doing?"

"Frank, I thought you already knew about Meyers. He passed away in the operating room. I was told that the gunshot wound caused too much damage for the doctors to do anything. I was told that you knew Meyers—I'm sorry Frank. I think that his lieutenant and some people from the F.O.P are on their way to notify his wife. How well did you know him?"

Frank stood there speechless. He would have slumped to the floor if it had not been for Nick holding him up. He had a lump in his throat that he could not have swallowed with several Dr Peppers. He could hear the captain talking but he could not comprehend what was coming out of his mouth. He began to get light-headed and sweaty. Nick was not much better. Nick put his arms around Frank. "Take some deep breaths Frank; I can't believe it either. This will be devastating for his family. It looks like you need to sit down for a while."

The captain asked Frank if he was all right. Frank looked at Nick and then at the captain. "You want to know how well I knew him. We grew up in the same neighborhood. We went to school together. I know his whole family; they are great people. Nick and I are a couple years younger than Billy. We always looked up to him in the neighborhood. He's a big reason why Nick and I came on the department. I can't believe he's gone. He was one of the nicest people you would ever want to know. I can't believe this is happening. I'm sick to my stomach. It's just not fair—he has a wife and kids. How in the hell will they go on without him?"

The captain gave Frank a big hug. "Frank, I'm heading back to the office. I'm really sorry that you and Nick have lost not only a great friend, but we have all lost a great police officer. It's senseless when this shit happens. I'm sure this is going to be an all night and all day operation until we catch that son of a bitch. I'm glad that you have the case Frank…keep me posted. If you need more detectives on this, let me know. Frank, don't make this personal; handle it like you would any other murder.

"Thanks Captain, I will keep you posted. You can rest assured that we will get whoever shot Billy. I take all murders in this city personal. I will do whatever has to be done to catch this coward."

The captain left the hospital. Frank and Nick sat in the waiting area. Nick had never seen Frank like this. It was as if time was standing still in the emergency room. Frank came out of his chair and asked where Lenny was. Nick said that Lenny is in the other room. He was told about Billy Meyers. Nick told Frank that Lenny also knew Billy. They had apparently worked together for a while before Lenny came to homicide.

Frank, Nick, and Lenny stood outside the hospital. The chilly air was doing Frank some good. He took a deep breath and said, "There will be plenty of time for grieving down the road. Right now we need to concentrate on Buster. Lenny, did you get any word from the office on him?"

"Sarge, I have all the information on our man Buster. I have his full description and his address. His last known address is 835 Chase Street. It's not that far from where the shooting took place. Do you want me to notify the dispatcher to broadcast the information over the city-wide channel?"

"Not yet Lenny, I don't want complete panic and chaos to take place in east Baltimore. I think the three of us need to take a ride over to see if our friend Buster is there."

"Sarge, if you don't mind me speaking up, I think that the officers on the street need to know right now about Buster. If we hold this information any longer, someone might get hurt. I would hate to see that happen."

"Lenny, you are right. I would hate to see anyone get hurt either, so let's get out of here and quit wasting time."

With a nod of reluctance, Lenny and Nick followed Frank out the door. Frank grabbed the keys from Lenny. He told the two of them to sit back and enjoy the ride. He told them to make sure their weapons were loaded to the max. As he raced across town, he told Nick and Lenny, "Gentlemen, we are about to administer some blue justice to someone that made the ultimate mistake and shot a cop in Charm City. It will be some Baltimore blue justice; the kind that has been handed down from generation to generation of Baltimore cops. We owe it to Billy Meyers. We owe it to every police officer that is wearing a badge. We owe it to the law-abiding people of this city. Also, on a personal note, we owe it to ourselves. That's right, I said it—regardless of what the captain said, it's real personal with me. I hope you feel the same way I do."

CHAPTER 36

Frank approached Chase Street. He had one block to go before he would be at Buster Mosley's address. He pulled into a space about fifty yards from the house. With the car lights turned off and a slight drizzle falling, it appeared very eerie on the street. There was a chill in the air. The slight drizzle and the chilly air resulted in very few people being on the street. Frank asked Lenny for a photo of Buster. He also asked Lenny what Buster's rap sheet looked like.

"Well Sarge, we are dealing with a real bad player. He has a rap sheet that would stretch a city block. I don't want to read them all. He has assaults, drug charges, robberies, and a couple of handgun violations. He is only twenty-eight years old, but his record is one of the longest I've ever seen. He is currently on probation for assault with a deadly weapon. I'm not sure why this dude is even on the street. I think we should call for some uniform backups. This guy has nothing to lose and will not go without a battle. Sarge, I think that with uniforms on the scene we have a better chance of nobody getting hurt."

"Thanks for the information, Lenny. I don't want to call uniform guys just yet. If we do, we will have a standoff that will go on forever. You know how it is when the SWAT units get on the scene. They want to put on a big show with all the equipment, all the fire power, and it could go on forever. I think that we can deliver the element of surprise to this asshole. If he is home and hears all the commotion with the SWAT guys, he might decide to take himself out. I don't want this bastard to go that way. I want him to experience what he gave to Billy."

Frank told Lenny to cover the back of the house. He said that he and Nick would go in the front. Frank advised them that he knew the layout of these types of houses. They were huge row houses with large rooms on the first floor, several bedrooms on the second floor, and a couple of rooms on the third floor. He told Lenny to be careful around back. The neighborhood had rats as big as dogs. He also alerted him not to use his flashlight unless it was absolutely necessary. He told Lenny that if they got in the house and took Mosley down without incident, he would notify him on his portable radio.

Frank was checking his gun and putting extra rounds in his pocket. Through the whole process, Nick did not say much. He did not disagree with Frank's plan—it sort of made sense. Frank asked if they were ready. Nick took a deep breath. "Frank, I know from working these neighborhoods that some of these houses don't even have electricity. I would suggest that when we get in and that's the case, we pull out and call for backup. Going through three levels of that house without lights would not be to our advantage. We know he has a gun. We could be perfect targets for someone that knows the layout of their house better than us. Also, Lenny, if someone comes running out the back, make sure you try to identify them before you do any shooting. People in these neighborhoods routinely run from cops even if they didn't do anything. You need to protect yourself Lenny; you also don't want to shoot an innocent person."

"Thanks Nick, I'll be careful out there. Talk to me on the portable and keep me up on what's happening. I hope the hell I don't see any rats, I hate those creepy bastards."

Frank didn't say much. From the dim street lighting you could see that he had his game face on. All three got out of the car. Frank gave Lenny a high-five. "Be careful back there brother. Stay alert and take a few rat bites for the team if necessary."

Frank patted Nick on the shoulder and gave him the thumbs up. "Listen Nick, we are doing the right thing. Stay close to me and watch my back. If there are no lights, we can use the flashlight sparingly. If any shots are fired, we will back out and call for help. Does that make you feel any better?"

"Not really, let's just do it and hope for the best. We still have time to change our mind and call for the uniform guys."

Frank moved toward the house staying close to the front of the houses. The street lights would give off a reflection if you were not close to the houses. Frank got on the left side of the door and Nick was on the right. Frank motioned to Nick that they would go in on the count of three. Frank got to three and pushed the unlocked door open. They both entered and sure enough the house was dark. Nick was thinking of his days in the Western District. Usually when you entered a house in that district, you could count on a lot of people being in there. This was unusual—was it empty for a reason? Did Mosley come home and tell everyone what happened? Did they all decide to get the hell out of the house before the cops came?

Frank and Nick were in the living room. It was dark with the exception of some of the streetlights streaming through the front windows. There was no need for the flashlight at this time. The room was very big, but you could see the entire room. Frank motioned for Nick to follow him to the middle room. Frank pushed a thin curtain which separated the rooms. When he walked into the middle room, the light was not so good. Frank turned on his flashlight and almost had a bathroom moment. "Don't move motherfucker!"

Frank not only scared the shit out of Nick, he was shaken a little himself. When he directed his light on the corner of the room, he saw an elderly female. "Who the hell are you and what are you doing hiding in this room?"

"How in the hell am I hiding in my own damn home? I know who you are—you the po-leese. I know why you here and I ain't gonna lie to you, officer. He's asleep in the second floor bedroom. That boy ain't been nothing but trouble all his life. What did he do this time?"

"First things first—what's your name?"

"I be Latisha Winkler. I be that boy's grandmother."

"Well Grandma, your little grandson has done something real bad. I want you to stay in this room and don't move no matter what. Do you understand?"

"I understand officer. What did Buster do that you need to break in my home this late at night?"

"Just do what I say and nobody will get hurt. Who else is in the house?

"I gots my granddaughter's children staying with me—they be on the second floor. It's two boys and they be good children. One of the boys is ten and the other is thirteen. Don't be hurtin those boys."

Frank whispered to Nick that they were going up to the second floor. He looked at Grandma and put his finger to his lips; she nodded back at Frank. Frank led the way up the steps with Nick close behind. A creaky sound emanated from some of the steps as they ascended to the second floor. Frank turned the corner and with gun in hand, he put his back to the wall. He motioned for Nick to take the other side of the hallway. Frank moved toward the front bedroom. With the light from the street, he could see two small figures on a mattress on the floor. He gave it a long look to make sure they were too small to be Buster. Frank made eye contact with Nick and pointed to the rear bedroom. The door to the room was closed. Frank tried the knob and it did not open. He whispered to Nick that he was kicking in the door. As Frank was preparing to kick in the door, he heard commotion and things breaking in the room. "Nick, get ready I'm kicking the door."

Frank hit the door perfect; the door came off the hinges. Nick ran by Frank and could see someone on the rear porch about to jump into the yard. Nick shouted, "Stop you bastard or I'll shoot." Nick started out onto the porch. "Frank, it's him and he has a gun. I need to call Lenny and let him know the dude might be coming his way."

"Nick, tell Lenny that I'm coming off the porch and into the yard after this guy. Tell him that Mosley don't have a shirt on and he has a gun. Call for some backup at this address and let them know what we have."

Nick screamed in the portable radio. "Lenny, the guy is coming your way and he is armed! Lenny, can you hear me?"

Nick ran down the steps to go out back. As he approached the rear door, he heard several shots. The shots were not in sequence—he heard two or three and then two or three more. When he was in the rear yard, he hollered in the portable again, "Lenny, are you all right— Lenny, are you all right—Lenny, please answer me!" Nick moved cautiously along the dark yard. Everything was silent and dark—no rats in sight. Nick called into the dispatcher that he needed backup units right away and gave the address. When he got to the end of the yard and near the rear alley, he saw Lenny on the ground. He saw Frank standing off to the side.

"Nick call an ambulance for Lenny—he's been shot. I have this bastard over here next to the garage, he's been shot also."

"Frank, I think Lenny is dead. I can't get a pulse. I need to try to resuscitate him. I can't believe this shit is happening."

"Keep trying with Lenny; help should be here any minute."

Nick could hear Frank talking to someone. He assumed that it had to be Mosley. Nick could not see Mosley as he was behind the garage just off the yard to the right. Frank leaned down to check Mosley. He had been shot also. "I think you're going to make it Buster. Are you done shooting cops tonight? Do you think you can get up and try to run from me? You shot two cops tonight and I know both of them personally. What do you think will happen to you Buster? Will you survive your gunshot wound? Will you be at your trial wearing a rosary and carrying a Bible? Will the stupid fuckin citizens on your jury decide that you didn't mean to kill two cops? Before I give you your sentence right here in this rat infested alley, do you have any final words?"

"What the fuck are you talking about? I didn't know he was a cop. He fired at me first. I need to get to a hospital. I'm bleeding to death out here."

"Buster, I found your gun in the yard. Do you feel helpless without your weapon? Well, here is what I am going to do for you. I'm going to give you your gun back. Here it is Buster, take it."

"What the hell is wrong with you man, are you crazy? Get me to the hospital or your ass will be in trouble."

"I don't think you will need a hospital, Buster."

Frank leaned down close to Buster. He could hear the sirens, both the police and the ambulance. Buster was bleeding from a gunshot wound to the right shoulder. Frank got up and stood about two feet from him. "Pick up the gun, Buster. Don't go out of this world being a sissy— pick up the gun."

Mosley grabbed the gun and shouted, "Fuck you bitch—I got the gun—what you going to do now?"

"Oh, one minor thing Buster, I took the bullets out of your gun."

Frank fired two rounds into Buster's chest. Nick left Lenny and came running toward Frank. "What the hell did you just do?"

"Nick, I was taking his dying declaration when he grabbed his gun. I had no choice but to shoot the sorry son of a bitch. How is Lenny doing?"

"Frank, you can't do shit like this. I know he deserved to die, but you can't be the judge and jury out on the street. Lenny is dead. I did the best I could for him."

CHAPTER 37

The city buildings were draped in black bunting for the funerals of Officer Meyers and Detective Wilkins. It is a tradition in most cities that the flags will be flown at half-mast for fallen police officers. Planning funerals for police officers killed in the line of duty was a monumental task. The streets were blocked off and traffic literally came to a standstill. The entire police command staff attended in full dress uniforms. Politicians came out of the woodwork for these funerals. They would all try to catch some camera time and talk about how we need to take back the streets from the thugs. People would line the streets from the funeral home to the grave site. The fire department would have their trucks along the route with the ladders crossed so the funeral procession could pass under the ladders. American flags would be flying from every overpass. Little kids and their families would be waving flags as the hearse carrying the police officers drove by. People that never knew the police officer would be crying. The news media would provide extensive coverage of the funerals. On this occasion, the news media also came from several other states. The coverage was on the national news networks.

In the church, the two caskets were together in the middle aisle—both draped with the American flag. The church was packed with law enforcement officers from all over the country. Officer Meyer's family and friends sat on one side of the church. Detective Wilkins' family was on the other side. The Mass was held at St. Patricks' Church and presided over by

Cardinal Edwin O'Toole. It was a massive undertaking just to get everyone in the church at the same time. The local TV stations were allowed to have cameras in the church. The overflow crowd could hear the Mass and eulogies over loud speakers outside on the lawn.

Frank and Nick sat together midway back on Officer Meyers' side. They knew his family very well. Most of the others on that side grew up in the same neighborhood with Nick, Frank, and Billy.

The cardinal was a well-spoken Irishman. He talked eloquently about both of the deceased police officers. He talked about how dangerous the streets of the city were. He called Lenny and Billy real American heroes. The church was deftly silent while the cardinal talked. You could have heard a pin drop in the church. The only real sound was the crying coming from both sides of the aisles. When the cardinal finished his remarks, he asked if the police commissioner wanted to say a few words. Commissioner Kelley walked to the podium and shook hands with the cardinal. "To the families of Officer Meyers and Detective Wilkins, I want to extend my condolences to you from the men and women of the police department. These fine men have made the ultimate sacrifice so that the citizens of Baltimore can be safe."

The commissioner went on for about twenty minutes. For a rough talking guy, he actually spoke very nice. He said all the right things. It was an emotional time for him and the entire department. At the end of his talk, he started to walk off the altar. He paused and returned to the microphone. "I just want to say one more thing. I want to thank the two officers who stopped the mad killer that took the lives of these fine police officers. I want to thank Sergeant Frank Favasi and Detective Nick Giango. We are proud of these two brave officers. Under some very dangerous conditions that night, they returned fire and stopped that crazed killer. I know this is extra tough on these two officers—they knew both of the deceased members that we are honoring this morning. To the families of the deceased officers, I want to let you know that your loved ones will never be forgotten. Also, you will never be forgotten—the department will always be there for you."

The commissioner stepped down from the podium. The cardinal said a few more words. He then asked if anyone else wanted to speak about the two fallen heroes. There was silence in the church as everyone looked around to see if anyone would talk. Frank patted Nick on the leg and said, "I have got to say something about these guys."

Frank walked nervously to the podium. He had his head down all the way to the altar. He let out a nervous cough. He reached into his coat pocket and pulled out a small card. He coughed again and said, "To the families and many friends of Billy and Lenny, I offer my deepest sympathy. I am saddened and have deep sorrow on the loss of your loved ones. I knew both of these fine men personally. I actually grew up with Officer Meyers. I worked in the Homicide Unit with Detective Wilkins. They were both extraordinary people, both on and off the job. They gave their lives doing what they loved to do. I only hope that the citizens of Baltimore can come together over this tragedy. We have tolerated a certain element of our city for too long. We need to stand together and fight those that want to destroy our city. The police department cannot do it alone. It will take a total effort on the part of law enforcement, the courts, the schools, and especially the law-abiding citizens of this city. This is a sad day for the families of these fine police officers. It is also a very sad day in the history of this city. I know that if we all work together we can make Baltimore a safe place to raise our families. I will never forget Billy and Lenny. I will dedicate the rest of my career in the department to these guys. I will continue to do the job that they would want us to do."

Frank stepped down from the podium—he smiled at the families of the deceased officers. He returned to his seat. The funeral service concluded with no others getting up to talk. Frank and Nick rode to the grave site together. Nick broke the deafening silence in the car. "Frank, that was a nice talk you gave in the church. I haven't really had a chance to talk to you since all this craziness happened. I guess this is as good a time as any. I know what happened in the alley that night. I have been thinking about it since it happened. I was mad as hell in the way you handled things that night. I know that if we had called for uniform officers to back us up that night, Lenny would still be here. Don't say anything Frank—let me finish. I understand all about the mission you are on to save the city from bad guys. I also know that you murdered Buster Mosley. He did not have bullets in his gun because you took them out when you found it in the yard. I have never before seen such a cold-blooded act as what you did to Mosley—even if you thought he deserved it. I don't know how you can live with yourself. I know that some of the other shootings that you have been involved in probably did not happen the way you reported them. Also, even if you had good intentions when you followed that guy that was seeing Janet, you murdered him also. I have known you all my life Frank and I have witnessed some crazy shit you have done. I don't know how long you can get away with what you do. You can't take the law in your own hands without drawing attention to yourself. I now feel that I am probably just as fucked up as you because I have stood by and allowed some of these things to happen. Now, before you say anything about what I have said, let me add one more thing. I have no intentions of talking to anyone about what I know. If I did, I would be dragging myself down with you. I also think that it would be in the best interest for both of us that I transfer out of the Homicide Unit."

"Nick, you were about as long-winded as I have ever heard you. I understand how you feel—I really do. I'm not on any mission to kill all the bad guys in the city. This city will be crime ridden long after I'm retired from the department. I do have a job to do as long as I am wearing this badge. Nick, we both took an oath to protect and serve this city. I don't like shooting anyone no more than you do. I, however, do not have a problem exterminating people like Mosley. I don't think either of us wants to see a long-drawn-out trial or appeals that would go on for years. Mosley is from the streets. He knew what he would get if he shot a cop. Nick, you are a really good detective. I don't want to see you leave the unit. I want you to think it over and down the road if you still feel like you want out, I will help you."

Nick did not respond. He felt that he had said all that he wanted to say. He also knew down deep inside that he did not want to leave the Homicide Unit. Frank assumed that because Nick did not respond, he would reconsider talking about leaving the unit.

Frank and Nick arrived at the grave site. The parking was horrendous. Cars were parked on the grass and anywhere you could fit a vehicle. The crowd was huge. They made their way as close to the gravesite as possible. After a brief talk from the cardinal and the playing of taps from the police department bugler, the ceremony ended. Leaving the graveyard was just as tough as it was getting there. While they were walking to their car, several uniformed officers came over to Frank and thanked him for what he had done. Frank shook their hands and told each one to be safe.

Frank drove Nick to his apartment. He asked Nick to go have a drink with him.

"I can't Frank…I'm totally drained from what took place today. I need to get some sleep. I'm probably going to take a couple of days off. I need to get away from police work and clear my head. I think you should do the same thing. You work too many hours, Frank—it's not good for you. Take some time off and go away for a while. Think about what's going on in your life."

"Nick, the last thing I need right now is to be away from the job. You know I thrive on working murders. I will promise you that I will consider taking some time off in the future. Maybe we can take some time together. We can get in the car and just go nowhere in particular. Does that sound like a plan, Nick?"

"No Frank, that does not sound like a plan. My time off will be spent with Janet. I'm more committed than ever to work harder on our relationship."

Frank drove away thinking that Nick was on the right track with his life.

CHAPTER 38

When Frank returned to work he was treated like a hero. The guys in the unit congratulated him on shooting Buster Mosley. Most of the guys knew that it probably did not happen the way it was reported—they didn't really care. It was a silent code amongst cops that whatever happened on the street was okay as long as it did not involve snitching on another cop. Several of the detectives in the unit came from police families. They were well aware of the long standing and traditional thin blue line. The detectives also knew that a criminal trial for a piece of shit like Buster Mosley would go on too long. It's not that they did not like long trials, they actually did—long trials meant lots of overtime.

The local media had rightfully portrayed Buster Mosley as a low-life career criminal. There was no outcry from the black community when Buster got shot. Sometimes when police were involved in shootings where the cop was white and the bad guy was black, it would cause some rift in the black community. On this shooting there was no such rift—not much to talk about. The criminal record of Mosley was talked about in the papers and on the TV. The only mention of Mosley after the shooting was that there was a small funeral service held at a black owned funeral parlor on the west side. Cardinal O'Toole did not preside over that service.

Frank was back with his unit and engrossing himself in work. It was Frank's way of thinking that everything was fine. The more you work, the less time you have to think about issues out of your control. To Frank, the few days away from the office only meant that he needed to stay late and catch up. He hated to be late with reports. He was also not happy when his detectives were late with their reports and he let them know it. Most of the detectives in the unit did not like to be prodded for reports. They knew that because of Frank's constant nagging, the final reports would be on time and very professional. They also knew that it made the unit look good. When the unit looked good—Frank looked good and everyone was happy. Even with Frank being nasty most of the time, there were some detectives in other squads that had put in requests to work for him.

Frank was deep into reviewing some homicide folders when Lieutenant Valentino came into his office. "Hi Frank, welcome back. We missed you buddy. Is everything okay with you?"

"Hi Lieutenant, I'm just fine. How in the hell have you been? Have a seat. What can I do for you?"

Lieutenant Valentino did not take a seat. He walked towards the window. He pulled out a cigarette. He asked Frank if it was okay if he smoked. "I know it's against the rules to smoke in the building. I sometimes need a smoke when I have something puzzling on my mind. You won't tell on me, will you?"

"Hell Lieutenant, you can smoke, you can have a drink, or you could have dancing girls in here if you want—you're the boss. I actually do have a bottle in my desk. Would you like to have a drink? You sure as hell look like a drink would do you some good."

"Frank, lock the door and get that bottle out. I have never heard of any rules about having a little drink in this building. They covered smoking, but there is no mention of drinking in the manual. It might settle me down—let's do it."

Frank pulled out a bottle of Crown Royal and two plastic cups. He made sure the door was locked. Frank poured two small shots into the plastic cups. He handed the lieutenant a cup and raised his cup, "To us and those that want to be like us—salute."

The two cups of whiskey were downed in no time flat. Both the lieutenant and Frank made a face and shook their heads. The reaction would be normal for cheap whiskey. This, however, was Crown Royal—

pretty expensive stuff for two cops drinking in the police headquarters building. It was actually smooth going down. There would be no reason for making a face or shaking heads. The making a face and shaking your head were a macho thing. It meant the whiskey was good and I will probably have another. Frank asked the lieutenant if he wanted another shot and he said, "Not right now Frank, but that was damn good."

"Well lieutenant, if you ever need a little something to get you through the day you now know where I keep my stash."

The lieutenant seemed at ease and took a chair opposite Frank who was sitting behind his desk. "Frank, I have something that we need to talk about."

"Well lieutenant, if it's about my drinking and being a nasty son of a bitch towards the detectives—I have already had that talk with the captain. As far as the drinking goes, you are now a co-conspirator with me because we just shared a drink. I'm just kidding lieutenant. What's on your mind?"

Lieutenant Valentino leaned back in the chair and lit up another cigarette. "I hope the smoke and booze ain't real evident when I leave this room or we will both be in trouble. Frank, I have a situation to discuss with you about a phone call I received while you were away. I got a call from a Carroll County detective who is working on a murder up their way. They are working on a murder of a man who was shot to death in his driveway. He discussed the investigation with me. They don't really have anything on the case. Have you heard about this murder, Frank?"

Frank showed no emotions or any facial changes. This was something he was good at—it came natural. He leaned forward on the desk as the smoke was getting a little overwhelming.

"Lieutenant, I think you better put that cigarette out. We don't need the guys to talk about us in here smoking and just kicking back. As far as that murder, I think I remember reading about it in the paper. When I read about it, my first thought was that the poor bastard got shot by his wife or one of the husbands of the broads he was messing around with. Other than reading about it in the paper, I don't know anything else. Why would they call you about their murder investigation?"

"Frank, I was told that they are doing everything possible to come up with a lead on their case. They actually told me two things they found out. They said that through phone records from this murder victim, they found the phone number of a female named, Janet Steele. I have done some snooping around Frank. I was told that Detective Giango is dating someone named Janet Steele."

"Damn lieutenant, you are not suggesting that Nick Giango had anything to do with that murder?"

"Frank, let me finish. I am not assuming anything. I'm only telling you what I was told. I was also told that someone in this office used the motor vehicle data base to get a listing on the victim's vehicle. I'm sure you know that whenever that system is used it leaves a footprint in the data base on who made the request. I was told that the system shows that the request for the information came from this unit's identification number. I told the detective who called me that I would check this information out and get back to him. He wants to interview Nick. He also wants to interview whoever got that listing on the dead guy. I have not informed the captain about this phone call yet. I wanted to talk to you and see what you know about this Janet Steele. Is Nick dating this woman and do you know anything about her?"

Frank was good at not flinching when confronted by surprises. He had been doing it successfully for a long time. He shook his head as if he could not believe what the lieutenant was telling him. He was also using one of his great strengths, the ability to look someone in the eye and lie like hell. He was very convincing and knew all the right things to say. The lieutenant looked hard at Frank and waited for a response.

"I don't know about you lieutenant, but I could sure as hell use another drink."

"No thanks Frank, I have a meeting with the captain later. I want to be able to tell him something about this. I also don't want to walk in his office stumbling and slobbering from the whiskey. I know that the captain keeps some booze in his office also. He is very secretive about it and has never offered me a drink while we are working. What do you know about what I have told you?"

Frank was dying for a drink, but was not going to pull out the bottle after the lieutenant had turned him down. He sat quietly for a few seconds and then pounded his fist on the desk. "Lieutenant, I'm not real sure what the hell is going on. I do know that Nick is dating someone named Janet. I know they have been dating for quite some time and are considering marriage. I have met her and she seems like a real nice girl. I do know that they have had some problems over the course of their dating. I think there was a period of time when they went their separate ways. I only know what Nick has told me, so I'm giving it to you second hand. As far as someone using the data base to get a listing on that dude's driving record—that's pretty serious. Could they have made a mistake about where the request came from?"

"Frank, let's be serious. Do you think it's a coincidence that the request for the information came from this office and Giango dates a girl named Janet Steele? The detective that I talked to was very excited that they have some little bits and pieces to go on. They have been working this murder day and night since it happened—this is all they have. Frank, it may be nothing or it may be real serious. Do you want to talk to Giango or do you want me to? As far as the information on the data base, it is what it is. The data on the computer base doesn't lie—it's not human."

"Lieutenant, I would like to have the opportunity to talk to Detective Giango. I promise you I will do it as soon as possible and get back to you. Can you hold off talking to the captain until I have a chance to talk to Giango?"

"Frank, this is something that I can't keep from the captain. When do you think you can talk to Giango? Not only do I need to talk to the captain, I promised the Carroll County detective that I would call him back as soon as I knew something. Make it quick Frank; I will give you until late this afternoon and then I need to do something."

Frank thanked the lieutenant. He knew he had to talk to Nick. He was leaving the office and it was all racing through his head. Maybe I can keep the lieutenant quiet, if I threaten that I will tell the captain that he was smoking and drinking in my office. I can tell the captain that the lieutenant is gay and made a pass at me while in my office. I could just kill the lieutenant. I can just stop thinking like an idiot and calm down. Yeah, killing the lieutenant is real fuckin smart. I need to stop thinking about killing people, especially people carrying the same badge. Valentino could have gone right to the captain with the information. He at least had the professional courtesy to come to me first. I'm Nick's supervisor. If he did anything wrong, I'm the one who should check it out. What the hell am I talking about? Nick didn't do anything wrong, it was me. I'm sure there is a way out of this. I need to calm down and think. I need to think like a normal person. In my case that might be a stretch, but this shit is about as serious as it gets.

CHAPTER 39

Nick was walking on the warm sandy beach. He was sucking up every bit of fresh ocean breeze he could. It had been years since he had made the three hour ride from Baltimore to Ocean City, Maryland. He had great memories of the quaint little vacation town on the Eastern Shore. He remembered the exciting trip over the Chesapeake Bay Bridge when he was a kid. He had to close his eyes and get on the floor of his dad's car to make it across. He had heard about friends and relatives who had to get in the trunk of their car to make it across. When you got to the top of the expansion bridge, it was like you could reach out and touch the sky.

This trip to the ocean was special because he had convinced Janet to take a few days off and come with him. He had promised her a quiet relaxing time to talk about their pending marriage and subsequent wedding plans. He wanted to get away from the craziness in the city. He needed a reprieve from the murders and all the chaos that goes along with policing in Charm City.

Nick loved the ocean. He made it a point when he was there to get up early and be on the beach while the sun was rising. He would stand there like many other early risers and wait for the day to start. He was mesmerized and in total amazement as the burning orange ball would slowly appear far off in the ocean. While he watched it slowly ascend from the never ending ocean, he had a calm feeling. The feeling was like no other calmness he had ever experienced. If only he could start every day this way. As he looked out over the ocean, it appeared as if the sun was being raised like the targets on the shooting range at Parris Island. The targets on the shooting range in boot camp would rise slowly from a distance of three hundred yards. When the targets were in full view, the shooting would commence. On this day there was no shooting. The shooting was back in Baltimore and that was the last thing on his mind on this beautiful morning.

Nick sat on the sparkling clean golden beach and buried his toes deep in the sand. He fell back on the sand and was lost in the wonderment of his surroundings. He was now away from all the chaos of working in one of the most dangerous cities in the nation. He was away from the rat race in the Homicide Unit. He caught himself and did not want to think anymore thoughts of Baltimore—it was Ocean City's time. He sat up and looked out across the expansive never ending ocean. The calm of the ocean was awe inspiring. If only he could reach out and touch it. How far did it go? Who was on the other side? How long would it take to get to the other side? Was someone on the other side sitting on the beach and wondering the same thing? Will it be here forever? How many people will sit in this same spot over the years and feel the way I do now?

Nick was calm and lost in his thoughts when he heard Janet calling him from the porch of the condo. It was early and when he left the condo she was sleeping. He waved at her and could see her great smile. The moment on the sand fit right in with the feelings he was having for Janet. He could not quite make out what she was saying. He waved and started walking back up the beach toward the condo. He was thinking how lucky he was to have Janet. As he got closer to the porch he could see she was in her two-piece bathing suit. He stood below the porch and just stared at her. The rising morning sun was bouncing off her body. She was beaming with radiance and that smile— it was powerful. Her smile could melt your heart. She never stopped waving until Nick asked what was up.

"I was wondering where you got to. I rolled over this morning and you were not there. I thought maybe you remembered something that had to be done on a murder and you went back to Baltimore. I'm only kidding, Nick. Do you want to go and get breakfast or are you living off love?"

"A little bit of both. To live off of love you also need some fuel in your body. Where do you want to go?"

Nick changed from his swim suit to shorts and his worn out FOP sweatshirt. Janet just put one of Nick's shirts over her scanty bikini. Nick watched as she stood by the large mirror in the condo and fixed her hair. He told her that if she wore that bikini to the beach, he would not be surprised if the lifeguard would tell her to put some clothes on. Nick grabbed her from behind and could tell she had already taken a shower. She smelled great and he could feel his heartbeat slow down. He had not taken a shower. He did not want to miss the sunrise.

The night before, had been a wonderful night. It was just he and Janet and the relaxing sounds of the ocean waves. They had a great dinner at a local seafood restaurant. They sat on the porch of the condo until midnight. Nick made sure he brought Janet's favorite drink to the ocean with him. She loved Baileys Irish Cream. She told Nick that it always went down so smooth and totally relaxed her. Nick liked it also, but it made him feel hot—he preferred Michelob Light. Janet, on the other hand, drank Baileys like it was water. The more she drank… the more relaxed she got. The more relaxed she got, the better Nick felt about paying thirty-seven dollars for the Baileys. Nick told Janet that he wished that every day and night in the future could be like being at the ocean with her. Janet kissed Nick. She told him that she really enjoyed the bubble bath last night before they went out for dinner. "Nick, I don't think I have ever been so relaxed in my life like I was in that bubble bath with you. I know the Baileys helped, but it was all you. You are very tender. You are the most sensitive man I have ever known. Did you enjoy it as much as I did?"

"I enjoyed last night like I have never enjoyed anything in my life. Oh yeah, the bubble bath wasn't bad either."

"Let's go to breakfast before I break out the remainder of the bubble lotion. I think you need some food in that body to keep up with me."

Nick and Janet went to the General's Kitchen which was a famous breakfast spot at the ocean. The only problem with the place was the waiting line. The restaurant was small, but the food was outstanding. They did not mind the wait—they had all day to be together. While waiting to get in the restaurant, Nick's cell phone rang. Janet grabbed the phone from Nick and told him not to answer it. "Nick, we are away from the rat race. Let the phone go to voice mail and you can check it later to see who called."

"I don't have to check later. I can see that it's Frank. He knows we are away for a few days. Why would he be bothering us? You're right, I will let it go to voice mail and check it later."

The breakfast was as great as always. Nick had not been to the General's Kitchen for a few years, but nothing had changed. The service was great and the creamed chipped beef on toast was everything he had remembered about it. Janet could not believe Nick ate it all. Nick told her that it was his first meal in the Marines. He told her that when he got to Parris Island for boot camp, he was awakened the first day at 5 A.M. After much screaming and attempting to march in some order, they were taken to the mess hall. He went through the line and the creamed chipped beef was slapped on his mess plate. He said that he ate it fast because the drill instructor was screaming for them to hurry up and finish. When he and the other new recruits got outside of the mess hall, Nick said he felt like he had to throw up. He said that he held it until about 9 A.M. and then it came up. He told Janet that when creamed chipped beef comes up, it pretty much looks like it did when it was going down. Janet was laughing, but did not appreciate the graphic description of the ups and downs of creamed chipped beef. Nick told her that in the service the meal was referred to as SOS (shit on the shingle). She told Nick he was gross—she had heard enough about his breakfast. Nick was laughing along with Janet. He had laughed more in the past twenty-four hours than he had in a long time.

They walked back to the condo from the restaurant. Janet wanted to pack some things and go to the beach. She told Nick that he might want to check that message—it might be important. Nick went out and sat on the porch. He could see that the beach was getting crowded with families. The umbrellas were sprouting up on the beach like mushrooms. Nick put his code in to retrieve the message.

"Nick, this is Frank. I need to talk to you as soon as possible. It's very important that you call me right way. I'll be waiting for your call."

Nick checked to see if there were any other messages. He was trying to think what was so important that Frank would call him in Ocean City. Did I do a bad job on a report? Did someone turn themselves in for a murder I worked on? Was Frank in some kind of trouble? Was there an emergency in my family?

Janet came out on the porch with her bag for the beach. "Nick, did you check to see who called?"

"Yeah, it was Frank and he sounded desperate to talk to me about something. I can wait to call him or I can call him now; what would you prefer me to do?"

"I'm sure he is just checking on his jarhead buddy. I would actually prefer that you don't call him at all. I know that your job requires you to call, so you might as well get it over with. Please promise me that you will not talk long. Nick, we are having a great time—don't let Frank or work ruin it."

"I'll call and hopefully he won't answer. I'll leave a message and tell him that his little jarhead buddy is in the middle of a bubble bath. I'll tell him to leave a message. If it isn't that I hit the lotto—please don't bother me anymore."

"Nick, be serious and just make the call; let's enjoy our time together."

Janet said that she would start down to the beach and get a good spot. She told Nick that she would wave to him when she put up the umbrella. Nick went back on the porch and dialed Frank's phone.

"Sergeant Favasi here, can I help you?"

"Frank, this is Nick. I'm down the ocean with Janet."

"Nick, I need to meet with you as soon as possible. Something has come up and I don't want to discuss it on the phone. I know you are off for a few days, but this is really serious."

Nick moved inside the condo as if he might say something to Frank that he did not want anyone to hear. He was holding the phone away from his ear and cussing out Frank under his breath. He knew by the sound of his voice that Frank was really upset. Knowing Frank, he knew he would not accept anything short of meeting him in person to talk. He knew that if he said no to meeting him in person, Frank would drive down the ocean. He paced the living room of the condo. He was trying to think of a good reason to tell Frank he could not meet with him. "Frank, I told you that I'm with Janet. We are having a great time and doing a lot of much needed talking. I will be back in town in two days. Can whatever you want to discuss wait two days?"

"Nick, I would not even call you if it could wait two days. It cannot wait two hours—this could be a real game changer for the both of us and Janet if we do not talk as soon as possible."

"What the hell does Janet have to do with us talking?"

"Nick, I promise you that I can't talk anymore on the phone about this. If it will help your romantic vacation with Janet, I can meet you halfway. How quick can you drive to Easton?"

"Frank, I can't believe this is happening. I take a few days off and I can't get away from you or the department. Janet is down on the beach waiting for me right now."

"Do you think I would bother you if it wasn't urgent? Now do the right thing and tell Janet that you need to drive to Easton to meet me. Tell her that it's an urgent matter. I'm sure she will understand."

"She is going to flip out. She is going to want to know what the hell is so urgent that I need to drive to Easton to meet with you."

Nick talked to Frank for just a few more minutes. He told Frank that he would leave right away. Easton was about an hour and a half drive back in the direction of Baltimore.

Nick looked down toward the beach and could see Janet under an umbrella. He paced the porch and was furious that Frank would do this to him. It was 10:45 A.M. and Nick was thinking that he could make it to Easton in about an hour if he drove like crazy. He would leave the FOP shirt on, that might help if the troopers stopped him. His pulse was racing in the anticipation of going down to tell Janet he had to leave and meet with Frank. He knew how she felt about Frank. She would think that Frank had come up with some scheme to ruin their time together. As crazy as it was, Nick knew that the only way to handle this was to go right down and tell her. As he walked down on the warm sand, his pulse raced faster. He had thought of turning around and calling Frank. He knew it would not work. Frank would just get in his car and drive down. He would knock on the door and make a big scene. By driving to Easton, at least Janet would not have to be confronted by Frank. The walk to Janet was tortuous. Nick's stomach was turning; he thought he would be seeing the shit on the shingle again.

"Hi honey, looks like you are real comfy. Make sure you have enough lotion on. I have a little problem that needs to be taken care of. Frank has some kind of an emergency. I need to drive to Easton and meet with him."

"Nick, what the hell are you talking about? You are on vacation. Can't that son of a bitch leave you alone for a few days? What the hell could be so important that you need to drive all the way to Easton to talk to him? Did he tell you what it was about? I'm really upset about this; I can't believe you are going to do it."

Nick decided that the best thing a man could do under these circumstances was to just listen to her and take his lumps. He was not married yet, but he knew that when a woman goes off on you, you just listen and nod your head in the affirmative. He also knew that no matter what she said or thought, he had to meet with Frank. Nick sat down on the blanket next to Janet. She moved over as far as she could before she was in the sand. He could not believe that just hours earlier, they were making love, talking about marriage, and just being together the rest of their lives. He knew that the longer he sat with her the worse it would get. He stood up and promised her that he would drive as fast as possible to Easton. "I won't stay any longer than it takes for him to tell me what's so important. I will be back before the sun goes down. I'll make it up to you tonight."

"I know there is nothing I can say to make you change your mind, so just go. Maybe I will talk to the lifeguard; I'm sure he would like a bubble bath. I'm only kidding—just go and get back as soon as possible. Don't drive too fast. That worn out FOP shirt is not going to keep you from getting a ticket."

"I will be careful. I'll be back before you're burnt to a crisp. I absolutely will make it up to you tonight."

Nick bent down and kissed Janet. She teased him and pulled him down on top of her. She put her tongue halfway down his throat. She knew what she was doing. She could feel that Nick was getting excited. Janet pulled away and told him that the beach patrol could get him for exposing himself. Nick rolled over and laughed. He grabbed a soda from the cooler and left for Easton.

CHAPTER 40

The town of Easton, Maryland was small. It was the last stop on a long drive from Baltimore to Ocean City. It maintained its economy by having the reputation as the place you stopped before you continued on to the ocean. It also generated revenue from the Easton Police Department who issued tickets on the weekends to sun-seeking travelers heading to Ocean City. As you entered Easton, the speed limit dropped from sixty miles per hour to thirty-five real quick. The police at times had cars backed up on the main drag issuing speeding tickets to families in a hurry to get every minute they could in the Ocean City sun.

The town had a couple restaurants, a gas station, a liquor store, and a Tastee-Freez. You could not drive through Easton without stopping and getting a milkshake at the Tastee-Freez.

The drive to Easton for Nick was not that bad. He was making great time and did not see any troopers. He thought about having to leave Janet and that was eating away at him. He thought that it was great that she seemed to understand. If they were going to get married, there would be many times he would have to leave home to do some police work.

Nick had to really concentrate on the driving. He would find himself thinking about Janet. What was in store for him when he got back down to the ocean? He thought about her so much that the time was just flying by. He finally saw a sign that said fifteen miles to Easton. He could not believe he was making such good time. A few minutes after the sign, he decided to call Frank. Frank answered on the first ring. "Nick, where are you? I've been here for about thirty minutes. I'm at the Hack and Gag."

"What the hell is the Hack and Gag?"

"It's a small restaurant. It has been here for years. When you get into the town of Easton, you will see it on the right side next to the Bob Evans. It's not called the Hack and Gag. I'm not sure of the real name—you'll find it."

"Why don't we meet in Bob Evans? It sounds a lot better than the Hack and Gag."

"Nick, I'm not going to argue over where to meet. This place is better because there are not that many people here. Just get here as soon as possible, the place smells like shit."

Nick spotted the place and pulled into the nearly empty parking lot. He saw Frank's car and parked next to him. He walked into the restaurant and it sure as hell smelled like shit. Frank was back in a corner and waved to Nick. "Sit down buddy—how about some coffee?"

"I think I'll have a soda—one with a cap on it. This is about the filthiest place I have ever seen. This place makes the Brew & Chew look like the Taj Mahal. Frank, I don't have much time. Janet has been really good about this stupid meeting. What the hell is so important that we need to meet? Talk quick dude—I'm racing back to Ocean City as soon as you're done."

Frank moved closer to Nick in the booth. When he did, he ripped the plastic seat more than it already was. Frank laughed about ripping the seat. "These bastards are probably the original seats. How many people do you think have sat in this booth over the years?"

"Frank, this is not funny. Who gives a shit about the plastics seats? You think that everything cops do has to be some crazy covert operation. We could be sitting in Bob Evans, but no, you pick this piece of shit place. Frank, nobody is watching you and me. We could have met at the Easton Police Department and it would not have mattered. Now please, what is it that you want to tell me?"

Frank sipped his coffee from a really dirty cup. Nick on the other hand, held his bottle of Pepsi. He had told the waitress not to take the cap off—he would do it himself. Frank looked around the room like they do in the old gangster movies. "Nick, how is Janet?"

"Damn Frank, tell me what's happening—Janet is fine. If you don't start talking I'm driving back to the ocean. Screw Janet, just tell me what the hell is so important that it can't wait."

"Actually Nick, I would like to screw Janet."

"That's it you sorry bastard...I'm going back down the ocean."

Nick grabbed his Pepsi and made a move toward the door. Frank went and grabbed him by the arm. "I'm sorry buddy; sit down and I will fill you in. How is the condo you are staying in? Is that the one that McCarthy told you about? McCarthy loves that place; he goes down there with his family every summer."

"Frank, you got one more shot. I can assure you that I will leave this nasty looking place if you don't get to the point. Yes, it's the same condo that McCarthy rents every year. It's a real nice place; you should rent it one year—it's fairly cheap."

"Sit down Nick. The reason I needed to meet with you is about the murder of Janet's one-night stand. Oh, I'm sorry Nick; I don't mean to refer to it as a one-night stand. I will use your words—it was just an acquaintance of hers. Well, the lieutenant came in my office yesterday. He was trying to be very blasé about what he wanted to talk about. We had a drink and he smoked a cigarette. He said that he got a call from the Carroll County cops who are working on the murder. Nick, you remember the murder—the murder of the guy Janet was seeing.

"Yeah, I remember it. How in the hell could I ever forget it? That's the one where you again took the law into your own hands and murdered the poor guy."

"Watch what the fuck you say, Nick. I did not murder that guy. He came at me with a baseball bat. I had no choice but to shoot him. Let me get to what the lieutenant had to say. He said he got the call and they told him that they found phone records showing that he made calls to Janet. He also told me that they found out through the data base we use that someone in our unit got a listing on Philbin's car and also checked his record. I told the lieutenant that I would check it out. I don't think he knows that you are dating Janet."

"Jesus Christ Frank—this ain't good. What the hell are we going to do? If they talk to Janet and she mentions that we are dating, their next step would be to talk to me. You said that they know that the record check on Philbin was done in our office. They did not have anything to go on and now they have two good leads. What the hell are we going to do?"

Frank slid against the wall and looked out the window. He was nervous, but his often used survival tactics were swirling around in his head. He looked at Nick. He reached across and slapped him on the arm. He told Nick that on the way down to Easton he had been running it through his head. What were the options? Was this all that the detectives in Carroll County knew or did they have more? "Nick, I have a plan. I see that you are shaken up by this. Let's just step back and I'm sure we will come up with something. You need to remember that Janet does not know anything about me shooting Philbin. If they interview her, she can only say that they were seeing each other. She knows nothing about the shooting. On the other hand, when they are talking to her and they mention the part about someone in the Baltimore Homicide Unit getting the data base information on him, that's not good. Whatever we do, we cannot tell Janet what happened that night. She will most likely tell the detective interviewing her that her boyfriend works in the Baltimore Homicide Unit. If she tells them that, the rules of engagement change."

"What the hell are you talking about—what rules of engagement will change? Frank, I really can't think straight right now. If I go back down the ocean and try to continue having a good time with Janet, she will know something is wrong. She reads me like a book. I could probably tell her not to mention that her boyfriend is a police officer. I'm not sure that would work; she would ask me why I would not want them to know. Frank, I think that you have finally put yourself in a bind. We have had this conversation over the years about you being the big bad crime fighter—the guy that takes the law in his own hands. I know you always talk about getting all the bad guys off the streets. You always talk about blue justice. This is not blue justice, that guy had nothing to do with crime in the city."

"I never said he had anything to do with crime. It got out of hand Nick; I did not want to shoot that guy. I wish I had it to do over, but I don't."

"Wait a minute Frank— I just remembered that I did not get the record check on Philbin. I told you that I thought Janet was messing around. You asked if I got the tag number of the car and I said that I did. You asked me if I got a listing on the tag. I told you that I did not want to do it in the office because it would leave a footprint in the system. So if I did not get the listing on him, who in the Homicide Unit did? Frank, maybe they know more about the murder than they told the lieutenant. Maybe they are throwing that information out to the lieutenant to see what he does."

"Hold on super sleuth. I need to clear up something with you right now. When you told me that you did not get the record check on Philbin, I said you that I would. I told you that we had ways to get information and it would not leave any footprints. Well, I actually lied to you. I can't believe I screwed up. I didn't think this whole thing would blow up like it did. I was in the office late one night and remembered that I said I would get the information. No one was in the office, so I used Lenny's computer. I had his user ID and password because I have all that information on the guys in my squad. Let me think about this, we might have an out."

"Frank, of all the dumbest things you have done, this is at the top of the list. I guess if necessary, you are going to use a dead detective to get yourself out of a mess. I won't have any part of it; I just won't let you drag poor Lenny into this."

"Listen to you, who the hell do you think you are? You talk about me getting out of a mess; well it's not just me buddy—it's us. I might have pulled the trigger that night, but you are as involved in this as I am. If you make anymore statements, make sure you say us and not you. Let's stop going at each other and we can figure this out."

The waitress came over to the table. "Is there anything I can get you boys? I'm getting off in a few minutes. I would like to clear my tabs. You can stay as long as you want, but I have things to do."

Frank threw a twenty dollar bill on the table. The waitress was quick to nab it and thanked them. Frank asked Nick to sit in his car for a while. He promised Nick that he would not keep him long. He told him that they needed to calm down and be rational in their thinking.

They left the restaurant and sat in Frank's car. Frank suggested to Nick that he needed to pull himself together, since he looked like shit. Frank said that he was not real sure about Lieutenant Valentino and under pressure he probably would not hold the bag for anyone—he was close to retirement. On many occasions he had mentioned to the sergeants under him that he would not allow anyone to screw up his retirement. Frank told Nick that he was also not sure if the lieutenant had informed the captain about the phone call he got.

Nick told Frank that he really needed to start back down the ocean and he would talk to him as soon as he got back to Baltimore. Nick started to get out of the car. Frank asked him to hang around a few more minutes.

"Frank, I understand the problem. I think that if we sleep on it and discuss it later, we might make some sense of it all. I know it is important, but for now, I have to get back to Janet."

"Nick, I'm sorry it got this far. I was hoping that the investigation would just fizzle-out and stay in their cold case files forever. I guess with as few homicides as they have in Carroll County, they can put all the manpower they have on it. If the murder was in Baltimore, we would be doing the same thing. Nick, this is serious and if we don't do the right thing, we could be looking at spending time in the slammer."

"Frank, I know it's serious. Is there any way you could say you shot him in self-defense? I guess I'm just grabbing at straws. I know that self-defense won't fly. If it was self-defense, then why would you leave the scene? Also, they would want to know why you were even in the area of his home that night. The kicker, after that, is why someone in the Baltimore Homicide Unit would get a record check on the guy. If that ain't enough, they would want to know about Janet dating a city detective while she was seeing this guy Philbin. I don't have any answers right now Frank—what do you think?"

Frank was writing down some stuff while Nick was talking. He told Nick that he did not have a good plan on how they would handle this. It was getting late and Nick wanted to start back down the ocean. He also did not want to leave Frank. Over the years, it always seemed like Frank had the answers. He had them when they were growing up. He had them when they were in the Marines. He had them in their early days in the police department. It wasn't that Frank was smarter—it was just that he was street-smart. Frank was bold and whenever he got into situations that were bad, he always seemed to find a way out. When they were growing up, it was always Frank that others looked to for guidance. He had nerves of steel. He didn't back down from anything or anyone. It was as if Frank cherished knowing that others looked to him to get them out of situations. But as they sat in the car, Frank knew that this time it would take all that he could muster to come up with a resolution. Nick wanted to get out of the car, but he felt frozen in his thoughts. He, at times, tried to talk but it seemed like he was just babbling.

Frank made the first move. He told Nick to head back down the ocean. "Nick, I will think of something. Just go back down and try to enjoy yourself as much as possible. Let's just remain calm. We will work it out. Don't discuss this with anyone, especially Janet. I know she will have a lot of questions when you get back. Just tell her that we discussed a murder you are working on. If she asks why we had to meet, tell her that I'm paranoid about talking about those things on the phone. You can tell her anything; just don't discuss what we have talked about here."

CHAPTER 41

Nick started the drive back down the ocean. The trip back was miserable. The time spent with Janet was now going to be much different. The information he got from Frank would get in the way of attempting to continue what had been a good time—up to this point.

He was doing the speed limit and before he knew it, he was driving up to the condo parking lot. It was still light out. He assumed that Janet was on the beach. The TV was on and the back porch door was open. The screen was closed, but the glass door was halfway open.

Nick went to the front of the porch and looked down at the still crowded beach. In the area where he had left Janet, there was an umbrella—but no sign of Janet. It appeared that there were some things sitting on the blanket under the umbrella. Nick jumped off the porch and walked down to the beach. When he got close to the umbrella, he saw her towel, a straw hat, and some lotion. He looked around the area thinking maybe she was walking on the beach. He walked a little way in each direction and did not see any sign of her. He approached the lifeguard and asked if he had seen the lady lying under the umbrella. Nick described her to the lifeguard. The lifeguard said that he thought he did see her earlier, but she had not been back since he returned from his afternoon break. He said that his break was about forty minutes. Nick thanked him and sat on the blanket under the umbrella. He figured she may have walked somewhere for something to eat. Maybe she met someone she knew and was talking. He sat there for about ten minutes. Between the mystery of where in the hell was Janet and the information he got from Frank, he nursed a really bad headache.

He decided that he needed something to drink. He put everything on the blanket and rolled it up. He left the umbrella on the beach; it was rented and picked up each day. On the way back to the condo, he looked in all directions but did not see her. He went in the condo by way of the back porch entrance. He went to the refrigerator and got a cold beer. He sat on the couch and flipped on the TV. As he sat on the couch, he thought how stupid he was; he had not checked the bedroom. Janet probably got tired and came up for a nap. After all, he had taken a little longer than he had thought. She probably left all the stuff down at the beach because she intended to go back down. He tried to be very quiet when he approached the closed bedroom door. He thought about just letting her sleep. He then figured he would go in the room quietly and snuggle up against her. He opened the door and could see her figure in bed under a blanket. He took off his shoes and the FOP shirt. He pulled the blanket back a little. He fell back on the floor with the blanket still in his hand. He started to scream. Janet was in the bed in a very large pool of blood. He tried to turn her to face him. He then saw the worst thing imaginable; her throat had been cut from one side to the other. He did what his cop training taught him, he tried to get a pulse. That was stupid—he knew from the extent of the cut on her throat that she could not be alive. He screamed for help and fell over an ottoman as he raced for his cell phone. He hit his head on the dresser. He had blood coming from the gash on his forehead.

He reached the phone. He was about to push 911 when he heard noise at the front door of the condo. He was still calling for help when he opened the door. Three Ocean City police officers came through the door and wrestled Nick to the floor. He was screaming and trying to tell them that his girlfriend was dead in the bedroom. The officers handcuffed him and put him on the couch. The blood from the gash on his forehead was pouring down his face. He was cuffed with his hands in the back. The blood was getting in his eyes. Two of the officers went to the bedroom. One of them returned to the living room and pulled out his police radio. "We have a homicide at the Sand Castle Condos, Fifty-Seventh Street on the ocean side in unit number ten. Could you please notify the on call detective and the duty officer? We will also need an ambulance here."

Nick remained on the couch. He asked if he could see Janet. He was told that he could not see her. He told the officers that he was a police officer from Baltimore. They asked if he had any identification on him and he told them that his wallet was in the dresser drawer in the bedroom. He tried to talk to the officers, but they advised him that he should not say anything at this time. Nick knew the routine, but this was different; he was now on the other end of the blue line. He asked if they could take the cuffs off and they said they needed to wait for the detectives. The blood was coming out of the gash on his forehead at a pretty good clip. One of the officers said he would put the cuffs in front so that Nick could press a towel on the wound.

Nick wanted to tell the officers a story, but they kept telling him to wait for the detectives. He sat there and could not believe what was happening. His world seemingly had come to a complete standstill. Earlier in the day, he was the happiest guy in the world. Now, as he sat there bleeding and Janet dead in another room—his world had crumbled.

CHAPTER 42

Frank drove back to Baltimore from Easton. He stopped for dinner; he had not eaten all day. After sitting in the Hack and Gag in Easton with Nick earlier in the day, he needed something that resembled real food. He also needed to go to a place that did not smell like shit. He stopped at the Harvey House which was a place where Frank was well known. The Harvey House was pricey, but Nick enjoyed being around the self-imposed elite of Baltimore. He always ate at the bar. On this day he told the bartender that he needed a cold beer and two shots of Crown Royal. The bartender had known Frank for a few years. He enjoyed having conversations with him about the murders happening in Baltimore.

Frank ordered a steak and that's all he had to say. Benny knew how he liked it—he also knew what he wanted with it. Benny was a well-traveled, old-time bartender—he was a good listener. He had told Frank that in his earlier life, he lived in Chicago. He often talked about how corrupt the Chicago Police Department was. Benny had a few scars on his face. He told Frank that they were the result of not paying some debts to the mob in Chicago. He related one story to Frank that he was picked up one night by people that he owed quite a bit of money. He said they took him to a local hangout on the south side of Chicago. They smacked him around a little. The boss of the gang told his guys to put Benny under the pool table. He said they lifted the table and slid him under the leg. Benny said they were going to drop the table on his face. He said he turned as the table was dropped. He went to the hospital with a broken jaw, fractured clavicle, and a partially collapsed lung. He told Frank that after that he decided that he had to leave Chicago for health reasons. He came to Baltimore and a friend got him the job at the Harvey House.

Frank was savoring the pleasant atmosphere and conversation with Benny. His meal was great. He was settling in to enjoy the evening. The drinks were good, his stomach was full, and he had his eye on a good-looking blonde at the end of the bar. His cell phone rang and he thought about letting it go to voice mail. He looked at the number and did not recognize it. The cell phone beeped indicating that there was a message in the voice mail. He told Benny to keep the drinks coming and to send one down to the blonde. Frank went to the men's room and looked at the phone number. He didn't recognize it and wondered if it was some broad he gave his number to. He went into his voice mail. The message stated that the Ocean City PD was trying to reach Sergeant Frank Favasi. The message went on to say that he should call the Ocean City Police Department immediately. Frank left the men's room and told Benny that he would be outside making a call. He dialed the number and he was put through to an automated system in the Ocean City Police Department. He punched in some number that directed him to the detective unit. "Ocean City Police Department, this is Corporal Perry can I help you?"

"Yes corporal, this is Sergeant Favasi; I'm with the Baltimore Police Department. I received a message to contact you at this number. What can I do for you?"

The corporal told Frank to hold on—he would rather he talk to the captain. Frank asked the corporal what was wrong, but got no response. He waited for about five minutes before a voice came on the phone. "Sergeant Favasi, this is Captain Clark… thanks for calling us. I have a situation down here that involves one of your detectives from the city. We are investigating the murder of a young lady that occurred earlier this afternoon. The murder occurred in a condo rented by your guy, Nick Giango. We have Mr. Giango in custody. He told us he was a Baltimore cop and asked that we call you. He said he was with you earlier today in Easton."

"Holy shit, you have Nick in custody for killing his girlfriend? That's not possible—Nick would not hurt that girl no matter what. I think they are engaged to be married. What can I do? Can I talk to him?"

"Not yet, we just want to know if you did meet with him in Easton earlier today. We don't think that he killed his girlfriend, but we have to check out a few things first. He is very distraught at this time. It was a very brutal death—her throat was cut. He said that he was with you discussing some investigation that you are working on in Baltimore. He said that when he came back down the ocean, he found her body in the bedroom. When our officers got to the condo, he was covered with blood. We do believe his story that he fell and hit his head on a dresser in the bedroom. Can you just confirm that he did meet with you in Easton?"

"Yes, we met in Easton and talked about a murder investigation. I called him and asked that he drive to Easton and meet with me. We talked for a while and he drove back down the ocean. He was happy as hell to be on vacation with Janet. This is unbelievable captain—Nick would not harm that girl. What can I do? Do you need me to drive down there and discuss this further? I'm sick to my stomach to hear about Janet. I don't know if Nick will ever get over this. Do you have any suspects? Did anyone see anything while Nick was gone?"

"It's early in the investigation. We do have a few things we are checking out. Someone in a condo in that block did see a black man walking near her condo. In Ocean City these days, it is not uncommon to see black guys walking around. Years ago, if you saw a black man walking in Ocean City, that was rare. I'm going to put the corporal back on the phone. He can tell you more about what we assume happened. I don't think we are going to hold Mr. Giango any longer. He's a nervous wreck. I think he needs to get some professional help. I am sure you can work that out for him when he gets back to Baltimore. Thanks for calling us and here's the corporal."

Frank talked to the corporal for a few minutes. He told Frank that he did not think Mr. Giango would be returning to the condo. He suggested that someone drive down to Ocean City and pick him up. He told Frank that Nick was in no condition to drive. He also had a large cut on his forehead. The corporal told Frank that Nick was treated at the lockup and did not need stitches. Frank thanked the corporal and told him that he or someone would come down to get Nick. He asked the corporal to make sure Nick stayed there. He did not want him to drive or even be by himself.

Frank went back in the Harvey House. He had a half of a drink in his glass and ordered another Crown Royal. Benny told him that he looked like he had seen a ghost. "Are you all right Frank? Is there anything I can do? If it will make you feel better, the blonde down the end asked about you. She wants to reciprocate and buy you a drink. Should I tell her that you will be down to see her? She looks like she could make you forget all your worries. What do you say, Frank?"

Frank downed the Crown Royal and paid his tab. He told Benny that he had to take care of something. He walked toward the door. The blonde left the guy she was talking to at the bar. She stood with her hands stretched out blocking the door. Frank could see that she was a knock out. He had business to take care of—but this was a sure thing. He asked if she was with anyone.

"I am with someone, but I'm sure he will understand when I leave with you. That is if you want me to leave with you. I don't want to force myself on you. I just think we could have a little fun together tonight. My apartment is close by and my roommate is out of town—need I say anymore Mr. Big Shot Cop. Yeah, I know you are a cop. Benny keeps me straight. I hope you are not thinking about locking me up for soliciting you. I'm not soliciting you. I am merely inviting you to my place for some fun and games. What do you say, Sherlock?"

Frank was taken aback by her bluntness and also her beauty. He knew that he needed to take care of the situation down the ocean with Nick. He also knew that what was blocking the door could be just what the doctor ordered. He put his hands on her waist. She moved close to him. He could feel the bone in her crotch press against his penis. Frank loved that feeling. It reminded him of his days in the old neighborhood. He loved to have girls dance close to him at the youth dances at his school. He and the guys called it the bone dance. When you got done bumping and grinding with a girl after the bone dance, you needed to have some serious adjustment of your underwear.

On the way to the blonde's apartment Frank told her that he needed to make a phone call. He felt bad that he was not heading back down the ocean to get Nick. He knew that in his condition, it would not be wise to drive. He also knew that this broad that was playing with his private parts while he was driving was going to be a once in a lifetime encounter. Frank pulled over in front of her apartment. He told her that he needed to make a very important call. She told him that she was in apartment 2C and she would be warming things up for him. She kissed him and pulled his hand down to her crotch. She told him to hurry up.

Frank called the Homicide office to see who was working. When he found out who was working, he decided not to ask any of them to get Nick. Instead, he decided to call McCarthy—he worked for Frank and would probably do it. He dialed McCarthy on his cell phone and got him on the first ring. "Hey Mack, this is Sergeant Favasi. I need to ask you a very big favor. I need you to drive down to Ocean City and pick up Nick Giango."

"What the hell sarge—do you know what time it is? It would take me three hours to drive down the ocean. Is this a joke?"

"Listen Mack, this is serious shit. Nick's girlfriend, Janet, was murdered while they were down the ocean. They thought Nick was a suspect. It's complicated, but it would mean the world to me and Nick if you could do this. I will make sure you are compensated for your time later. I need someone that I can trust and you are the guy. What do you say?"

"Damn sarge, are you telling me that Janet was murdered? This will devastate Nick. They were planning on getting married. I can't believe this. I'll go down and get him. Where in the hell is he?"

"He's at the Ocean City Police headquarters. I asked them to keep him there until someone comes down to get him. I appreciate this, Mack. I will call you later and I won't forget this. I've got something real important to take care of here or I would do it myself."

CHAPTER 43

The benches in the city, especially the ones at the bus stops, had a quote stenciled on them. The quote was, "The City That Reads." Not quite sure who in city hall came up with that quote. It did not last long. The quote was quickly changed by anyone that had a paint brush. The quote painted over the old one, now stated, "The City That Bleeds."

The slaughter of people continued in Baltimore. A lot of the murders in Baltimore were drug related. In parts of the city you had street corners where a young guy could get wealthy really quick. He could also get killed and replaced in the blink of an eye. The youngsters in those neighborhoods did not seem to care. They could work in a fast- food joint for minimum wage or stand on the corner and make a few hundred dollars a day. If you ask where the parents were—they were the prior generation selling the drugs on many of the same corners. Maybe Frank was right with his attitude of eliminating as many of the bad guys you could. With enough cops thinking like Frank, it might get done and the streets would be much safer.

The police department had problems in other areas besides murder. The corruption investigations by the FBI took its toll on the department. The commissioner, who came up through the ranks was probably no exception. The rumors were widespread in the department that he would take anything that was not nailed down. He was close to retirement and building his nest egg. He was frequently interviewed by the TV and radio media and denounced corruption in the department. He formed a special investigative unit that reported directly to him; they were supposed to investigate corruption. He, however, put his closest friends in that unit. Just to keep the media off his ass, he would occasionally announce that his special unit uncovered a corrupt cop. His corruption fighting efforts were a joke amongst the men in the department. It seemed like the more murders that occurred in the city—the better it was for the commissioner. He could talk about all the violence and hope that the corruption questions did not come up.

Frank Favasi for the most part, was a fairly straight cop. He knew that corruption existed in the department, but never really participated. He had certainly been approached while working in the district. It was pretty much a given that your sergeant would approach you and tell you that if you avoided contact with certain people, there might be a couple of bucks in it for you. Most of the people you were asked to avoid were in the gambling business. If payoffs occurred to allow drug dealers and suppliers to operate, it usually happened at higher levels than the uniform cop on the beat. Everyone in the department would talk about the fact that they would never take money to allow a drug dealer to operate. In most cases it was just talk. Cops that worked in drug infested neighborhoods were driving nice cars, taking expensive vacations, and buying things that probably could not be purchased on their salary. Some cops to avoid any attention on them would drive old beat-up cars to work.

There were certain areas of the city where the cops had been on the same beat for many years. It was a standing joke that when a veteran retired or died, there would be transfer requests from all over the department to get certain posts. Many cops avoided taking the promotion test because they would lose money if they got promoted. The police department needed a complete overhaul and the newspapers wrote about it often.

What Frank was doing was not considered corruption in his mind. The fact that he was killing people, planting weapons on them, and lying about them was just his vigilante style of making the city a better place. He had no qualms about what he was doing. He often talked to Nick about those thieving cops who are on the take. He actually told his squad once at a meeting, that if he ever found out anyone was taking money he would make sure they got fired.

Nick returned to work after a week of bereavement leave. He was told by the captain that he could take as much time as he needed. He was also offered counseling. He turned down both offers. He needed to be at work. It had been the toughest thing he had ever done when he faced Janet's family and friends at the funeral. Every minute in the funeral parlor was agony. He stood with her parents and greeted people. He did not know what to say to most of them. Each time he looked in the coffin at Janet, he could still see the blood gushing from her throat. As with most funerals, he stood there and discussed as much of the story of her death that he thought needed to be told. He did not get any feelings that her family held him responsible. He did not need any of those feelings; he absolutely felt responsible. From the time since he found her body, it has always been on his mind. Did I have to leave her to talk to Frank? Should I have told her to be more careful? Should I have taken her with me to Easton? He knew that his life had changed for the worse. The recent times that had been the most exciting of his life were gone. The dreams that they shared about marriage and having children would never happen.

Nick kept his distance from Frank for the first week back on the job. Frank did approach Nick to express his sorrow over Janet's death. He did it every time he saw him. Nick told Frank that he needed time to think. He later told Frank that he did not entirely blame him for what happened.

Nick kept in touch with the Ocean City PD about the murder investigation. They had been good to Nick after they cleared him of any involvement in Janet's death. Some of the Ocean City detectives came to Baltimore for the funeral. His latest update from them was that they did have a few leads. Nick was told that they have a composite drawing of a black man who was seen in the area of the condo that day. He was told that no murder weapon was found on the scene. It was believed that the assailant possibly used a box cutter or a straight razor. The lead investigator in the Ocean City PD stayed in touch with him. Nick had gone back down the ocean after the funeral to give a more detailed statement about what happened that day. He also related to them many more details about his long involvement with Janet.

The detectives in Ocean City had done a nice job on the crime scene. Although the only strong lead was the composite drawing, they felt confident they would solve the case. The Ocean City Chamber of Commerce went on all the media outlets and offered a ten thousand dollar reward for any information leading to an arrest in the case. The FOP in Baltimore came up with an additional five thousand dollars for the reward money. Nick knew from being in the business of catching murderers that money talked. If anyone was going to come forward, the fifteen thousand dollars would be a big enticement.

Nick tried to work his investigations in Baltimore as best he could. Every murder reminded him of Janet's senseless killing. There were times when he would go to other areas of the building to be alone. He never wanted the guys to see him crying...Marines don't cry. There were times when he thought about the meeting with Frank in Easton. Why hadn't the Carroll County detectives contacted him? If they knew that the data on Philbin was obtained from a computer in the homicide office, why is there no follow-up? They must know that Janet was killed. It seemed simple to Nick that with all they knew...what were they waiting for?

The autopsy on Janet was completed in about ten days. The cause of death was obvious. The blood work and other forensic procedures had to be completed. Nick got a call from the lead detective on the case. "Hi Nick, this is Detective Mitchell. How have you been holding up?"

"I'm doing okay. I would be doing a lot better if you are calling to tell me you caught that son of a bitch."

Detective Mitchell paused for a minute. The tone of his voice led Nick to believe that something bad was coming. "Nick, I have received the final report on the autopsy performed on Janet. I have also talked to the medical examiner that did the autopsy. I wanted to make sure that what he has in the report was accurate. I'm not going to read all of it to you. I'm sorry that I have to be the one to let you know what the doctor found."

"Detective Mitchell, you do not have to be sorry—at this point in my life, there is nothing that will shock me about Janet's death."

"Nick, the medical examiner has confirmed through their examination that Janet was raped before she was murdered."

CHAPTER 44

Frank paced back and forth in the office. "Hey sarge, you look like an expectant father in the maternity ward."

"Ronny, it ain't anything like that. I got a lot on my mind. You know I always pace the floor when the pressure builds up—I'm fine."

Frank went back in his office and shut the door. He dialed a number from the directory on his cell phone. He did not get an answer—he left a short message. It was obvious to the guys in the office that something was bothering him. Frank had nerves of steel. He also showed a worrisome side when it came to clearing the murder investigations in his squad. He came out of his office and had some small talk with the detectives. He loved to talk about their open investigations. The detectives also knew that he was always in their files looking for something they should have done. When he would ask them a question, they knew that he probably already knew the answer. When the questioning started, they did not try to dance around the answer. They gave him the answer if they knew it and smiled at him. It was a give and take; Frank was usually on the giving end.

Frank kept looking at the clock and then he would look at his cell phone. It was about nine o'clock. He had a few more hours before the midnight shift would be coming in. "Guys, I will be back shortly. I have the police radio and my cell phone. If anything goes down, give me a call."

Frank was heading out the door when Nick asked if he needed anyone to go with him. Frank thanked him and told him that he needed to take care of something by himself. He went to the garage and got an unmarked vehicle. Most of the cars assigned to the unit were old. The detectives bitched all the time about the condition of the cars. One of the cars had the floorboard eaten away by rust. When you were driving, you could see the street under the vehicle. There had been occasions when detectives going out to a murder scene had to call for help—the car broke down on the way out. It was something that the captain knew about, but did not seem like he cared. When the supervisors would attend meetings with the captain and the lieutenant, it would come up. The captain would tell everyone that they needed to stop bitching about the cars and solve the murders. At one meeting when he was in a bad mood, he told them to take the bus. It was times like this that the detectives did not like being in the Homicide Unit. If it were not for all the money they were making in overtime, most would transfer out.

Frank found himself just driving with no particular destination in mind. He was waiting for a phone call. He was getting agitated that the call was not coming. He was driving in the Western District. As he passed different corners, he remembered when he worked in uniform in those areas. He also could point out spots where he and his squad handled murders. Driving in that district could really make you appreciate being a sergeant in the Homicide Unit. It was amazing to just ride and still see the same old shit—nothing had changed.

Frank found himself thinking out loud. Where do these people shop? What the hell were they thinking when they burned down everything? Frank saw a lot of old stores that were now churches. It seemed like there was a church on every other corner. It was a challenge to find one that had all the spelling correct on their signs. The signs on most of the storefront churches were handmade. Frank laughed at one sign that read, The Church of Jesus Crist. Then there was the one that read, Church of the Ladder Day Sants. Frank spoke out to no one but himself, "If these people are so fuckin holy, why do they commit all the crime?"

He was heading back to the office when his cell phone rang. "Sergeant Favasi, can I help you?"

"Yeah, it's me. Do you still want to meet me tonight? You got my money?"

"I have been waiting for you asshole. Meet me in Druid Hill Park next to the tennis courts in thirty minutes."

Frank called the office to see if anything was happening. Michaels answered the phone. He told Frank that they had two detectives out on a shooting in Cherry Hill. He told Frank that he thinks the victim is still alive. The uniform guys had made an arrest. He told Michaels that he still had something to do and would be in the office as soon as possible.

Frank did not like driving in Druid Hill Park. He had handled too many murders in that park. It was a dumping ground for murders that were committed on the west side. It was a beautiful old park during the day, but at night it was dangerous. Frank drove into the park and went directly to the tennis courts. He parked alongside the first court and turned out his lights. He checked his equipment—that included the two guns he was carrying. He had one gun in the holster in his waist and the other gun was in an ankle holster.

He was listening to calls on the police radio when he noticed a vehicle driving slowing toward the courts. He flashed his lights. The vehicle pulled next to Frank's car. Frank got out and motioned for the driver to follow him behind the courts. Frank used his flashlight sparingly; he did not want anyone to see him. The area behind the courts was pitch dark with the exception of some light coming from the old mansion house on the hill. Frank flicked his light to show where he was standing.

"What's up sarge, you got my money?"

"Well, let's not be in such a hurry. I can't believe I'm standing here talking to the badass Kenny Jackson. I put your butt away years ago and now you get out and shoot a dude on the east side. You should have never been released— the system sucks"

"I ain't here to talk about shooting some dude or how the system sucks. That dude deserved what he got. I did a job for you. I want my money. You put me away once—I ain't going away anymore."

Frank moved a few feet back into the wooded area. Kenny on instinct followed him—that's exactly what Frank wanted. "Kenny, when I got in touch with you and asked you to do something for me, I must have been crazy. You have been a piece of shit all your life. I asked you to do one thing and you fucked it up. I got your money, but I feel like I have been cheated. You didn't follow my instructions. You did it your way and that ain't good. You let me down"

"I did the job—that's all that matters. You owe me."

"Yeah Kenny, I sure do owe you. I'm going to give you everything that you have coming to you."

Frank pulled his gun from the holster in his waist. He fired one shot that hit Kenny in the stomach. Kenny fell to the ground, "You motherfucker, you double crossed me. I did the job for you and now I get this. What the hell is wrong with you?"

Frank stood over Kenny and had his gun pointed at his head. He knew that he had time—gunshots in Druid Hill Park would not arouse anyone. Kenny was screaming that he was bleeding and needed some help. Frank put the gun closer to Kenny's head. "You want help. You didn't give Janet any help when you cut her throat. I told you to shoot her, not to cut her throat. I specifically told you what to do and you went and did it your way."

"Please Frank, get me to the hospital. You don't even have to pay me."

"I had no intentions of paying you anyway. I do have intentions of killing you. I'm not going to let you get busted and spill your guts about what I asked you to do. You made that poor girl suffer. I told you I wanted it to be quick. Oh yeah, one more thing I want to know before I kill you. Why did you rape her?

"Keep the money, Frank. I won't tell anybody about what you asked me to do. I don't know why I raped her. She fought me real hard. I lost it. I'm sorry, Frank…please get me some help."

Frank stood over Kenny and laughed. "You people are all alike. When you got the upper hand, you are badasses. When you are at someone's mercy you cry like a baby. Kenny, one thing is for sure—you won't ever fuck up again in this world."

Frank pointed the gun at Kenny's head and fired one shot. He backed away from the splatter of blood and brain matter. He fired another round into his chest. Kenny kicked for a few seconds. He then went motionless. Frank stood over him and talked as if Kenny was still alive. "You didn't think this would end any other way. I had no intentions of paying you to kill her. But even if I did want to pay you— you screwed up. You had to rape her. That was the last thing she experienced before she died. I have been thinking about what I would do with you ever since I heard that she was raped. You deserve what you got. I was going to bury you in the park, but I ain't going to waste my time. I hope the animals eat your sorry ass."

Frank walked back to his car. He wasn't surprised that no one heard the shots. They either didn't hear them or they accept it as part of the mystique of the park. Frank knew that when daylight came someone would find the body. Kenny was lying next to the tennis court; he would be in clear of view of anyone coming to play tennis.

Frank was satisfied that with Kenny's extensive criminal record, not much effort would be put into the investigation. He knew that any family that Kenny had, would not even press for a thorough investigation. It was perfect as far as Frank was concerned. Kenny did a job for him that he could not have done himself. The problem as far as Frank was concerned was that Kenny took it to the extreme. In Frank's sick mind, he contemplated that hiring Kenny to kill Janet was okay; raping her was not acceptable.

Frank was in no hurry to leave the park. It was quiet and gave him time to think about what else needed to be done to keep the Carroll County detectives off his ass. He had a miniature of Crown Royal in the glove box. He pulled it out and downed it with a little bit of Dr Pepper. Frank leaned back in the seat and thought about all that was happening. He knew in his mind that he had crossed the line in a big way.

It was times like this that Frank always thought about his survival training in the Marines. Sergeant Stafford made it a point to stress to the trainees in boot camp that survival was not only for you; survival was for the unit as well. The big picture with survival was that you did whatever it took to complete the mission. Survival meant kill or be killed—there was no time to second-guess your actions. Frank knew that he had basically been in a survival mode ever since he joined the police department. He also knew that in the police department he could get away with more than he could in real combat. In combat, you had other members of the unit that could tell about your random killings. In the police department you were usually alone when your survival mindset would kick in. He justified killing Kenny because he did not follow orders. Frank was all about following orders. Kenny was not a solution to anything; he was just a part of the big problem. Therefore Kenny was expendable—just someone that was in the way.

The killing of Philbin was different to Frank. He actually believed that he had the right to kill him, because Philbin came at him—he assessed that he had no other options. The fact that Frank stalked the guy and approached his car was irrelevant. It was just another case of survival.

The Crown Royal relaxed Frank; he knew that he needed a few more. He called the blonde that he met in the Harvey House. He had her number, but he could not think what her name was. There was no answer and he did not leave a message.

While driving out of the park he passed several cars that were parked near the reservoir. The area was a secluded spot that couples would come to the park and make out. In some vehicles you could see two heads; in some you only saw one head. Cops in that area would ride by the vehicles and shine their searchlights on the unsuspected couple. You found out early in your police training, that the powerful light reflecting off the passenger side window acted like a mirror. You could see everything going on in the vehicle. Sometimes you could sit there for minutes before anyone in the car knew you were watching. When they knew you were watching, they popped up and arranged their clothing. They would smile at you. You usually smiled back and drove off. What the hell could they do? They were having sex in a public park. Some of the older cops made it a point to sneak up on the cars with their lights out; they had it down to a science. They probably jerked off watching the X-rated movie playing on the car window.

Frank tried the phone number again. He got no answer and decided to give up on the blonde. The bars were still open. He headed for the Pirate's Den. Maybe Pam was horny tonight.

CHAPTER 45

Nick was making every effort to move on with his life. It was tough, but he knew he had no other choice. He had his moments when he thought of all the possibilities he and Janet might have had. They were so in love with each other. Would he ever love anyone like he loved her? He immersed himself in his investigations; that's what cops do when they have emotional problems. It was the time off from the job that was the toughest for him.

There were things in his apartment that belonged to Janet. He gathered them up and tried to get rid of them—he could not do it. He put the articles in boxes and placed the boxes in his storage locker. They were out of sight and hopefully out of mind. He wondered how older married couples handled it when they lost their loved ones. He heard stories from his parents about spouses smelling the scent of their deceased spouse long after they were gone. He wasn't married to Janet, but he had those moments and it was mentally draining.

Nick decided to talk to his pastor at Saint Joseph's Church. Father O'Neal had been around a long time and was a very close friend of the family. He knew every family in the parish; that's what priest did in his neighborhood. He also thought about getting some professional counseling. His medical plan would pay for it. He didn't really have anyone that he could sit with and discuss his feelings. In the past, he had relied on Frank to talk him through troubled times. The last person he wanted to talk to about Janet's murder was Frank. He knew that it would lead to the meeting in Easton. It ran through his mind like a bad movie. Why didn't I take Janet with me to Easton? Even if Frank in his covert crazed mind wanted to talk in secret, Janet could have shopped or just rode around Easton.

Nick could not shake the awful feeling that he was somehow responsible for Janet's death. He only hoped that the detectives in the Ocean City PD would make an arrest in the case. He knew they would not let him talk to a suspect. He would love to ask the suspect why he murdered Janet. He needed to know if it was a planned act, robbery, or just a spur of the moment craziness on the part of the murderer. Why did he rape her? If it was a robbery, why not take her money and jewelry and get the hell out of the condo. Nothing made any sense in her death. If only they knew the motive or why she was singled out.

The guys at work and friends would tell him that time heals all wounds. Nick was not buying it for a minute; he knew that the wounds were too deep. His friends would tell him that he was young and he would meet someone. He would just shake his head. He knew that everyone meant well, but it wasn't working. He tried to be his old self at work, but it was difficult working murders all the time.

He enjoyed his talk with Father O'Neal. The old salty priest tried to say all the right things to Nick. The part about God knows best for us mortal souls on earth was a tough pill to swallow. The priest also talked to Nick about how God had better things for Janet. What better things could he have for such a wonderful person? He also said that God took her early, but she did good things while she was here. Nick had talked to Father O'Neal for about two hours. When he left, he sat in his car and wanted to believe the priest. Nick was a Catholic and he was taught to just believe a priest. On the other hand, he wanted to race back in the rectory and tell the priest it was all bullshit. Why would God take her in such a horrible manner? Why didn't she just get hit by a car? What better things did God have for such a young person? Did God decide to have some crazed killer rape her and slice her throat? What kind of God would end someone's life like that? Nick pounded on the steering wheel. He cried uncontrollably. He knew that the priest meant well, but deep down inside did Father O'Neal have the same questions that Nick had. Would the good priest feel that way if it were his sister, his mother, or his fiancée?

Nick got a call from Jimmy Jordan. "Nick, I'm sorry I have not called you about Janet's murder. I'm really sorry buddy. I know how much in love you guys were. Nick, I would love to have you come down to the bar and have a drink with me for old times' sake. We don't have to talk about the murder. I just want to have a drink and talk to you. I heard you haven't been going anywhere. This would mean a lot to me, please say yes."

"Jimmy, I do appreciate you calling. I really haven't been out much lately. I think I will come down and have a drink with you. You have always been a great friend over the years. I could use someone to lean on. I have a few things to do today. I can stop in to see you later, if that's okay with you." Jimmy was elated that Nick had accepted his invitation. He told Nick that it would be like old times again.

Nick arrived at the bar at about 8:00 P.M. and it was a sparse crowd. Nick knew that the bar business was falling on hard times since the neighborhood was changing. Jimmy grabbed Nick and kissed him on the cheek. He directed him to the back of the bar. As Nick walked to the back, he was startled by who he saw at the table.

"Damn it, Jimmy—I thought you and I were going to talk like old times. What the hell is Frank doing here? Why didn't you tell me he was coming?"

"Hold on kid. I thought that for old times' sake we could all get together like we used to do. I know you guys haven't been talking lately, so I took it upon myself to get us all together. Let's at least give it a shot. You guys go back to far together to give it all up. Do this for me."

Frank just sat in the booth. He did not want to say anything. Jimmy was doing all the talking. He knew how Nick felt since things between the two of them had soured. Frank motioned to Nick, "Nick, please sit down. Jimmy called me and told me you would be here. I miss you dude. We need to talk. I can be a good listener, I promise."

"Frank, I only need to talk to you at work. I have no obligation or desire to talk to you on my own time. I understand what Jimmy is trying to do; he should have told me you were coming. I'll stay for a few minutes, but only because of Jimmy."

Jimmy talked about the neighborhood and how it had changed lately. He told them he missed the good old days. He surprised them both when he said that he may have to sell the bar. He tried his best to bring up some stories that he knew would get them laughing. It was gradual, but he did get a few laughs. The laughs were as subtle as laughs can be. He told them that things were not like the old days. He missed them coming in the bar. He said that the new crowd was different. He told Frank and Nick that everyone always talks about them. He said that the whole neighborhood was very proud that they both were cops. Jimmy did most of the talking with Frank and Nick just nodding approval of the stories. Jimmy ordered more drinks and was running out of material. "How in the hell have you guys been? Frank, tell me what you have been up to lately."

"Well, I have been working most of the time. I'm sure you know Jimmy that crime is a bitch in this city. Nick and I have been working some long hours. It seems like there is not a day that goes by that there are not murders in the city. I never realized it until I went on the department, how dangerous this city is. Nick knows this, as well as I do that there is an element out there that just terrorizes the city. The courts are malfunctioning—they just operate like a revolving door. The bad guys get put away by one judge and a few years later, another judge lets them out. The cops do their best, but in my opinion, we are losing the battle. Do you agree with me, Nick?"

Nick was actually enjoying the drinks. It had been a while since he had any alcohol. He did not respond to Frank, other than nodding his head in agreement. Nick took a deep breath and said, "Jimmy, I do appreciate your intentions and your hospitality, but I'm really tired. I need to get some sleep. Frank is right—the city sucks and if he had his way, he would just round up the bad guys and exterminate them. Frank never talks about the conditions that some people in this city are living under. He never mentions the poor education system that just passes kids so that the teachers don't have to put up with them. He never talks about the lack of any real rehabilitation going on in the prison system. He never talks about the fact that most of the kids in the bad neighborhoods are living in a one parent home. He only talks about one thing, getting rid of all the bad people. Well Frank, like I have told you on many occasions, everybody in this city is not bad. We work in the Homicide Unit and we see nothing but bad all the time. I think there are about six hundred thousand people in this city. If they were all bad, we would not have enough jails to put them in. If you had your way, we would not have enough graveyards to bury them in. I think I'm going to hit the road."

Frank sat and listened to Nick. He knew Nick was blowing off steam and that was okay with him. Nick was still suffering from the loss of his best friend. Frank knew that in the past, he would have jumped in and stopped Nick from his rambling. Nick started to leave and Frank asked him if he would stay for a few minutes. "Nick, you made some good points in what you said. I know that the city is full of holes in all departments. We don't work in the education field, the court system, or corrections. We are law enforcement officers. Our concern is keeping the peace and arresting the bad guys. Jimmy knows what's wrong with the city. He is now operating his business in a bad neighborhood. Nick, you and I were raised in a different time. We were not angels, but we didn't go around killing people for the hell of it. I'm only saying that times have changed. I don't see it getting any better. The murder rate in this city keeps going higher and higher each year. We are just peas in the pod, Nick. Nobody in government gives a rat's ass how many murders we have each year. They only care about the big money line and that is keeping certain areas of the city safe. You and I know that if they cared, they would take the cops that work in the downtown area around the hotels and tourism spots and put them in the high crime areas. They don't do that Nick and the reason is that the areas they want to protect bring in big bucks to the city. There is no big money coming into the city coffer from the west side. We live in an imperfect world Nick. I do what I do on a daily basis to make sure people like Jimmy can operate a business and make a decent living. You do it for the same reason; you just look at it through different lenses."

Nick stood up. He had listened to everything Frank had to say. Jimmy was staring at Frank. It seemed like he was ready to applaud. Nick sat back down. He knew that most of what Frank said was correct. He did not like some of what Frank had done over the years, but he did respect him. He also did not agree whole heartedly with Frank on a lot of things, but admired him for sticking to his belief and hardly ever wavering.

Nick was tired, but he wanted to show Jimmy that everything was okay between him and Frank. "I'm not sure why I'm staying. I guess this place will always remind me of the good times we had here. Who would have known years ago when we were in here drinking under age, that we would both turn out to be cops? I'm sure if Jimmy would tell the truth, he would probably say that he thought we would end up in jail."

Jimmy could sense that the rift between Frank and Nick was loosening up a little. Even if it was the drinks, it was a good thing. Jimmy also knew that these two guys had been through a lot together. He believed that down deep inside they cared deeply for each other. It was the old neighborhood, the Marines, and now the police department that bonded them.

The night was moving along quickly and the laughter was getting to be more frequent. Frank and Nick were actually exchanging old stories. Jimmy was the host and moderator; he jumped in when there were breaks in the stories. He left the two of them together on occasion and tended to the few customers in the bar. When he would return to the table, he smiled. He told them both how much it meant to him that they came to the bar. "You guys don't know how much this means to me to see you here. I have bragged about you for years. I feel in a way that you are my adopted sons. I probably know more about you guys than your parents. You have made my day. I hope that you can move forward and patch things up."

Nick was feeling pretty good—not drunk—just feeling good. He was facing Frank and Jimmy across the table from him. In a move that was reminiscent of an old cowboy movie, he pulled his gun from his waist. "Don't make a move. Don't turn or do anything until I tell you to."

Frank and Jimmy were shocked. What the hell was happening? One minute Nick seemed happy and telling stories and now he is holding a gun on us. Nick's eyes were as wide as eyes can get. His stare was not on Frank and Jimmy, but just over their heads and to the left. He repeated himself, "Don't do anything until I tell you to. Keep looking straight ahead and focus on me."

Frank was both confused and pissed off at what Nick was saying. Did he go off his rocker? Was he at his wit's end and going to shoot the both of us? What the hell was going on? Why did it come on so fast?

"Nick, what the hell is happening? Put the gun away."

"Frank, don't do anything until you follow my lead. The place is being robbed. Two black dudes are at the end of the bar with guns. I'm going behind the bar to see if I can surprise them. When I make my move, wait a minute and then get on the floor. Trust me and it will work out. I don't even think they know we are back here."

Nick had a look in his eyes that Frank had not seen since their combat training in the Marines. For some reason, Frank trusted what Nick was saying. He was itching to turn around and see what was happening. He decided that he would go along with Nick's assessment of the situation. Frank had already pulled his gun and had it under the table. Nick didn't know it, but Frank pulled it out when Nick first pulled his gun. Frank was not sure at first what Nick's intentions were and if warranted, he was prepared to shoot Nick in the knee from under the table. Jimmy was making a slight turn to see what was happening. Frank grabbed him and told him to follow what Nick had said. He told him that everything would be fine.

The bar had emptied earlier and the only people left were Jimmy, Frank, Nick, and the poor bartender who was being held at gunpoint. Nick had a dead-on stare on the two black guys. He was waiting for the opportune time to make his move. "Okay Frank, I'm going behind the bar—wait about thirty seconds and turn. Make sure you stay behind the booth for cover. I'm going to use the element of surprise. When you hear me holler police, slowly make your way a little closer to the front. Frank, remember to stay out of my line of fire. If they get frisky, they will try to make it to the door. I will have a line of fire across the bar and you should have a bead on them from the right side. We okay with all of that?"

Frank had his gun on top of the table. He was feeling the same adrenaline rush that he had often felt in the past. He was proud of Nick taking the lead. He hoped that it would go well and nobody got hurt. He told Jimmy to fall to the ground when he heard Nick holler police.

Nick made his move. The bar was long enough that he was not seen as he dove to his left and behind the bar. He worked his way down toward the front. He was uncertain when he should pop up and announce police. He estimated the length of the bar. It raced through his head that he had been in the bar so many times in the past, that he should at least know the length. He passed the beer tap section and knew he was close. For some reason he was calm. Frank was getting nervous, so he edged his way toward the end of the booth. He wanted to turn around and just rush the two hold-up men. He promised Nick that he would do it his way. He did not want to have a crossfire and one of them get hit by their own bullets. He fought like hell to not just turn around and see what was happening.

Nick knew he was very close to the end—maybe a little too close. He checked his gun. He made sure the safety was off and a round was in the chamber. He could see that the bartender was about fifteen feet away. He was putting money into a paper bag. Nick was hoping that the bartender would not see him and panic. The last thing he needed at this moment would be for the bartender to look at him and say something. He took a few more steps and made his move. "Police— don't move motherfucker or I'll shoot!"

Nick was crouched in a military style firing position behind the bar. He hollered for the bartender to hit the ground. The bartender just stood there with the bag in his hand—obviously in shock. One of the black guys turned toward Nick and raised his gun. Nick fired three shots in rapid fire. The guy went down. When Frank heard Nick holler police, he did not get behind the booth like Nick had told him. He ran closer toward the front, staying on the right side. The second black guy panicked and tried to make it out the front door. Nick continued to holler for him to stop and drop his weapon. Nick had a clear shot on the second guy as he moved toward the door. He decided not to fire. He wanted to see if he would comply with dropping his gun. The guy turned and fired a shot at Nick and shattered the mirror behind the bar. Frank saw that the guy's attention was on Nick. He ran the distance of the bar and dove on the floor. He rolled to his right and fired two shots at the guy. With the diving and the rolling movement, he did not know if he hit the guy. He got up and fired two more shots. The second guy fell backwards and halfway through the front window. Nick came around the bar and approached both guys. Frank joined Nick. It was no doubt that both the robbers were dead. The bartender was shaking so bad that he could not move from his spot and was still holding the bag of money. Jimmy came to the front and told Frank that he had called 911 to report he was being robbed. He told Frank that he also told the 911 operator that two cops were in the bar and everything was under control. Frank hugged Nick and asked him if he was okay. The nervousness that was not there a few minutes ago was now prevalent in both of them, especially Nick.

The bar was one hell of a crime scene. Both of the hold-up men were dead on the scene with multiple gunshot wounds. It was determined later that none of the shots that Frank and Nick fired missed their targets.

Jimmy sat at the bar for a couple of hours while the bodies were removed and the crime lab did their job. At one point he started to laugh— an obvious very nervous laugh. He looked around the bar. He told Frank that it was like old times again. He told him that he always enjoyed a little excitement from them in the old days, but this was taking it a little too far. He walked through the bar shaking his head in disbelief and still laughing.

The crime lab and the Homicide Unit were finishing up their work. It was getting really late. Jimmy had some friends come down to the bar to clean up and board up the front window. They did a little cleaning behind the bar, but it was too much damage. Jimmy told them to just leave things the way they are and it can be taken care of in the morning. Frank and Nick had talked to the homicide detectives and given their account of what happened. It was backed up by the bartender and Jimmy.

When everyone had left the bar, Jimmy asked Frank and Nick to have one last drink with him. Nick said that he wasn't in the mood for a drink. Jimmy said, "Guys, I'm asking you to have one last drink with me for a reason. When I say last drink, I mean last drink. I'm selling the bar as soon as possible. I have had a great run in this bar. The memories will be with me forever. I would keep the bar open if you two could be in here every night. I can't do it anymore. I'm getting up in age. I have a wonderful wife and some beautiful grandchildren. I want to be around for a few more years to enjoy them. With the neighborhood changing the way it is, I take a chance every day I open the door. Now, I insist that you two heroes have a final drink with me."

Frank and Nick hugged Jimmy and could see the emotions building up in him. He had the bar for many years and to give it up would be tough. Jimmy went behind the bar. He was searching in a cabinet for what he told them was a special drink for a very special occasion. Jimmy pulled out a bottle of Jameson Irish Whiskey. He told them that it was a very expensive blend of Irish whiskey. It had been in the bar ever since Jimmy took over the bar twenty-two years ago. The bottle looked a little dusty and the label had worn off. Jimmy told them that the whiskey was named after John Jameson and was first brewed in 1780 in Dublin, Ireland. Jimmy said that Jameson was a lawyer back then, but made his fortune from whiskey. He said that the whiskey is still produced in Cork County, Ireland. Frank was impressed on what Jimmy knew about the whiskey. He started to put the shot glass to his lips and paused. "You sure this shit is still good? How long have you had it?"

"I got that bottle when I first opened. I think the owner before me had it for a few years. Drink up you asshole—it's better than the shit you are used to drinking."

Frank looked at Nick and then at Jimmy. He held out the glass of whiskey. "Here's to you guys—I love you both."

With the lights out in the bar and only the street lights providing any light, they had the last drink at Jimmy's bar. It was now very quiet and you would have never known that a few hours earlier two more murders took place in a bar in Charm City. The only difference was that these two would be ruled justifiable homicides and no need for any additional investigation.

Jimmy's bar would be just a memory now. He had succumbed to the terror of the city. The doors would now close forever. Frank and Nick had administered swift justice in Jimmy Jordan's Bar. The drinks were good up to the last drop of the old bottle of Jameson.

Frank and Nick took Jimmy to his car and wished him well. They told him that they would get together again for old times' sake. Frank and Nick walked to their cars. They were now back talking—life was good again. Frank offered to buy Nick breakfast. "Come on dude, I'm going to treat you to the best breakfast available in the city of Baltimore. It's the best breakfast, because it is the only place that is open at this time of the morning."

Nick was hungry; he was more tired than hungry. "I haven't been to the roach palace for a long time. I thought the health department would have closed the Brew & Chew down by now. Let's do it. What the hell—some good old Irish whiskey, some eggs, and scrapple. You can't beat that combination."

CHAPTER 46

The Homicide Unit office was not the most professional looking place in the headquarters building. It showed its wear and tear from the years of murder investigations. It was also filthy from the lack of care from the detectives. Most detectives shared a desk with another detective from a different shift. Even if a detective wanted to take care of his space, it was almost impossible. There was no other place to keep the witnesses when they were waiting to give statements. It was not unusual to see potential witnesses lying on the floor or sleeping at a detective's desk. The walls were dirty. They were covered with nicotine from the years of smoking before it was banned. Smoking was not allowed in the office. It was hard to enforce that rule. How could you tell the guys not to smoke if they were putting in twelve to fourteen hour days and seldom leaving the office?

The cleanup crew came through early in the morning. All they did was a fast walk through. They ran the dirty mop across the dirty floor. On occasion, they would actually make an effort to remove blood stains, coffee stains and God only knows what some of the other stains were. One of the unofficial jobs of the early morning cleanup crew was to turn on the lights and wake up the detectives who were sleeping on desks, couches, and chairs. When the lights got flipped on, it was a sight to behold. Guys were moaning and pissed off that the lights got turned on. The sleep time was actually rare, so you had to take advantage of it when you could.

The small rooms where the murder suspects were held were the pits. They had no windows, nothing on the walls, no trash can, and smelled of urine. The only furniture in the room was a table and two aluminum chairs. Nobody really gave a shit how this room looked. The dirtier and nastier it was, the better chance you had that a suspect would tell you what happened. On occasion, some suspects would spend ten or more hours in that room. They would fall asleep with their head on the table or crawl up in a corner. If those rooms could only talk, they would tell you about many times when the suspects got the shit kicked out of them. It wasn't that the detectives routinely beat the suspects—it was mostly for the ones that broke bad while being interviewed.

In the Homicide Unit there were many infamous investigative games played—all done in the effort to get a confession. The detectives knew all the tricks in the book to get someone to confess to a murder—even if they didn't do it. The games included things like entering the room and just staring at a suspect's shoes. This would work well when the murder scene you were investigating had a lot of blood. The detective would just stare at the suspect's shoes. He would walk around and get different angles on the shoes. Even if the suspect would ask what you were looking at, you never said anything. You would then leave the room. You would come back in about thirty minutes and ask for their shoes—still not saying anything. The detective would put the shoes in a bag clearly marked "EVIDENCE". The detective would wait about another thirty minutes and go back in the room. He would tell the suspect that what he thought about the shoes has been verified by the crime lab. You can now imagine at this point the suspect is thinking – what the hell is on my shoes. The detective has to be real cool and not deviate from the plan. Staring at the suspect works wonders in a game like this. The detective would then ask the suspect what he thought the crime lab found on his shoes. Usually the suspect would say he didn't know. The detective would then break the game open and go for the kill. He would lean in as close to the suspect as possible and tell him that the victim's blood was on the shoes. Without waiting for a response, the detective would leave the room. He would wait a short time and go back in. He would ask the suspect if he wanted to give a statement or would he rather just be booked for the murder. It was amazing how many times the suspect would tell the detective that he would now give a statement and confess to the murder. As stupid as this game seemed… it worked.

Another game that was a favorite of the detectives was one that you really needed a stupid suspect to pull it off. It was fairly simple and went like this… you would ask the suspect if he wanted to take a lie detector test to prove his innocence. If the suspect said that he would take the test, you would have another detective act as the operator of the lie detector equipment. The lie detector equipment in this case, was actually a big copy machine. The way it worked is that before you took the suspect to the room where the copy machine was, you placed a piece of white paper in the copy machine. On the paper you would print in big letters…YOU LIED. You would take the suspect to the room and put a large leather weight lifters belt around his waist. If you wanted to be real creative, you could put some small wires hanging from the belt. You needed to act professional and look the part. The so-called operator would explain to the suspect that the machine was very accurate. When he was convinced that the suspect was on board, he would tell him that to save time he would only ask one question. The operator would ask, "Did you commit the murder that you are being investigated for?"

The suspect would say, "No."

The operator would push the button and the piece of paper would come out with the words, YOU LIED. It sounds crazy, but it worked. It was used in court to convict some of the dumber suspects. The judges that would try these cases usually stated that the mere fact that some resemblance of trickery was used in the investigation, the fact remained that if you did not commit the murder, you would not have confessed.

As time went by in the Homicide Unit, Frank used some of these tricks more than most. He would do anything to put a bad guy away for life. He always told his men that whatever means necessary they used, was okay to get a confession. Nick, being more of straight arrow than some in the squad did not like the games played to get confessions. He did not openly object, but it was obvious to others that he would rather do it the old fashion way. He would prefer not to trick the suspect into a confession.

Frank's influence on the men in the unit was ever present. They knew that he would approve of pretty much anything to get a murder cleared. Nick, however, had a great reputation with the attorneys that prosecuted his cases. They knew that with Nick, you got a good clean investigation. The witnesses were reliable and could be counted on to show up for the trial. The evidence was properly collected and marked. The confessions made by suspects were very thorough and no funny business was used to get the confession.

Nick, although having the tag of being a guy who worked by the book, was respected by everyone in the unit. The pressure that the others felt from Frank was not felt the same way by Nick. It was a relationship between the two of them that was understood by the other members of the squad. Everyone knew that Frank and Nick were tight. Frank didn't get on Nick like he did the others. Most of the detectives knew that Nick was a perfectionist. He was always praised for his investigations. His conviction rate in court was one of the highest in the unit. On occasion, the detectives in the unit would come to Nick for advice on their cases. They trusted his knowledge of murder investigations. Nick sometimes would give his professional opinion. Most of the time, he told them to check with the sergeant. He knew that the last thing he wanted would be for Frank to find out guys were coming to him for advice.

Nick was often called upon to assist with the training for new investigators coming into the unit. He would spend many hours with them that could have been spent on his cases. He always preached to the new investigators that they were special. They would not have been chosen to come to the Homicide Unit, unless they stood out in patrol. He always warned them about the pitfalls of the job. He encouraged them to make sure they maintained their home life. If they were married, he told them to be careful that the job did not interfere with activities at home. If they had kids, he told them to always be there for their kids. He preached that the family was first and the job was second.

He also made sure that they were well aware of the huge plaque on the wall as you entered the homicide office that read, "No greater honor could be bestowed upon a human being than to investigate the death of another human being." He told them that if he was in charge of the Homicide Unit, he would have each detective touch that plaque when they showed up for their shift each day. It would be like the sign at the Notre Dame Football Stadium. When the football players enter the field, they first go through a tunnel and reach up and slap a sign that reads, "PLAY LIKE A CHAMPION".

Nick actually enjoyed the role of a father figure—even though he was not much older than the other investigators. He felt like he was giving back to the department and at the same time keeping busy.

At times when things were quiet—which was not that often, some of the guys would ask about his personal life? He always tried to skirt the issue. He knew that most of the detectives were well aware that Janet had been murdered. How much they knew about the murder was not clear. The conversations would sometimes get around to guys asking Nick if he wanted to meet a real nice girl. It seemed as if every guy in the unit had a wife who had a friend that would be perfect for Nick. The guys were sincere, but Nick was still not ready to move on with his personal life. The memories of Janet were still quite fresh in his mind.

CHAPTER 47

Monday morning in the Homicide Unit was always crazy. With all the murders and shootings over the weekend, the office was routinely filled with the members of the command staff and the media. On this particular Monday, it was quite different. Most of the detectives were standing around in the office. It was definitely much quieter than usual.

Frank arrived for work and walked toward his office. "Can somebody tell me what the hell is going on—this place looks like a funeral parlor." The sergeant on the night shift, Bob Barnes, who had not gone home, motioned for Frank to come in his office. "Frank, I got some real bad news—the captain died early this morning."

"What the hell are you talking about? He ain't that old. What the hell happened to him?"

Barnes told Frank to sit down. He asked Frank if he wanted a coffee. Frank did not sit down; he nervously paced back and forth. He asked Barnes again what had happened to the captain.

"Frank, the most we know at this point, is that his son called the office about 6:00 A.M. this morning. He was extremely upset, as you can imagine. He said that his dad was feeling ill last night but he would not go to the hospital. He said that his dad went to bed about midnight. He did not respond to the alarm clock this morning. His wife tried to wake him up. She realized he was not breathing and called the ambulance. When the ambo got there, he was already dead. They tried to resuscitate him but it was too late."

Frank sat in his chair. He was speechless for a few minutes. He had grown fond of the captain over the time he was in the Homicide Unit. He considered the captain a true friend. There had been a few times when he and the captain did not see eye-to-eye, but overall he got along great with him. Frank asked Barnes if there was anything the unit could do at this point for his family. Barnes told Frank that the arrangements for the viewing and the funeral were being made. He said that nothing else needed to be done at this time. He told Frank that he was going home. Frank thanked him for staying around.

Frank went out into the main office area. Most of the detectives were still milling around. He did not see Lieutenant Valentino. He assumed that he was the only supervisor in the office at the time. He walked back to the captain's office and looked around. There were papers on the desk that were probably waiting for the captain's signature. He looked at all the photos of the captain's family. Numerous certificates and plaques were hanging on the walls. In the far corner of the office, on a small table, there were two trophies. One of the trophies was for bowling in a league the captain was on. He always bragged about how good a bowler he was. The other trophy was for the unit winning a softball league several years ago. Frank was not sure why the captain kept that trophy in his office—he did not play on the team. The unit had a separate trophy case in the main office that had all the trophies from bowling, shuffle board, and softball. I guess the trophy in the captain's office had some special meaning or it would have been in the big trophy case.

Frank looked around for Lieutenant Valentino. Nobody seemed to know where he was. The detectives were still hanging around; it appeared that they wanted more information on what happened. Frank walked into the main office. "Gentlemen, I'm sure you all know that the captain passed away last night. We really don't have much more to add to that at this time. I would suggest that you all attempt to go about your day and try getting some work done. The guys that are off duty should go home. We will get in touch with you when we find out the arrangements. I would like to see the guys from my squad in my office—in about ten minutes."

Some of the detectives slowly started to exit the office. It was a somber office. It was definitely not a typical Monday morning in the Homicide Unit.

Frank went to the fifth floor to get a Dr Pepper. He stood in the rear of the cafeteria. He was thinking what a loss the captain would be. Who would take his place? Would the new captain be different? Would he be someone who wanted to come in and make a lot of changes? Frank finished the Dr Pepper and went back to his office.

He wanted to get his squad together and just talk about nothing in particular. "Good morning men, I just wanted to get together for a few minutes to talk about the captain. I'm sure you are as shocked about his death as I am. He was a really good man. He will be sorely missed in this unit and the department. He gave his life to this job. He will never get to enjoy his retirement—that sucks. I guess the saying... life's a bitch and then you die has some truth to it. I assume that Lieutenant Valentino will be in charge until they pick another captain. I will keep you posted after I talk to Valentino. In the mean time, just keep working hard. Does anyone have any questions? That's all I have for now. I'm sure we will hear more about the funeral arrangements before we leave today."

Frank asked Nick to stay back for a few minutes. He asked him if he wanted to go get some coffee. Nick said that he had too much to do and wasn't really in the mood to go anywhere. Frank told him that he would not keep him long. "Just a couple of things I want to talk about. I talked to the sergeant in IID and he said that the final report was done on the shooting in Jimmy's bar. He said that the shooting would be ruled justifiable. As far as they are concerned, the investigation is closed. I also talked to the captain last week about the incident. He wanted me to tell the lieutenant to write us both up for a bronze star for what we did in the bar. I told the captain that I would write you up. I don't want to be written up."

"Sarge, I don't want a bronze star for what happened in that bar. It was just something that happened. Any police officer would have done the same thing we did. If you want a bronze star, that is fine. I really have no desire to receive any medal for what I did."

"Nick, I think you should take whatever the police department wants to give you; it looks good at promotion time. I know how you feel about shooting people. What you did that night was absolutely heroic. You took control and handled it like a pro—you should be rewarded. As your supervisor, I'm writing you up for the medal. I really don't want any more discussion about it."

Nick shook his head and started for the door. Frank asked him to stay for a minute. Nick gave Frank a look that pissed him off. Frank stood up behind his desk. He made a motion with his hand for Nick to sit in the chair. "I have one more thing to say and then you are dismissed. Don't get a fuckin attitude with me. I have been trying like hell to be nice to you lately... apparently it's not working. Don't make me revert back to my nasty old self. I would rather we got along as friends—even if I am your boss. Now if you don't mind detective, have a seat. I will finish what I have to tell you."

Nick sat in the chair and looked at his watch. "Frank, I mean sergeant, what is it that you need to discuss with me? My investigations are all up to date. What is it that needs to be discussed?"

"What needs to be discussed is more important than all of your cases and all of the cases in this unit. Nick, I'm worried about the investigation in Carroll County. It has been real quiet since they called and talked to Valentino. I just want you and I to be prepared if they would want to talk to us. We know that they got Janet's phone number from the guy's cell phone. Valentino said that they knew about Janet and they knew about someone in this office getting the record check on that Philbin dude."

"Sergeant, let me stop you right there. I don't know what the hell they have so far. Janet is dead, so whatever they wanted to ask her is not going to happen. The crazed bastard that killed her in Ocean City ended that aspect of their investigation. You used Wilkins' computer to get the information on Philbin. Lenny is dead, so that throws another wrench into their investigation—they can't talk to him. I would assume that if they are checking around on Janet, they would have found out by now that we were engaged."

"So let me stop you, Nick. If you were in their shoes, what would you be doing with the investigation? They have no witnesses on the scene of the shooting. They are probably checking out everyone that was in his cell phone. Janet was probably not the only female in his phone book. The part about the record check on Philbin coming from a computer in this office is what bothers me. They have to be asking— why would someone in the Homicide Unit get a record check on Mr. Philbin?

Sergeant Favasi got up and walked toward the window. Nick could see that he was upset. He always had the answers… this was not one of those times. He slapped his hand on the window. It was a good thing the windows in the office were thick. They were solid glass and could take a good hit. There had been occasions when suspects thinking they could jump through the window, found out the hard way that the windows were solid. On one occasion, a suspect was in another sergeant's room and locked the door. With the door locked, he took a chair and beat it against the window. He continued for several minutes until they could get a key and open the door.

"Nick, the only other thing that comes to mind is that Valentino talked to the Carroll County investigators. I like Valentino, but he's not the kind of guy that would share information with you. He has one mission in life. That mission is to retire and move to Florida. He has said on many occasions that he has survived a lot of years in the department and nobody is going to ruin his retirement.

I don't know if he is telling me everything that was talked about on the phone with the Carroll County investigator. I have noticed lately that he seems to be avoiding me. Now that the Captain Jenkins is gone, he will probably get the job for a while. I think that would make him shakier than usual."

"Sergeant, we could sit here forever and think of lots of scenarios. We don't know what the Carroll County guys will do. The only person that could hurt you is me. I'm the only living person that knows what happened that night, other than you. I wish it would have never happened, but it did. If I'm ever approached by them, I can only say that I was engaged to Janet. I will say that I don't know anything about the murder. If push came to shove, I guess I could say I got the record check because I saw that car in front of her apartment house. I guess I could say that I was a jealous bastard and wanted to know who owned that car. On the night he was shot, I know that I was either working or could vouch for where I was. I'm only talking and thinking out loud. Let's leave it alone for a while and see what happens. Is it okay if I leave and get some work done?"

"Nick, thanks for talking about it with me. I didn't mean to jump in your shit. Remember, this is something we can't share with anyone. I know we have our moments that we argue, but we have a bond that goes deep. If you are contacted by anyone about this, you need to let me know right away."

Nick pulled the door open—"Oh, hi lieutenant, I was just leaving. I guess you want to talk to Sergeant Favasi. I'm really sorry to hear about the captain—he was a good man. He will be sorely missed around here."

"Thanks Detective, the captain was a great guy and yes, he will be missed."

Lieutenant Valentino pushed the door shut and locked it. He turned as Frank was sitting down behind his desk. He had a somber look on his face—more somber than usual. Valentino was a big man and took up a lot of space. He was hardly a fashion bug—his wardrobe was sketchy at best. He was from the old school and his appearance backed that up. Nothing seemed to match, especially his selection of ties. He wore a black belt that was part of his police uniform. He often wore white socks. His shoes were noticeably very old and worn. He had smoked for too many years. His parched voice and constant hacking confirmed that.

Frank walked over to greet the lieutenant. He shook his hand. The lieutenant walked toward the window; he did not say anything. He then took his fist and pounded the file cabinet. "Frank, why in the hell did the captain have to die at this time? I was very content in my job and now they will probably put me in charge of the unit. That damn position can get you in all kinds of trouble. Hell, I'm retiring soon; I don't need all the aggregation that comes with that job. I don't mean to downplay the captain's death, Frank. His death puts me in a spot that I don't want to be in."

"Have a seat, lieutenant. We haven't had a chance to talk for quite a while. I know you are upset. It's early, but would you care for a shot of my favorite whiskey. I know that with all that has happened, you probably could use something to calm you down. If not some whiskey, I can get you a coffee. What's your pleasure, lieutenant?"

"Frank, I appreciate your concern and your offer. I only want to talk to you about a few things. I need to be in the colonel's office in about twenty minutes. I'm probably going to take command of the Homicide Unit. I think the colonel wants to go over a few things. The last thing I need this early in the morning is whiskey on my breath."

Frank pushed the drawer shut—no whiskey today. The lieutenant looked really down. Valentino was about to get the job that most lieutenants in the department would be honored to have. Frank, being the go-getter that he was, could not understand why Valentino was acting this way. He was thinking—if only I was a lieutenant and was asked to take over the Homicide Unit, I would be ecstatic. On the other hand, Frank could sympathize with the lieutenant. He had worked hard his whole career. Now towards the end, he would be put in the spotlight.

Valentino was not like Jenkins—he did not have the savvy to handle the pressure of being the commanding officer of the Homicide Unit. Jenkins was smooth and a real good bullshitter. He prided himself on getting out of jams. He had what it took to be in charge. Valentino did not possess any traits that Jenkins had perfected over the years.

"Lieutenant, I'm sure things will work out fine for you. You have some good people in this unit. I am sure they will not let you down. Did you ever consider that the chief might make you a captain? If he would, you could work a few more years and retire on a captain's pension instead of a lieutenant's pension. Think of the positive side of this and not the negative. I'm sure you will be fine."

"Thanks Frank, I knew you would make some sense of all this. I wish I had more supervisors like you in the unit. I think you make a good point—they might just make me a captain. I like the sound of that already, Captain Valentino—it has a certain ring to it."

"You will be fine—you sure you don't want a little shot of whiskey. I have some gum you can chew on the way to the colonel's office."

The lieutenant reached out to shake hands with Frank. He assured him that he would not turn down the chance to be in charge of such an elite unit. He thanked Frank for being a good listener. He told him that he felt a little ashamed that he thought of himself, at a time when everyone should be grieving the loss of a good man. Frank wished him well and walked out of the office with him. He slapped the lieutenant on the back. "Good luck with the meeting with the colonel."

Chapter 48

The viewing for Captain Jenkins was held at the Dominic DiPasqualle Funeral Home. It was an old funeral home in the Little Italy section of the city. It was a typical viewing for a well-respected senior member of the police department. There were police officers standing as honor guards next to the casket, in full police dress uniforms. The captain's casket was draped with the American flag. He had served in World War II and in Korea. He never talked about it much; it took a few drinks to get it out of him. Some of the medals he had earned while in the service were mounted on a beautiful display near the casket. The attendance at the viewing was overwhelming. The entire command staff showed up. The captain was well liked and it was obvious from the number of people that attended. The viewing was for one night, with the funeral service to be held the next day at St. Patrick's Cathedral.

The captain was a very religious man. He sometimes was a little overbearing with his religion. On numerous occasions, when he had to discipline someone in the unit, he would end with telling the person that they should have God in their life. He also made it a point to let everyone know that he was on the building committee at St. Patrick's Cathedral. A few times during the year, he would ask for donations from anyone that wished to make a contribution to the church. He kept a small box outside his office for the donations. It was known throughout the unit that detectives would put money in the box when they knew the captain was watching. It was also talked about amongst the unit members that when you drove around Baltimore with the captain, he always made the sign of the cross when he passed a church.

Frank attended the viewing along with all the members of the Homicide Unit. The viewing lasted until 9:00 PM. The word was spreading around the funeral parlor that everyone was stopping at Flanagan's bar for some drinks. Flanagan's was a watering hole for detectives who stopped after their shift to beat the traffic. Beat the traffic was always the line used to have a reason to stop for a drink, especially after the day shift. Most guys would get there at about 5:00 P.M. and would leave a few hours later; some would stay until closing time. The ones that stayed…sure as hell beat the traffic. The only good thing was that when you left the bar, there was no traffic. The bad thing was that you were drunk and hoping that you could make it home safely.

Ray Flanagan was a great guy—he treated all the cops that frequented his bar with respect. He was a retired captain with the Maryland State Police. He opened the bar after he retired. He had a partner at first. After a few years owning the bar and doing quite well, he bought the partner out. He would often sit with the detectives from the city. He would try to match them story for story. The city detectives would make fun of his stories. They would jokingly tell him that the MSP guys were nothing but traffic cops. Flanagan was a true Irishman. He would take the kidding for a short time and then he would get loud. The more worked up Flanagan got, the more drinks he would order for the guys. Everyone loved Flanagan and he loved the fact that they came in and spent so much money. It was a regular routine in the Homicide Unit that when your shift ended, someone would ask who was going to Flanagan's. Everyone felt secure there. It seemed that on most nights the place was filled with just cops.

Frank was with his guys in one corner of the bar. The drinks were coming fast. Flanagan had a lot of respect for Captain Jenkins. He was deeply moved when he heard that the captain died. He would make his way around the bar and make sure everyone had a drink. As he stopped at the tables, he held up his glass. He asked that the table salute Captain Jenkins.

Well, with all the saluting that was going on, it was very obvious that most of the detectives sure as hell would beat the traffic on this night.

Frank and Nick were having a good time. A lot of the talk from everyone was about different incidents that involved the captain. Some of the stories were being told for the first time. It was assumed that now that the captain was dead, who would rebut the story. The drinks were flowing. Flanagan decided to close the bar to the public. He told the bartender to give the guys whatever they wanted. He announced that all drinks were on him.

The night moved along and everyone was having a great time. It was all in honor of Captain Jenkins, of course. At least that is what most of them would tell their wives when they got home, after beating the traffic.

Frank went over to Lieutenant Valentino and put his arm around him. "How did you make out with the colonel today?"

"Well Frank, I'm not sure how it went. We talked about the death of Jenkins; the colonel really liked that guy. He did ask how I felt about taking over the unit, until they decide which captain they will put in that spot. He never really got around to asking me if I wanted the job. We talked about some of the issues that have been around in the unit for some time now. I really did not get a good feeling from the colonel. I'm not sure if he wants to promote me to captain and take over the unit."

Frank motioned for the bartender to get them a drink. It was obvious that Valentino was in need of a drink. Frank was a little surprised that Valentino had even come to Flanagan's and hung out with the peons. He was a heavy drinker, but it was not known in the unit where he did his drinking after work. He acted at work like he wanted to be one of the guys, but on his off-duty time he did not associate with anyone. Frank talked with Valentino for a while. He invited him to come and sit with the men from the unit. Valentino told Frank that he had to leave. He said he was glad he came to Flanagan's, but he was starting to feel a little tipsy. Frank told him not to worry, that if necessary someone would drive him home. He told him that the guys in the unit always looked out for each other and would take anyone home if they needed a ride.

The party continued well past midnight. There were no signs that it would be breaking up anytime soon. Flanagan was having a great time and the doors were locked. There was no reason to stop the party. There were toasts every few minutes for Captain Jenkins. Frank was leading the group in stories. He was drinking shots of whiskey and chasing them with beer. Nick could see that Frank was on his way to making a fool out of himself, as usual. Nick had seen this act too many times in the past. He knew that most of the time it ended with bad results. He tried to talk to Frank about slowing down a little with the booze, but to no avail.

Frank stood on a chair and said, "Gentlemen, I want to make a toast to the best captain that ever commanded the Homicide Unit. He was a good cop, an honest cop, and a dedicated cop. He will be sorely missed. I salute you Captain Jenkins and may you now patrol the streets of heaven."

Everyone raised their glasses or bottles in salute to the captain. Frank got down from the chair. He grabbed Gus Buckley—Gus had been in the Homicide Unit for quite a while. Frank knew that Gus also worked a part- time job driving a hearse for the DiPasqualle Funeral Home. "Hey Gus, are you still driving part-time for the funeral home?"

"Yeah sarge, I still drive once in a while for them. Why do you ask?"

"I was wondering if you would like to do something for Captain Jenkins. I know he would be damn proud of you for it. I assume that you have the key to get in the funeral home? Let's go down there and bring the captain back to the bar for a real celebration."

"What the shit are you talking about—are you crazy?"

Frank grabbed Gus by the arm and told him that the two of them could do it. He said that everyone in the bar would be shocked. He told Gus that sometimes you have to do something memorable, so that the next generation of cops that come along will have great stories to tell. Gus put his beer to his mouth and downed his beer. "You know what sarge, you are a crazy son of a bitch and so am I—let's do it!"

Frank announced to the bar that he and Gus had to leave for a few minutes. He asked them to remain until they got back. He told them that when they got back, it would be a moment that nobody would ever forget. Most of the guys in the bar were already drunk. They did not have any thoughts about leaving. Nick was curious, but he was feeling pretty good. He wondered what Frank was up to. He grabbed Frank as he was leaving the bar.

"Frank, what the hell is going on? Where are you and Gus going? What are you up to?"

"Nick, you will love what we are doing. Just stay in the bar until we get back—this is going to be the caper of the year."

Frank and Gus left the bar and drove to the funeral parlor. Gus parked in the driveway leading to the basement. He told Frank that there is no security on duty at night and there is no alarm system. He said that the bodies were kept in the basement overnight because it's cool down there. Gus opened the door and he and Frank went in. Gus knew the layout of the basement. He did not need any lights. He moved along looking at the different coffins.

"Hey sarge, here it is—this is the one with the captain in it. I'll get the keys to the hearse. It will be easier to take him back to the bar in the hearse. We need to make sure we get him back here before 6:00 A.M., that's when the day workers come in."

"That's great Gus, let's wheel him out and get on our way. The guys are going to shit when we bring the captain back to the party."

Frank and Gus loaded the coffin into the hearse. They drove back to Flanagan's. Frank was laughing his ass off so much in the hearse that he pissed in his pants. Gus was laughing just as hard. It was probably quite a sight for other vehicles on the road, to see two people in the front seat of a hearse laughing their asses off.

The trip took about forty minutes total, from the bar to the funeral home and back to the bar. They parked the hearse close to the front door to the bar. They parked in a no parking zone. "Sarge, this is a no parking zone—we might get a ticket."

"Gus, are you fuckin goofy? Who the hell is going to write a ticket on a hearse that is parked in front of a bar? Hurry up and grab the other end and put the captain on the gurney. I'm going to open the door to the bar and announce that someone special wants to join in the fun. After I say that, we will wheel the captain in. I'm sure all hell will break loose. I can't wait to see the faces on those guys when they see the captain."

Frank knocked on the door. Flanagan opened the door and almost shit himself when he saw the casket. "Frank, what the fuck is going on? Who's in that casket?"

Frank and Gus moved quickly past Flanagan and into the bar. Guys were standing on chairs to get a better look. You could hear one common theme—"What the hell is going on? Who's in that casket?"

Frank stopped by the pool table and announced, "Folks, we have someone here that we have been talking about all night. Gus and I thought that we would go get him. If we are going to talk about him, I figured he might as well be present."

Gus opened the casket. Frank stood on a chair so everyone could see him. "Gentlemen, raise your drinks for the finest captain that any of us ever worked for. I present to you, Captain Bobby Jenkins."

Needless to say, everyone was shocked. Most of the guys were drunk and shocked. When they saw the captain, they could not believe what was happening. Frank asked Gus to help him lift the captain onto the pool table. Gus was against this and told Frank that it was best that they did not move the captain around. He worked in the funeral parlor and knew that it took a lot of preparation to have the body look so good in the casket. Frank agreed to not move the captain. He did ask each person in the bar to come by and pay their last respects. It had been very loud in the bar prior to the casket arriving. It was now eerily quiet, as the guys walked by the captain.

Flanagan suggested that they sing some Irish songs as a tribute.

Somebody told Flanagan that the captain was not Irish, but it was too late. The bar broke out in a bad rendition of "When Irish Eyes Are Smiling", followed by "It's a Grand Old Flag". No one was quite sure how the "Grand Old Flag" got in the act—no one cared either. Some knew the words and most did not—it didn't matter. As each person passed the casket, they reached in and touched the captain. A few people left miniatures of whiskey in his coat pockets. Flanagan said that it was an Irish tradition to make sure the deceased took some booze for the trip to heaven.

The party got louder after the singing. What at first looked like a really bad idea by Frank and Gus, turned out to be something that no one had ever been involved in. It was one of those incidents that would be talked about by generations of police officers in the future. It would be included with the numerous wild and crazy stories that get passed down over the years.

It was now showing some daylight outside. Nick told Frank that it would be very wise to get the captain back to the funeral parlor as soon as possible. Frank said that he need not worry; he and Gus would take care of getting the captain back in time for his funeral service.

Frank had a little too much to drink. He was being unusually friendly toward the guys in the unit. Nick was surprised that Frank hadn't started some trouble or said something to get a fight going. Frank walked to the back of the bar and was surprised that Lieutenant Valentino was still hanging with the group. "Hey Anthony, you old bastard, I'm proud of you. See what you have been missing all these years. You should have been hanging with us over the years. You would have had a great time. What the hell are you and Nick talking about back here in the corner?"

Valentino was feeling no pain. He was still belting down drinks. He told Frank that he and Nick were just discussing a few things. Frank asked if he could join in the fun or was it a private discussion. Nick started to walk away. Frank grabbed his arm. He grabbed it a little harder than he meant to. Nick pulled away and told Frank not to grab him again or he might find himself on his ass. Frank made a motion to grab Nick again. Nick was a little more sober than Frank and avoided him. Nick walked away and Frank sat down next to Valentino. "What the hell is up with Nick? What could you two be talking about that would make him act like an asshole? Is it personal between you guys or can you share the secret with me?"

"Frank, we were not talking about anything personal. We were just having a discussion—is that okay with you? I know that you and Nick go back a long way and are good friends. I also sense that Nick thinks that you watch over him too much. Maybe we should move Nick to another squad. I think it would make him feel more relaxed. What do you think, Frank?"

Frank moved in closer to Valentino. It was actually a little uncomfortable for the lieutenant. He held out his arm to maintain a separation. Frank picked up on the gesture and sat back in his chair. Frank asked Valentino if he wanted another drink. He told him that he had a full drink and that it would be his last—he was leaving. Valentino leaned over the table. He told Frank that although the gesture of bringing the captain to the bar was commendable, it might not have been a good thing to do. He told him that cops loved to talk about their drinking escapades. He said that he was worried that this incident would get around in the department. Frank told him not to worry—he and Gus would get the captain back to the funeral parlor soon. Valentino made a move to get up to leave. Frank asked him if he would discuss with him what he and Nick were talking about.

"Frank, if you must know, I was talking to Nick about the murder of his girlfriend. I think he is still suffering from that tragic event. I also told him about the phone call I got from the Carroll County detectives working on that murder. I haven't had a chance to tell you, Frank. They called me again the other day. They said that they wanted to interview Nick. They said that they do not believe that he had any knowledge about the murder. They only want to talk to him as they have found out that he and Janet were engaged. They feel that Janet must have fooled around with this guy and that is why he had her phone number in his cell phone. The detective that I talked to said he found it very interesting that someone in our unit got a record check on the guy. He also said that it was interesting that a member of our unit was dating someone that was listed in the murder victim's phone. I told Nick that he should talk to them and clear up anything he might know about Janet seeing this guy."

"So you think it would be best for Nick to talk to those assholes in Carroll County? Those guys are desperate to charge someone with that murder. I'm going to advise Nick not to talk to them. He can tell them over the phone that he dated Janet. He can tell them that if she dated the murder victim, he didn't know anything about it. I'm not going to let Nick get involved in something that could backfire on him. I'm surprised that you think otherwise."

Lieutenant Valentino pulled himself up from the chair. He had been sitting too long. He needed the wall to assist his getting upright. He was a tall man and towered over Frank. He was adjusting his clothes for the ride home. He knew that he would be facing the almost certain questioning period from his wife. He had made the number one mistake that most cops that go out drinking make—he did not call his wife. He looked at his watch and told Frank that it was probably about time for the party to break up and everyone go home. He also told Frank that he and Gus need to get the captain's body back to the funeral parlor. As he was standing erect, it appeared from his demeanor that he was usurping his position as Frank's supervisor. He started to say something and Frank stopped him.

"What the hell is going on? You stay out with us most of the night and now all of sudden you put on your lieutenant's hat and dish out orders. This is a social function, so what you have to say doesn't really matter right now. You can save all the orders for another day when you are back at the office. As far as Nick talking to those detectives, it ain't going to happen. I know Nick better than you or anyone else. I will make sure he says nothing to those guys about his involvement with Janet or anything else. For the sake of everyone involved, I would suggest that you not talk to those detectives anymore."

"Who the hell do you think you are talking to? I stayed out tonight with all of you because of my respect for the captain. I'm your boss and you need to remember that—do you understand?"

"Lieutenant, I have one thing to say to you, so listen up. I'm more of a cop than you ever were or ever will be. You have hidden in office jobs your whole career in the department. Everyone knows that you are a paper-pusher. You couldn't investigate a homicide if your life depended on it. The guys in the unit know that you are a complete joke. I've been wanting to tell you this for a long time. I'm glad no one is around right now, so that I can get this off my chest. I also know that I have to face you tomorrow at work. I don't give a shit—I will deny I said anything to you. I think the colonel would probably believe me before he would believe you. Now, if you have to get your pansy- ass home, get the hell out of here!"

Frank just stood there and stared at the lieutenant. Valentino was speechless for a while. He started toward the door and came back. He appeared to be at a loss for words. He waved his finger at Frank and gritted his teeth—no words came out. He made another move toward the door and returned again. "Frank, you will be sorry you talked to me like that. I can make life miserable for you and you know it. I have been good to you the entire time you have been in the unit. I have probably saved your ass on more occasions than you know about. I can't help but to think about all the shit you have been involved in over the years. The shootings and all the other bullshit that you got yourself into could have gotten you fired. I was usually the one that told the captain and the colonel that you were a good cop. This is my reward for looking out for you—you are an ungrateful bastard! I will talk to Nick tomorrow about calling the Carroll County detectives and giving them a statement. I don't know what the hell you two are hiding, but whatever it is will come out soon. Now, as far as what you have said to me tonight, that will be between you and me. I just want to let you know that if you screw up in the future, your ass will be out of the Homicide Unit. Don't say another word to me—I'm going home."

Now Frank was the one at a loss for words. He sat down as he watched the lieutenant walk toward the side door. The door was locked. He motioned for Flanagan to let him out. Flanagan tried to shake hands with Valentino, but was snubbed. Flanagan walked over to Frank and asked what was up with the lieutenant. Frank told him that it was personal between the two of them. He said he did not want to discuss it. Flanagan told him that he was going to ask everyone to leave. He told Frank that it was a great night and one that he will never forget. "Frank, you did the captain right. You should be proud of yourself. I'm sure that the captain is looking down on you and the guys. He is thanking the hell out of you all. Frank, I have been around for a long time and I'm full of advice. Do you mind if I convey one good piece of advice to you?"

"Sure Flanny, go right ahead. I'm always open for some good advice from a man of your stature. If it's to stop drinking and quit messing around with the women, you can save your breath."

"No Frank, I would not give out that kind of advice. My advice to you is based on what I hear from the guys in the unit. You need to relax and not be so hard on the troops. You also need to stop thinking you can solve the crime problems in Baltimore. Frank, it seems like you are always in the news for something. You need to improve your image if you ever want to get promoted. I know a lot of people in your department and most of them think you are in a self-destructive mode."

Frank smiled at Flanagan. Nick walked over and interrupted the conversation. "Frank, I have had too much to drink. I'm going home and get some sleep."

"Okay Nick, we are all leaving. Gus and I will take the captain back to the funeral parlor. It should only take a short time. How about if we meet at the Brew & Chew for breakfast? I would really appreciate you meeting me. I need to talk to you."

"Frank, I don't think I can stay awake any longer. I really need to go home and get some sleep. We can talk tomorrow."

Frank found Gus and they took the casket out to the hearse. It was turning daylight and there was much more traffic in the area than earlier. They tried to act professional as they loaded the captain into the hearse. As they were about to leave, Frank asked Gus if he could take the captain back by himself. Gus balked at that idea, but Frank begged him. He told him that he had to do something that could not wait. Gus agreed and Frank thanked him and went to his car.

Frank sat in his car and fought the urge to just lie down and get some sleep. He was furious about what the lieutenant had said to him. He was more concerned that the lieutenant would convince Nick to talk to the Carroll County investigators. He ran it all through his mind—what was going on up to this point. The Carroll County investigators were just fishing. They had nothing good to go on in their investigation. They only knew that Janet's phone number was in the dead guy's cell phone. They knew that someone in the Homicide Unit got a record check on the guy.

They probably knew by now that Janet had been murdered in Ocean City. They know that Nick dated Janet. Do they know more or are they hoping that Nick can shed some light on the murder?

Frank was now thinking straight in spite of all the drinking that went on in Flanagan's. Who can implicate me in the murder of that guy? Janet is not around any longer. I used Lenny's computer and he is gone. The only one that can hurt me at this point is Nick. He and I are too bonded together for him to go in and give me up. I'm not sure about the lieutenant. He is weak and he doesn't know anything. I have eliminated Janet. Lenny is not around to say anything bad about me. The only person that can do me in is Nick. He would never say anything bad about me or tell them I shot the guy. If he did tell them, he would also lose everything. That leaves me with the lieutenant. I can't trust him, but he is in no real position to hurt me.

If I am fighting to stay out of jail for the rest of my life, I need to make sure that anyone that can hurt me is either eliminated or is on board with me. I know that Nick would never put me in. We have too much history together. We have fought in the trenches over the years. I have considered Nick a brother and I hope he feels the same way about me. He has just as much to lose in this mess as I do. I need to stay focused. I know things will work out—they always have in the past.

CHAPTER 49

The sun was shining and sunglasses were in order for the large crowd that stood outside the cathedral. When senior bosses in the department died or a police officer was killed in the line of duty, it was a time for the politicians to make a showing. If it was also an election year, they came if they were running for anything from street cleaner to governor. It was a time to get in front of a TV camera. They would talk about how wonderful the deceased was and how they made a difference in the fight against crime. It was all bullshit; most of them didn't even know anything about the deceased.

The church was packed. Captain Jenkins was very well liked and it was obvious from the huge congregation in attendance. Frank sat in the back of the church with two guys from the unit. Nick sat a little closer. The service went off well. It was a full-blown Catholic Mass. As it ended, a black lady with a voice that appeared to rattle the walls of the church, sang Amazing Grace. The tears were flowing. If you didn't cry after that rendition of Amazing Grace, you probably have ice in your veins.

The police commissioner spoke after the song. He talked about when he worked with Captain Jenkins in the old days. He told a couple of funny stories—one seemed a little inappropriate for a funeral. The story was about when he and the captain were rookies. They went out drinking after their shift when they were in patrol. They were so drunk that they woke up the next day sleeping in a graveyard—propped up on a tombstone. I think the commissioner realized he was telling an inappropriate story, but had to finish what he started. Some of the older cops laughed—most of the immediate family just looked at each other. The commissioner rebounded and stuck with the normal stuff. He talked about what a difference the captain had made in every unit that he commanded during his years with the department.

The mayor got up and basically just thanked the captain for his service. He told the family that it is people like the captain that make the streets of Baltimore safe. When the mayor finished his talk, he told the crowd that it was an honor to be the mayor of Baltimore. He stepped over the line when he ended his talk by stating that he would appreciate everyone's support in the upcoming election.

A couple of family members got up and talked about what a great husband, father, grandfather, and friend that the captain was to so many people. The last speaker was the captain's son. He talked about wanting to follow in his father's footsteps. He said that he admired his dad. He said that the family will sorely miss him. He broke down halfway through the talk. He finished by thanking everyone for honoring his father with such a large turnout. When he finished talking he asked if anyone else had anything to say. Nick looked back at Frank as if to say you should get up and say something. Frank just shook his head and mouthed the word "no" to Nick.

The funeral procession to the gravesite was huge. It stretched for several city blocks. The intersections were all manned by cops and this allowed the procession to move through the city at a rapid pace. Frank and Nick drove to the gravesite with Gus Buckley and Sam Gimble. At the gravesite, it was very somber as the family was crying as the final prayers were said. The casket was lowered into the grave. Frank and Nick stood on a hillside overlooking the somber event. The captain was a veteran and the casket was draped with the American flag. The flag was removed as Taps was played by a member of the police department honor guard. It was a beautiful day and the flowers in the cemetery were in full bloom. The ducks in the nearby pond were splashing around. It was so calm that you felt like lying on the grass and just taking it all in. Maybe lying on the grass in a cemetery might not be the smartest idea.

Frank and Nick did not talk as they watched from the hillside. When the ceremony ended, the four of them got in the car and drove toward the police building. During the ride, Gus talked a lot about what he thought the unit would be like without the captain. Sam jumped in on occasion and said that he did not think there would be any changes. Frank just smiled at the two of them. When they approached the entrance to the police garage, Frank told Gus and Sam that he and Nick had someplace to go. Nick looked surprise. He reattached his seat belt and asked Frank where they were going. Frank thanked Gus and Sam for attending the funeral and told them that he and Nick would be back in the office in about an hour. Frank had never answered Nick. As they pulled away from the garage, he said, "Nick, I just need to talk to you away from the office. It won't take that long. It's private and I don't want the whole office to hear what I have to say."

Frank drove the unmarked police car at a high rate of speed. Nick asked him to slow down. Frank just laughed. Nick was frustrated. He asked Frank to just pull over and talk. "Where the hell are you going for this private talk?"

"I thought Clifton Park would be a good spot to talk. I always liked to pull in and relax in that park when I was in patrol. Hang in there Nick, it won't take long. I just have a couple of things that need to be addressed."

"I hope this isn't going to be one of those talks about me getting on board with eliminating all the bad guys in the city. If that's what this is about, you can drive me back to the building."

Frank knew the park very well as he drove across some grassy areas to find a secluded shady spot next to the golf course. "Here we are Nick—this was always one of my favorite spots. I could park here and do some serious thinking when I was in patrol."

"That's great Frank. Now what is it that is so important? I really need to get back to the office and get some reports done."

Frank got out of the car and leaned against the front fender. He did not say anything to Nick. He knew Nick was pissed and would follow him out of the car. Nick got out and walked over to Frank. "Frank, is this a game or something? What the hell do you have to say?"

"Nick, I have been thinking about the guy I killed in Carroll County. I'm not sure what those detectives have on that case. I think about it daily because it could cost me my job, not to mention some serious jail time. I'm concerned that they want to talk to you. You do understand that if they pin that killing on me, you will also be involved. I don't want you to talk to those detectives. Valentino has talked to them and that worries me. I don't trust that bastard. I have played this over in my mind. They know that Janet went out with the guy. They also know that someone in the Homicide Unit got a record check on him. Beyond that, I'm not sure what they would have. I do know that the only person who could possibly implicate me in that killing is you. I think that Valentino has an inclination that I was involved in killing the guy. He associates me with you. He feels that you could not have killed anyone. On the other hand, he thinks I'm a mad man. He thinks that if anyone in the unit killed the guy, it had to be me. I need to get your feelings on this Nick. This is about as serious as it gets. I never thought it would come to this. What do you think we should do?"

"Frank, I don't want to sound like Tonto... 'What you mean we white man?' I haven't done anything wrong. You took it upon yourself to go out that night and stalk that guy. You then made the stupid mistake of approaching his vehicle. I know you said he came at you with a baseball bat. What the hell did you expect him to do? He was in front of his house...it's dark, it's raining, and some guy is approaching his car. It was a big mistake on your part Frank. I have no idea what to do."

Frank listened intently to Nick. Usually Frank acted like he was listening, but he was always thinking ahead. Frank very seldom asked others what they thought about anything. He was the sergeant and he thought he had all the answers. Frank paced around the car. He occasionally picked up a rock and threw it at the trees. The more rocks he picked up, the harder he was throwing. It was obvious that he had come upon a situation that was about as serious as any he had ever faced. "Nick, I wish I had it to do over, but I don't. I know it was probably stupid shooting that guy. I set myself up for failure. That is against everything you and I ever learned in the Corps. Marine training teaches you to always think about the mission. I didn't think—I just haphazardly made my move without thinking about my escape plan."

"Frank, knock off the Marine bullshit; it has been years since we were in the Marines. You talk as if you're always in combat. You can talk about plans, escape routes, and all the other bullshit—you screwed up and that's all there is to it. I think we should just let it go and see where it takes us. The more we talk about it and the more you plan, the crazier it gets. We don't know what they have in their investigation. Until they make a move, we should forget about it."

Frank was actually listening to Nick. Over the years, it was always Frank that did the talking when they were in sinister situations. It was obvious to both of them that those days were over. Nick sat in the car and fastened his seat belt. Frank stared at him from the driver's side of the vehicle. Nick's actions made it very obvious that he wanted to leave and get back to the building. Frank threw the last of the rocks and got in the car. "Nick, before we head back to the building, listen to what I have to say. I know I don't have all the answers. I have been put in positions my whole life where people expected me to make decisions. In the Marines, I got promoted at a young age. I made decisions that affected others. In the police department, it's the same thing. I was making decisions as a small kid when we were growing up. After all these years, it's something that's supposed to come natural to me. This situation is different—I'm actually scared for the first time in my life. It would have never happened if I didn't go to check out that guy for you."

Nick listened and he felt that Frank was being sincere for a change. This was something that he had not seen for a long time. He got the feeling that Frank was actually hurting inside. The last thing he needed was for him to pour fuel on the fire. Frank started the car and headed for the building.

On the ride to the office, Nick changed the subject and asked Frank how he was doing outside the department. Frank told him that things were going okay. He said that he was dating a girl and really felt good about her.

He told Nick that the girl had been around the block a little, but he had hit it off with her. Nick asked what he meant by around the block. Frank laughed and told Nick that she has had some drug problems in the past. "Damn, Nick you're getting into my personal life. I didn't think you gave a shit about what I did outside the job."

"That's not the case Frank—I do care about you. I just wish you could relax more and not take things so serious. Who's the girl? Maybe we can all go out some night and have some drinks. Where did you meet her?"

"Well asshole, if you have to be so nosy, I met her in a bar years ago. You remember the bar—the Pirate's Den. Her name is Pam. I've been wanting to get with her for a long time, but she had a boyfriend. The guy died about three months ago and we started dating. Before you say anything else, no, I did not kill the guy. He died while being operated on for a heart problem. I know you were thinking that I killed the poor bastard."

Nick laughed and it seemed like things were back to the way they were in the old days—it didn't last long. Frank pulled into a parking spot in the headquarters building. He asked Nick if he could say one more thing about the Carroll County investigation. Nick shrugged his shoulders and told Frank to fire away. "I don't like the fact that Valentino is taking calls from the Carroll County detectives. I know he don't like me. I'm sure that after the conversation we had the other night at Flanagan's, he is out to get my ass. I need to think of a way to silence that fat bastard."

Nick and Frank were walking toward the elevator. They were both talking in a low voice. It was something about talking loud in the building—you never knew who was lurking in the background. They got on the elevator and Nick told Frank that Valentino was just an old crusty fart that was biding his time in the department. He told Frank that even if Valentino didn't like him, he would not want to make any waves.

On the fifth floor, a patrol major got on the elevator. "Hi Frank, how in the hell are you doing? Have you killed anybody in the last ten minutes?"

"No major, I have been waiting for someone to get on this elevator. My friend Nick and I were going to take the first person who got on and slice their ass up in pieces."

"It's nice to see that you still have a morbid sense of humor Frank. The department needs people like you. Without you who would the IID investigators have to investigate?"

The elevator stopped on Frank's floor. He and Nick got off. Frank held the door open with one arm. "Major, I hope you have a nice day. It's always a pleasure to have such an intelligent conversation with someone of your stature."

As the door was closing, Frank made the statement that the major was the biggest asshole in the department. Frank said it loud enough that the major probably heard it.

"Damn Frank, you can't talk to majors like that. He's in a position to make trouble for you if he wanted to."

"Piss on him…he's a wimp. He works in the commissioner's office flipping papers from one desk to another."

Frank asked Nick if he wanted something to drink. They walked to the small room next to the homicide office where there were soda machines and candy machines. Frank got a Dr Pepper and asked Nick what he wanted.

"Damn Frank, how many Dr Peppers do you drink in a day? You know that shit is probably not good for you—I'll have water."

They stood in the small room for a while. Frank told Nick that he wants to know if Valentino talks to him about giving a statement to the Carroll County detectives. He told Nick that it was important that they stay in touch. Frank told Nick that he appreciates him taking time to talk. He whispered to him as they were walking out of the room. "I will do whatever is necessary to stay out of jail."

CHAPTER 50

Nick was in the office working the day shift when he got a phone call from the Ocean City detectives working on Janet's murder. It had been a few weeks since he had any contact with them, even though he had sent them e-mails once or twice a week. The last time he talked with them, he was told that they had followed some very good leads and still had nothing. Nick was frustrated. He was not sure if they were giving a hundred percent effort on the investigation. He felt at times that he wanted to get in his car and drive down to confront them. He felt like he wanted to talk to someone in command about Janet's murder. He thought that after all, how many murders occurred in Ocean City that they could not put all their resources on Janet's murder.

Being a homicide cop frustrated him even more. He, however, did not think they would appreciate a cop from the big city telling them what to do. He was so frustrated that he often thought about asking the chief in Ocean City if he could come down and help with the investigation. He knew that would never happen—he was too close to the victim.

Nick put the call on hold. He told the investigator that he wanted to go to a private room to talk. The lead investigator on Janet's murder in Ocean City was a former NYPD cop. He had retired and moved to Ocean City and started a second career in law enforcement. He was not only their lead investigator in serious cases, he also taught in the Ocean City Police Academy. Nick at first felt good about having him in charge of the investigation. He had come from one of the largest police departments in the country—so he must know what he is doing.

Nick locked the door to the small interview room. "Hello, this is Nick Giango."

"Hi Nick, this is Sergeant Vince Pantalone. How have you been? It has been a few weeks since we talked. I hope things are well with you. I did get your e-mails, but I have been too busy to answer them. I need to go over a few things with you about the murder. Do you have time now to talk about it or should I catch you at another time? It won't take long…I have some good news. I'm sure you want to hear what we have."

"Sergeant Pantalone, I have all the time in the world. I'm really excited that you have good news. I hope the news is that you caught the sorry bastard that murdered Janet. I will drive down there and kiss you on the cheek. I will do it in front of your whole department on the beach, if that's what you are calling about."

"Well, as tempting as that sounds Nick, we really don't physically have anyone in custody. However, I do have some very good news. We sent all the evidence recovered on the murder scene to the FBI lab at Quantico. I mean we sent just about everything that was in that condo on the day Janet was killed. We got notified late yesterday that they have recovered some latent prints that belong to a guy who lives up your way. The problem is that we checked him out and he was a murder victim in Baltimore a couple months ago. I need you to check your records and give me the particulars on his murder."

Nick leaned back in his chair. He felt a calm come over him that he had not felt in a long time. Finally a breakthrough…maybe it all could be put to rest. Nick was thinking that it was not much satisfaction hearing that the killer was dead. He would have preferred a trial, with the suspect getting the death penalty. Nick would have loved attending the execution of the murderer. Throwing the switch would be the ultimate thrill for him. "Thanks sergeant, I'm at a loss for words. I am just wondering why some dude from Baltimore would go to Ocean City and kill someone. Are you sure you have the right person?"

"Well Nick, if you let me finish, I will tell you the rest. We are positive that we have the right person. When the prints came back we were elated. We also got a hit on the DNA from the victim's underwear. So, with a hit on the prints and a positive test on the DNA, we are certain we have the right guy. I need to you to check on the circumstances of his murder in Baltimore. His name is Kenny Jackson. He last resided at 2112 Division Street in Baltimore. Can you call me back as soon as possible with the information? I hope this makes you feel a little better. I know you think we have taken a long time to clear this murder. I can assure you that we have been working feverishly on this case. I wanted you to be the first to know about this information."

"Thanks Sergeant Pantalone, I do appreciate all your efforts. I know that you were working hard. I will check this guy out in our system. I will get back to you as soon as possible. Thanks again, this is the best news I have received in a long time."

Nick hung up from the sergeant. He went directly to the file cabinet. He pulled the index card on Kenny Jackson. He saw the folder number was H-139-10. It had a red sticker on it. The red sticker meant that the murder was still open—no arrest had been made. Nick went to the file cabinet. He pulled out the Kenny Jackson file. It was next to the Maurice Jackson, Wendell Jackson, Bernard Jackson, and the Leroy Jackson files. Nick could not help but to think—did the whole Jackson family get wiped out in Charm City.

The office was empty, with the exception of a few detectives and Sergeant Favasi. Nick took the file and went to his desk. He went through the official report made by the patrol officer. The report stated that the body of Kenny Jackson was found next to the tennis courts in Druid Hill Park. It went on to say that the body may have been there for several days, as it had animal bite marks. The report stated that Jackson had multiple gunshot wounds to his upper torso. Nick went through the reports by the detectives. He saw that the case was handled by Detective Jimmy Mulligan. Nick knew Mulligan—he was on the night shift. Nick had the paperwork spread out over his desk. He was going through the material when Frank came out of his office. He asked Nick what he was working on.

"Frank, you won't believe it. I got a call from the Ocean City detectives. They know who killed Janet. I just talked with Sergeant Pantalone. He confirmed that they have fingerprints and a DNA match on the killer. I'm so excited. I'm sure Janet's family will be relieved when they get the good news."

Nick wasn't looking up at Frank. He couldn't see the pale look on his face. Frank moved closer and looked over Nick's shoulder. He immediately noticed the name on the folder with the red sticker.

"Frank, say something—can you believe they finally nailed the bastard? The sad part about it is that he was a murder victim here in the city. This is his folder. He was found dead in Druid Hill Park next to the tennis courts. Detective Mulligan worked the case. Don't just stand there Frank, say something."

"Oh, that's great Nick; I'm happy for you. You will finally have some relief from all the agony you have been through. I think we should turn the information over to Mulligan. Let him handle it from here on out. I really don't think you should be going through the folder without Mulligan's permission. You know how we have talked about security of the case folders."

"Frank, you're worrying about the security of the folder at a time like this. Don't you have any questions about how they got the prints or how they got the DNA? I would think that you would be as excited as I am. Screw the security of the folder. I promised Sergeant Pantalone that I would check it out. I'll call him back with all the information. I'll get with Mulligan soon, but for now, I'm so excited that I can't think straight."

Frank did not want to be so obvious about his lack of interest in the folder. He patted Nick on the back. He told him to be careful what he shared with the Ocean City Police. He walked back to his office and shut the door. He sat facing the window. He could not believe the sudden turn of events. The thoughts were racing through his head, that not only was he worrying about the Carroll County investigation, he now had to think about being connected to Kenny Jackson. He thought about bringing out the good whiskey from his desk. He changed his mind—the last thing he needed at this point was for Valentino to catch him drinking on the job.

He locked his door and popped two aspirins. He chased them down with what was left in the Dr Pepper can.

Nick was making notes from the folder. He came across the arrest record for Jackson—it was quite long. Nick figured he would just fax it down to Pantalone. He put it on the side of the desk. He continued making notes. When he was finished, he picked up the phone and started to call Pantalone. While dialing the number, his attention was drawn to the arrest record. He put the phone down and scanned down the sheet until he got near the bottom. "Holy shit—Frank locked this guy up for murder."

Nick took the folder and the arrest record and knocked on Frank's door. Frank opened it without saying anything. "Frank, you locked Kenny Jackson up in the past for murder. What a coincidence—do you remember anything about him?" Was he found guilty?" Did he do much time?" What can you tell me about him?"

"Slow down Nick, relax and take some deep breaths. Let me look at that folder. I don't remember everybody I locked up."

Nick gave Frank the folder and stood over him. Frank was getting a little nervous with Nick being so excited. He told Nick to give him a few minutes and maybe he could recall something about Jackson. Nick tried to be calm. He told Frank that most cops would remember the people they put away for murder. Frank slammed the folder on the desk and told Nick that he really needs to calm down. "If the son of a bitch is dead and they are convinced that he is their guy—why are you getting so worked up?"

"Frank, I can't believe you. They got the bastard that murdered Janet and you want me to calm down. It doesn't matter if he's dead or not. I want to call them back and tell them something about this guy. They want to know how he died. My big question, which seems like a mystery to me, is—why this guy would go to Ocean City to commit a murder?"

"Nick, it was most likely a random act. He was probably down there looking to break into some places. He broke into your condo thinking no one was there. He came across Janet and killed her. I'm glad the dude is dead. They can clear their case and everybody is happy."

"Frank, he not only killed Janet, he raped her. Something is not right with the whole event. He could have raped her—he didn't have to kill her.

I want to get with Mulligan and see if he knows more about this guy. What do you recall about the case you had that sent him away?"

Frank got up and paced the floor. He told Nick that he does not remember all the facts about the case. He told him that he does remember that the guy was a real beast. Nick was taking notes as Frank was talking. Frank said that he had a great case on Jackson but the jury only found him guilty of manslaughter. He said that some of the witnesses refused to show up for the trial. The case was not as strong as they would have wanted. He told Nick that Jackson got ten years. He only served about three years and was out on the street. "Wow, what a coincidence that I locked this guy up once. Now they have him for the murder of Janet. You're right Nick, this is as crazy as it gets."

"Yeah, what a coincidence. I'm calling Sergeant Pantalone and letting him know what we have. He may want to talk to you about Jackson. It would be great to know more about what happened that day that led Jackson to that condo."

Frank got a call to go see Lieutenant Valentino. Nick took the Jackson folder and went back to his desk. He was excited about knowing who killed Janet. He was perplexed on why she was singled out.

Nick called Sergeant Pantalone on his cell phone. He answered on the first ring. He thanked Nick for getting back to him so soon. Nick told him what he had found out from the homicide folder. He read all the reports, including the autopsy report. He told Pantalone that the detective who worked on Jackson's murder was on another shift. He promised Pantalone that he would have the detective call him and discuss the matter in detail. Nick told Pantalone that he was shocked to find out that his sergeant had arrested Jackson for murder. Pantalone was silent on the other end. Nick asked if he was still there.

"Yeah, I'm still here Nick. Let me ask you a question. By any chance is your sergeant's name, Favasi?"

"Yeah, his name is Frank Favasi. Didn't I mention that to you before?"

"No, you did not mention his name. Nick, I want to be totally honest with you and share what we have. When we examined the condo for evidence, we found some paper that we think Jackson dropped when he was struggling with Janet. The reason we believe this is because the paper has blood on it—it's Janet's blood. The paper could not have been in that condo prior to the attack on Janet. I want to tell you something, but I will ask that you do not share this with anyone at this time. Do I have your word that you will not share this with anyone?"

"Sergeant, I appreciate all that you and your men have done up to this point. I promise that whatever you tell me, I will not share with anyone until you tell me to."

"Nick, I trust you. It may be nothing, but we found a piece of paper with Sergeant Favasi's name and phone number on it. The paper also had the address of the condo where the murder occurred. It could mean nothing, but for now I need to keep it confidential. Do you understand where I'm coming from?"

"Wow, you have floored me with that information. I know Frank arrested Jackson, but why would he have Frank's phone number and the address where we were staying. I got a lump in my throat right now the size of a softball. What the hell is going on?"

Nick was grasping for words. Weird thoughts were racing through his head. Sergeant Pantalone again asked Nick to keep this information between them. Pantalone asked Nick if there was anything else he knew about the relationship between Jackson and Sergeant Favasi—other than the arrest. Nick said that he knew of nothing. Frank had never talked about Kenny Jackson. Pantalone told Nick that he would get back to him soon. Before he hung up, Pantalone said, "Nick, on the day that Janet was murdered, why did your sergeant want to meet you in Easton? What was so important that he wanted you to drive to Easton when you were on vacation? He could have driven to Ocean City and met you. Why meet in Easton? What was that all about Nick?"

Nick hesitated to respond to the question. The softball was getting bigger in his throat. He wanted to say—that is the way Frank operates. He wanted to say that since Frank made sergeant, he called the shots. He got a little quieter on the phone. He looked around to make sure no one was listening. "Sergeant, I'm not really sure why he insisted on meeting in Easton. He could have driven the rest of the way to Ocean City. He certainly knew that I was on vacation with Janet. I never really gave it much thought. Frank never takes no for an answer. He always has to have things his way. All the years that I have known Frank, he always has to have things his way. Now that I think about it and after what you have told me about the paper you found, I'm a little confused. What do think about the whole situation?"

Sergeant Pantalone told Nick that it might mean nothing. He said that at some point he would have to talk to Frank about it. He asked Nick to cooperate with him. He again told Nick not to discuss anything with Frank. He also told him that he would probably contact Frank later. Pantalone thanked Nick for getting the information on Jackson. He told him that he would stay in touch. He made it very clear to Nick again that he should not discuss anything with anyone—especially Sergeant Favasi.

Nick hung up from Pantalone. He walked out of the office. He went to the ground floor of the building and went outside. He sat on the bench in front of the building. There were a few smokers out there, but no one that Nick knew. It was a hot and humid day. There could be better places to sit, but for now Nick just needed to be out of the building. He sat and just stared across at the War Memorial Building. The transit buses that came by emitted fumes that could gag you. He was trying to make some sense of what he was just told. He was thinking of what a predicament it could have been if he had told Pantalone the real reason he met Frank in Easton. This would have been a shocker for Pantalone if he told him that he and Nick met in Easton to discuss what they were going to do about Frank killing Janet's friend.

Nick thought if over in his mind—what the hell was Jackson doing with Frank's phone number and the address of the condo? He was thinking that it would not be so bad if Jackson just had Frank's phone number, but having the address of the condo was puzzling. Frank could probably justify Jackson having the phone number—having the address is the weirdest thing ever. Nick went back inside and up to his office. The air conditioning was a welcome relief from the bus fumes and heat.

Nick was visibly shaken and wanted to stay as far away from Frank as possible. He knew that Frank would notice that something was wrong.

The last thing he needed at this point was Frank grilling him about the conversation with Pantalone. Nick went to his desk and packed a few things in his attaché case. He headed for the door. He didn't quite make it out when he heard Frank call his name. Before Frank could say anything, Nick told him he was going out on the street to locate a witness. Frank walked in the hallway with him toward the elevator. "Nick, it's great that they broke the case in Ocean City. I'm sure you feel relieved knowing that they found out who committed that awful act on Janet. You seem to have been on the phone a long time with them. Is there anything else they found out that I should know?"

"No Frank, they were just going over a few things with me. You know the normal stuff in a murder investigation. They are just tying up some loose ends. I'm sure they will close the investigation soon. The sergeant did say that he might want to talk to you about Kenny Jackson. I guess they just want to get a feel for what you know about the guy."

"Nick, they said they wanted to talk to me about Jackson. What else could I tell them other than I locked him up for murder? It's not like I know anything personal about the guy. Why would they want to talk to me?"

"I don't know, Frank. He said that he would probably get in touch with you and discuss Jackson. I really need to get on the street and get some work done."

Frank stood in the hallway by the elevator and watched Nick leave. Nick pushed the button for the third floor where his car was parked. He got to his car and could feel his hand shake as he put the key in the door. He sat behind the wheel. He did not start the car for a few minutes. He knew that he had just told the biggest lie to someone that he had never lied to before. He tried to justify it in his mind by thinking that Pantalone did say he wanted to talk to Frank about Jackson. It's not a lie that I told Frank, but there was some deception in the way it was worded. Nick was feeling bad as he drove from the building. He knew that if Pantalone wanted to talk to Frank about Kenny Jackson, there would be no doubt that he would get into the bloody paper found in the condo.

He turned the air conditioner on full blast. It seemed as if everything was coming to a head all at once. Pantalone wanted to talk to Frank. The Carroll County investigators were determined to talk to me about the Philbin murder. Nick was just talking out loud to himself. He usually did this when he had real concerns or was trying to figure out how some of his murder investigations should go. I know what Pantalone is thinking. He may be on the right track. Frank has always said that he would do whatever it takes to stay out of jail. I just don't want to believe that he would send Jackson down to Ocean City to kill Janet—that's absurd. I need to stop thinking like that. How else would Jackson have found Janet—if in fact he was looking for her? The bloody piece of paper with Frank's name and phone number on it is crazy. The paper also had the address of where we were staying. This is all crazy. I only wish I would have been a little stronger and told Frank to drive to Ocean City. This sounds like a crazy horror story. I drive to Easton to meet my sergeant and while I'm gone, someone murders my girlfriend. Not only does someone murder my girlfriend, it turns out he was at one time arrested by my best friend. Now I find out that the killer also had the address of his victim. I'm so damn confused—I don't know which way to turn. I told Pantalone that I would not discuss anything with Frank. I just have to hang loose and wait for him to contact Frank.

Nick decided to actually try to do some real police work. He needed to look for a witness. He drove to southwest Baltimore and sat in front of a house on Washington Boulevard. The area was a nasty run-down neighborhood with a drug dealer on each corner. Nick could recognize a drug dealer a mile away. He was not there for drug dealers. They scattered when they saw the unmarked car. He fumbled through his paperwork looking for the name of the witness. He found the paper and could not make out the last name of the person. He had the right address. He just could not read the name. Nick banged his fist on the steering wheel. I got it—I'll ask Pantalone if I can see the paper he found in the condo. I have been around Frank all my life. I sure as hell can identify his handwriting. Now what the hell is the name on this paper?

CHAPTER 51

Frank walked back to the captain's office that was now being occupied temporarily by Lieutenant Valentino. Frank knew he was going to catch some serious flak. Hell, the way he slammed the lieutenant at Flanagan's bar—what else could he expect. The lieutenant was sitting in a chair next to the captain's desk. He had set up a small table. He was not using the captain's desk or chair. Frank walked in and said, "Good morning lieutenant, how are things going?" Valentino did not even look at Frank. He motioned with his hand for Frank to sit down. Valentino continued reading some papers without acknowledging that Frank was even in the room. Frank knew he was getting the silent treatment for a reason. He also knew he despised Valentino. He sat quietly waiting for him to finish whatever he was reading. Frank was surmising that Valentino was probably just staring at the papers and not even reading them. It would be his way of saying—I'm the boss—you will wait until I'm ready to talk. Frank got up and asked if he could close the door. Valentino told him to sit down and don't worry about the door.

"I was just thinking that with the door closed, our conversation could be more private. I'm not sure what you want. Before you start, I do want to apologize for talking to you the way I did at Flanagan's. I know I was out of line."

"Sergeant Favasi, I will be with you in a minute. You don't have to apologize to me for anything. You were obviously drunk, as usual—so whatever you said at Flanagan's is over."

Frank sat and knew that whatever was coming was not going to be good. His thoughts raced through his head about the information he got earlier from Nick about Kenny Jackson. He had a lot going on in his mind and this was a good time for the survival mode to kick in.

Valentino put down the papers and looked at Frank. He didn't say anything; he just rubbed his jaw with his hand. "If you are wondering why I'm sitting in this chair with this table, it's out of respect for Captain Jenkins. His desk is still cluttered with the paperwork he left on his last day in this office. I have decided that until I find out who will get this job, I'm not touching his desk. Let's just say it's sort of a memorial to him for now. As far as our relationship, for the time I have left in this unit, it will be strictly professional. I hope you feel the same way. Let me make one thing clear to you. Until I leave this unit, I'm your boss. I expect you to do your job as if Jenkins was still here. If I leave or retire I hope that the next person in charge of this unit can deal with your bullshit better than I can."

"Lieutenant, let me say one thing before you continue. I work hard around here. The results that my squad members show on a daily basis prove my point. I will continue to work hard whether you or someone else is in charge. I'm a team player and my main interest is to solve murders. I admit that I may have some tactics that are different than the other sergeants in the unit. I'm passionate about what I do. I admit that sometimes I go a little overboard, but we get the job done. The bad guys in this city are vicious people and handling them with kid gloves is not the way to go."

Valentino was listening, but Frank could tell that it was going in one ear and out the other. He had heard this spiel from Frank before. Valentino got up and closed the door. He told Frank that he was on a slippery slope. He said he knew how hard Frank worked in the unit. He said that he also knew that Frank's squad was one of the best in the unit. Frank sat there and was waiting for the good stuff to end and the bomb to be dropped. He knew Valentino very well. He knew this was a prelude to something bad. He felt like telling Valentino to just give me the bad shit and forget about all the good stuff. Valentino was talking, but it was obvious to Frank that he was waiting for the precise moment to get to what he really wanted to talk about. "Frank, you have been very lucky in your brief career. You have gotten away with some stuff that others would have been fired for or possibly indicted. It seems like you could fall down a shit hole and come out smelling like roses. You treat your men like dirt. You are nasty as hell to the black detectives in the unit. You have a lack of respect for most of your supervisors. You have a reputation with the command staff of the department as someone who is a know it all. I wanted to bring you in here today to let you know that until the colonel tells me that I do not have this homicide job permanently, I will be watching you very closely. If you screw up, I will not hesitate to have you moved back to patrol. I know you don't believe me Frank, but I have a lot of friends in the command staff. Some of them have worked for me over the years and they owe me big time. I will not tolerate your shenanigans any longer.

I also want to let you know that I talked to the chief of the Carroll County Police Department this morning. He is very concerned that we are not cooperating with his detectives. He told me that they know that someone in this unit got a record check on their murder victim just days before he was shot. He also knows that Nick Giango dated the woman that their murder victim was seeing at one time. They got her name off the cell phone of the murder victim. He also knew that the same woman was murdered in Ocean City recently. He told me this morning that if Nick did not cooperate soon and give a detailed statement, he was going to have him summonsed to the grand jury. I told him that we would cooperate with him. I also told him that I would order Nick to go up there and give a statement. I'm not sure what they have, but we will cooperate. Frank, if you two know anything about that murder, you have an obligation to cooperate. If Nick thinks he needs a lawyer and does not cooperate, I will have to report that up my chain of command. I'm sure the legal department would then get involved."

Frank was squirming around in his chair. He was listening intently. He was thinking ahead as he usually did. So far the lieutenant had not really said anything that had not already been talked about. Frank knew that it was going to be inevitable that Nick would have to give a statement. The only connection back to the Homicide Unit would be getting the record check on the murder victim. Frank was thinking that if only he had not done the record check, things would be a little better.

Frank waited for the lieutenant to stop talking. "Lieutenant, I'm not going to address all the things you said about me. I would however like to give my opinion on Nick giving them a statement. Nick dated a girl name Janet Steele. They were very serious about each other. She told Nick that she needed some time away from him. He found out that she was seeing this guy, Paul Philbin. He told me about it and I told him not to worry. I told him that if she really cared for him, she would be back. He took it really hard. They eventually did get back together and worked things out. I think they were talking about getting married. They went on a trip to Ocean City. She was murdered and raped one day in their condo. Nick has not yet recovered from that horrible tragedy. As far as someone in this unit getting a record check on Philbin, I don't know anything about it. I'm not pointing the blame—maybe Nick wanted to find out who the guy was and where he lived. As far as knowing anything about that murder, I have no knowledge. I'm sure that Nick doesn't know anything either. I do know that the Ocean City police have cleared their case on the murder of Janet. They feel that some guy from up this way killed her. I don't know anything about that case, except for what Nick has told me."

Valentino listened to Frank and shook his head on occasion. When Frank stopped talking, Valentino told him that he would have to tell Nick to get in touch with the Carroll County detectives and make arrangements to give a statement. Frank started to leave the office. Valentino stood up. He told Frank that he better be real careful in the future. "You are walking a fine line with me. I want to again make things perfectly clear between us. I know you don't like me and the feeling is mutual. I'm in charge of this unit until I'm told different. I know you think you have a lot of friends in the department, but you are losing them because of your stupid acts. I will have no problem having you transferred out of this unit if things don't improve. It's about time you knocked off the attitude that you are better than the rest of us. We work as a team in this unit and you need to get on board if you want to stay."

Frank had no choice but to tell the lieutenant that he was on board. He walked out the door and headed back to his office. "What a crock of shit that fat bastard is. He'll be out of this unit before I will. The bosses think more of me than they do of him. If I didn't feel they would fire me, I would have knocked him on his fat ass right there in his office."

Frank locked the door to his office. He decided to call the Carroll County Homicide Unit and talk to the investigators. He figured that he could talk to them and see what they had before Nick agreed to give them a statement. He dialed the number and was thinking maybe I should just drive up there and talk to them in person. He decided against driving up and continued dialing the number. He got the secretary and asked for the investigators working on the Paul Philbin murder. She asked him for his name and told him to hold on.

"Hello, this is Sergeant Roger Neely, can I help you?"

"Yeah, this is Sergeant Favasi with the Baltimore City Homicide Unit. I was calling to talk about your request to take a statement from one of my men about a murder you are working on."

"Yeah, we want to take a statement from Nick Giango. You can have him give me a call and we can make the arrangements. It's important that he contact us as soon as possible."

"Can I ask what this is all about? I feel a little funny telling my man to give you guys a statement about a murder. Can't you just talk to him on the phone? We are all cops and should be able to talk freely. I'm actually against him giving a formal statement without first knowing at least what this is about."

Frank figured he would push the inquiry as far as he could. Maybe he could get some information on the phone.

"Sergeant Favasi, I can understand your concern. I also would assume that as a homicide supervisor you would agree that the purpose of a statement is to find out information that someone might have. We are not accusing him of anything. We merely want to talk to him about any contact he may have had with our victim. We know that he dated Janet

Steele. We also know that our victim was seeing Miss Steele on occasion. We obtained her name from the victim's cell phone. We talked to her family and they told us about Detective Giango. To be very honest with you and as one supervisor to another, we don't have anything on this murder. We are following up on all the leads we have. We need to talk to Detective Giango. We need to do it in our office and not on the phone. I really can't go into much more than what I have already told you."

Frank knew that he had pushed the envelope as far as possible. He found out as much as he was going to get from the sergeant. He wanted to ask more questions. He knew that if he did, he might say something he would regret. He told the sergeant that he would talk to Nick. He said that it would be entirely up to Nick if he wanted to give a statement. He said that the Baltimore Police Department would not force him to give the statement. Frank knew that was a lie...Valentino had already told him that he would order Nick to give the statement. Sergeant Neely thanked Frank for calling. Before they hung up he told Frank that to be very clear about the whole thing, he would have to summons Nick if he refused to give a statement. Frank told Neely that he had known Nick his whole life. He told him that Nick was not a vengeful guy and was not really upset that Janet was seeing another guy. Sergeant Neely stopped Frank and told him that it would all come out in the statement. He told Frank that he would treat Nick as a fellow police officer until such time as the circumstances might change.

After talking to Sergeant Neely, Frank called Nick. He reached him on the police radio and asked him to come in the office. Frank was going to discuss with Nick what he would tell Sergeant Neely. He kept thinking of the options. Sergeant Neely had already told him that they did not have anything on the murder. Was Neely playing the same game that Frank and others in the Homicide Unit played with suspects and witnesses? Get them in the office under the pretense that they had nothing and lay a bomb on them. Were they going to do the good-guy, bad-guy with Nick? Should he take a lawyer with him?

Nick came in Frank's office and asked what was up. Frank closed the door and asked him how he was doing. Nick stated that he was real busy with his cases. He said that he can't stop thinking about the guy that killed Janet in Ocean City. He told Frank that he has been running it around in his head. He said that he could not come up with any logical reason for the guy to drive to Ocean City and murder Janet.

Nick knew that Frank wanted to talk to him about something, but he was dying to ask Frank more about Kenny Jackson. To Nick, it just seemed like Frank wanted to dismiss any talk about Jackson. Nick decided that before Frank would talk, he would throw out a line to him and see what his response would be. "Frank, tell me more about Kenny Jackson? What was the arrest like? What occurred at the trial? Did you have any contact with him while he was in prison? Did you know when he got released? What is your theory on him being the one that raped and murdered Janet? Do you think it's a coincidence that you arrested him and he is the one who killed Janet? Frank, what are the odds of this happening?"

"Nick, you have rattled off several questions. Are you interrogating me or are you baffled that a no-good son of a bitch like Jackson could find his way to Ocean City and commit a murder. I agree that it's a hell of a chain of events that occurred. Yes, it's a real coincidence that he murdered someone that was close to my best friend. I can only tell you that when we arrested him for murder, we had a great case. Like a lot of cases in this city, we lost some of the witnesses. The jury found him guilty of manslaughter instead of first degree. When he was in prison, he did write to me. The letters were just gibberish; he could not even put a decent sentence together. He talked about stupid shit. He accused me of lying on the witness stand. He would then talk about the fact that he understood that I was only doing my job. He would then write that he had a bad childhood. He said that cops had harassed him his entire life. He talked about some of his drug charges and said that cops planted drugs on him. His letters were crazy. I just threw them all away. That was the only contact that I had with him. I did know that he was released. I was notified because as you know, when a murder suspect you put away is released, they notify the arresting officer. You asked me if I thought it was a coincidence that Jackson would be the one that would murder my friend's girlfriend. I would have to say that nothing surprises me anymore in this city. If you're thinking that it

Dick Ellwood

was some kind of revenge directed toward me, I would have to say that is crazy. If he wanted revenge on me, he would have come after me or my family."

Nick was listening and more importantly he was watching Frank's demeanor. After all these years of knowing Frank, he still realized that Frank was a master at lying and manipulation. Frank was convincing. Nick did not really see anything that would lead him to believe that Frank was blatantly lying. It all did not make any sense, but Nick knew also that he had to let up on Frank for now.

Nick was excited that he was going to drive down to Ocean City and look at the paper found on the crime scene. The last thing he wanted at this point was for Frank to find out about that piece of paper.

"Nick, let's get off of Jackson for now. I talked to Lieutenant Valentino and he has talked to the chief in Carroll County. He wants you to contact them and give a statement about your relationship with Janet. Valentino said that if you refuse, he will order you to give them a statement. Nick, I'm still against you giving a statement. I'm not sure how you can get around it—it's entirely up to you. I want you to be sure that you are totally comfortable with giving the statement."

"Yeah Frank, I'm sure you want me to do the right thing. Why don't you go give the damn statement? Just tell them that you killed the guy. I guess you could say that you just happened to be in the area. You thought the guy was going to break into his own home. You could say that as a dedicated police officer from Baltimore City, you took it upon yourself in a jurisdiction that is about thirty miles out of the city to take action. You could then tell them that the guy pulled out a baseball bat to protect himself from some crazed asshole that snuck up on him. You could say that you shot him and everything would be fine."

"Just hold on Nick—I understand how you feel. I'm not going to let you hold the bag. I just want to make sure that when you give the statement, you stick to a simple story."

"Hold the bag—what the hell does that means Frank? I can only say that I dated a girl named Janet. I can say that maybe this guy was seeing her during the period that we broke up. I can then say that Janet was raped and murdered in Ocean City. I guess I could say that the Ocean City cops have determined from prints and DNA that she was murdered by Kenny Jackson. I'm sure that they already know she was murdered in Ocean City. I'm also sure they have already talked to the detectives down there. If they are real smart, which I'm sure they are, they have had the time to check everything out. Hell, they only have about ten murders a year in that county. I would then assume that they would check the record of Jackson and find out that he was arrested for murder by my sergeant. My sergeant just happens to be the best friend of the guy they are taking a statement from. Frank, you started this conversation by saying that you did not want me to give a statement. Well, based on everything that I just said…I don't want to give a statement either. What is your master plan for this situation? You always seem to have a plan for everything."

Frank got up and told Nick that he needed to calm down. He told him that the walls were thin in the office. He told him that they needed to discuss exactly what to say when giving the statement.

Frank told Nick that he needed something to drink. Nick said that he could use something also and he told Frank that he would go get the drinks. Frank said that he wanted a Dr Pepper—Nick already knew that. Nick walked to the other side of the office and got the drinks. On the way back, he convinced himself that he had to calm down. He realized that he was in the middle of what now seemed like total chaos. He had too many things going on and needed to prioritize them. The statement was the most urgent. He knew that giving a statement relative to a murder investigation was as serious as it gets. He would listen to what Frank had to say. He knew this could be a life-changing experience. The final decision on giving the statement would be his and he would have to live with it.

CHAPTER 52

Frank took a few days off to be with Pam. Ever since he had moved in with her, things had been different. Prior to living together, they appeared to have the perfect relationship—at least that was Frank's take on it. She continued working at the Pirate's Den. They got together when Frank was not working murders. Frank had told her one night when he was drinking that he had it made. He told her that he could drink and screw around whenever he wanted to. He said that he would then go over to the apartment and get laid anytime he wanted. Sometimes he said it jokingly, but over time it got to be a sore spot with Pam. She knew that the relationship was going downhill fast. She wanted to break up with Frank, but she was actually afraid of how he would handle it. Pam also enjoyed the fact that he paid most of the bills. She enjoyed working at the bar, but she knew that most of her income revolved around tips.

There had been times when Frank was drunk and accused her of sleeping with some of the patrons at the Pirate's Den. He could be about as nasty as anyone when he drank. She talked to him often about cutting back on the booze. The more she asked, it seemed like the more he drank. It was also very apparent that he would not confide in her like he had in the past. He would brush things off and tell her that she did not understand what he went through on a daily basis. There were also times when he got so mad that he would break up some of the furniture in the apartment. He had a temper that was fueled to the max by the drinking. He would sometimes go to the Pirate's Den and sit at a table in the rear of the bar. He would watch Pam tending bar. She was nervous when he did that. She didn't know when he would just go off. He had on occasion even asked guys in the bar if they ever slept with her. Most of the patrons in the bar knew Frank and put up with his bullshit. They knew about his temper and tried to avoid him. The temper, along with being a cop, kept most people away from him. Pam also knew that he had told some of the guys in the bar that if they wanted to get laid, he could get Pam to take care of them. When she first heard that, she laughed, but over time she knew it was his sick sense of humor. She asked him to stop saying it. He told her that she was nothing but a whore before she met him. What started out to be a great relationship between the two of them was now a raging war when they were together. There were many times when he came home drunk in the early hours of the morning. He would accuse her of messing around. They would argue and sometimes it got physical. It usually ended with Frank forcing her onto the bed and overpowering her to have sex with him. He would tell her how much he loved her. When his forced sex was satisfied, he would resume calling her a whore.

Frank made it a point to always leave the bar about fifteen minutes before closing time. He would usually be drunk by then. He would sit in his unmarked police car across from the bar and watch Pam leave. She refused to drive in the police car when Frank was drunk.

The neighborhood around the bar was not the greatest. When Pam left the bar and was not meeting Frank, she usually had someone walk her to her car. She always assumed that Frank would be close by watching. Sometimes he would just fall asleep and didn't even know she left the bar. She always told whoever walked her to her car to just leave when she got close. She knew that any outward signs of affection by anyone would set him off—if he was awake.

Friday night at the Pirate's Den was their busiest night. Pam had a great night with tips—she was excited. She hung back in the bar at closing time to have a drink with the owner and two longtime patrons. The owner, Clyde Wilmont, was in his seventies. He had owned the bar for about twenty years. He didn't come in the bar every night—usually on Friday and Saturdays. Pam was counting her tips and ready to leave. They always locked the front door after the last call was announced. Clyde would open the door to let customers out as they finished their drinks.

The last two customers were leaving the bar. A short time later, she heard Clyde say, "We're closed…what the fuck." When she looked toward the door she saw two men with hoods over their heads. It was dark in the bar but there was enough light from the street that she could make out the hooded men. She knew right away it was a robbery. Her first instinct was to pull the silent alarm that was next to the cash register. She changed her mind, knowing that any sudden movement would be seen by the intruders. Pam could observe that one of the men had Clyde by the throat and was walking him toward the rear of the bar.

She knew that Clyde had a bad heart. "Please don't hurt him. I'll give you whatever you want. Just take the money and leave us alone. Please, he has a bad heart—just take the damn money."

Neither of the two hooded men responded, they just mumbled something to each other. Clyde was pushed behind the bar. One of the men pointed toward the cash register and said, "Put it all in the bag." He threw a plastic bag at Pam. She fumbled with the bag. She could clearly see that both of them had guns. Pam was filling up the bag when her cell phone rang. Instead of ignoring it, she picked it up. The larger of the hooded men told her not to answer it. She told him that it was her daughter and she only had to tell her she would not be home. Pam could see on the cell screen that it was really Frank. She was surprised when the hooded guy said, "Answer it and that's all you say."

"Hi honey, I won't be home tonight. I will probably be spending the night with a friend."

The hooded man grabbed the phone from her and threw it in the sink. He did not know that the call had not ended. "Fill that bag up bitch or your friend here gets one in the head."

She deliberately talked loud. She was hoping that Frank was still on the cell phone. "Please don't hurt him. I will give you all the money. We won't even call the police when you leave. We don't know who you are, so please don't hurt us."

Pam filled the bag with whatever money was in the register. It did not seem to please the robbers. They told Pam and Clyde to put all their jewelry in the bag. Outside the bar, Frank sat in his car stunned at what he was hearing on the open cell phone. He had been drinking from a fifth of Johnnie Walker Red. He took a large swallow from the bottle. "Holy fuck—the joint's being robbed!"

Frank could have called in on his police radio, but he decided against it. He figured that if he called in that there was a robbery in progress, the whole damn police department would respond. He pulled his revolver out and made sure it was fully loaded. He also retrieved his second weapon from under the seat. He was parked about a half a block from the bar. He got out of the car and ran toward the bar. He took up a position behind Clyde's car that was parked just off to the right of the entrance to the bar. His plan was to take them down when they exited the bar. As he waited he could not believe that Pam did not pull the alarm. He was glad that she did have the presence of mind to answer the cell phone. Frank had his phone and could still hear some of the talking in the bar. He flipped the phone shut—he had heard enough to know what was happening.

The door to the bar opened. Frank did not know that Clyde and Pam had been locked in a walk-in freezer in the rear of the bar. The two black men had removed their hoods. Frank waited until they were clear of the door. He had a great angle and Clyde's car was good cover. The men stood in front of the bar and seemed to be folding their hoods. They were looking up and down the street. Frank could see the bag of money. He could also see the taller of the two holding a small gun to his side. He took a deep breath as he jumped out from behind the car. "Police, motherfucker—drop the gun!"

Frank did not wait for any guns to drop. He opened up on the two men. He had the element of surprise as he moved closer. The one with the gun went down with a thud after Frank's first burst from his revolver. The second guy was fumbling to get his gun from his waist. Frank fired again from his second revolver. This burst hit the guy in the leg. Frank saw him fall to the ground, screaming in pain. The first guy that was shot was lying motionless on the street. The second guy was attempting to crawl up the street with an obvious gunshot wound to his leg. The bag with the money was on the sidewalk and the wind was blowing some of the bills down the street. Frank could hear sirens in the background. He caught up with the crawler. "You think you are going to just crawl away dude? You were a fuckin big shot a few minutes ago and now you are squirming away like a wounded animal. Well, I hate to see wounded animals. I like to take them out of their misery. You ready asshole for some justice—blue justice. I love to eliminate people like you. You make my job so much fun when I get to do things like this. Is there anything you want to say before I end your sorry fuckin life?"

"Fuck you cop—that's what I got to say!"

"No, my good man—you and all the other no-good bastards that have not yet met their fate at the hands of Charm City's finest. Now, let me just put this gun that you dropped back in your hand before I waste your sorry ass. Oh, in case you're wondering, I did take the bullets out."

Frank waited until he could hear the sirens were getting closer. He moved back a couple of feet and fired three rounds into the guy on the ground. As the first of the responding police cars were pulling up, Frank spit on the guy. "Happy trails motherfucker; I hope you meet up with your partner on the dark side."

Frank told the first officer on the scene who he was. He told them to go in the bar and find the owner and Pam. Frank stayed outside and gave a report to another officer. It was perfect as far as he was concerned. It was just another exciting night. The best part of the whole incident was that he could make up any story he wanted. The two hooded dudes took their shot and tried to rob the bar—they don't have a story. They got the money and put the fear of God in Clyde and Pam. They thought it would be just another robbery—an easy night's work.

Frank gloated in the spotlight as more officers arrived on the scene. When they got the story and looked over at the two dead guys, there were high-fives all around. For the newer cops that arrived on the scene, it was thrilling to hear Frank go over the story. For the older cops, it was just another incident where Sergeant Favasi added notches to his gun.

The senior cops were all too familiar with the escapades of the infamous Sergeant Frank Favasi.

Pam came running out of the bar and hugged Frank. "Frank, are you all right? I can't believe that you were on the phone. I didn't think they would ever leave—they wanted more money and we didn't have any. I don't know what would have happened if you didn't call me. We could have been in that freezer all night. Frank, please just take me home and be with me. I'm still shaking. I won't ever forget this night."

Frank kissed Pam and told her to just sit in the bar for a few minutes. He said he wanted to talk to the night duty officer and make sure everything was okay. Frank talked to Major Bobby Batson, the night commander. Frank knew Major Batson—they had done some drinking together in the past.

"Frank, are you all right? I think I will send all the troops back to their post—everything seems to be under control here. Frank, it looks like it went picture-perfect. Two guys hold up a bar and super cop Frank Favasi is on the scene and everything is copasetic—or should I say that everything is SNAFU... (Situation normal—all fucked up). I have to be honest with you, Frank. Whenever you get involved with something, it's always larger than life. As far as I'm concerned, they need to set you lose in this fucked-up city. Charm City would be a safer place with Sergeant Favasi on the prowl."

Frank was gloating in the spotlight. Major Batson had just added the frosting to a delicious cake. Frank and Batson were just kicking stories around about the old days when they would go bar hopping together. Most of the cops had left the scene. The bodies were picked up by the very busy ME's office. The crowd that had gathered early in the morning to see what was happening had gone. It was Frank and Major Batson just standing there laughing their asses off. You would have never known that two guys were just gunned down. They were two guys who chose to put on hoods and try for some easy money. Two guys that before they met Sergeant Favasi thought that they could push their weight around and terrorize anyone they wanted to. Two guys that probably left their homes and figured they would return a little richer. Two guys that in a few days after the family mourn will be portrayed as wonderful and loving human beings. Two guys that departed this crazy city at the hands of one nasty son of a bitch, Sergeant Frank Favasi.

Frank went in the bar after Major Batson went back to being the night duty officer for the city. Pam and Clyde were sitting in the dark and empty bar. Both were still very upset over the ordeal they had been through. Clyde was drinking Crown Royal whiskey straight. Pam commented that she had not seen Clyde drink for years. She actually had known that he was an alcoholic years ago. This was no time to ask why he was drinking—the answer was obvious. Pam was drinking something that had a little umbrella in it. Frank always called them sissy drinks. He walked behind the bar and asked Clyde if he could make a drink.

"Frank, you can make anything you want. You can have anything you want. You saved my life and Pam's also. I will never bitch about you again as long as I live. You gave those two bastards just what they deserved. I have never been so scared in my entire life. Maybe it's time I retired and went off in the sunset to some old age home."

Frank made a drink, a very strong drink. He sat at the table with Clyde and Pam. He put his feet up on an adjoining chair and let out a big sigh. He downed the drink and Pam went to make him another.

"Clyde, don't let these assholes force you to close your business. That's what they want. They figure they can just run rampant in this city and get away with whatever they want. Just be a little smarter in the future. Maybe you need to hire some big dude to be here late at night. Make sure he has a gun. He can help close the joint. He can also make sure you and your employees get to their cars. Clyde, you need to out think these cretins—we are smarter than they are. They roam our neighborhoods just looking for people to prey on. They are like animals waiting for another animal to die so they can eat the carcass. Those two assholes that robbed you tonight are the lowest scum of the earth. Do you really think anyone will miss those bastards? Maybe somebody claiming to be their mother will try to sue the city. They will be on TV tomorrow crying and saying what great boys they were. They will claim police brutality and some shyster lawyer will take the case. If they really push it, the city will fold and give them a couple thousand dollars. It's all a game with those people. We need to be strong. We need cops on the street that will not take any shit from them. Too many cops are getting hurt in this city. Cops need to take control and gain back the streets. I do my part, but we need all the cops to be pissed off and stand their ground."

"Frank, a few years ago I would have told you that you are full of shit. I have changed my mind. I agree with everything you said. Decent people in this city trying to make an honest living don't have a chance."

Pam was listening—she had heard most of this from Frank in the past. She used to tell him that he was cynical and even accused him of being a racist. At this moment, sitting in a dark closed bar drinking to calm her nerves, she had nothing to rebut Frank's theory. All she wanted to do was go home with Frank. He might be the biggest asshole in the world at times, but right now, he was her hero.

CHAPTER 53

The ride up to meet the Carroll County detectives was a pleasant and very scenic ride. Although it was only about thirty-five miles up to their headquarters, it gave Nick time to think. It also gave him some time to reflect on his life. He took the back way through Worthington Valley. He looked at the very expensive homes. He thought about what it would have been like living in a nice house with Janet. Even if he could not afford those houses, it was nice to dream. He could imagine their kids running around on the expansive property.

He stopped at a Royal Farms store to get a coffee and a doughnut. He was hungry—he was also trying to control the butterflies in his stomach. A coffee and doughnut would hold him over until lunch. He smiled when he thought about lunch. I might not be getting lunch if they decide to charge me with some crime—my lunch might be slid under the bars.

On the drive up, it also gave him time to go over what he would tell the investigators. He had to make it simple and keep his attention on the questions. He was smart enough to know if they were fishing or if they actually knew something. As he drove closer to the Carroll County Police Building, it started to hit him that he really didn't do anything. Why in the hell am I always looking out for Frank? I don't know where this whole thing is going to go. I know it won't go away. These guys are cops and have the same job that I have—they need to solve a murder.

Nick arrived and parked his car in a police only parking spot. He went in the main entrance instead of the entrance marked for police only. He approached the front desk and the sergeant behind the desk said, "You must be Detective Giango, we've been expecting you. Let me call Sergeant Neely."

Sergeant Neely came out from a door off to the side of the desk sergeant's area. He was with another man who was carrying a large stack of papers. Nick was thinking that if I could only look through those papers, before they take my statement. Too bad that's not the way it works and he knew it.

"Hello, I'm Sergeant Roger Neely and this is Detective Mark Holland. Thanks for driving up from the city to give us a statement. Detective Holland is the lead investigator on the case. He will be taking your statement and I'll sit in with him. Can I get you something to drink before we get started?"

"No thanks—let's just get on with it."

Sergeant Neely motioned for Nick to follow him. They went in a small interrogation room. Nick was familiar with the procedure—small room, no fixtures on the walls, small table, and three chairs. Nick had taken many statements in the past, but this was different. He now knew the feeling that people had when he would be taking their statements. The unknown is a little unsettling, especially when you are on the answering end of the statement.

Sergeant Neely and Detective Holland sat on one side of the table. Nick sat on the other side. Holland was positioning his papers. He was covering up some of the papers—probably the more important ones. That's the way it's done and Nick knew exactly what Holland was doing. Nick grinned while Holland was arranging the paperwork. The three of them were uncomfortable. Interviewing a police officer about a murder was out of the ordinary. Nick tried to look relaxed, but his stomach was turning. He could also feel beads of sweat forming on his neck. Holland appeared to be a neat freak of some kind as he moved papers in a very annoying fashion. It was as if he was preparing for a magic show. He rolled up his shirt sleeves, he positioned his legal pad, he placed a highlighter next to the legal pad, he put the tape recorder in the middle of the table, he moved his chair a few times, and he cracked his knuckles. Even Sergeant Neely appeared a little perturbed at all the magic moves. Finally, Holland squared back his shoulders, smiled at Nick, flipped on the tape recorder, and said, "Testing one, two, three, and four." Nick was thinking that if this was a Saturday Night Live episode, he would reach over, smack Holland, and say—"Take the damn statement asshole." But this was not a TV show, it was real. The magic show was about to begin.

Nick was asked all the personal questions before Holland even got to the main reason for the statement. He knew the process—you ask all the personal questions to relax the subject. You then proceed to get into what is called the meat of the statement. You would close with going over some of the more important questions to see if anything changed. You would then end the statement asking the subject if there is anything else they want to say.

Nick did seem a little more relaxed after answering all the personal questions. When he knew Holland was beginning the meat of the statement, he asked if he could take some notes. The questioning actually started off with Holland making a general statement. "Mr. Giango, we do appreciate you coming in today to give a statement. I'm sure you know that we are investigating the murder of Paul Philbin. He was murdered in front of his home at 5527 Talbot Road, here in Carroll County. He was shot as he was exiting his vehicle to confront a person while he was in his driveway. He later died at the hospital. He actually died before he reached the hospital. He could not give any information to our officers. I'm sure you must have read about this in the paper. We are following several leads in this murder investigation. I hope you understand as a homicide investigator yourself, we need to check everything out. We have very little physical evidence from the scene. The victim's wife was home at the time but she only heard the shots that were fired. We have asked you to give a statement because we found out that you were dating a female that the victim was also seeing."

Nick was paying strict attention. He nodded on occasion when he agreed with what Holland was saying. Sergeant Neely was just staring at Nick. The staring made Nick a little uncomfortable. Neely was watching

Nick's body movement. Most detectives received training in kinesics—the study of the movements of certain parts of the body. It dealt with how a person sat, how you positioned your arms, how you reacted to questions, facial expressions, and any other movements of the body that would seem out of the ordinary. Nick started to doodle on his legal pad. He caught himself and stopped. The last thing he needed was for them to think he was nervous. He pushed the paper to the side and focused on Holland.

Holland went over several things with Nick. He asked him where he grew up, where he went to school, if he was ever married, where he lived, and other routine personal questions. Holland got to the part about dating Janet Steele. Nick was prepared and glad that Holland was finally moving to the meat of the statement.

Nick pulled his legal pad back in front of him. He told Holland that he would be jotting down some things on the pad to make sure he has the dates correct. He started off by telling Holland that he did not know Mr. Philbin. He told him that he and Janet had been dating for at least a couple of years. He said that it was a casual relationship at first and escalated as time went on. He said that Janet told him that she wanted to spend some time away from him. He said he was surprised when that happened because things were going great at that time. Nick told Holland that without going into a lot of mundane details—he saw Janet with a guy. He said that he was very upset that she would be seeing someone so soon after she said that she needed some time apart. He said that he did not approach Janet about the guy. He said that he checked the tag number of the vehicle and found out who it was listed to. As soon as Nick said that, he realized that he had just made a split-second decision to say that he got the record check on Philbin. Nick ended by saying that he never talked to Janet about Philbin and he knew nothing about the murder until he read about it in the paper.

Holland did not follow up immediately about Nick saying he checked out the tag number. He proceeded with some short rapid-fire questions that Nick answered quickly. Did you know Philbin? Do you know how Janet met him? Did you ever go near his home? Have you ever talked to Philbin? Do you know who killed him? Nick answered no to all the short questions. Holland leaned back in his chair and smiled. "Nick, is it okay if I call you Nick?"

"You can call me Nick if you want."

Nick knew this tactic also—you are very formal in the beginning of the statement and toward the end you try to cozy up to the subject. He played along with Holland. He was actually looking at it as a contest between the two of them. Who was going to outsmart the other?

"Nick, do you know anything about the murder of Paul Philbin?"

"No, I only know what I have read in the paper and what you have told me today."

"Nick, don't be offended by this question. Did you kill Mr. Philbin?"

"I'm not offended because I know you have a job to do. I did not kill Mr. Philbin."

"Nick, do you have any knowledge about who killed Mr. Philbin?"

"No, I do not."

Holland smiled at Nick. He then made the formal remarks on the recorder that the statement was ending. He recorded the date and time and turned off the recorder. Holland reached over to shake hands with Nick. He thanked him for taking the time to come in and talk to him. Sergeant Neely also thanked Nick for giving the statement. Nick pulled his chair back from the table and was about to stand. Holland said, "Nick, can I ask you something off the record?"

"Well, I know that nothing is off the record, but go ahead with the question."

"We have heard a lot about your sergeant. I think his name is Frank Favasi—is that correct?"

"Yes, he is my sergeant."

Nick was not surprised that they were asking about Frank—after all, he is in the news all the time. So why ask the question off the record? If they wanted to discuss my relationship with Frank, they should have asked the question on the record. Nick told Holland that he did not feel comfortable talking about his sergeant in such a formal setting. Sergeant Neely agreed and thanked Nick again for coming in. Nick started toward the door when Holland popped another question at him. "Nick, your sergeant is a real cowboy, isn't he?"

"Listen Holland, I came in and gave you a statement. I'm not sure where you are trying to take this with that kind of question. What the hell does that mean?"

"What I mean Nick is that he seems to be a one-man hit squad. He's always in the paper or on the news for shooting someone. I have some friends in your department. They think the guy is an accident waiting to happen. I was just wondering what you think about all the shootings and the trouble he seems to get into?"

Nick was getting pissed off and made a move toward Holland. Sergeant Neely stepped in and told Holland that he was getting a little out of line. He thanked Nick one more time and told him that they would be in touch if they needed any additional information.

Nick quickly left the building. He got in his car and was fuming. Who the hell does that half-assed investigator think he is? Nick started to pull out of the parking lot. He realized that he had silenced his phone for the statement. He flipped the phone back on and saw that he had messages waiting. He went through the messages and two of them were from Frank. He listened to the messages and both were asking Nick to call him as soon as he left Carroll County.

Nick was hungry. He pulled into the first fast food joint he saw. He did not want to go in, so he went through the drive-thru line. The clown spoke, "Welcome to McDonalds...can I take your order?" He got his food and pulled his car to the rear of the McDonald's lot. He devoured his hamburger and fries. He dialed Frank's cell phone. He did not want to talk on the office phone. Frank answered and without saying hello, he said, "Well, how did it go?"

"Frank, I think it went okay. I really didn't like the investigator who took the statement. He got a little weird at the end when I was leaving. He asked about you."

"What the hell did he want to know about me?"

"Frank, it went okay. I just finished my lunch. Can we talk when I get back to the office?"

"I don't think that we should talk in the office. Meet me in Clifton Park in about an hour—you know the spot."

Nick finished what was left of the fries. He was not a big fan of fast food. He had been trying to eat healthy, but it's tough when you are always on the go.

He was driving back to the city and took the same route through Worthington Valley. He passed one of the horse farms that the valley was known for. It was beautiful seeing the horses in the fields just eating all the grass they could. He pulled over. He sat there and admired the beauty of the horses and the land. He pushed the seat back as far as it would go. He felt relaxed. He was thinking about meeting Frank. What would Frank want to do next? It's always what Frank wants to do next. It's as if I have no brain. I go along with Frank and that's the way it has been for most of my life. Frank gets us in trouble and I have to go along with it. I really need to be my own person for once in my life. I have to realize that Frank is dragging me down with him. In the past I would have done anything for Frank—it has to change. There is too much bullshit going on. I need to make some decisions that are in my best interest. We have been a team for a long time. I need to start to think about myself and my future.

CHAPTER 54

The Chesapeake Bay Bridge is an awesome structure. Nick always admired it every time he crossed it on his way to Ocean City. His thoughts were always the same—how in the hell did they build this monstrosity? Nick admired the bridge, but it was not always that way. When he was young, he was scared of the bridge. He remembers being with his parents in their car as they approached the bridge on the way to Ocean City. He would get on the floor in the rear of the car until they said they were across the bridge. In more recent years as an adult, he had conquered his fear of the bridge. The bridge was known simply to everyone heading to the Eastern Shore of Maryland as the Bay Bridge. The bridge connected the Baltimore-Washington metropolitan area with Ocean City and all points on the Eastern Shore of Maryland. Nick's approach to calming his fears and safely crossing the bridge was to stay in the right lane, roll up the windows, turn the radio up loud, and get a death grip on the steering wheel. He also taught himself to breathe as he approached the very top of the four mile long bridge. He would always experience his heart racing when he reached the highest point. The controlled breathing helped. He would calm down a little when he could see the shoreline on the other side.

Nick had called Sergeant Pantalone and told him he was driving down to discuss the identification of the suspect in Janet's murder. He also wanted to check out the piece of paper found on the murder scene—the paper that had Frank's name, phone number, and the address of the condo. The drive usually took about three hours. Nick, in the past, had always stopped in Easton to get something to eat or get gas. On this trip down, he could not bring himself to stop in Easton—too many bad memories. He stopped in Cambridge instead.

He thought about the last ride down to the ocean with Janet. They were laughing and having a great time on the ride. He had brought along a trivia game. He loved it when Janet would ask him questions. If he did not know the answer, he would make one up. He was good with the sports questions—she tried to avoid them and ask about history. She was as bubbly as he had ever seen her. She was happy. The talk on the way down was about their future. They talked about where they would live and their future wedding plans. Nick remembered every moment of that day. It was a memory that he cherished and wanted to hold onto forever.

Nick pulled into the Ocean City Police parking lot. He was early for his appointment. He sat in the car for a few minutes and then decided to go in. The suspense about the piece of paper was killing him. He sat in the lobby and waited for Sergeant Pantalone. He had not said anything to Frank about driving down to Ocean City. He took the day off and said he had some personal things to take care of. Frank was so controlling that he usually would ask what you were doing on your day off. He did not ask Nick about this day off; he probably had a lot on his mind. Nick looked at his watch and the desk sergeant picked up on it. The desk sergeant came around from the desk. "Sergeant Pantalone will be right with you, detective."

Sergeant Pantalone came out from a secured private door. Nick was surprised at how tall he was. He must have played basketball. Nick shook hands with Pantalone and from the size of his hand, he was sure he played. They went to the back of the building. Pantalone directed Nick into a small room where another person was already sitting. "Nick, this is Pete Cummings…he's our top forensic expert. He worked on the case with us."

"I appreciate you taking time to talk to me. I also want to thank you all for the great work you did in identifying the guy who killed Janet. I hope I was not a bother to you guys. I know I made a lot of calls down here while you were working the investigation."

Sergeant Pantalone offered Nick a seat and asked if he wanted a drink. Nick said he was fine. He told Pantalone that he didn't want to take up much of their time. He asked if he could see the paper found at the scene. He knew he was pushing a little bit. He wanted to see that paper and then they could talk. Nick noticed that Pantalone looked at Cummings with a half-smirk and a half-smile. He saw that they had a lot of paperwork. He wanted to ask again to see the piece of paper. He could sense that they would show it when they were ready.

Sergeant Pantalone told Nick that he was really sorry about the death of Janet. He told him that a lot of work went into the investigation. He said that the forensics was very important in identifying Jackson. Sergeant Pantalone told Nick that he had a few concerns that he wanted to discuss before he showed him the piece of paper.

"Nick, I have been talking to your lieutenant. I have talked with Lieutenant Valentino several times during our investigation. He has been very helpful to us. Nick, your sergeant seems to be a real character. I know that he is not only your sergeant, but a lifelong friend. I actually know a lot about your relationship. I don't want to sound like we have been snooping around on you. I hope you understand that in a murder investigation everything and everyone is fair game. When we saw the name of your sergeant on that piece of paper, we needed to check it out. In a minute, I will show you that paper. We were not so much concerned about Jackson having Sergeant Favasi's name on a piece of paper. We were not even concerned about having his cell phone number. We were however, very concerned that the address for the condo was on that paper. Nick, that paper somehow must have fallen out of Jackson's pocket while he was viciously murdering Janet. The blood on the paper is Janet's. It means that the piece of paper came there that day with Jackson. I want Pete to take over and explain some of the forensics."

Nick did not say anything. He knew about the paper having Frank's phone number and the address of the condo. Somehow hearing it again from Pantalone in a formal setting really hit home. He had also thought that it was very disturbing that the address of the condo was on the paper. He was hoping that Pantalone did not think that he was covering up anything. It's incredible that a cold-blooded murderer like Jackson would make that kind of mistake. It reminded Nick of a case he handled when a guy held up a drug store and on the way out, he dropped his wallet.

"Hi Nick, I'm Pete Cummings. I can only reiterate what Sergeant Pantalone already told you. My team worked for days on that crime scene. We felt like it was personal when we found out Janet was dating a police officer. Basically what we have are prints that have now definitely matched up with Jackson. We have DNA from the scene that is also a match with Jackson. We actually have enough to go to court and win a murder conviction—that's if Jackson was still alive. As far as the piece of paper, I can tell you that we almost overlooked it. We did recover it and it has Janet's blood on the paper. I will let Sergeant Pantalone take over from here."

Sergeant Pantalone reached over and pulled a red folder from the stack near Cummings. He went through some papers and pulled out a piece of plastic. Nick could see that there was a white piece of paper inside the plastic. He could also see clearly that there was blood on the paper—Janet's blood. Pantalone pulled the paper out from the plastic casing. He told Nick that he wanted him to look it over. He asked Nick not to handle it too much—just look it over. He slid the paper over in front of Nick. He got up and walked around the table and was looking over Nick's shoulder. Cummings leaned forward in his chair as if they were about to watch someone identify the Hope Diamond. Nick also leaned forward a little and was directly over the paper.

"Sarge, that's Frank's handwriting."

"Are you absolutely sure that's Sergeant Frank Favasi's handwriting?"

Nick stared intently again at the paper. "Sarge, I have known Frank for my entire life. I have no doubt whatsoever that is his handwriting."

Pantalone moved back around to his chair. He carefully put the paper back in the plastic case. He put the case back in the red folder. He looked at Nick and just shook his head. He told Nick that he would need a statement concerning his positive identification of the handwriting on the piece of paper. Pantalone asked Cummings if he would leave him and Nick alone for a while. Cummings got up to leave the room and told Nick that it was a pleasure meeting him. He said that he wished it would have been under better circumstances.

Pantalone told Nick that he needed to go over some information that he had received. He told Nick that the information he was going to tell him should remain confidential. He told Nick that he had been working with Lieutenant Valentino and a few others from the Baltimore Police Department. Nick was surprised and wanted to interrupt and ask who they were. He decided that Pantalone so far had been on the up and up with him, so he would just listen. Pantalone told him that he had been to Baltimore and met with Valentino. He said he also met with some members of the Internal Investigation Division (IID). He told Nick that when he gets back to Baltimore, he will probably be called into Valentino's office to discuss things a little more. Pantalone told Nick that he wanted to be perfectly honest with him and not pull any punches. He told him that Frank was in some serious trouble on many different fronts. He asked Nick if he needed anything to drink. Nick asked if he could just get some water. Pantalone told Nick that he would have Cummings get the water. He told him that he wanted to call Valentino and get him on the speaker phone. Pantalone said that he wanted to make sure he and Valentino were on the same page. Cummings came in with two bottles of water. Pantalone asked him to stay.

Pantalone dialed the phone without even looking for the number. Nick picked up on this and assumed that he had talked to Valentino on enough occasions that he knew the number. Pantalone put the phone on speaker. It rang a few times and then Valentino answered. Pantalone told Valentino that he was sitting in an office with Detective Nick Giango. Valentino responded and without saying hello or anything else, he told Nick that he was doing the right thing. He told Nick that if he cooperates, he will be just fine. Nick spoke up and asked the lieutenant what he meant by cooperating. The lieutenant asked Pantalone if had told Nick about the task force. Pantalone moved toward the speaker part of the phone. "Lieutenant, I have told Nick that there is an investigation going on concerning Sergeant

Favasi. I have not gone into the task force part of the investigation. I have not really covered what you and I have talked about."

Valentino was quiet on the other end for a minute. You could hear him clear his throat, "Nick, we have formed a task force and the subject of the investigation is Sergeant Favasi. I will have to order you not to discuss this with anyone, especially Frank. We will be having a meeting in a few days and you will learn more at that time. We have found out a lot about what has been going on with Frank in the past. I'm sure Sergeant Pantalone has told you that we think Frank contracted Jackson to kill Janet. I know that's a god-awful thing Nick, but everything points in that direction. Nick, I know you want to do the right thing. I'm again telling you not to discuss this with anyone. I will let you know when the meeting is and then you will find out more."

Nick slumped back in his chair. He was shaking his head as he heard Valentino telling Pantalone that he would be in touch with him soon. Valentino told Pantalone that the meeting of the task force would be in Baltimore. Pantalone hung up the speaker phone. "Nick, I didn't know he was going to talk about the task force. I was going to tell you before you left. I just wanted to make sure Valentino talked with you. I know you have a lot on your mind right now. I would only encourage and advise you to cooperate. I don't think you are in any serious trouble. I do know that Sergeant Favasi is probably going to be indicted. I don't know when—I guess we will all find out when the task force meets. I'm sorry that it now appears that your best friend hired Jackson to murder Janet. I can't imagine what you're thinking right now. Don't do anything that you will regret. I'm available if you need to talk to someone. Let it all play out Nick. Favasi has made a lot of mistakes. I don't know him like you do, but he appears to be a person who won't stop at anything to protect his image. He didn't play by the rules, Nick. He's a rogue cop and needs to be stopped."

On the ride back, Nick was thinking that he had not quite been so honest with Pantalone. He could have opened up and told him all about Frank. He was shaking as he drove the vehicle toward the bridge for the trip back to Baltimore. As he approached the highest point of the bridge, he realized he had not shut the windows, he had not turned the radio up, and he didn't have the death grip on the steering wheel. What a way of breaking the curse of the bridge— finding out that your best friend had your girlfriend murdered.

When he was at the very top of the bridge, he stopped the vehicle. Nick was crying as he got out of the vehicle. The bridge was crowded and the horns were blasting. He walked to the rail. Several people got out of their cars and were hollering at Nick not to jump. Nick held onto the rail oblivious of the chilly choppy waters below. He put one foot on the second wire of the rail. A man approached and was very careful not to excite Nick. "Sir, I'm not sure what your problem is. Please move away from that rail."

Nick looked at the man. He turned back and stared out at the Chesapeake Bay. He put a fist in the chilly air and shouted as loud as he could. "Fuck you Frank Favasi—I owe it to Janet to make sure you rot in hell!"

Nick stepped back from the rail. He felt a calm come over him. He was approached by two men who asked if they could take him to the hospital. Nick pulled out his badge and held it up. "Thank you gentlemen—I'm a police officer. I was just getting a feel for what it would be like to jump off the Chesapeake Bay Bridge."

Nick got in his car. He rolled up the windows, turned up the radio as loud as he could, started to breathe, put the death grip on the steering wheel, and drove toward Baltimore.

Chapter 55

The Internal Investigation Division offices were located in the basement of the World Trade Center in downtown Baltimore. The reason they were not in the main police headquarters building was to keep the unit away from everyday police activity. The investigators that worked in the Internal Investigation Division were not well liked by the rank and file of the police department. Their job was to investigate cops. When you took the assignment in IID you were a marked man for the rest of your career. Getting into IID was voluntary. Once accepted, you were constantly being checked out by supervisors in the unit. It was like having a top-secret clearance. Although you were supposed to have the highest integrity and honesty possible, some got in the unit because they just didn't like working the street. The common theme throughout the police department was—don't talk to or even associate with anyone in IID. The only way out of the unit once you were there was to either get promoted or screw up. With either one, if you left the unit, no one would talk to you. If cops were talking or just standing around when an IID member came by, they would stop what they were doing. It was common to hear them referred to as rats. The age old adage of the thin blue line was alive and well in Charm City.

The meeting at the IID office was well attended. The captain in charge of IID was Wendell Golden. Captain Golden was a black man who had risen through the ranks at a record pace. He was thirty-five years old. He had been on the job for twelve years. There was no doubt within the department that Golden would go very high and would probably be the police commissioner one day. He was somehow tied in with several black politicians in the city. He frequented city hall and made it known that he could get things done. He also made it known amongst the members in IID that he didn't care who the police officer was that was being investigated—he would go after anyone. He dressed meticulously. It would not be unusual to see him with a white suit, pink shirt, black tie, and very expensive alligator shoes. He was a well-built man and it was obvious that he worked out. If you would see him on the street and didn't know he was a captain in the police department, you might think he was a pimp. He was very friendly and would go out of his way to greet cops. Everyone was respectful to him because they either feared him or knew that sometime in the very near future he might be the police commissioner.

The room where the meeting was being held was not that big. It started to fill up quickly. Captain Golden came in the room and most stood up. He looked good in his light blue suit, dark blue shirt, striped red tie, and those good-looking black alligator shoes. Golden walked to a podium in the front of the crowded room. He looked out over the crowd and adjusted his tie. "Gentlemen, please have a seat. If we need more chairs, we will get them. If you wish to stand that's fine. I have asked my secretary to attend this meeting to record what is said. Before I start I would like to introduce some of the attendees at this meeting. My name is Wendell Golden; I'm the commanding officer of the Internal Investigation Unit. The police commissioner has asked me to preside over this very important meeting. As I acknowledge you, could you please stand so that others can see who you are. We have with us States Attorney Mark Cohen, Lieutenant Anthony Valentino, Sergeant Roger Neely from the Carroll County Police Department, Sergeant Vince Pantalone from the Ocean City Police Department, Lieutenant John Trader from the commissioner's office, Dennis Hall from the public information office, and there are a few investigators from my office."

As the introductions were being made, everyone nodded as that person stood. Captain Golden started to fumble through his papers. He said something to his secretary and then pulled a piece of paper from the folder. "Gentlemen, I have a detective in the other office who is going to join us in a minute—his name is Nick Giango. The reason that he is in the other office is so I can briefly tell you about him. He is a member of the Homicide Unit and works for Sergeant Frank Favasi. I know that most of you have been briefed about the investigation of Sergeant Favasi. Before I ask this fine detective to join us, I want to make some things clear to you. Detective Giango is cooperating with our investigation. He has agreed to testify against Favasi if necessary. The unique thing about this is that Giango works for Sergeant Favasi. He not only works for him, they grew up together. They have been the best of friends for their entire lives. I want everyone in this room to talk to and treat him with respect. He has made some mistakes through his affiliation and friendship with Favasi. He now realizes those mistakes and that is why he is cooperating with us. One other thing before I bring him into the room. His fiancée was murdered in Ocean City. We feel that Favasi was responsible for hiring the person that killed her. When he joins us, I will not be questioning him. I do want him in this room when I go over the results of our investigation on Sergeant Favasi. I have discussed with Giango that we are not out to get him—we are out to get Favasi. I have told him that his cooperation will go a long way in any decision that the commissioner makes about his future with the police department. I have also discussed this with State's Attorney Cohen. Some of what Giango did may be criminal, but his cooperation in this investigation will help him in the long run."

Captain Golden motioned to a detective in the rear and asked him to bring Giango in the room. Nick came in the room. He looked a little surprised at how many people were attending the meeting. He had been briefed by Golden and Valentino. They only told him it would be a meeting. They didn't say how many people would be there or use the term, task force.

Nick sat in a chair off to the right side of Captain Golden. He was really nervous. He had talked to Lieutenant Valentino and Golden about the meeting. He knew from the size of the group that this was very serious. He knew that the sole purpose of the meeting was to work out the details on how and when they would arrest Frank.

It was strange to hear everyone talking about Frank. In a different time, he would have jumped up and defended him. He sat and listened to a lot of discussion. He tried to listen intently but his thoughts were on Frank. Why would he go so far as to have Janet killed? Was there ever going to be any end to his madness? Would he ever realize that he could not solve all the problems in such a dangerous city as Baltimore? Would having Frank arrested and put away make the city any safer? Would it be better for the city that Frank is allowed to continue his reign of terror?

Nick caught himself drifting away from the purpose of the discussion. He realized that he needed to pay more attention. His career and for that matter, his future depended on his total cooperation with the task force. There could be no holding back of any information he had. It had to all come out. If he held anything back and they found out about it down the road he would be fired. He didn't even know if he would be allowed to keep his job after Frank's arrest.

Captain Golden passed out some documents to the task force. He told them that it included bullet points on what was known about Sergeant Favasi. He said that some of the information is spelled out in general terms. He said it would be in more detail prior to the indictments. He started to read from the document. "Gentlemen, let me start with what we know about Favasi. He was a good cop when he worked in the district. He had a lot of promise and had some good cases. He was promoted to sergeant and assigned to the Homicide Unit. It seems like when he got to the Homicide Unit, he took the burden upon himself of ridding the streets of Baltimore of what he referred to, as the bad guys. According to reliable sources within the department, he would go to any means to make sure the so-called bad guys would either be arrested or killed. We know that he has planted weapons on suspects that were shot by cops. We know that he always told his detectives that they should do whatever was necessary to protect patrol officers when they use deadly force. We also know that he had a complete disdain for the black detectives that worked in the Homicide Unit. Here are a few of the more serious things we know about Favasi. He will be indicted by the Carroll County Grand Jury for the murder of Paul Philbin. Detective Giango will be the key witness in that case. Mr. Philbin was shot as he returned home and was in his driveway. It's a long story, but Philbin was dating a woman that had also dated Detective Giango.

He will be charged as a co-conspirator in the murder of Janet Steele. She was murdered in Ocean City, Maryland. He will be indicted by the Worcester County Grand Jury. Janet Steele was dating Giango. When they briefly broke up, she dated Mr. Philbin. Favasi later hired Kenny Jackson to go down to Ocean City and murder Janet Stelle. She was not only savagely murdered—she was also raped. We know that Favasi was involved because a bloody piece of paper with his name, phone number, and the address of the condo were on the paper.

On this particular incident we feel that Favasi also murdered Kenny Jackson in Druid Hill Park in the city. Jackson was shot with a .38 caliber. We feel that we will be able to match the ballistics on that case showing that the bullets recovered from Jackson's body were fired from Favasi's weapon. On this case we got real lucky. The crime scene investigators that were on the scene that night recovered an empty can of Dr Pepper soda. The can was next to Jackson's body and the investigators saw fit to recover that can. We have now recovered a partial fingerprint off that can and it belongs to Favasi."

Captain Golden took a long drink from a water bottle. He told the group that he would only be a few more minutes. He looked over at Nick and asked him if was okay. Nick nodded that he was. Golden proceeded, "We also have a black man that has come forward with information on a shooting that occurred at Linard and Jefferson Street. The man was arrested on drug charges recently and told the detectives he had information on that shooting. He said that he saw Favasi shoot his partner. He said that they did have intentions to rob him, but Favasi got the jump on them. He said that he was on the ground with a gun to his head. He said that his partner came around the car and Favasi just shot him. The guy said that Favasi told him that he was giving him a break and let him run away as the sirens could be heard coming to the corner. He has identified Favasi from photos. He is currently in jail on drug charges and wants to testify against Favasi. He wants to get some consideration on his sentence. We will leave that up to the States Attorney.

Recently, Favasi was involved in a shooting outside the Pirate's Den bar. His girlfriend works at that bar. He was outside when two holdup men exited the bar. He shot both of the holdup men. He shot and killed one guy as he exited the bar. The second holdup man was wounded according to Favasi's report. Favasi said that the guy crawled up the street. He said that when he caught up to the one crawling away, the guy raised his gun and pointed it at him. Favasi said that is when he fired and killed the second holdup man. We have gone back over this entire shooting and Favasi's account of what happened. It appears that the gunman had apparently dropped his weapon. Favasi shot the guy while he was on the sidewalk. He made a couple of mistakes. He put the gun in the guy's right hand. Our investigators have determined that the guy was left-handed. Also, the gun that the guy had in his right hand did not have any bullets and had not been fired recently."

Captain Golden took a deep breath and told the group that he had covered a lot in a short period of time. "I have one more incident to talk about. This may be the most ruthless of all the acts committed by Sergeant Favasi. In East Baltimore, after Officer Meyers had been murdered, Favasi took it upon himself to execute a man. The man was Buster Mosley. He was wanted for shooting Officer Meyers. Mosley had exited the rear of his home after Favasi, Giango, and Detective Lenny Wilkins went there to arrest him. When confronted by Detective Lenny Wilkins in the rear of the home—Mosley shot and killed him. Detective Giango has reported to us that he saw Sergeant Favasi shoot Mosley. Favasi put a gun with no bullets in Mosley's hand and fired several shots into him—killing him instantly. Detective Giango witnessed that act. We probably all agree that Mosley certainly deserved to die. It should have been in the electric chair—not in an alley in East Baltimore.

Captain Golden told the group that all of what he said is being compiled into one document and will be shared with the various jurisdictions. He started to say the meeting was over. He said, "One more thing about the shooting in Carroll County. It was obviously a cold-blooded murder by Favasi. He had told Detective Giango that Mr. Philbin had come after him with a baseball bat. He told Giango that he had no choice but to shoot

Philbin. Investigation by our partners in Carroll County has determined that there was no baseball bat on the scene when the police arrived. So, he told his best friend about the murder, but he didn't tell him the truth."

Captain Golden told the group that they are not to discuss this investigation with anyone. He told them that we are dealing with a deranged man. He said that the task force would move swiftly to arrest Favasi. He told them that any information leaked out could put Detective Giango in grave danger. Golden thanked everyone for coming to the meeting. He said that they would break for lunch. He told Nick that he would like to meet with him privately and buy him lunch.

CHAPTER 56

Roll call was just starting when Nick walked into the office. Sergeant Favasi was conducting the roll call. Usually the lieutenant presided over roll call, but on occasion the sergeants handled it. Just seeing Frank standing there reading about crime in the city made it difficult for Nick to look at him. Nick knew that in the very near future, Frank would be arrested. He would most likely spend the rest of his life in prison. At the far end of the office, Nick could see Lieutenant Valentino. He purposely did not want to make any eye contact with him. After roll call, Frank asked his squad to hang back in the office for a very short meeting. The squad assembled in Frank's office. Nick stood in the back. He was still trying to avoid direct eye contact. Frank knew Nick like the back of his hand. If Nick would act in any way out of the ordinary, Frank would pick up on it.

The meeting lasted about ten minutes. Frank talked about the unsolved homicides that the squad had. He asked the guys to make every effort possible to clear the open murders. He thanked them for all their hard work. This was a little out of line for Frank's meetings. It was commonplace when Frank held a meeting that he would get very loud. He would usually single out someone in the squad for not clearing a case. Very seldom did he praise anyone for good work. This meeting was different from others. He acted as if he was mellowing a little. The guys didn't know how to react to Frank being nice.

The meeting ended. He thanked everyone again for working hard. As Nick was leaving, Frank grabbed him by the arm. "Hey dude, what's up? You look like the cat's got your tongue. I nodded at you in roll call and you looked away from me. Is everything okay? How was your day off? Did you go anywhere?"

Nick put on his best face. He told Frank that he was fine. He told him that his day off was great. He said that he relaxed and did a little shopping. Nick started out the door and Frank asked if he wanted to go get some breakfast.

"I don't think so Frank. I have a lot to catch up on. Maybe we can go another time."

Frank slapped him on the back. Nick left Frank's office and went to his desk. He wasn't at his desk a minute when the intercom on his phone buzzed. He picked up the phone. Nick was surprised that it was Lieutenant Valentino. "Nick, I saw you go in Frank's office; what did he want?"

Nick felt uncomfortable talking to Valentino. Frank was only about twenty feet away. He tried to turn and face the wall. He had his hand up to his mouth as he talked. He knew this would appear strange. He could not believe Valentino would even call him on the office phone. "Lieutenant, Frank called a short meeting and we didn't really talk about anything. I don't think it's wise for you to call me on an office phone. I'm going out on the street in a few minutes. Let me get out of this building and call me on my cell phone."

"Nick, I talked to Captain Golden this morning. We are going to have to move a little quicker than we had originally planned. Golden has briefed the police commissioner and he wants this matter resolved immediately. Nick, I will call you in fifteen minutes on your cell phone."

Nick packed up his briefcase with any papers that were on the desk. He knew that Frank and others could see him packing. He was leaving the office when he heard Frank call him. He pretended he did not hear him. Frank followed him into the hallway. "Nick, what's up? You are acting strange this morning. Why such a rush to get on the street? What were you shopping for yesterday?"

"What the hell are you talking about Frank? What kind of question is that…what was I shopping for yesterday? It's none of your goddamn business what I was shopping for. My time off is none of your business. You can be a control freak on the job, but when I'm off, that's my private time. I can't believe you sometime. You think we are all puppets in your little charade. You pull the strings when you want us to jump. Well, that's not the way it is Frank. We are real people and we all have private lives. What I do when I'm not under your control is none of your business. I got to go now."

Nick walked briskly to the elevator. He was hoping that Frank was not following him. He also regretted talking to him that way. It was bad enough that he was about to get busted and possibly put away for life. Frank did not follow him. Nick went to the garage and got in his car. He drove away from the building as fast as he could. His cell phone rang—it was Captain Golden. Nick was surprised—he thought it would be Valentino.

"Nick, how are things going? Did the lieutenant tell you that we need to move a little quicker on Favasi? I mean that we need to get together right now and make some plans. I have some of the task force people together already. We need you to come in immediately. I know how Favasi watches people, so park your car in front of the courthouse. Walk down to the Sheraton Hotel. Come in the front door and go to the front desk. Ask the clerk for Mark Twain and he will direct you to our room. We have been working out of a hotel suite. How long do you think it will take you to get here?"

"I'm almost in front of the courthouse now. It should only take about fifteen minutes to meet you."

Nick parked the car and started to walk to the Sheraton. He took a different route. He knew no one was following him, but he wanted to make sure. He walked up to the front desk of the hotel and asked for Mark Twain's room. The clerk told him he would call the room and let someone know that he was in the lobby. A few minutes later a man approached Nick and told him to follow him. Nick did not know the guy and asked who he was. The guy waited until they were on the elevator and produced a badge and told Nick he was an FBI agent. Nick had not remembered any FBI agents being in the room during the task force meeting. As they were getting off the elevator, Nick asked the agent why they were involved. The agent said, "Nick, I wish I could tell you more. My job right now is to bring you to the room. I'm sure you will find out soon why we are involved."

The agent was friendly, but he was typical FBI—tell me all you know and I will tell you nothing. Nick entered a very large suite that was crowded with people. Some of the people he recognized from the prior meeting. Some were new to him. He was approached by Captain Golden. "Nick, we have included the FBI in this task force because of the seriousness of the crimes. I have already briefed them last night. They know everything about this investigation. Nick, we have a plan that we think will seal the deal on this investigation."

Captain Golden directed Nick to a large round table. He asked everyone in the room to please take a seat. Nick saw charts on an easel and lots of paperwork on the large table. Captain Golden stood at the end of the table. He looked as sharp as ever. He didn't have a suit on. He had yellow pants, a light green shirt, a blue cashmere sweater, and white boat shoes. He gave the alligators a break today.

The others in the room were dressed casually except for the FBI agents. They never wore anything except expensive looking suits. If they were ever shot in the line of duty, you could take them right to the funeral parlor and lay them out.

Nick was beyond nervous. He knew from the urgency displayed that the time was approaching that he would play a big role in taking down Frank. It was no turning back. Frank had led his life on the edge and now he was about to fall off. Nick wished that none of this was happening. He also wished that Janet was still alive. He knew his motivation at this time was to punish Frank for having Janet murdered. He knew that even down the road at a trial, he would have no problem telling Frank that he did it for Janet.

Captain Golden thanked everyone for responding so quickly. He told the group that the police commissioner and the mayor had been briefed earlier this morning. He said that he was given orders to move forward with the arrest of Sergeant Favasi. He told the group that the State's Attorney believed that they had enough to arrest Favasi on warrants. He said that they felt that a little more would be beneficial for a strong case in court. Golden said that a plan has been devised and if it went off smoothly Favasi would be arrested today. He looked directly at Nick and said, "Detective Giango, this is where you play a big part. We feel that Favasi would open up to you if you provoked him enough. We are going to ask you to arrange a meeting with him. We prefer that the meeting be away from the police building. We have asked our partners in the FBI to assist with some technology. We know that Favasi is as sharp as they come. We also know that if you meet and provoke him, he will probably search you to see if you are wired up with a recording device. The FBI has some sophisticated devices that can be installed in the front of your vehicle. The listening device can pick up a conversation at a lengthy distance. They also have a camera that can be installed in the front of the vehicle that can videotape. Because we know that Favasi is so sharp, we will put a fake wire on your body so he can find it. He will be pissed off and tear it off of you. I would think this would then make him talk. He would not know we have devices in the front of the vehicle. The problem is identifying a good meeting place. Also, for your safety Nick we need to have some people in the vicinity. Is there a spot where you can get him to meet you?"

Nick was almost speechless. His first response to what he had heard was—"wow." Golden picked up on Nick's nervousness. He told Nick that he knew it was a lot to swallow at this time. He said that they had very few options and needed to act now. He told Nick that agents would be close enough to him. If they heard that it was going bad, they would act immediately. Captain Golden waited for a response from Nick.

"Well, I guess—I mean like do I have any choice in this matter? I have agreed to cooperate, but I didn't think it would come to something like this. As far as a spot to meet, Frank likes to meet me in Clifton Park. He feels comfortable in that park. The area where he always parks has very little cover for anyone. Your agents might be seen by Frank."

Captain Golden looked over at an agent and asked him to do the work-up on Clifton Park immediately. Golden asked Nick again if the plan is something that would get Frank to talk. Nick shook his head and told Golden that it's possible. Golden didn't like the answer and came back at him. "Nick, let me know what you think. You are the main player in this plan. I need your total honesty."

"Captain, I'm sure you have a lot involved in this plan. I can only assume that it will work. Regardless of whether this works or not, you still have enough to arrest him."

Golden looked at an agent and asked if the car had been taken care of. The agent informed him that it is being worked on as we speak. Golden went to the map of Clifton Park that was brought in the room by an agent. He asked Nick to come up to the map. Several agents gathered around the map as Nick pointed out different areas of the park. The area of concern was the exact area where Sergeant Favasi always parked his car when they met. Golden placed markers on the different spots. He drew a large circle around the parking spot. He asked everyone to have a seat again. He went over the map and pointed out certain areas of concern. He told Nick that he would hope that the meeting could take place while there is still some light outside. He assured Nick that his investigators and the agents would be close by in the area. He said that they might be on the golf course, riding bikes, or just jogging in the area. He told Nick that a command post would be set up a good distance from the park. Golden said that they would be listening to the conversation. He assured Nick that if anything appeared to be going bad, he would have all units move in as quickly as possible. He said that he hoped they would get enough on the recording, but the most important thing was Nick's safety. The captain paused and asked an agent how Nick's car was coming along.

"Captain, did you ask him how my car was coming along?"

"Oh yeah Nick, I forgot to tell you that we towed your car from the courthouse. Your car is now at the FBI garage and they are installing the audio and video devices on the car. We wanted to just tow it as if you were illegally parked. Sorry, I didn't tell you about that. We thought that would be the best way to handle it."

Nick just smiled. He was wondering what else they had not told him. He knew from past experiences that when a major operation went down, there were always a few things that were not shared with the peons. He also knew that on this operation, he was not exactly a peon. He was the leading man. Nick was thinking about what Golden was saying about provoking Frank. To provoke Frank it would have to be something that was clearly a threat to him. It would have to be something that would get him to Clifton Park.

CHAPTER 57

The meeting with the task force ended. Nick was driven to the FBI garage to get his vehicle. At the garage he was given a quick class on how the audio and video devices worked. He really didn't have to do anything. He was told that he should not stand directly in front of his vehicle. He was also told that the devices would be remotely controlled by agents in the command truck. The last piece of advice he got was the most important. If at any time while talking with Favasi and it appeared that something was wrong—they would move in. He was assured that his safety would be a priority.

Nick decided that he would stay out on the street riding around as long as possible. He would avoid any contact with Frank until later in the day. It had been decided by Captain Golden that it would be up to Nick to decide how he would provoke Favasi enough to get him to Clifton Park. Nick knew that with the way things were, it would not be hard to provoke Frank.

Nick was given the direct phone number to the command post. He was told to check in periodically during the day. Golden had told him that he would have members of the task force go to the park and check out good vantage points. Golden told Nick that he was not to go to the park until he had notified the command post. He wanted all task force members to be in place before the meeting.

Nick thought about getting something to eat before the big plan went down. He could not however bring himself to eat. His stomach was upset. He knew he would not be able keep anything down. He drove for most of the afternoon. He drove around the city. It was weird that while driving around, he found himself in his old neighborhood. He parked for a few minutes alongside what was left of Jimmy Jordan's Bar. The bar had closed. It was now a small run-down grocery store...the neighborhood had changed.

While parked, he thought of all the good times he and Frank had in the bar. He was not even sure if Jimmy was still living. Jimmy would not be proud of what was about to go down.

He drove by his old school. Even back when they were just kids, Frank always looked out for him on the playground. He passed the church that they attended. He had some great memories of him and Frank making their First Communion together. He also remembered when Frank grabbed some money out of the church collection basket. He thought about the time Frank listened to Harry Salk giving his confession to Father O'Neal on Saturday afternoon. When Salk left the confession booth, Frank could not wait to tell Salk everything he had just told the priest. Salk was mad as hell. He and Frank fought over it—Frank won.

Then there's the playground where the guys played baseball on a black asphalt surface. The cover would come off the baseball from the pounding on the asphalt. We would put black tar tape on it. Whenever we needed a new baseball, Frank would make a short trip to the Sears store. He had it down to a science on how to steal a baseball. He would have one of the guys stand near the entrance. Frank would go to the sports section—get a baseball, throw it to the guy near the door, and off they went to the black asphalt baseball diamond. I'm not sure where we got all the black tar tape. We sure used a lot of it.

Nick parked his car next to the small park where he and Frank would spend some late summer nights sleeping on the grass. Johnson Square was always packed in the summer. Without air conditioning, the park was a reprieve from the scorching summer nights in the city. Nick noticed that the grass was gone from the small hills in the park. It was replaced with cement. What the hell is that all about? How in the hell can you sleep on cement? It finally hit him that sleeping on the grass was totally out of the question these days. The neighborhood was so bad now that nobody even came out at night—no need for grass. As he looked around he did not see many air conditioners in the old row homes. How in the hell were they coping with the same oppressive sweltering summer nights?

The more Nick drove around all the old familiar sites, the less he wanted to go through with the demise of his once best friend. He racked his brain to see if there were any alternatives to what was about to happen. Each time he would feel sorry for Frank, he would catch himself. Why should I feel sorry for someone who took the best thing in my life away from me? He has to be stopped. It would not end—Frank would continue to connive and manipulate people. It's all he knows. He has done it for so many years. It's a way of life with him. He needs to be stopped. Nick found himself talking out loud. He even looked in the mirror on occasion—he wanted approval from the guy looking back at him.

He kept checking his watch, even though there was a clock on the dashboard. He was fidgety and was getting very nervous. The sounds coming from his stomach were getting louder. It was now very obvious to him that he definitely had to eat. He needed to stop the rumbling noises. He wanted to go to Lombard Street and get a corned beef sandwich. He, however, thought better of going there. He knew that the guys in the unit also went there. He did not want to run into anyone at this time. He decided that Lexington Market might be a better choice. It wasn't in the greatest of neighborhoods, but they had great sandwiches. He also knew the odds were better that he would not find Frank or any of the guys there. Frank had told Nick when they were at the market that he did not like eating around so many black people. He said it made him nervous. Nick never could figure that one out—a sandwich was a sandwich. Frank made remarks sometimes that were a little off the wall. He frequently said that black people only ate hog maws and hominy grits. The black detectives in the unit got a kick out of that. Nick only said it to piss them off. The black detectives were quick to point out to Frank that hog maws were the stomach of the pig. They told Frank that during slavery when the pigs were slaughtered, the slaves only got to keep the chitterlings or the chitlins as most people called them. Frank laughed at the stories about slavery. The guys in the unit knew that if Frank had his way, the blacks in Baltimore would be kept in a cage. They would occasionally be fed hog maws, hominy grits, and maybe some chicken wings thrown in if they behaved.

Nick knew that the time was approaching that he needed to make the call to Frank. He had thought hard about the best way to get Frank provoked enough that he would ask Nick to meet him. He would try to act calm. He would tell Frank that he decided to talk to the Carroll County investigators about the murder of Mr. Philbin. He would tell Frank that it has been bothering him—he wants to tell them the truth. He knows that Frank will go off and scream over the phone. Nick was sure that Frank won't want to talk in the police building. He just hoped that Frank sticks to his favorite spot—Clifton Park.

Nick made the call to Frank's office phone. This would be even more reason for Frank to not want to talk on that phone. Frank did not answer. Nick left a message that it was urgent that they talk. He was going to try the cell phone but wanted the conversation to be on the office phone. All calls on the office phones were recorded. Nick waited ten minutes and called again. Frank answered the phone.

"Frank, this is Nick. It's very important that we get together and talk. I have been thinking about what's been going on lately. I want to set things straight with the Carroll County investigators—it's been bothering me."

"What the fuck are you saying? Have you lost your mind? I don't want to discuss anything on this phone. Meet me in Clifton Park in about twenty minutes. Don't talk to anyone until we meet."

"I don't think I can make it in twenty minutes. I'm tied up on something. I can meet you in about an hour. I will meet you on the hill in the same spot."

Nick could tell that Frank was furious. He was a little more than provoked. Nick stayed away from the police building. When he was in a spot near the city line, he called Captain Golden. He told Golden that Frank was pissed and they had arranged to meet in about an hour. Golden told Nick to stretch the meeting time into two hours if he could. He told

Nick that most agents were in place. He preferred the later time to make sure most civilians were off the golf course in the park. Nick said he would just show up late. He did not want to call Frank back.

Nick stretched it out as much as possible. He then headed for the park. He could feel the jitters coming over him. The roaring sound in the stomach was back. He knew that he needed to control himself. If he went there and Frank started screaming like he always did, he might not get the confession they needed. The weather was a little overcast, but no rain. It just seemed like a dreary miserable day. The real misery had not started yet.

Nick drove into the park. From the road he could see Frank's car on the hill. Before he entered the park, he had notified Golden. He was told that everyone was in place. He was told to make sure he parked his vehicle facing Frank's vehicle. This was a must for the devices in the front of his vehicle to work properly. As Nick approached Frank's vehicle, he remembered that he always pulled alongside Frank's car in the past meetings. Would Frank pick up on this and think it's unusual?

Nick stopped his car facing the front of Frank's car. He got out of the car and walked to meet Frank. He stopped before he got to Frank. He was thinking about his instructions—don't block the devices, don't be too far from the devices, and stand off to the side.

Frank was so pissed off at Nick that he walked directly to the spot where Nick had stopped. "Why in the hell are you parking like that Nick? Pull your car closer to mine."

"Frank, I don't give a shit how the cars are parked. I came here to let you know I'm not playing your silly games any longer. I have decided to tell the Carroll County investigators about what happened that night. I can't live with it on my mind any longer. I know we will be in trouble. I just got to do it."

Frank paced in front of Nick. He didn't say anything. He kicked up some dirt. He walked up directly in Nick's face. Nick held his ground although Frank was right in his face. He knew he had to maintain his position so the audio could be recorded. Frank put his finger on Nick's chest. "You sorry bastard, are you out of your mind? You say that you think we will be in trouble. If you talk to anyone about that night, they will charge me with murder, you stupid shit! They will charge you with being an accessory to murder. I could get life in prison. You could get thirty years. Do you want to see us go to prison? I can't let you do that Nick."

Nick didn't say anything; he wanted Frank to do all the talking. When Frank started to pace a little away from Nick's car, Nick asked him if he would just turn himself in. Frank started to laugh. "Turn myself in, is that what you want me to do Nick? I have done some crazy shit Nick—I shot that guy for you. I went there that night just to watch the guy and find out where he lived. I didn't know he was going to get out of the car and come after me. He had a baseball bat. Nick, I couldn't do anything else but shoot the guy. You understand Nick— don't you?"

"Frank, I really don't understand much of what you have done over the years. I know that it can't go on. I have to talk to the Carroll County investigators about that shooting. By the way Frank, I talked to the Ocean City investigators about Janet's murder. They have a piece of bloody paper with your name, your cell phone number, and the address of the condo on it. The paper had to be on Jackson. They feel that during the struggle to murder and rape Janet, he dropped that paper. I know you hired Jackson to go down to Ocean City and murder Janet. You lured me away from the condo so Jackson could kill her. You're a sorry piece of shit Frank. I'm going to make sure you are stopped. You're a ruthless cold-blooded murderer!"

Frank smiled at Nick. "Well buddy, I'm glad to see that you are finally becoming a good detective. Looks like you got it all figured out. You need to get over Janet—she wasn't any good for you. I knew it would be a matter of time before those investigators would bring her in and talk to her. She would have involved us as soon as they told her about someone in homicide getting a check on her friend. Nick, she was messing around on you—I did it for you buddy."

Nick could hardly take it any longer. The words from Frank's mouth tore at his heart. If not for the recording, he would have beaten the shit out of Frank right there in the park. He started toward Frank. He stopped when he realized the recording was definitely needed to convict him. Nick told Frank that he was a sick person. Frank had that stupid damn smile on his face. It was the same smile that he had seen so many times over the years. The smile that said, I'm Frank Favasi— you ain't shit.

"Nick, we will be okay in all this. You can't talk to anyone. In time, all of this will pass. You and I will be fine. I have a way of covering my tracks. Yeah, I had Jackson go down to murder Janet. I didn't tell him to rape her—I'm sorry about that. Jackson will never be able to say anything about me. When he came back from the ocean, I met the no- good son of a bitch in Druid Hill Park. I shot him. He's dead Nick—he can't talk to anyone."

Nick knew that at this point he had Frank talking about three murders. He was only hoping that the devices on the car were working properly. Just as Nick was about to try and end the meeting, Frank grabbed him from behind. He threw Nick over the front of the car. He was going over Nick's body. "I get it buddy—they wired you up to get a confession from me."

Frank ripped at Nick's shirt and found a small black plastic recording device. He was aware of recording devices. He had used them in the past. He ripped the device from Nick's chest and threw it on the ground. "You common bastard, you were taping me. Where's your gun?"

Nick told Frank that he had left his gun in the office. Frank checked Nick's ankles for a second weapon. He looked in Nick's car; he checked under the front seat. Frank pushed Nick farther away from his car. He pulled out his gun and smacked Nick in the face with the barrel. Blood began streaming down Nick's face. "You common no-good bastard, all I have done for you over the years and you do this to me. I should shoot your ass right here. I can come up with another bullshit story. I'll just say we were being robbed and some dude shot you. I'm good at making up stories Nick—wouldn't you agree?"

"Yeah Frank, I know you're good at it. Like the guy you shot after he robbed the Pirate's Den. You made a mistake there, Frank. When you put the gun in his hand after you shot him, you put it in the wrong hand. You put it in his right hand—he's left-handed. You have made a lot of mistakes over the years, Frank. Do you remember shooting a guy at Linard and Jefferson Street? Well, the one guy you didn't shoot and let go has now picked your photo out. He said that you just shot the other guy point blank for no reason. I'm sure there is much more. Do you get the gist of what I'm telling you Frank? Your reign of terror in Charm City is over."

"Who are you working with Nick? Who put you up to all this bullshit? Are you trying to save your ass? Yeah, I did all that shit. I probably did a whole lot more than that."

"Was Janet a bad person Frank? Why did you have her killed? She never did anything to you. She was a sweet person Frank. She didn't deserve to die the way she did. Well, you want to know who I'm working with. I'm working with anyone that will listen to me. You need to be stopped Frank and I'm going to see to it."

Captain Golden had everything he needed to take Frank Favasi down. They had checked the recording and the video. Everything came out perfect. Golden needed to make a decision real soon about moving in and making the arrest. He told all the units on the detail to stand by to move in.

Frank pulled his revolver out again. He motioned for Nick to move away from his car. Nick was sure that Golden would hear what was taking place. Was there going to be a shootout? Nick noticed that off to one side there were two men in a golf cart approaching. He then saw other golf carts coming in his direction. What kind of plan was this? Were they going to just drive up in golf carts and take Frank down? Frank pushed Nick to the ground. "Well my good buddy, I think this is where I say goodbye to you. I don't know who's in those golf carts, but they won't make it in time to help you. I told you I would never go to jail. I love you like a brother Nick, but I got to do this."

Frank put the gun about six inches from Nick's head and pulled the trigger. Nothing happened—he pulled the trigger again with the same result. He looked at the revolver and pulled the trigger again. "What the fuck is going on?"

Nick leaned back against his car; he was dumbfounded about what had just happened. Why didn't the gun fire? What was stopping Frank from killing him? The golf carts moved closer. Before Frank could get back to his car, the agents wrestled him to the ground. He was screaming that he was a Baltimore City Police sergeant. "What the hell is going on? Who do you think you are dealing with? I'm Frank Favasi; what are you doing to me? Nick, tell them who I am."

Frank was handcuffed and placed in an FBI vehicle. He didn't go easy— he was kicking and screaming. He spit on one of the agents. Nick slumped to the ground—he was exhausted. He was relieved that it was over. He was a little sad to see Frank taken away like that.

Captain Golden came on the scene. He helped Nick to his feet. "Nick, you did a great job. We have enough on Sergeant Favasi to send him away for the rest of his life. Nick, I have also talked to the police commissioner. He told me that if there are no formal criminal charges placed against you by the State's Attorney, he would consider minor disciplinary actions from the department. I think you will be able to keep your job."

Nick was not so much interested in keeping his job—he was grateful that he was still living. "Captain, Frank pulled the trigger several times on his weapon and nothing happened. Tell me what that's all about."

"Well Nick, I asked Lieutenant Valentino to inspect all the sergeants' guns yesterday. It was routine as you well know. However, when he inspected Frank's weapon, he made a switch. He gave Frank a gun that had a filed down firing pin. We thought that would be the best way to go. Also, we searched his vehicle prior to the meeting. We recovered two other guns. One gun was under the front seat and the other was in the trunk. I'm sure our ballistics people will be going over all his guns. I know it must have scared the shit out of you Nick. I'm sorry. We now have another charge of assault with intent to murder to go along with all the other charges."

Nick went back to the command truck in a golf cart. He was in no condition to drive his car. His car was being driven back to the FBI garage to dismantle the audio and video devices. He sat in the command truck, still in disbelief of what had just happened. He heard Captain Golden talking with the police commissioner about a news conference to be held in the morning. "Nick, I guess you heard what I was telling the commissioner. I want you to be at the news conference tomorrow when we announce the indictments on Frank Favasi. I want the citizens of Baltimore to know that when cops go bad, we will catch them. I think it's a great story. In spite of your many years of friendship with Favasi, you still did the right thing. Nick, you are a credit to the police department."

"Captain, I'm no credit to the police department or to Baltimore City. I would rather not be at the press conference. I did what I did for Janet. I did it because it was the right thing to do. I'm ashamed that I did not come forward sooner—maybe some lives would have been saved. I have disgraced my name in the police department. I'm not sure if I can continue in police work. I would like to take a leave of absence and think about my future. The news media will play this up for a long time. When something like this happens, they paint the entire department with the same brush. I know that there are so many hard working dedicated police officers that go out on the street each and everyday to protect the citizens of Baltimore. The trial will come up and the department's image will be dragged through the mud. The people who hate the police department will hate them even more. Captain, I had an uncle named Carmen Giango who gave his life in the line of duty. I didn't know him that well. I remember my dad talking about him. He was a real hero. I don't want to be mentioned in the same vain as him. In a way, I wish that Frank's gun was working. I might consider myself a hero under those circumstances."

Captain Golden and a few members of the task force were listening to Nick. As some of them were leaving the command truck, they patted Nick on the back. A few of them told him to hang in there—he did the right thing. Golden reached out to shake hands with Nick. Instead of shaking hands, he put his arms around him. He hugged him for a few seconds. "Nick, I understand how you feel. We will do whatever you want to do. Let me take a minute and tell you about my dad. He was a cop in the city also. When he retired he gave me his somewhat tongue-in-cheek definition of a police officer. He said a police officer is a person whether active or retired, who at one point in their life wrote a blank check made payable to the city of Baltimore for an amount up to and including their life. Nick, your uncle would be very proud of you. He would not want you to cash your check yet."

CHAPTER 58

Homicides in Baltimore continued at an alarming rate. Sergeant Favasi was now out of the picture. It seemed as if the bad guys knew he was gone. Nick had moved on with his life. It had been a year since the trial of Frank Favasi. The trial was without a doubt the most demanding and nerve-racking time Nick had ever gone through. It was no cake walk for Frank either. The trial lasted three weeks. Each day that Nick sat in the courtroom was pure mental torture. During the first few days of the trial, he found himself getting emotional as he listened to the prosecutor portray Frank as a monster. Nick wanted to jump up and say—stop all the talk—just find the son of a bitch guilty and send him away. He tried to make as little eye contact as possible with Frank. He did, however, look directly at him when he was on the stand testifying. He couldn't help but look at him; the witness stand was about five feet from where Frank was seated.

The jury was made up of twelve of Frank's peers. Well, they were not exactly what Frank would call his peers. The jury consisted of nine blacks, two whites, and a Hispanic. The testimony during the trial was riveting. The jurors took notes throughout the trial. They were very attentive. None of the very graphic testimony seemed to bother them. Hell, they were from Baltimore—they had heard and seen crime all their lives.

Frank was found guilty of first degree murder. He was given a life sentence without the possibility of parole. He would spend the rest of his life in jail with the same bad guys he tried to eliminate from the streets of Charm City.

The judge took the opportunity at the end of the trial to admonish Frank. The judge knew Frank from some murder trials that he had testified at. The judge was a veteran with over twenty years on the bench in Baltimore. He had convened over many murder trials in his days as a judge. He was an elderly man, probably in his late sixties. He leaned forward on the bench. His wire rimmed glasses were down on his nose at the point they looked like they would fall off. He looked over the glasses. He asked Frank to stand. It was sad to see Frank on the other side of the justice system. It was even sadder to see him in handcuffs and leg irons. He had a nice suit on, but that would be the last time he would wear it.

The judge cleared his throat and said, "Mr. Favasi, I have a few things I would like to say before they take you away. In the past when you were in my court, I had the utmost respect for you as a police officer. Having heard all the testimony in this lengthy trial, I am shocked. I'm appalled at what I have heard in these past few weeks. You took an oath to serve and protect the citizens of Baltimore. You not only violated that oath, you disgraced the police department. The badge you carried meant that people looked up to you. It was not a license for you to commit such heinous crimes. You will spend the rest of your life thinking about what you have done. At this point in a trial, I would normally say good luck to the defendant as they are led away. I can't bring myself to say that to you. I can only say that I hope that everyone you have hurt feels that justice has been served. I hope that the families of the many people that were harmed during your reign of terror can find solace in the fact that you will never be on the streets of Baltimore again."

Nick stood as Frank was led from the courtroom by the guards. When he was almost at the door to the cell block area, Frank hollered to Nick—"Semper Fi, buddy."

Nick said nothing as Frank was taken through the doors. He felt like hollering back—Semper Fi my ass—you were never faithful. He decided to leave it alone. What good would it do?

Frank would be serving his time at one of the oldest prisons in the nation. The Maryland Penitentiary was built in the mid 1800s. Frank was tough, but he was about to live the rest of his life with some of the most dangerous criminals in the state. As Frank disappeared through the doors to the lockup, Nick could not help but think what a waste of life. Frank could have gone as high as he wanted in the police department. He was smart and at one time very dedicated.

Several months after the trial, Nick was busy as ever in the Homicide Unit. He had made the decision after he took a short leave of absence from the department that he actually enjoyed policing too much to give it up. He received an official disciplinary reprimand from the department for not coming forward with information about the Philbin murder. It was interesting to Nick's friends that one week he received a disciplinary action and the following week he received a departmental award for his actions in stopping Frank. He also received letters of appreciation from the mayor, the governor, and the police commissioner. Nick accepted the accolades, but it was bittersweet that the recognition was for putting his best friend away for the rest of his life.

Nick was promoted to sergeant and stayed in the Homicide Unit. His promotion was not based solely on what he had done to nail Frank. He had studied for the promotion test and finished high on the list. He used most of his off-duty time to study.

The promotions were held at the Baltimore Civic Center. As in all promotions, it was a time for the dignitaries in the city and state to show up. It was a large promotion—ten lieutenants and twenty sergeants were getting promoted. Nick was excited. This is what he had wanted since he joined the police department. His family and many friends from the department showed up. He had recently started to date a girl named Darlene. He met her at the University of Maryland while taking some courses in the evening. She was working toward a law degree. Nick was taking criminal justice courses. She attended the promotion ceremony. Nick smiled when he saw her in the audience. He really cared for Darlene, but he wanted to take it slow. He would need more time to get over the tragic death of Janet.

Nick paraded across the stage and received his promotion certificate from the police commissioner. He received his sergeant's badge from Captain Valentino. Yes, Valentino had been promoted to captain and decided to stay in the police department a few more years. He loved the Homicide Unit and wanted to go out on top. He had told Nick that he wanted to again make the unit one of the most respected in the department.

The badge that Nick received was special. Prior to the promotion, ceremony he had approached Captain Valentino. He told him that if it was possible, he wanted Frank Favasi's old badge. At first, Valentino tried to talk Nick out of it. He told him that it would probably remind him of Frank and that might not be a good thing. Nick persisted and Valentino gave in. He made arrangements for Nick to receive the badge. Nick knew down deep inside that he wanted the badge so that it would remind him that no one is above the law. He also thought that maybe one day in the far off future, he would write to Frank. He would let him know that he carried the badge his entire career. It would not be in honor of Frank, it would be to make things better under the badge that did so much wrong.

When the ceremony ended, all the promoted personnel were invited to attend a reception in the lobby of the civic center. Nick met with all his friends, fellow investigators, family, and Darlene. After the reception, he thanked everyone for attending. He told Darlene that he needed to go back to work for a while. He had made arrangements for them to go to dinner later that night.

Nick walked into the Homicide Unit office. Immediately the detectives in the office stood up and saluted him. It was a caring gesture. Nick enjoyed it and laughed. He asked the guys assigned to his squad if they would gather for a few minutes in his new office. The guys were laughing and kidding Nick about only being promoted for minutes and already calling for a meeting. Nick laughed along with them. He remembered Frank's meetings and his would be nothing like that.

"Good morning gentlemen. I know most of you personally. The ones I don't know, I look forward to finding out about you. I want to just say a few things. I want to emphasize that we are a team and no one person is larger than the team. I'm not going to give a pep talk. You are all in the Homicide Unit because you are the best in the department. I want you to know that I'm here for you. We can discuss anything you want to talk about—it can be personal or job related. This is a tough job. Remember that the families and friends of the people that are murdered in this city expect us to do everything possible to bring the offenders to justice. We will do that in a professional manner. There are no shortcuts in a homicide investigation. I'm sure all of you are aware of the Sergeant Frank Favasi reign of terror while he worked in this unit. We need to work hard to gain back the respect of the citizens."

Nick stood near the door and as each investigator left the meeting, he shook their hand. He sat behind the desk; the same desk that Frank had ruled from for a few years. The walls were bare. He could not wait until he could hang some personal photos, various awards, and of course his promotion certificate. He started to fumble through the drawers of the desk. Most drawers were empty. The bottom drawer on the right side of the desk was hard to open. He yanked at it—"I'll be damn. Frank is not completely out of this office yet." Nick saw a fifth of whiskey and a can of Dr Pepper. He was moving toward the trash can with the whiskey and soda when the door opened.

Captain Valentino walked in. "Nick, what the hell are you doing with that whiskey?"

"Don't get excited captain. I'm cleaning out the last of Frank Favasi. I'm throwing it away. Do you want it?" The captain laughed and shook his head. He didn't even answer Nick. He smiled and headed back to his office.

Nick told the captain he would be back in the office in the morning. He walked down the corridor toward the elevator. He heard several people saying, "Good morning sergeant." It didn't hit him at first, but they were talking to him. He got on the elevator and pressed the button for the main floor. On each floor when new riders got on, they would say, "Good morning sergeant." Nick liked the attention. By the time he got to the main floor, he was walking a little taller.

Sergeant Nick Giango is the new supervisor in the Homicide Unit. Watch out bad guys—all is well in Charm City and we're coming after you.

All that is necessary for the triumph of evil is that good men do nothing...

Thomas Jefferson